Lantern for the Dark

"Is that what Peterkin calls to you in your dreams? Does he cry out 'Stop, Mama, please stop'?"

She straightened, arching her back until the boning of the dress crackled audibly. She was too angry now to bother with poses and posturing. The Edinburgh advocate had touched her as she did not want to be touched. She was suddenly afraid of him and in her fear, struck out. "He was only a baby. He could not speak."

"He could say 'Mama', could he not?"

"He could say my name. He knew who I was. But I did not poison him. God, how could I? My own child, my own flesh." Anger got the better of her. She shot to her feet. "Yes, I do still see his face when I close my eyes at night. I will see his sweet wee face until the day I die. But if you suppose that I killed him then you are wrong." Clare plunged on. "I was with another woman's children when he was taken from me. I should have been with my own lamb. I should have been there to hold him in my arms. That's why my Peterkin cries out to me in dreams."

About the author

Born in Glasgow, Jessica Stirling is the author of nearly thirty
heartwarming novels, many with Scottish backgrounds.

Lantern for the Dark

JESSICA STIRLING

CORONET BOOKS

Hodder & Stoughton

Copyright © by Jessica Stirling 1992

First published in Great Britain in 1992 by Hodder & Stoughton
A division of Hodder Headline
First published by Hodder and Stoughton in paperback in 2003
A Coronet paperback

The right of Jessica Stirling to be identified as the Author
of the Work has been asserted in accordance with the
Copyright, Designs and Patents Act 1988.

3 5 7 9 10 8 6 4 2

A CIP catalogue record for this title
is available from the British Library

ISBN 978 0340 82220 3

Typeset in Plantin by Hewer Text Ltd, Edinburgh
Printed and bound by
CPI Group (UK) Ltd, Croydon, CRO 4YY

Hodder & Stoughton
A division of Hodder Headline
338 Euston Road
London NW1 3BH

Contents

The Tolbooth

Chimes, on the hour, from the Tolbooth steeple divided the day monotonously. Each afternoon about one o'clock, however, the city's musical master came to the tower and played a selection of Scottish airs on the bells. Over the weeks the old tunes so impressed themselves upon Clare Kelso's memory that throughout the lonely evenings and long, wakeful nights she would croon them softly to herself as if she had no care in the world and was in all respects content to endure imprisonment.

Snow had long since gone from the sill of the barred window and more recently frost had melted from the thick glass panes. Bells and weather told Clare that her term in the Tolbooth's narrow cell was drawing to a close. If she returned here after her trial it would not be for long. Every morning she marked off the passage of another night with a pencil stroke on a leaf of the Testament that Mrs Rossmore had sent in along with warm stockings and a little basket of hazel nuts. The gifts had been made before town gossips put about that her guilt was unimpeachable and not even the interventions of highfalutin' Edinburgh advocates could save her pretty white neck from the rope.

The lawyers employed to plead her case were Advocates Thomas Walcott and Angus McKay. They had assured her that with their aid the truth would certainly emerge and she would be acquitted without stain on her character.

Seated on a stool by the side of the cot Mr Walcott had spoken to her so gently and intimately that she was almost tempted to believe his promise of a miracle. 'By God, Clare,' he'd told her, 'I'll not let the will of the Glasgow mob triumph. I'm damned if I'll see you condemned to the gallows just to appease their Calvinistic sensibilities.'

She had not allowed herself to be flattered by Mr Walcott's extravagant compliments. In the course of the past two years she had learned that men were by nature attracted to her. From the lawyer's amorous disposition, however, Clare had taken much comfort. Mr Walcott might competently defend her to earn his fee and bolster his reputation but he would plead the case a great deal better if he believed that, after acquittal, he might possibly possess her.

For this reason she had not rebuffed his exploratory advances, not even when his fat hand had circled her waist and his ponderous belly in its flowered silk waistcoat had delicately brushed against her breasts. In fact she had promised herself that when he came again she would permit him, within reason, fresh liberties by way of compensation for his sympathy and to keep him up to snuff for trial day. Unfortunately, Mr Walcott did not come again.

Throughout February Clare had awaited his attendance with mounting impatience. No scratch of a pen from Edinburgh, not a word from Mr McKay in Glasgow, no answers to the letters she wrote enquiring after her cause. She could not understand why Mr Walcott had suddenly abandoned her. Eventually she had become sufficiently agitated to ask Jailer Hinchcliff if he knew why she was being ignored. Hinchcliff had laughed at her conceit and had told her in no uncertain terms that *he* would not neglect her after judgment came down and she was left to *his* tender mercies without the protection of her influential friends.

Magistrates' offices, Dean of Guild's courts and Halls of Justice were all crammed into the Tolbooth building, cheek by jowl with the jail. From street level the civic edifice had seemed strong and austere. Since she had become a prisoner within its walls Clare, though, had learned that corruptions small and large flourished behind its handsome facades.

On reflection she realised that the city fathers had never been anything else but callous. Vividly she recalled a morning three or four years ago when, to celebrate King George's birthday, the Provost and his henchmen had spilled drunkenly on to the platform that joined the external staircases and had pelted the crowd with chicken bones and toasting glasses. She remembered too last summer's executions, when Hanging Johnnie Harkness had been employed to dispatch, among others, two young girls caught and convicted for theft. In full public view Provost Hay had bussed the girls and groped their haunches as if they were so much meat for the market. The mob had brayed and hooted and egged him on to further indecencies before Johnnie knocked the pegs away and the girls had plummeted down to dangle, squirming and thrashing, on the ropes' ends.

Jailer Hinchcliff had made a point of showing Clare the iron room where the condemned spent their last days, a bleak, narrow, straw-littered cell, reeking of rat-dirt. Once she had been found guilty, he had pointedly informed her, she would be confined there without comforts and privileges, except those he chose to provide out of the goodness of his heart. Hinchcliff was not a paid servant of the city. He was a mere contractor who culled his profits from the debtors who occupied the lower wards of the jailhouse. He sold them food and liquor and permitted them to entertain relatives and friends as if the Tolbooth, or that part of it, was a public tavern. Felons, of course, were kept apart, secured behind deadlocks and iron bolts to await the arrival of the Circuit Court and judgment day.

Clare felt no affinity with common criminals or sympathy for their plight. For the spring term she was the star in the jail's firmament. Well the jailer and his turnkeys knew it. The charity of black velvet gentlemen had bought her privacy and privileges, their influence had kept her safe from harm; yet their involvement, however marginal, in the crime with which she had been charged had invested the case with scandalous overtones and, in some stuffy quarters of the town, instinctive and unwavering condemnation not yet justified by facts.

Clare had been snatched from the nursery in Purves's Land some time before midnight on December 31st, in the dying hours of the year 1787. Confused, shocked and shivering, she had been marched by four town officers up Saltmarket Street and across the breadth of the Trongate to the jail. In those first hours there had been nobody of power or authority to protect her, not Andrew, not Eunice and certainly not Frederick. She had been at the mercy of clerks, constables and jailers who, unaware of her connections, muttered and smirked over the papers of charge and admission that a magistrate had signed late that very evening.

As soon as the documents had been checked and approved, sleepy Billy Turner, the turnkey, and a wide-awake Hinchcliff had whisked her upstairs and had thrown her into the iron room, which happened to be without an occupant. Billy had been dismissed while Josiah Hinchcliff had gotten on about the business of discovering just who it was that lay sobbing on the straw at his feet and what pleasure or profit he might wrest from the unfortunate wench.

Hinchcliff was a small, squat, ugly man about forty years of age, heavy-thighed and barrel-chested. From his left hand had hung leg-irons plucked from a hook in the admissions room. He had dangled them ponderously before Clare's face and had grinned. Everybody knew that it was no longer legal to fetter female prisoners but Clare, in shock, had not had the wit to challenge the jailer, had imagined, perhaps, that Josiah Hinchcliff had been appointed judge, jury and executioner all rolled into one.

The man was bad but the woman was somehow worse. Fay Hinchcliff, the jailer's wife, was a gaunt black spider with pale grasping hands. At first she had remained in the shadows at the head of the stairs. She had watched in silence while her husband had fondled the lawn tucker at the neck of Clare's dress and, when Clare had tried to crawl away, had tugged the skirts of the dress itself as if he intended to strip her to the skin. Enveloped in the stink of his body, his frost white breath in the lantern's beam, she had been too terrified to scream when he tore the tucker from her breast and tossed it casually over his shoulder to his wife.

The woman had caught the floating cloth in mid-air. Rubbing it between her fingers she had lifted it to her nose then held it close to her glaucous eyes.

'What, Josiah, is a servant doin' wi' the likes o' this?' she had asked.

'Hand-me-downs,' Hinchcliff had answered. 'You know how it is these days, m'love. You can hardly tell mistress from maid, sometimes.'

'What has she on below?'

'Chinese slippers an' gartered stockin's.'

'Silk?'

'Nah, white cotton.'

'I'm thinkin',' the woman had said, 'that what we have here's a favoured party. Mark my words, some fine gentleman will be scamperin' upstairs before breakfast anxious to protect her.'

'She's pretty enough.'

'You'll have to wait for your pleasure, Josiah, just as I'll have that pretty dress she's wearin'. She will swing, though, won't she?'

'For murder? God, aye!'

'Fetch her tea, then,' the woman had said.

'What! Who'll pay for such a luxury?'

'I told you, Josiah, this one's bound to have a fancy friend.'

Clare had gathered herself stifled her sobs and had told him 'Mr Purves will be here soon.'

'Purves the banker?'

'Yes.'

'Oh, so you're *his* little toy, are you?'

'I am – his cousin.'

'Lyin' bitch,' the woman had said. 'You're not Andrew Purves's cousin!'

'I am. I am.'

'We'll see,' Fay Hinchcliff had said. 'We'll see who arrives tomorrow.'

Mr Rossmore, not Mr Andrew, had been first to the jail. He had hastened early to the Tolbooth on the express instruction of old Mr Purves to assure Clare that the family would stand solidly behind her. The accountant had been followed by Mr McKay, one of Glasgow's more respected legal agents, then by the two Mr Purveses. The following afternoon, just in time to plead against the indictment, Mr Jonathan Brown, Writer to the Signet, and the famous advocate Mr Thomas Walcott had arrived from Edinburgh.

By that time the jailer and his wife had been sufficiently subdued to treat Clare with grudging respect. It seemed that Purves's generosity had given tone to the half-lie that she was a close relative, not merely an encumbrance who had been wished upon the banker's family and charitably taken in as a servant.

Gifts and payments had elevated her from grey indecipherability, from being nothing but the daughter of a woman who had once been married to a man who had been distantly related to the partners in a banking firm. Substance had been added to Clare's claim to be a lady by the dresses that accumulated in the deep wicker basket that Mr Shenkin, at Clare's request, brought in. The dresses, both second mourning, had been gifted to her by Eunice Bates, who had come in person to deliver them, together with ribbons, buttons, scissors, thread, needles and other useful appurtenances. Eunice had not stayed long. She had been too much moved by Clare's predicament, and had wept into her handkerchief for much of their time together. Like Clare, she had mourned not for Frederick but for the poor dead child, her nephew.

In the first weeks of her confinement – after Mr Walcott's pleading at arraignment had failed to prevent committal – Clare had thought not at all of her appearance or the impression that she might give to visitors. She had thought of very little except Frederick – Frederick and Peterkin, Peterkin and Frederick, endlessly trapped in a web of tears. Gradually, though, boredom had soothed her terrible grief, and grief had given way to pondering and to calculation eventually. She had occupied her hands by sewing, by stitching, tucking and exact repair. She had even managed to scrounge the use of a flat iron and a hot brick from the jailer's wife and had thereafter secreted herself away behind the fabrics.

There was irony in it. The more vain she seemed to those who observed her the more calm and determined she became within. Words too had become fabric. Questions and answers, truths and lies stitched and seamed to cover facts that Clare was driven to conceal. She had laboured hard on that garment too. She had plied the needle of her imagination so well that even Mr McKay, an expert in unpicking the perjured testimony, had appeared in part deceived.

Clare was wary of Mr McKay. He had dry skin, a dry voice, dry manner. He was not enchanted by her. He would not have been impressed by the Queen of Sheba laid out on leaves of gold. When Mr McKay had visited her cell, which he did not do often and not at all during February, Clare had said very little. She would sit modestly on the stool, sewing and crooning one of the Scotch airs to herself. Even that performance had earned no sympathy from the Glasgow lawyer. He treated her as if he *knew* that she was hiding something, some secret that it would not be wise for defending counsel to bring to light. Nonetheless, it was McKay who brought Clare news about Mr Walcott and put an end to the misery of uncertainty.

One afternoon in early March Mr McKay had turned up unannounced. He hadn't wasted his time by beating about the bush. 'Mr Walcott will not be pleading at the diet after all,' he'd told her drily. 'Instead you will be represented before the bar by another Edinburgh advocate, a younger man.'

Clare had realised that McKay was angered at the new appointment. Puckers of flesh at the corners of his mouth and peppery flecks in his pupils had told her so.

'What is this younger man's name?' she'd asked.

'Adams.'

'And would this Mr Adams not be your choice of a depute?'

'No, he would not.'

For a few seconds the tables had been turned. Clare had become the inquisitor, McKay the defendant.

'Is Mr Adams Mr Walcott's choice?' she'd asked.

'Aye, foisted upon us whether we wish it or not.'

'Then,' Clare had said, 'he must have some merit.'

'He has never before appeared in a criminal case,' McKay had said. 'He is, however, an "Edinburgh" man, and that seems to be enough to elevate him above me.'

'He is, you say, young?'

'Too damned young, a mere pup.'

'Will he come to ask me questions too?'

'I expect he will, though one never knows what "Edinburgh" men will do,' McKay had said.

'When will he come?'

'When it suits him.'

Every morning thereafter Clare had made herself ready to greet the man who would plead her case before the bar.

She had not thought badly of Mr Walcott. She had not thought of him at all. She had instantly concentrated her mind and imagination upon Mr Adams, sustained herself with the fond belief that anyone who riled McKay could not be entirely without virtue.

Patiently she would dress her hair. Weeks without powder or pomatum had lengthened and refined the

bob-curls that Frederick had so admired. It had been all
that Clare could do to control the blonde locks and keep
them neat about her ears. She had no mirror and had to use
the reflection on the water basin to give back her image.
She had no cosmetic preparations either, and could im-
provise little to make up for this deficiency. A trace of
mutton-fat tinted with carbon from the candle had helped
elongate her upper lids and make her clear blue eyes seem
even more crystalline. She would work hard at it, fuss until
her arms ached, until she grew tired of staring at her
features in the water and would be more relieved than
annoyed when a dray rumbled over the ruts of the Trongate, shivered the image in the basin and atomised it into a
thousand trembling parts.

Once all was ready she would seat herself on the stool by
the window with the Testament open upon her lap. And
wait. She would not stir when Billy brought in her breakfast, would not stir after she had devoured the gruel, eaten
the bread, drunk down the ale. Motionless as a painted
statue, she waited for Mr Adams to discover her, waited
while the sun shifted round or rain came and went and the
chimes mechanically counted out the hours and the musical master pecked out the day's tunes and the light
wanted and the evening breeze came up Saltmarket Street
from the river and the debtors below grew rowdy and the
air became charred with the stench of pork fat and fried
mutton and the tart, astringent smell of spirits from
Hinchcliff's taps below.

Only then would Clare admit that another day had
ended, that Mr Adams from Edinburgh had not deigned
to call. She would rise stiffly, take off the pretty dress,
brush it with her hand and put it safe away then, with a
musty blanket wrapped about her like a shroud, she would

wait for supper, would eat it and would lie wearily down to
wait for sleep.

From Glasgow's lacework of streets and causeways
would come the laughter of free and honest citizens, from
the wards below the muffled cries of debtors and felons.
Clare would draw her knees to her belly, cowl the blanket
over her head, cower down. She would hear the calls of the
Watch and would murmur over and over again, 'Mr
Adams, Mr Adams, come, come, come,' as once, not so
long ago, she had sought to summon Frederick back into
her arms. When she wakened in the night, though, it was
not the lawyer's name that sprang to her lips, nor that of
her lover. She would cry out in the dark for Peterkin, whom
she would never see again, Peterkin, her son, who was
dead.

Advocate Cameron Adams emerged from breakfast in the
Tontine Hotel at a little after ten o'clock and set out to walk
the short distance to the Tolbooth. In greatcoat, topboots
and a fantail hat, he cut quite a dashing figure. He was
thirty-one years old, slender in build and somewhat above
average height. He did not hide his chestnut hair under a
wig of any sort for he was far too busy carving out a career
to waste time fussing with tailors and barbers.

Cameron had been nine years accepted by the Scottish
Bar and in that period had built a considerable reputation
for diligence and tenacity in the handling of civil actions
and disputes. Though reddendo casualties, conditions of
tenure and other matters of conveyancing might butter
one's bread they were not the stuff of which a young
advocate's dreams are made of. Cameron had never before
matched himself against the shrewdest courtroom brains in
the land, most of whom were to be found not in the Court

of Sessions but in the High Court. There life itself was the
lawyers' stake. If they were daring and quixotic and willing
to put all thought of pecuniary profit behind them, de-
fenders could make names for themselves in criminal
proceedings almost overnight. It was to satisfy this natural
urge that Cameron had temporarily abandoned his Edinburgh practice to travel across the breadth of Scotland to
plead a single case at the Glasgow spring assizes.

Jonathan Brown, the defendant's appointed agent and
an old school chum of Cameron's, had obtained the brief
from Walcott. Apparently Jonathan had had to use all his
persuasive gifts to convince old Walcott that he, Cameron
Adams, could master documents in short order and lead
defence with some hope, albeit faint, of saving the poor
creature's neck. The fact that Thomas Walcott could not
abide Angus McKay, whom he thought to be a stiff and
passionless pleader, was certainly a mitigating factor. Perhaps, uncharitably, Walcott's surrender had more to do
with disbursement of the fee. The hefty sum required to
obtain the services of the gravel-voiced old tyrant had
already been partly paid, and partly consumed, not in
purchasing the testimony of witnesses but in feeding Mr
Walcott's vast appetite for good food and fine wine.

Alas for Kelso and her benefactors, in February the
gigantic advocate had fallen ill. Badgered by doctors, his
wife and daughters and spurred by kniving pains in his
belly, he had been forced to retreat to bed. Physic had
failed to cure him in time to trust his precious bulk on the
spring circuit. Finally, belatedly, the great man had taken
heed of Jonathan's suggestion, had summoned Cameron
Adams to his house and, with tears in his bloodshot eyes,
had entrusted. Miss Kelso's fate to the untried young buck
from Newington.

Initially Cameron was less puzzled by evidence in the case than by Tom Walcott's sentimental appeals to save the poor lassie, come what may. Old Walcott was known to have a heart of flint. To see tears coursing down the great man's mottled cheeks was a chastening, intriguing experience.

Admittedly old Walcott had been at the girl's side from the first. Even so, his faith in female integrity seemed at best misplaced and at worst beyond reason and logic. To Cameron's way of thinking the evidence gathered in writing painted Kelso not as an innocent victim but as a cunning Delilah hellbent on snaring a husband at any price. The deeper he delved into witness statements and Kelso's own declaration the more convinced Cameron became that his client was as guilty as sin.

Kelso had been arrested at her place of employment on the day of the year's end and brought on charge before a sitting of Glasgow magistrates on the second day of January. Though Walcott had devised an involved rigmarole in technical Latin he had failed to have the charge against the panel dismissed. Kelso had thereupon declared herself Not Guilty and had begged for a chance to clear her name of calumny before the court.

Bald facts and personal opinion did not deter Cameron Adams from agreeing to lead the defence. He might remain unswayed by the girl's tale of accident and coincidence but nonetheless felt himself challenged by certain peripheral mysteries, not least of which was Walcott's emphatic assurance that Clare Kelso was completely innocent.

'Do *you* think she's innocent?' Cameron had asked Jonathan Brown, soon after he had received and read the transcripts and declarations.

'If she isn't,' Jonathan had answered, 'she ought to be.'

'In Heaven's name, what do you mean by that?'

'Wait until you see her,' Jonathan had said.

'You mean she's attractive?'

'Oh, yes.'

'Is that why old Walcott's fallen for her?'

'Not entirely,' Jonathan had said. 'Old Walcott actually thinks she didn't do it.'

'On what evidence?'

Jonathan had shrugged. 'None that I can discover.'

'Ah, a pretty face and a neat figure and—'

'It's more than that. True, a disreputable old *bon vivant* like our Thomas might nurture hope that she will bed with him out of sheer gratitude—'

'If he gets her off.'

'Quite! But it's more than that.'

'So you keep telling me,' Cameron had said, testily.

'It's her vulnerability that's so appealing, I suppose.'

'Good God, Jonathan! I cannot go before judges and jury and plead "vulnerability" as mitigation in a case of infanticide. I would be laughed to scorn.'

'I'm not sure that you would.'

'Oh, come now!'

'Patience,' Jonathan had told him. 'You'll see.'

'*What* will I see?'

Jonathan smiled infuriatingly and had refused to be drawn further upon that aspect of the case.

As soon as the Court of Session closed at the end of the winter term, Cameron said farewells to his mother and sisters and had left the family home in Newington to catch the early-morning fly for Glasgow. He had much to do before the Circuit Court flung open its doors and took the business of truth and justice roughly by the hand and yanked it inside. He had reached Glasgow at noon. He had left his luggage in the Tontine's least expensive room and, armed with a little sketch map that Jonathan had provided, had set off at once to familiarise himself with landmarks that had bearing on the fatal case.

Cameron had not sought out Angus McKay or arranged a meeting with Kelso's benefactors. He preferred to find his own way about, to survey in passing the jail, courtroom, bank and cottage. He paused for a while before the Apothecaries' Hall, then wended a mile or so along Argyle Street to the westward suburb of Grahamston to inspect the trim new villa which Striker leased and where his sister, Eunice Bates, still lived.

In cold, blustery twilight Cameron had lingered at the villa's gate. He had peered down the garden at the front door and had found himself wondering behind which window the acts of seduction had occurred. He also found himself wondering if the girl had been a virgin when Striker had taken her or if she had been enjoyed by another man or men. He gave himself a shake to knock such prurient thoughts out of mind and turned away to hurry through the flurrying March dusk in time to take tea in the Tontine.

All that evening Cameron Adams kept himself to himself. He supped alone and then confined himself to his room where by candlelight he read again the one pathetic letter that had passed between Kelso and Striker.

The letter was not the original, of course, but a copy. Tom Walcott had let him see the original, however, and Cameron had been impressed by Kelso's steady hand. The duplicate did not do her credit. The copy-clerk had failed to capture the girl's flowing stroke or the haste with which she ran one word into another and with quick little dashes of the nib separated them again. If character could be read from manuscript, Cameron reckoned that he was dealing with a young woman who was rash, impulsive and passionate, though, really, he had no notion of what murderous passion would look like when set in ink on paper.

By contrast Frederick Striker's letters to the court showed a hand that was elongated and upright. Control marched in every consonant. It was difficult to imagine what the man looked like. Jonathan Brown and Walcott could give no first-hand account of Striker's appearance for the fellow had not been seen in Glasgow since October, ten weeks before the murder had occurred.

Though Striker had kept himself out of sight he had not been silent. He had written at length to Tom Walcott and to the agents of the court who would prosecute the libel against Kelso. He had answered all their questions as speedily as the mails would allow. He had posted letters from Shrewsbury, Liverpool, Dublin, Belfast and Larne. He seemed eager to help Clare Kelso in every way possible – this side of marriage. Marriage, Cameron supposed, had never been on the cards, however much Kelso might have wished it. Striker was too cynical to squander himself on a penniless waif, even if she did have some blood kinship with merchants and bankers.

Striker's sister Eunice, who lived with him in the Grahamston villa, had acted as go-between. She had stretched out a helping hand to Clare Kelso on her brother's behalf. In Cameron's opinion, however, that was not enough. The excuse that Striker had been detained abroad on matters of urgent business did not ring true, though it would probably sound perfectly reasonable to judges and jurymen, to whom affairs of business always took precedence over affairs of the heart.

Boisterous March weather matched the spirit of Glasgow rather well. Horse traffic spilled through wynds and closes. Carters and porters pushed barrows and kegs hither and thither. Glimpses of backstreet markets suggested that there was still money about even though the city's monopoly in tobacco had been lost in the war with America. Trongate, broad and spacious and less populated than the narrow sidestreets of the Stockwell and Saltmarket, was dominated by handsome frontages, including those of the Tontine Hotel and the Tolbooth, five storeys in height and heavily embellished with turrets, cupolas, pediments and cornices. Under its double staircase and long piazzas a number of scarlet-clad merchants strolled and chatted soberly, their clerks and valets trailing respectfully behind them.

Though Cameron had never met McKay before he picked the lawyer out instantly from Jonathan's description. Dry McKay, indeed! Braced like a helmsman, legs apart, arms folded over his thin chest McKay was more alert than the guardian of the gate at the base of the Tolbooth. He'd had Cameron in sight for several minutes, eyes fixed like ballshot on the young advocate who had stolen away a case that should rightfully have been his to lead. McKay was dressed in rusty black, his sad old bushy wig backed by a tiny, knobby pigtail that stuck out like a pistol hammer at full cock.

'Lawyer McKay?'

McKay offered no hand. 'Aye, Lawyer Adams, I am he.'

Jonathan and Tom Walcott had told him what to expect. Cameron was not daunted by McKay's severity, thought it did not bode well for professional co-operation.

'I see that you received my letter,' Cameron said.

'I did, sir, as must be obvious from my presence.'

'Yet you did not see fit to reply to it, Mr McKay?'

'It needed no reply.' McKay could not help but add, 'It

was not after all an invitation to supper, or even to break-fast.' He spoke with a queer accent, neither the Broad Scots of his ancestors nor the pinched and cultured tones that a younger generation cribbed from English associates. There was something mean about it, grovelling and haughty at one and the same time.

If the brief had been his from the first Cameron would not have employed such a man to assist him. He was saddled with the grey imp now, though, and could do nothing but make the best of it. With more enthusiasm than he felt, Cameron said, 'Well, sir, shall we venture within the prison walls and see what our client has to say for herself?'

'She will say nothing, sir,' McKay told him. 'She will sit silent as Patience on a monument and pretend she doesn't know what she's doing in prison or why she is being persecuted.'

'Indeed?' Cameron glanced at the barred windows over-head. 'Is she then addled in the brain?'

'No, she is a woman like all women,' McKay answered. ' "There's a language in her eye, her cheeks, her lip. Nay, her foot speaks; her wanton spirits look out at every joint and motion of her body." '

'I am not much for playgoing,' Cameron said.

'It is liter-a-chure that I paraphrase, not theatre.'

Cameron stifled a groan. He hoped that McKay was not going to turn out to be one of those advocates who prove their erudition by hurling obscure quotations at the jury.

'Come then,' Cameron said, 'steer me into your Tol-booth and let me judge this wanton Cressida for myself.'

Stubbornly McKay stood his ground. 'Wait.'

'Wait for what?'

'Have you no question for me first?'

Cameron hesitated then asked, 'Do *you* believe that Kelso is innocent?'

'I do not, sir.'

'Is it the character of the woman or evidence amassed against her that persuades you of her guilt?'

'She *is* guilty, Mr Adams. Take my word on it.' McKay added, 'Of course, my opinion carries no legal weight. Whatever feelings I may nurture about the panel, I will give her the full benefit of my wisdom and experience.'

'With solemn conviction, Mr McKay?'

'My convictions are always solemn, Mr Adams,' said Angus McKay and thereupon led Cameron across the flagstones to the wicket that formed the Tolbooth's first scant line of defence.

Cameron was relieved that he had not been offered the position of junior counsel. He doubted if he could have ably supported a man who had already made up his mind that the client was so tainted by Original Sin that she could not possibly be innocent. He wondered why the Purves family, who were apparently footing the bill for legal services, had condoned the appointment of such a fellow. On the one hand Tom Walcott cried to Heaven that the girl was as pure as a marigold, on the other Angus McKay was willing to have her hanged that very morning. Cameron's own assumptions were no longer quite so clear cut as they had been yesterday. Written evidence had paled somewhat now that he was here in Glasgow, a queer, quaint, rumbustious little city as different from Edinburgh as chalk is from cheese. He pulled his greatcoat about his flanks and followed McKay across the varnished floor to the staircase to the right of the entrance hall.

The prison was not dilapidated. It did not have about it

the mottled, suppurating meanness of Edinburgh's Tol-booth. Even in the morning hour there was a to and fro of visitors to the debtors' wards and high above somebody was singing a shanty in a merry, muscular voice.

The jailer had been alerted to their visit. He waited on the first landing, by the niche where the turnkey had his chair, not far from a half-open door that gave access to communal rooms and kitchens. In the background Cameron noticed a gaunt, spidery woman dressed in black. He thought irreverently what a perfect wife she would make for Angus McKay.

Catching the direction of Cameron's glance, the jailer said, 'That's my good lady, sir. She sees to the comfort o' your client.'

Jonathan had also warned him about the Hinchcliffs. Cameron peered through sun-banded angles of wood and iron. 'Why is Miss Kelso kept in the tower?'

'It's usual, sir, to put a prisoner in her position away from the rest,' Hinchcliff blandly explained. 'For her own protection.'

'I find it hard to believe that an untried young woman can be in serious danger from her fellows,' Cameron said.

'Infanticide is a crime against nature,' McKay put in. 'She'll be regarded as in league with the devil.'

'What!'

'It's no lie, Mr Adams,' Hinchcliff added. 'Besides, there are some within these walls who'd seize advantage of a young woman, given half a chance.'

Cameron nodded. 'Take me up, if you please, Mr Hinchcliff.' He was suddenly eager to see the girl for himself.

If the public opinion was dead set against her it would make his task doubly difficult. Judges were notorious for pandering to galleries and Crown prosecutors would not be slow to exploit the fact.

The case had already been listed and would be led by Advocate Depute, Robert Ordway, a formidable opponent. Lords Pole and Drumfin would be presiding judges.

Cameron was breathing heavily by the time he reached the cell on the top landing. Hinchcliff unlocked the studded oak door and pushed it open. 'Your client, sir,' he said.

She was seated on a stool beneath the high barred window. Sunlight shone on soft golden hair. She had delicate features, not harmoniously regular but with a childlike sweetness about the mouth that made Cameron Adams catch his breath. What had Jonathan said? If she isn't innocent, she ought to be. She wore a dress of second mourning, not ashamed to announce to the world that she grieved for the child she was purported to have murdered.

From his sisters' interminable conversations Cameron had learned a little of feminine fashion. Kelso's dress was made of twilled silk, not best material but expensive enough, a midweight, dark grey tabby with a fine rib to the pattern. It showed off a figure that, though slender, was not in the least childlike. Knees together, shoulders straight, she remained motionless. She stared primly into space as if she was reluctant to be drawn from contemplation of the meaning of some passage in the little Testament that lay open upon her lap.

'Visitors,' Hinchcliff barked. 'Stand up.'

She looked round, not hastily, not guiltily, but with resigned detachment. March sunlight brushed her cheekbone and illuminated the long line of her throat. Cameron reminded himself that Kelso was no ordinary servant but one of that indigenous class whose family could claim some slight edge of advantage by accident of birth and kinship to the well-to-do, in this instance, the Purveses.

McKay growled, 'Well, Kelso, what do you have to say for yourself?'

Her eyes were blue as azures. A single teardrop trembled on one lash until, with a gesture that was in itself apology, she flicked it away with her fingertip. She gave a shuddering sigh and addressed herself directly to Cameron Adams.

'I'm sorry, sir,' she said.

From the moment Clare clapped eyes on Cameron Adams she knew this was a man she could trust. Mr Adams was impressed with her too. She'd noticed his favourable air of surprise when she'd first turned to face him, and a light, brusque manner that pleased her.

'What are you sorry for, Clare Kelso?'

He had come forward from the crowded doorway. He stood before her, hands behind his back, greatcoat fanned out, hat tipped back. He had dark brown hair with a natural curl to it, dark brown eyes that figured amusement as well as curiosity.

'For my bad manners, sir.'

'Is it not a crime you are sorry for then?'

'I have done no crime, sir.'

When she made a half-hearted effort to rise, Mrs Rossmore's Testament slipped from her lap to the straw. Cameron Adams stooped, retrieved it and laid the book lightly upon her knee.

'If you have not done a crime,' he said, 'why are you locked away in the Tolbooth?'

'Because – because others say I have done wrong?'

'Why would they say such a dreadful thing if it were not true?'

'Because they suppose it to be true?'

She answered question with question as if he was a schoolmaster putting her through an examination of Catechism. Cameron said, 'They must have some reason for supposing it to be true.'

'I did not do it, sir.'

'Come now, Lawyer Adams, she has continually denied her guilt. Why do you not ask her about—?' McKay interrupted.

Without taking his gaze from the girl for so much as an instant, Cameron Adams snapped, 'I'll formulate my own questions, thank you, Mr McKay.'

Clare said softly, 'What I have told you, Mr Adams, is the truth.'

Cameron nodded then straightened and turned. He jerked his thumb at Hinchcliff who was lingering in the doorway, ears cocked and a smirking expression on his face.

'You,' Cameron said. 'Out.'

'The door has got to be locked,' said Hinchcliff.

'Then, damn it, lock the blessed thing. I'll summon you when I wish it opened again.'

Reluctantly the jailer stepped back, crashed the heavy door and rotated the key in the lock. He did not move away, however, but loitered with his ear near to the spyhole until Cameron called, 'Miss Kelso is not a creature in a menagerie. The matters I have to discuss with her are private. Go away.'

Footsteps, diminishing, echoed from the stone stairs.

'Will you be requiring me to leave too, Mr Adams?' said Angus McKay.

'Certainly not, Mr McKay. Why would you think that?'

The Glasgow lawyer lifted his shoulders and assumed an

expression that reminded Clare of one of Edwina Purves's prissy simpers. 'So that you might be alone with the panel. That was how Mr Walcott preferred it.'

Cameron uttered a soft 'huh' to indicate that he would have no truck with the sort of games that Thomas Walcott played then, turning his back on McKay, devoted his attention to Clare once more.

'How do you sleep at nights, Miss Kelso?'

'I do not understand.'

'Do you rest easy here?'

'No, sir, I do not sleep well.'

'Are you troubled by noises from the street?'

'Yes, sir.'

'And by dreams?'

'Yes, sir, by dreams too.'

'Bad dreams?'

Frowning, Clare nodded. She had been prepared for the sort of questions that she had answered many times before, but Mr Cameron Adams seemed to have no interest in unvarnished fact. She was suddenly afraid that the Edinburgh advocate might lure her into confidences against which she had shut her mind. For the first time in weeks she felt vulnerable.

'Do you dream about your son, Miss Kelso?'

'Sometimes.'

'Peter, was that his name?'

'We – I called him Peterkin.'

'Do you see Peterkin's face in your dreams?'

'Yes.'

'Does he hold his arms out to you?'

'I – I do not know what you mean.'

She was ruffled by the strange interrogation.

'I think you do know what I mean,' Cameron Adams

said. 'Is it the memory of your son that keeps you awake at night? Peterkin's little face twisted with pain, blotched by the poisonous effects of sulphide of arsenic?'

'Stop, please stop.'

'Ah! Is that what Peterkin calls to you in your dreams? Does he cry out "Stop, Mama, please stop"?'

She straightened, arching her back until the boning of the dress crackled audibly. She was too angry now to bother with poses and posturing. The Edinburgh advocate had touched her as she did not want to be touched. She was suddenly afraid of him and, in her fear, struck out. 'He was only a baby. He could not speak.'

'He could say "Mama", could he not?'

'He could say my name. He knew who I was. But I did not poison him. God, how could I? My own child, my own flesh.' Anger got the better of her. She shot to her feet. 'Yes, I do still see his face when I close my eyes at night. I will see his sweet wee face until the day I die. But if you suppose that I killed him then you are wrong.' Cameron Adams said nothing. He offered no comfort but made no further challenge. He watched and listened, hands behind his back, head cocked. Clare plunged on. 'I was with another woman's children when he was taken from me. I should have been with my own lamb. I should have been there to hold him in my arms. That's why my Peterkin cries out to me in dreams.'

'I see,' Cameron said. 'If you had known he was going to die you would have made an effort to be by his side?'

She breathed hard, sucking the cell's chill air into her lungs. His devious questions had revived feelings that had been smothered for weeks, for months. Later she would realise just how close Cameron Adams had come to manoeuvring her into telling the truth, and her brow would become damp with sweat and her hands tremble at the narrow escape.

She cried out, 'I could not go so far as that, to hold him while he died.'

'Oh, so you knew—' McKay interrupted.

The Glasgow lawyer's intrusion brought Clare immediately to her senses. She saw the trick at once and, cheeks fiery, seated herself upon the stool, folded her hands and, mute as sculpture, gazed up through the window at the blue sky beyond.

Cameron Adams sighed, then yelled, 'Jailer, you may let us out.'

The key clacked in the lock. The weight of the door creaked on its hinges. Clare longed to glance at Cameron Adams to gauge the effect of her outburst. She resisted, maintained her pretty pose, calm and silent in suffering. When he rested his hand upon her shoulder, though, she started, drew in her elbows, hunched her neck as if in expectation of a blow.

'Thank you, Miss Kelso,' he said quietly.

And then he was gone, and the Glasgow lawyer with him. The door clanged shut and the key grated.

Clare sat stock still, waiting until she was certain that the lawyer did not intend to return. Only when the roads and chains of the steeple's clock jarred and whirred to strike eleven did she begin to weep, not for her son, or her lover, but in fear of the clever young advocate who had come so close to breaking her resolve.

Cameron Adams strode out as if he must reach his destination before the old clock sounded the last note of eleven. In fact he was going nowhere in particular. He had no clear idea of whether he was headed west or east, towards the

Tontine or away from it. He charged on in the hope that he might outstrip his frustration and possibly shake off the damned Glaswegian blabbermouth.

'Did – did you hear her, Mr Adams?' McKay panted along at his side. 'Did you – hear how she – condemned herself?'

'I heard nothing of the kind,' Cameron retorted.

'Come now, it was as close to a confession of guilt as ever I've heard,' McKay said.

It was on the tip of Cameron's tongue to inform the lawyer that Clare Kelso's confession might have been even more complete if he, McKay, had not butted in. However, he did not wish to antagonise the man further and kept his mouth firmly shut.

In spite of McKay's intervention he had succeeded in drawing from the girl certain admissions that seemed to substantiate her guilt. He had to admit, though, he now knew why Jonathan and Walcott had been taken in. He too had been impressed by Clare Kelso. As one cluster of little mysteries was solved, however, another appeared to take its place. He must be careful not to fall under her spell, must remain impartial and rational enough to uncover the whole truth if only to separate out those parts that must be buried from sight of judges and jury.

Puffing, McKay caught at Cameron's sleeve. 'Why do you hurry, Lawyer Adams? I cannot keep up with you at this lick.'

Cameron stopped in his tracks, 'In that case, sir, perhaps we should go our separate ways at a pace that suits our separate temperaments.'

'Will we not be taking dinner together?' McKay asked, indignantly.

'I think I will forgo dinner today.'

'May I remind you that we have much to discuss?'

'Time enough to discuss strategy, Mr McKay, when we have more facts at our fingertips.'

'If it's your intention to call upon the witnesses, perhaps I might help by makin' introductions?'

'Your offer is appreciated,' Cameron said, 'but the witnesses will have to wait.'

'If you will not dine with me, perhaps you will do me the honour of takin' supper at my lodging?' McKay was obviously anxious to make amends.

'May I have a stay on that kind invitation?'

'A stay until when?'

'Tomorrow. Perhaps.'

'Damn it, Adams, we've precious little time until court's declared.'

'I am well aware of it, Mr McKay. It's for that reason I ask you to excuse me.'

'What do you intend to do?'

Cameron Adams beggared the question by offering his hand. The wind had been blown out of McKay's sails a little, anxiety had replaced his superciliousness. 'Let's breakfast tomorrow. Half past nine o'clock in the coffee room of the Tontine?' Cameron suggested.

'Very well, breakfast it is,' McKay agreed then, as the Edinburgh advocate swung away, called out, 'Do you know where you are, sir?'

'Oh, yes, Mr McKay,' Cameron answered. 'I always know where I am,' and, with a wave of the hand, sallied round the corner into High Street, out of sight.

Billy Turner did not bring her midday dinner and when she called for fresh water and for the night tub to be removed she was pointedly ignored. Perhaps Hinchcliff was punishing her for her lawyer's high-handed behaviour. She did not care what the jailer thought, or did. She was pleased at that positive aspect in the Edinburgh advocate's character. In case she had to go supperless too, however, she saved a last cup of fresh water from the earthenware jug to last her, sip by sip, throughout the night.

It was a beautiful spring evening. Stripes of light turned the wall primrose. The bars were like stalks of lavender and Clare imagined she could smell the scents of herbs and grasses, moist with twilight dew, floating in from the Plant Garden in Seville Street. One afternoon she had taken Peterkin to the Plant Garden. She had held him up to the wrought-iron gates to enjoy the refreshing perfume of the herbs, but he had not been impressed. He had girned to be taken away to the grill at the back of the Tontine where there was a heavy blast of roasting coffee and basting beef to enjoy. Even in his unweaned state it had seemed that her son shared his father's taste for the finer things in life. It was not painful to remember Peterkin so. Since she had been in prison, detached from the routines of Purves's Land, Clare had fallen into a sort of limbo. It was not difficult to imagine that Peterkin remained alive and well, safe with Mrs Handyside. He would be growing apace, tucking into mince collops like a tiger cub, and sprouting out of his small clothes. She wondered if he enquiried when his Mama would come to take him out again or if in the swift exuberance of childhood he had forgotten her existence entirely.

Such pleasant waking dreams kept Clare content until the sun had gone down and the cell grew cold. Billy Turner did not bring a taper to light her candle and, as she'd expected, no supper was served. Though food and lights had been paid for in advance she would not complain. Darkness and hunger were but minor punishments.

The folk in the debtors' ward were in good voice tonight. Singing had started early. Later it would grow raucous and be accompanied by stamping feet and shouted curses as beer and spirits flowed. She felt no affinity with the debtors and did not yearn for their company.

In darkness she removed her dress; hand-brushed it and folded it along the tucks. Her stomach was cramped through lack of food and she was cold to the bone. She placed the dress across the table and fumbled the blanket from the bed, draped it about her body. And then, arrested by a glimmer of light in the spyhole, she froze. Perhaps she was going to be fed after all or perhaps Hinchcliff had simply come to squint in at her in the hope of catching her in a compromising state. She had no modesty left tonight. She did not scuttle to the inner wall to hide in the only corner that afforded her a measure of privacy. She heard the key turn, hinges squeal. She saw the shadow of a man swarm across the strawed floor. She slipped back and seated herself on the bed, drew up one knee and pressed her fists into the fold of her thighs.

'Do not be afraid,' Cameron Adams said. 'I have come, with your permission, to join you for supper. I apologise for giving no warning but I assumed that you would be "at home", shall we say, and not averse to a measure of company.'

Clare did not have it in her to devise a witty reply. He had caught her unprepared.

He said, 'I take it that you haven't supped yet?'

She managed to shake her head and murmur, 'No.'

'Are you hungry?'

'Yes, I am.'

Mr Adams snapped his fingers and a servant in Tontine livery and a little black boy in pantaloons and brocaded waistcoat entered the cell. They carried huge wooden trays decked with silverware and crystal, each tray centred by a candelabrum. Already lighted, the candles conveyed such a glorious glow into the room that Clare felt immediately warmer and more cheerful.

'Do, please, put on your dress, Miss Kelso. I am not the sort of fellow who sups with ladies in *déshabillé*,' Cameron said.

Clare was decent enough in shift and petticoats. She had not even removed her stockings and slippers yet it embarrassed her to struggle into the dress while men were present. Sensing this Mr Adams turned his back and supervised the arrangement of the supper table. The Tontine waiter and his little assistant paid her no heed and, with an agreement to return in the morning to collect the dishes, were swift to depart once their tasks were done. Gallantly offering Clare his arm Cameron Adams escorted her the two steps from the bed to the table. He drew out the chair and waited while she settled herself upon it, then divested himself of his greatcoat and hat and produced a little folding contraption of pine and canvas that opened into a stool. He seated himself gingerly upon it as if unsure that it would actually bear his weight then, finding that it did, let himself relax. He smiled. Clare smiled back.

Candlelight glistened in his dark eyes and on his glossy dark-brown hair. He had a squarish face, a full under lip, even white teeth. He was not so attractive as Frederick but he was handsome enough, she supposed, for a lawyer. He poured wine from a bottle that a servant had uncorked and offered Clare a glass. 'To your health, Miss Kelso. And your freedom.'

The rims of the glasses chimed on contact and Clare felt the vibration in her fingertips.

Cameron lifted the cover from an entrée dish and released the succulent aroma of hot beef into the air.

'What will you have first? This, I believe, is fillet of roast beef on a ragout of sweetbreads. In this dish there's boiled fowl in rum sauce.'

'Beef, if you please.'

He ladled meat on to her plate, adding a helping of yellow turnip spiced with ginger. Clare watched, as round-eyed and eager as Master William at tea in the Purveses' nursery, and when Cameron Adams nodded, promptly lifted her spoon and fell to.

One day, Cameron told himself, he would dine out on the tale of how he took supper in a cell with a lovely young murderess. His sister Mary would probably refuse to believe that a woman so wicked could have such dainty manners. Evil, to Mary's way of thinking, was the province of the lower orders and she tended to equate it with breaches of etiquette rather than lack of morals. Clare Kelso, in fact, bore more than a passing resemblance to his youngest sister.

She ate quickly, neatly. She drank in quick little sips like a finch at a dish in a cage. The last slice of preserved gooseberry tart defeated her, however, and she pushed away her plate. If she had been privileged to be a man, Cameron thought, she would have unbuttoned her waist-coat and loosed a trouser string or two.

'Are you satisfied with your supper?'

'Yes, sir, I am. And I thank you for it.'

There was colour in her cheeks now and a drowsy softness in her blue eyes. When she smiled her gratitude

Cameron felt himself weaken. He was obliged to look away before he spoke. 'Is it too late to talk?'

'Too late?'

'I mean, are you too weary for conversation?'

'No, Mr Adams. I am weary with being shut up here on my own. I would welcome conversation.'

He contemplated a patch of night sky through the high window. 'I'm afraid that I must ask you some questions.'

'That is your business, Mr Adams.'

He realised with a little shock that she was observing him just as keenly as he observed her. Feeding her had not made her easy and relaxed, rather it had fortified her and brought strength from its hiding place. He was suddenly aware of perspiration on his upper lip, a pulse throbbing in his wrist. He got noisily to his feet, pushed the little stool from under him and said, 'I want you to tell me everything.'

'About—?'

'The incident, the – the murder.'

'It's all in the paper I wrote down for Mr Walcott,' Clare Kelso said. 'My deposition.'

'That is not sufficient.' Cameron hated himself for sounding so testy. He pushed on regardless. 'We are not seeking clemency but acquittal. You must, therefore, convince me of your innocence before I can convince a jury. Do you understand, Clare?'

'Yes, sir, I do.'

'On soul and conscience, Clare, you must answer me truthfully.'

In the light of certain things he had discovered that afternoon and certain judgments made he had doubts about her guilt. Doubts too, alas, about her innocence. He was balanced exactly between two opposing opinions, like a copper weight on a wire. For instance, he had begun to wonder if Striker really was the father of the murdered child. If not, who might the father be? Why had Clare Kelso protected Striker and why did she continue to protect him even at the risk of her life? It had even crossed the advocate's mind that the child had not been born to Clare Kelso at all but to some other woman.

Cameron said, 'Was Frederick Striker the father of your child?'

She answered, 'Yes, sir, he was.'

Cameron said, 'Is there no doubt, no shadow or question on that score?'

She answered, 'None, sir.'

'Clare, do you know what I'm asking?'

She hesitated then said, 'Frederick is the only man I have been with. There has been no other.'

Cameron inhaled a long breath and with as much composure as he could muster seated himself on the unsteady stool once more. He propped his elbows on the table and stared straight into Clare Kelso's blue, unblinking eyes.

'Very well,' he said. 'Now I want you to tell me everything, everything you can remember. I need to know it all. Will you do that for me, Clare?'

'I will, sir,' the girl answered and, without further prompting, began.

BOOK ONE

I

The Captains' Bank

She had had her first sight of Frederick Striker on a stormy morning in October. She remembered the day well for the sloop *Marie* laden with printed calicoes and four days late, had weathered gales in the North Channel and had finally limped into harbour at Port Glasgow. The Purveses had no stake in the ship but Andrew had put out capital to enable an independent agent, Mr Frederick Striker, to purchase and trade cargoes from Dublin and he was, Clare gathered, worried about the security of his investment.

Certainly, there was a buzz of relief about the banking hall and in the domestic apartments above it. Accountant and clerks – Rossmore, Shenkin and McCoull – were just as excited by the news as were the Purveses, father and son. Even Moresby, the porter, had cracked a joke about it with Elsie Gollan when he hobbled into the kitchen for bannocks and tea at half past ten o'clock. By that time Mr Andrew Purves had set off hot-foot for the Port and Old Mr Purves had been given a shake and a dust and chased downstairs to fulfil the morning's quota of appointments.

Old Mr Purves was not so old as all that, nor so lazy. Since his son had entered fully into the partnership, however, he had acquired the habit of lying long in bed and did not much care for morning labour. Though he had never been to sea a day in his life old Mr Purves was nonetheless 'the captain'. Mainstay of the family concern, he knew when to take his place at the helm. By half past nine he was in full occupation of the worn walnut and cane armchair that reposed behind an old oak table in the parlour office behind the banking hall, and was ready to tackle the first of the day's petitioners.

Purves & Purves was Glasgow's only private bank. The firm was a relic of the initiative of three buccaneering sea captains who, back in the Forties, had scraped up cash to finance their own trading ventures with the Americas. Like many other Glasgow merchants the captains had ridden to prosperity on the back of the tobacco monopoly. Unlike their brethren, however, they had not managed to survive the onset of colonial wars and only the perspicacity of old Mr Purves's father had rescued the partnership from ruin.

By shaving away material assets like ships and warehouses and cutting off liabilities like three old seadogs, the Purveses' illustrious ancestor had saved the bank for his descendants. He had put it on such a firm, if unambitious, foundation that it had struggled intact through the fierce banking wars that had decimated the ranks of the city's largest investors and dampened the ardour of its entrepreneurial fringe. All of this tradition had accumulated in old Mr William Purves who was both shrewd and cautious and, if his son's mutterings were to be credited, as immune to change as a Dodo bird.

Mr Striker, agent for the Dublin cargo that had given them all such concern, had called casually at the bank in Purves's Land in the hope of finding Mr Andrew there. Instead he had engaged in conversation with old Mr Purves and, being a relative stranger to Glasgow, had enquired for information – gossip really – about the workings of its social circles. Edwina, Mr Andrew's wife, had been summoned to provide the gentleman with a package of current news about who was in and who was out in the drawing-rooms of the embroidered class. Edwina, however, had been toiling in the closet as the result of the morning's excitement upon a sensitive digestion. She had hissed at Clare through the door, had told her to trot downstairs and offer an apology for her in hospitability. Clare had given charge of the Purveses' three children over to Maddy, the young nurserymaid, and had hurried down the steep side staircase and across the back of the banking hall to the partners' office.

She had knocked, entered, dropped a curtsey, then reeled off a polite excuse for Mrs Purves's absence, an excuse to which the stranger paid not the slightest attention.

Even before Clare had finished speaking, the stranger had put an overly familiar hand on old Mr Purves's shoulder and was asking, 'And who, pray tell me, sir, is this?'

Old Mr Purves had never quite known how to explain Clare's position in his household. Everyone who was anyone in the city understood that she was just another skeleton, albeit a beautiful one, who had rattled out of the depths of the family cupboard some years ago and had been taken in out of charity. But it was not the first time that a stranger had mistaken her for a niece or a full cousin.

'She's – ah – she's Kelso – our – ah . . .' the old man muttered.

'Well, I'm damned!' Frederick Striker said. 'Andrew has never mentioned her. Keeping her to himself, perhaps.'

Clare glanced at Mr Purves. She expected him to object to such an indelicate remark but Mr Purves said nothing. He put his hands up, as he sometimes did when his wife was going on at him, cupped the cauliflower curls of his old wig and gave it a tweak of adjustment.

'Have you a name, young lady?' Frederick addressed Clare directly.

Clare watched Mr Purves's buckled shoe dip and jig with embarrassment. 'I told you, Mr Striker, her name is Kelso.'

'Indeed, you did, sir,' Frederick Striker said. 'My question was but a ruse to induce Miss Kelso to speak, so that I may hear if her voice is as beautiful as her appearance.'

Clare said, 'I am called Clare Kelso.'

'Ah!'

'You may leave us now, Clare,' said Mr Purves hastily. 'Mr Striker and I will continue with our business. And perhaps Mrs Purves will find a moment free to join us later?'

As Clare turned to leave, she heard Frederick Striker say, 'My God, Purves, what a beauty you have there.'

And Mr Purves's dry response, 'Quite!'

Edwina Purves had emerged from the closet and was waiting for Clare in the little drawing-room at the rear of the first floor apartments. Ringlets bobbing, Edwina asked anxiously, 'What did he say?'

'Mr Purves said—'

'No, not Papa. What did Mr Striker say?'

Since the birth of her third child Edwina had been unable to control her girth. She covered areas of distention as best she could with frills and flounces, and laced herself into stomachers of appalling tightness. At thirty she was still pretty but her pertness was being submerged in shapeless fat. Clare had heard it said that Edwina was paying the price of being a daughter of Cathcart of Orbiston, a family more noted for its corporeality than its bloodline.

'The gentleman did not say much, Mrs Purves.'

Eagerness and anxiety in Edwina's tone indicated that she had met Mr Striker before. 'Did he not enquire about *me*? Did he give you no particular message for *me*?

'No, Mrs Purves.'

'I should have ignored my discomfort and gone down,' Edwina tutted to herself. 'What are they *doing*, Clare?'

'Discussing business, I think.'

'Business! Business! Fiddle-faddle!' Edwina wrung her plump hands then assumed her high-nosed, haughty look. 'Inform Jinty that I will take tea. Camomile, lightly infused. If it settles me quick then I will attend Mr Striker as soon as I am able.'

'Do you wish me to request Mr Striker wait?' Clare said.

'No, let him wonder.'

'Yes, mum,' Clare said, and hurried away through the warren of small rooms and passageways to the stairs that led down to the kitchen.

Marriage had not rid Edwina of the vanity that had once made her gay and vivacious, the belle of Assemblies and, with a not unreasonable dowry, the catch of the season. An only child and sole heir to the Captains' Bank, Mr Andrew had been something of a catch himself in those days. He was handsome if not debonair, courteous if not charming. His value as suitor and husband lay in his no-nonsense approach to Edwina's conceits. He was, of course, too sensible and decent ever to have dabbled with mistresses let alone prostitutes and to be bringing something other than love to the marriage bed. William, first child of the marriage, had been born within a year and it was some six months, and two nurserymaids, after that that Clare had first been brought to Purves's Land.

From the first Mr Andrew had been Clare's champion

within the crowded household. Loyalty to the menfolk and
their liking for her had kept her apart from the servants and
had prevented her from becoming the confidante of either
the old wife or the young.

For two or three years after her arrival in the big,
sprawling tenement house off Saltmarket Street, Clare
had indulged herself from time to time in the silly fantasy
that she was really the natural child of old Mr Purves. She
could not imagine where or when her mother and the
elderly banker might have encountered each other but
that did not matter. It was all nonsense, of course. Clare
knew it to be so even as she lay in the wooden-walled
closet just off the nursery and dreamed that somewhere,
somehow, the deed had been done and she was really Mr
Andrew's half-sister. The phase passed eventually. She
had not been born out of wedlock. Whatever his other
failings, her father had been no ghostly stranger but a
figure all too real. She had two older brothers and had had
a baby sister who had died. Somehow she had pushed her
childhood so far into the past that she had but dim
recollections of all of them, except her mother whom
she would never forget.

Robert Kelso had been a strange, wilful man whose only
claim to fame had been his connection with the banking
clan. Even that had been so inexact and tenuous that in the
telling the relationship shifted and changed as often as a
Greenock weathercock. It was only much later, when Mr
Andrew dug out and studied certain dusty family records,
that the line was settled once and for all: Robert Walter
Kelso had been the son of a half-brother of old Mr Purves's
father, though the father had married twice and the half-
brother three times.

'Do you think your father really knew who he was?'

Andrew had asked Clare after they had pored over the documents together.

'No,' Clare had answered. 'And my mother certainly didn't.'

When Clare had reached an age when such things mattered she had once asked her mother how many living relatives she had. Her mother had taken her to the kitchen door and had pointed to a beech tree that grew at the end of the garden. 'As many as there are leaves on yon tree, dearest.'

'But where are they all?'

'Scattered, scattered like the leaves in the autumn,' her mother had answered. 'Blowed away by the wind.'

Robert Walter Kelso had turned out to be so light a character that he too was blowed away by the wind.

One Thursday afternoon in the month of September, when Clare was twelve years old, Robert Walter Kelso had left the tenement room above the little chandler's shop – latest and last of many fruitless adventures in commerce – and had run off to England with a lass of fourteen.

What was worse was that he had taken with him every penny the family possessed. He had even sold the shop's paltry stock for a lump sum and thus left Clare's mother with nothing – nothing that is except two sons, a daughter, a table of small debts, and a fatal impostume of the breast.

At this crucial point in her life Clare had learned what sort of steel had been bred in her, not through the Kelso or Purves line but via her mother, a Gibson from the Perth-shire hill farms. Within a half hour of Mother Kelso discovering the scribbled note that had informed her that her husband had run off, Clare and her brothers had the best of the shop stock roped under canvas on a handcart and were running with it for the Greenock quays. Panting hoarsely, mother had followed hard on their heels, dragging two packs stuffed with clothing and domestic possessions. She had leaned against the cart for two or three minutes, coughing, then she had climbed on to the cart's tailgate and at the top of her voice had announced to fishermen and sailors that a great bargain sale of ironmongery was now in progress.

Packet boatmen, lightermen, skippers from the herring busses and white fish market had been quick to take advantage of the opportunity. Most of them knew what was going on. They had seen Kelso dandling his little miss in harbour taverns and had heard him brag how he would one day cast off for foreign climes with her. They were sympathetic towards the abandoned family. Inside an hour Jenny Kelso had sold again every spike and cleek, every hitch of rope, boll of canvas, bucket, nail and dowel that husband Robert had already sold that very morning to Mr Fortallis, Greenock's most successful chandler. If Mr Fortallis had been less of a skinflint somebody might have run to tell him what was going on – but nobody did. With the September sun just beginning to slip behind the hills of Cowal, Jenny Kelso had finally sold the cart itself and with her three children, her bundles and her profits had dived into Mr McAllister's boat and paid him for passage up river to Bowling Landing and something extra to keep his mouth shut when Mr Fortallis came hunting to find out where they'd gone.

They had spent the night huddled in a thicket above the river's edge then they had boarded another boat that had brought them up river on the dawn flood and had landed them, as in a dream, at a mooring by the Old Brig in the heart of Glasgow.

Clare had looked like a child of eight or nine, not twelve.

She had been dressed by her mother by the riverside so that she resembled a little lady and not the daughter of a profligate chandler. She had come into her woman's state there on the green by the Clyde. It had been that, Clare believed, that had made her lack fortitude and cry so hard when her mother had explained what the future would be and how it was time to tug the string that attached them to money, to request not charity but mercy from the mighty Purveses.

'What about Davy? What about Ross? Will they be comin' with me?' Clare had sobbed.

Mother Kelso had shaken her head. Clare had hugged her brothers and wept more and more. Davy and Ross had been educated in the rudiments of reading, writing and arithmetic – Clare too had attended school in Greenock Wynd for a time – and, Mother Kelso said, she would see them signed on to a good ship or, if she could find out how it was done, recruited into the King's navy. Clare had never been particularly close to her brothers. She had sensed, though, that when the seas took them she would probably never see either of them again and she had wept and clung to them for quite a while. Then her mother, speaking in a soft voice, had told her to be Good and Obedient and to Pray for Her Soul for, when Clare was settled and the boys too, she would be off to the farmstead in the Perthshire hills where she had worked as a lass and would stay there for as long as the Lord allowed. 'Now, Clare dearest, you must stop your cryin', let me wash your face fresh, an' promise me not to cry again while we do what has to be done.'

Mother Kelso had left the boys by the riverside to look at the ships and had taken Clare, dry-eyed now, by the hand. She had led her up to Saltmarket Street, into the lane where the Captains' Bank was and, beside and above it, the old, black-tarred tenement of Purves's Land. Somehow she had persuaded Moresby, the porter at the door, that they were relatives and even if they did not have an appointment were entitled to claim ten minutes of Mr Purves's time.

Clare had been good for her mother's sake, quiet and calm while old Mr Purves and then young Mr Purves had scrutinised her, listened to Jenny Kelso's sober tale and had peered, frowning, at the little purse of silver that the woman had spilled upon the table to pay for her daughter's indenture.

Old Mr Purves had hemmed and hawed but Mr Andrew had spoken out strongly in his brown-bread voice. 'Keep your money, Mrs Kelso. Yes, we will take her here.' He had spoken so decisively that Clare had been comforted and had not wept even when her mother had kissed her and had gone out, all stooped, and had closed the door behind her without glancing back.

Before Martinmas word had come down from the minister of the parish of Comrie that Jenny Kelso was dead. Clare had wept then, certainly, wept until Mr Andrew feared that she would make herself ill. It was the one and only time that Mr Andrew had ever touched her. He'd had a bed made up for her in the quiet little book-lined room that was his study. He had personally sat with her there for a good three hours. He had even put his arm about her and had led her awkwardly through a prayer of sorts. Then he had just sat, still and silent, with her head resting against his waistcoat until at long last grief had released her and she had fallen asleep.

Frederick Striker did not rouse in Clare the same emotions as did Mr Andrew. In spite of his extravagant compliments she was not particularly attracted to the stranger, less so when she learned that Edwina Purves had met him previously at a tea-party in Sinclairs' Land where, according to Edwina, Mr Striker had flirted with her quite outrageously.

How much of Edwina's story was true and how much fancy remained moot. Mr Striker had wound up his business that October morning and had been on his way to another engagement long before Edwina got herself ready to receive him.

'Did he say anything about me before he departed?'

'No, my dear,' her father-in-law answered.

'Did he, perhaps, leave a note?'

'No, my dear.'

'Did he indicate when he would call again?'

'Edwina, Mr Striker is your husband's client not mine,' old Mr Purves said. 'If you require further information on the English gentleman, may I suggest that you enquire from Andrew and not badger me? I hardly know the fellow.'

'That,' said Edwina, not at all put down, 'is because he has not been with us long.'

'Long enough, it seems,' old Mr Purves said and then, with a muttered excuse, went out into the banking hall before he could be called upon to explain his last remark.

If there had been talk about Mr Striker among the servants before that morning Clare had not been privy to it. But then the kitchen crew, cook Elsie Gollan in particular, tended to regard Clare with suspicion and distrust.

For practical purposes Clare was more servant than kinswoman, but she had been with the Purveses longer than most of the other females and had acquired skills that enabled her to fill any household post. When Edwina's sharp tongue had chased away yet another cook, Clare had even taken charge of the kitchen for a spell. Edwina Purves was too lazy to be a dedicated housekeeper. She could not be bothered with planning, with overseeing the chores needed to keep the tenement society ordered and comfortable. She did not, as a rule, even make her own market. Consequently she leaned heavily upon the goodwill of the women below stairs to work without supervision which, for the most part, they did. The cost, however, was a yielding of too much power to the cook, Elsie Gollan.

Eight women, two men and a couple of lads were employed to keep the Purveses in comfort. Old Mr Purves refused to shell out for a footman or butler; to Edwina's way of thinking another example of her father-in-law's niggardliness, like his refusal to contemplate the purchase of a country estate. Of course, Edwina had no head for business, no clue as to the manner in which menfolk made their money. It did not occur to her that the Purveses were not as rich as the Sinclairs, the Johnstones or the Dreghorns or that it was only her father-in-law's modest caution that kept the family solvent in troubled times.

If the Purveses' domestics were rather a shiftless lot, the bank clerks were exactly the opposite. They had served Purves & Purves, man and boy, and had learned the rules of financial hurlyburly at the very desks which they now occupied. Mr Rossmore was the accountant. Mr Shenkin, a converted Son of Israel, and Mr McCoull were the clerks. All three were as loyal as lions and as honest as bullion. Perhaps they were not gentlemen born but they had been bred in the right degree and knew their places to a tee. They treated Clare with affectionate respect and received affectionate respect in return. Even after she had been made up to nursery-maid Clare continued to act as an unofficial link between house and bank.

A special bond between Clare and the penmen had been

forged when she was young. On Mr Anderw's instruction the clerks had taken time from their duties to round out Clare's education in grammar, geography, history and arithmetic. Mr Rossmore had even gingerly introduced her to the joys of Latin and Greek and had provided her with a little library which she studied whenever she had the time. Therefore it was not to the kitchen crew that Clare went when she required information that did not concern her but to her friends in the banking hall.

Something in Mr Frederick Striker's arrogant manner suggested that he was wealthy. For her own satisfaction Clare wanted to find out what she could about the English stranger to whom her mistress seemed so attracted.

'What's your interest in such a fellow, Clare?' Mr Shenkin peered mildly over his inch-thick spectacles. 'I find it hard to believe that you find him attractive too.'

'Too?'

It was quiet in Saltmarket Street. The banking hall was deserted. Varnished panels rejected the sun's rays and even the brass around the door and along the edges of the counting table seemed dull that afternoon.

Mr Shenkin tightened his waistcoat tapes and tweaked his cravat. He was about fifty-two years old, had fathered seven children, not one of whom had died, and his wife, Bea, liked to splash out in society. 'Striker's the current darling of the Sinclair set, the talk of all the tea-tables. My youngest, Becky, has even raised his name in polite conversation and my wife is quite dazzled by what she has seen and heard of him.'

'Well, I found him very rude, very forward,' said Clare.

Spectacle glass enlarged Mr Shenkin's jet black eyes. 'That was Becky's opinion too – at first. She quickly changed her tune. Though I know not why.'

'What do you know of his circumstances, Mr Shenkin?'

'He would not make a husband for you, Clarey.'

'A husband!' She was genuinely taken aback. 'I am not in search of a husband, Mr Shenkin.'

'It would be natural if you were, quite natural.'

'I am perfectly content where I am, thank you.' Clare tried to sound indignant. 'Besides, I would not be at all right for a man like Mr Striker.'

'Why ever not?'

'He – he's a gentleman.'

'No, Clarey, I do not think that he's a gentleman. He may have money, wear a bright blue coat with silver buttons, take dinner with Mr Andrew and tea with Betté Sinclair—'

'Does he?'

'– but none of that makes him a gentleman.'

'He's too old for me,' said Clare.

'Nonsense! He's not a day over forty, if that. Dissipation ages a chap very quickly, you know.'

'Dissipation?'

'Clarey, Clarey, have you been eating the parrot's seed?' Mr Shenkin extracted a heavy ledger from the shelf before him, propped it open on the lectern and pretended to peer at columns of inky figures. 'I think – opinion has it – the word is out – that your Mr Striker is a rake.'

'Gossip!'

'Ask Mrs Purves.'

'How can I?'

'Put it to her discreetly. She has an ear more finely tuned to scandal than I have.' Mr Shenkin glanced up suddenly and frowned. 'Oh! Did she send you here to ask me these questions?'

'Certainly not.'

'Phew!' breathed Mr Shenkin.

Clare had teased mild and kindly Mr Shenkin often in the past, but always pleasantly. She could not fathom why, today, there was such an edge to her statements.

'Perhaps I should inform Mr Andrew that you have a very poor opinion of his client,' she said. 'And let *him* find out the reason for it.'

Mr Shenkin caught her arm. 'No, Clare. Please do not do that. I would not have told anyone else what I have just told you. What's wrong with you today?'

'Nothing. I am perfectly well.'

'Are you so struck with this Mr Striker that you would betray your old friends?'

'No. No, I'm sorry.'

'Clarey, Clarey, put this man out of your mind.' Mr Shenkin patted her arm. 'Try to remember what it was that killed the cat.'

'Curiosity, do you mean?'

'Curiosity I do mean,' said Mr Shenkin. 'Now go away, please. I have interest to compound before tea.'

Clare had never before thought of herself as a wife. She had been casually pursued by Coachman Bob and by the valet that Mr Andrew and his father shared. But Bob and Peter-Pierre had not been after her hand but other parts of her and she had not been flattered by their attentions. In fact she had scolded them with such vehemence that the kitchen crew's sympathies had fallen on the males and she, Clare Kelso, had been dubbed a snoot for not allowing herself to be kissed and fondled without complaint.

In the shortening late-autumn days the tedium of life in Purves's Land demanded some diversion, however, and gossip about Frederick Striker provided it.

Fuel was added to the fire by the fact that Frederick Striker was a not infrequent visitor at the bank that fall. He took tea upstairs once or twice and seemed to be slipping into a close friendship with either Mr Andrew or with Mr Andrew's wife. Opinion on that vexed question was divided.

Jinty, Maddy, Nancy – the young maids – were full of talk of Mr Frederick. They were attracted as much by his wicked reputation as by his looks. His long, mismatched features somehow added up to irresistible manliness, enhanced by height and an insinuating swagger. Besides, he was no dour, grunting Scotsman. His flat English accent made him seem contained but approachable.

In the meantime, of course, those mothers who had eligible daughters on their hands were falling over themselves for introductions to Mr Striker. And the gentleman himself – if half, nay, a quarter of the market rumours were true – was keeping his bridal parts in trim by bedding any woman who would tumble with him which, apparently, included several of the most genteel wives in town.

'How does he get away wi' it?' Maddy, agog, asked. 'Why has he no' been shot by an angry husband?'

Elsie Gollan tapped the side of her fleshy nose with her forefinger. 'Well, you know the old sayin': Them as has gold aplenty may plate sin with brass.'

'What does that mean, Mrs Gollan?'

'You'll learn, dear, when you're older.'

'Is she one o' them?' Jinty asked.

'Who's that?'

'Upstairs?'

'My God, girl, that's no' a very nice thing to be thinkin' about your mistress.'

'Is she, though?' Jinty persisted.

'Pym tells me she isn't,' Elsie said.

'But would she no' like to be?' said Nancy.

'Well, Pym tells me she's takin' to callin' round regular at Mrs Phoebe Johnstone's just in the hope of meetin' him there,' Elsie said.

'Does Pym go with her?'

'Nah, nah. She's careful to leave Pym at home.'

'What'll happen if *he's* there when *she's* there?' Maddy asked.

'Who knows!' said Elsie Gollan, darkly.

'Och, but he could hardly – you know, right there on the parlour rug,' said Jinty.

'No sayin' what a man like that might not do,' said Elsie.

'It's chance he's after, I'll wager,' said Nancy. 'He'll be in search of opportunity.'

'Well, given time, it's my guess she'll make sure he gets it.' Elsie Gollan nodded smugly.

'Unless,' said Jinty, 'he finds a better fish to fry.'

'Oh, I reckon Freddy Striker's got pan enough for all the fish he can catch,' Elsie Gollan said.

And the girls, sniggering, crouched closer round the table to discuss the pecularities of male anatomy and Mr Striker's attributes in particular.

Slackness and disrespect were inevitable consequences of Edwina's neglect of matters domestic. Whatever discipline was handed down to the servants came not from the boudoir but from Mr Andrew and was applied by Bob McIntyre, who ruled the courtyard with a rod of iron. What went on indoors, of course, was another matter. Rules and regulations for servant behaviour, rotas and tallies, count-sheets of linen and candles, coals, flints, blankets, preserves and the hundred-and-one other comestibles that crammed the presses had been drawn up and written down years ago, by old Mrs Purves: and long ago lost. Edwina did not seem to care and Mr Andrew, though quite aware of what was going on, was by nature generous and saw no reason to cheat the servants of comforts or to curb their natural appetites excessively, provided no theft for resale was involved which, Bob assured him, it was not.

Lack of proper discipline and moral example in the female head of the house manifested itself in more insidious ways. Edwina cared little or nothing for her children. Provided they were kept out of sight and out of earshot and did not inconvenience her, she was content to let Clare take care of them and run the nursery as she wished.

On that particular evening Clare had been up with the newest little Purves, baby Margaret, who was breaking teeth and feverish and fretful because of it. Clare had cradled the child in her arms and walked with her for a couple of hours while Maddy snored in the bed by the wall as if she was deaf. There was nothing particularly unusual in this. Clare had nursed Dorothea through teething phases and did not blame the latest arrival for her crossness. What made Clare tense that evening was the fact that Frederick Striker had been invited for supper.

If Edwina had imagined that Frederick was coming just to admire her then she was doomed to disappointment. No sooner had supper been concluded than Andrew carried Frederick off to the cosy little lair of a room at the corridor's end with two bottles of port, a dish of walnuts, a bowl of tobacco and a quiver of new clay pipes. It must have borne hard on Edwina to realise that it was male business not feminine company that had brought Frederick to Purves's Land that night.

Though Clare had only glimpsed the Englishman on his arrival upstairs, the knowledge that he was nearby made her uncommonly restless.

Up and down Clare walked, up and down, between and around the little beds, shushing and crooning to the whimpering infant. She would pause now and then to rub poor Margaret's inflamed gums with a lotion that Maddy had fetched from the Apothecaries' Hall just before it closed at ten.

In spite of its rambling passageways there was precious little privacy within the wooden house of Purves's Land. Clare was well aware that her mistress was sitting up, with Pym for company, in the marital bedroom. She guessed that Edwina was also listening to the faint rumble of masculine conversation and sporadic laughter that filtered from Andrew's study. Perhaps she was trying to catch a word here or there, to separate Frederick's voice from the dreary tones of her husband. Edwina would be dressed in her silk night-gown and silk stockings. Perhaps she was awaiting an opportunity to emerge – accidentally – from her bedroom in time to let Mr Striker view her unstayed charms.

Outside, midnight had been called. Tobacco fumes and the rich, rubicund smell of wine drifted through the usual effuvia of coal and candle smoke like red threads in a grey wool shawl. It was obvious that the port would go round until both bottles had been polished off and that Mr Andrew, who had no stomach for strong drink, would be sick again tomorrow.

Though Clare was calm and soothing to the baby, inwardly she was irked that Mr Andrew's wife should plot so shamelessly to catch the eye of an eligible bachelor while she, Clare Kelso, spinster and maid, was dressed like a cocklegirl in petticoat, shift and shawl. It was only to foil

Edwina's plan, not to show herself to Mr Striker, that Clare yielded to impulse and, when the study door finally opened, stepped from the nursery into the passage with the drooling infant cradled to her breast.

The glow from the study was brilliant with coalfire, and candlelight the colour of whisky. Mr Andrew was in shirtsleeves and unbuttoned waistcoat. Mr Striker carried his coat over his shoulder like a countryman. Both men were ruddy-cheeked and laughing, more like rakes than men of business. They were so engaged in the taggle-end of convivial conversation that they did not notice Clare at first or for that matter Edwina, who had also stepped out into the passage. Frederick, blinking through the haze, was first to spot the woman. Edwina paused as if the presence of the Englishman had caught her completely by surprise. She raised one plump arm, curled her fingers and assumed an expression of modest astonishment that she had probably been rehearsing for hours.

'Why, Mr Striker, I did not realise that you were still with us.'

'Madam, what a vision is this to greet a gentleman half in his cups,' Frederick said. 'I believe I must be dreaming – though, damn it all, my dreams have never been so sweet before.'

'What the devil are you doing, Edwina?' Andrew said.

The woman stammered prettily, 'I was awakened by – by the cries of my daughter and thought to go to her.'

Only then did Clare realise that Edwina was unaware of her presence in the passageway. At the same moment little Margaret opened her sticky eyes and let out a piercing scream. With grim satisfaction and more than a little malice Clare watched Edwina's amorous playlet degenerate into farce.

'Yes, mum,' Clare heard herself say. 'I thought you might be worried so I was just bringing little Margaret in to you for comfort.'

Stepping along the passage, she offered the squalling baby to her appalled mother.

Roused at last by Margaret's screams, Maddy poked her head from the nursery door. Pym appeared from the bedroom, while Mr Andrew, fuddled by drink, tried vainly to shoo his wife out of Frederick's sight by flicking at her with a moist red handkerchief.

'What?' Edwina spun towards Clare. 'Why?'

'I thought a wee drop of milk might—'

'Milk!' The very word filled Edwina with horror. She shuddered, recoiled from the noisy bundle and crossed her hands over her ample bosom as if some extreme form of robbery was contemplated. 'Me! Milk!'

Revived by cool air, Andrew had regained some control of his senses. Without doubt, he would have managed to take charge of the situation and preserve the dignity of all concerned if he had been allowed ten or twenty seconds longer to recover.

At this juncture, however, young Master William burst sobbing from the nursery and sent Maddy flying in his rush. At almost six years old the boy was a toddler no more. He had sturdy legs and a bullcalf head which he butted directly into his father's most sensitive region before the man could defend himself.

'PAP-AAAAAAH!' William yelled, and butted again for attention.

Andrew uttered a soft round sound, clutched at his breeches with both hands and doubled over while his son and heir tried to climb upon his back in search of protection from the terrors of a dark, deserted nursery.

Even as Andrew sank to his knees, four year old Dorothea, rubbing her eyes and snivelling, tottered too into the passage.

Bemused, she headed straight for her mother. Edwina recoiled once more and cried out, 'No, get back, get back,' as if her offspring was a hobgoblin or horrid sprite.

To his credit Frederick Striker saw the humour of the situation. Just as old Mr Purves, lantern in hand and nightcap askew, appeared on the stairs, Frederick began to laugh. He straightened, like a totem pole among Indians, planted his hands on his hips and laughed aloud. Laughter changed his character completely. Unlike his smile his laughter was devoid of cynicism or calculation.

With tears running down his cheeks and a catch in his throat he held out his hands to Clare and found just enough breath to say, 'Here, lass, give the morsel to me.'

Old Mr Purves had come down into the passage and Dorothea, still snivelling and in search of comfort, trailed damply towards her grandfather.

Edwina was quivering with rage and shame. Charms unwrapped for Mr Striker's delectation were pointed like blunderbusses at her husband. She commanded him to do something. Andrew, however, was in no fit state to do anything at all. He crouched gasping on all fours while his son pulled his hair and yelled.

Frederick eased the baby from Clare's arms. The fact that the child was wet about the bottom did not seem to trouble him at all. He held Margaret tenderly, big pale hands cupping her while he inspected the little pink mouth.

'It's a teething fever.'

'Yes, sir. I know it is,' Clare said.

'Have you tried a borax lotion?'

'Yes, it has been administered.'

'Poor thing,' Frederick said. 'How she suffers.'

Raising little Margaret, he draped her comfortably over his shoulder, let her fix her mouth upon his shirt frill and suck and dribble to her heart's content.

It was a small, still lull in the confusion, a moment that Clare would remember and cherish. Frederick looked down at her with a candour she no longer found humiliating. She knew that he could see the lines of her figure through her thin petticoat and shift. But she no longer cared.

By a discreet lift of the brows Mr Striker indicated that he was impressed by what he saw.

'Should – should I not take her back?' Clare whispered.

'No, not just yet,' said Frederick.

Behind and around them Maddy and Pym were herding the older children back into the nursery. Old Mr Purves helped his son to his feet.

As soon as Andrew was vertical again he minced towards his wife, gripped her shoulder, gave her a push towards the bedroom, growled at her to remember who she was and, when she had gone in, dragged the door shut behind her.

Rocked by the big safe hands and with cambric to gnaw on Margaret had gone quiet. No longer drowsy, she gazed with chocolate-brown eyes over the stranger's shoulder at her father and grandfather.

The smile was back on Frederick Striker's face, the smile that Clare did not much like. She drew the folds of the shawl over her breasts, whereupon Frederick delivered Margaret to her with a little careless toss of the arms and, that done, apparently lost all interest in infants and servant girls.

'An evening to remember, Andrew.' He adjusted his shirt, drew on his coat and put an arm about his host's sagging shoulders. 'By God, sir, you certainly know how to lay on an entertainment.'

Andrew had no stuff left with which to do the honours. It fell to old Mr Purves to see his son's client downstairs and light him by lantern out into the yard and Saltmarket Street. Andrew, meanwhile, shuffled away into the study to inspect the damage to his sensibilities and soothe the throbbing with a snifter of brandy, taken internally of course.

Clare waited in the passage, Margaret in her arms. She heard the clank of the chain that secured the back door and then old Mr Purves, grumbling and puffing, climb upstairs again. He glowered at Clare, his normally equitable features displaying annoyance and perplexity.

'Where's my son?'

'Gone into his parlour.'

'I do not like to see him drink.' Mr Purves sighed. 'He'll be ill tomorrow, you know.'

'Yes, sir, I fear he will.'

'I'll take on his morning's appointments. He had better remain in bed. Tell him that, Clare, if you see him.'

'I will, sir.'

Sighing again, Mr Purves paused long enough to chuck his grandchild affectionately under the chin.

'Goodnight, wee lassie,' he said. 'And to you, Clare.'

'Goodnight, Mr Purves,' Clare said then, carrying Margaret, she returned to the nursery and closed the door behind her with her heel.

All was quiet in the tenement of Purves's Land. William and Dorothea were asleep, sprawled in a heap with Maddy on the servant's bed, all three of them snoring lightly. It was against the rules for children to share a cot with a servant but that was another tradition that seemed to have withered through neglect in this lax household. Margaret had at last found peace and slept in the high-sided crib by the embers of the fire. Clare lit no candle. She sat close to the infant on the old short-legged nursing chair and watched, musingly, over her.

She wondered if Frederick was striding homeward, hat in hand and coat unbuttoned, vigorous and refreshed by the cold November air, or if – she could not ignore the thought – he had been sufficiently inflamed by the sight of Edwina Purves to have gone prowling down the Briggait in search of one of the wantons who served the urgent needs of lusty gentlemen. She wondered what Frederick would do with those long, strong, flat-fingered hands, which of all the details she had heard in Elsie Gollan's kitchen were true and real, which fantasy. She could not quite imagine what would happen when money had been paid and dirty sheets stripped down. She had not enough experience to put herself in a street girl's place. Her lack of knowledge was no longer innocent, however. It was tinged with a delicious itching sort of guilt, made all the more vivid by her ignorance.

Thumb to mouth, Margaret whimpered, 'Mum-mmm-mmm.'

Clare soothed her and brushed away the little beads of perspiration that had formed on the child's brow. She touched her fingertips to her lips and tasted, faintly, salt.

'Hush, lambkin, hush,' she murmured softly. 'Clare's here. Clare's here.'

And outside, like an echo, a watchman cried the hour.

2

A Gentleman's Pursuit

After that late-night episode nothing was seen of Frederick Striker at Purves's Land for several weeks. When tackled on the subject Andrew merely shrugged and informed his wife that what the Englishman got up to was really none of his concern but that he did not doubt that Mr Striker would turn up again in due course, like the proverbial bad penny.

The onset of a spell of particularly cold weather soon put the doings of the fascinating Mr Striker temporarily out of mind. The kitchen crew were far too busy to engage in random gossip. They were kept on the hop from morn till night, venting chimneys, cleaning grates, ferrying kindling and coals, filling up warming pans and chopping ice from the yard pump to get fresh water flowing again. Old Mrs Purves was taken poorly. Even when she was over the worst she continued in her bed, boosted by cordials, philasters, coltsfoot candy and occasional pipes of black tobacco. Old Mr Purves, of hardier stuff, was out and about as usual. Wrapped in knitted muffler and coachman's greatcoat he looked more like a footpad than a gentleman, as if he was setting out to conk his friends and not simply dine with them at one or other of the city's clubs.

The shallows of the Clyde froze over. On suitable ponds and watermeadows skating contests and curling matches were confidently arranged and, out on Coulter's Loch, a great bonspiel organised by the Merchants' House roared on and on, with stones and sweepers lit by bonfires that could be seen from every hillock and garret in the city. But the cold grew grey, then black as the month wore on, and soon became too severe for recreation, too sore for most folk to want to do anything except huddle about the hearth with a bowl of broth or tassie of hot toddy cupped in shivering hands.

Alone among the servants, Clare had no aversion to the bitter weather. She preferred to be out of doors. She had no compunction about sacrificing fashion for comfort. She dressed like a Highland tinker in thick ribbed wool stockings and clumsy shawls, strapped pattens to her shoes, wrapped one of Edwina's discarded scarves about her head and ventured out into the near-deserted streets with only William for company.

Unlike his mother and sisters, Master William thrived on fresh air. His demands provided Clare with perfect excuses to quit the smoky, smothering tenement for an hour or so each early afternoon. Now almost six, William was a sore trial to all those who lived in Purves's Land. His restless energy found its best expression in mischief. He was for ever leaping downstairs or pounding along the passage-ways or sneaking out into the gardens, barefoot, to crunch the rime of frost under his toes or lick at the icicles that hung from the washhouse eaves. Maddy would rush out to drag him indoors again and the little devil would kick Maddy's shins or tug her hair, secure in the knowledge that she was forbidden to raise her hand against him. He was more respectful of Clare who had the power to administer a slap or clout or report him to his father for a taste of the strap if and when he went too far.

William was always going too far. He would spit, curse, strut and glower like a miniature guildsman or one of the councillors whom he encountered about the Merchants' House steps or on the pavé by the Trongate. Many of the town's noble citizens, knowing fine whose child he was, would pause to pat the wee chap's head and fuss over him. They thought him no end of a man-in-the-making because of his punch and precocity. They also appreciated the opportunity to pass the time of day with Nursemaid Kelso who was a jewel for beauty and wasted on the Purveses.

Edwina wanted Willy put to school just to be rid of him. Andrew and his father would have none of it. They had been boys too once and were boys still at heart. They would not deprive the lad of childhood liberty and actually regretted that he would soon have to be handed over to some formidable dame or cadaverous master who would no doubt thrash the nonsense out of him.

Clare was encouraged to take the boy with her whenever she performed errands about the town. Edwina had even expressed the faint, fond hope that Clare might stumble upon a gypsy band that would steal away the little horror to trade for drink, or that one of the wild beasts from the showman's caravan might consume young William in lieu of lunch. No such luck. Clare was careful of her charge. She seldom let William stray beyond the reach of her hand and never turned her back on him, not for an instant.

Fire-eaters, naturally, were William's favourite diversion, followed by freaks, jugglers, menageries and Horace the Learnéd Pig. Grand fairs and carnivals rolled into Glasgow only at Whitsun and Martinmas, however. Usually William had to content himself with a horse sale or cattle mart or a stroll down to the flesh markets to watch mutton being butchered or fowls wrung and plucked. The

King Street market's paved courts and rusticated entrances made it the best in Europe. Each stall had its own waterpipe and a drain to carry blood away. William loved the rasping saws and flashing knives, pens of sheep and cattle awaiting their turn on block-and-tackle. He was impatient with Clare's shopping, especially on cold days, and would hop and strut, growling under his breath, until Clare guided him at last to King Street to buy the butcher meat.

Cow tripe, giblets and a flank of good beef ham were on Clare's provision list that bitter, black afternoon. Cold air sharpened men's appetites and both Mr Andrew and his father had declared themselves home for supper, so a satisfying spread would be necessary. Clare had William firmly by the hand. Her elbow was clamped against the leather purse that rode in her dress pocket and she was walking quickly for even she felt the bite of the frost and did not want to tarry too long out of doors. She rounded a stone pillar with William dragging behind her. The sight of a sheep's head stuck on a spike with blood frozen into a long pink icicle from its purple tongue had caught the boy's fancy and he was lagging behind. Clare turned to remonstrate with him and collided with two men, one short as a gnome, the other tall as a totem.

'Oh, sirs, I'm sorry,' Clare apologised.

Willy crammed into the back of Clare's knees and projected her forward. She stumbled. She felt the tall man's arm encircle her waist and his hand support her. It was a natural gesture, gallant in its intention. He did not, however, release her once her balance was regained. He drew her closer and leaned his long, hard thigh into the folds of her dress, contour against contour, like spoons in a velvet case.

'Clare Kelso, is it not?'

She recognised the English voice a split second before she looked up and identified Frederick's face framed by a fur-lined collar and fur-brimmed hat. 'Mr Striker! What a surprise.'

Cold had brought out the character in his features. He had a burnt-sugar complexion that suggested he had spent more time of late out in the weather than snuggled in feathery boudoirs or drawing-rooms.

Frederick's companion was clearly not a gentleman. He had the loose-shirted, grubby look of a farmer and sported thigh-length hessians that had been long out of fashion. What the gnome-like man shared with Mr Striker, though, was an arrogance that indicated he was no humble servant whose livelihood depended upon a master's whim. The wee man carried a canvas sack tucked under one arm. A cursory glance at the bag was sufficient to tell Clare, and Willy too, that it contained a living creature.

' 's'at?' William demanded, scowling from behind Clare's apron. ' 's'at a rat?'

'How gratifying that you should remember me.' Frederick Striker ignored William and devoted his attention to Clare. 'Are you faint with cold, Miss Kelso?'

'No, sir, I just stumbled. Perhaps you should release me now that I have safely found my feet.'

'If it was not a faint then perhaps you threw yourself upon me deliberately,' said Frederick teasingly. 'May I live in hope that you will do so again at a more convenient hour?'

'Why, sir, I did not intend—'

'I know that you did not. I see that there is not much practice of wit in Purves's Land.'

'Wit enough, Mr Striker.'

'And propriety?'

'Aye, sir.'

'More propriety than wit?'

Clare could not think of a sharp reply. She was relieved when William, furious at being ignored, stalked out from behind her skirts and demanded, 'Is that a rat ye have in that bag?'

'William, do not be impudent.'

Frederick's companion was not in the least dismayed by the behaviour of the lordly whelp. Only a foot or so taller in height than Willy, the little man kept the canvas bag tucked under his armpit and, in a tone as icy as it was low, told the boy, 'Speak only when spoken to, sonny.'

'I want to know what's in that bag.'

'Willy!' Clare put a hand on William's shoulder but had it rudely shaken off. She would have picked him up if Mr Striker had not intervened.

'Let him see for himself,' Frederick said.

The wee man glanced enquiringly at Frederick, cocked an eyebrow and received a nod by way of sanction.

'Well,' said the wee man, 'I canna let you see what's in ma bag, sonny, but I'll let you ha'e a feel.'

'Feel?' William frowned.

'Aye, an' if you can tell me how many teeth ma pet has got then ye shall have it for your own.' He stared at William, on the level, eye to eye. 'How's that for a bargain?'

' 's a rat,' said William, without certainty.

'Is it really?' The wee man eased the bag into his hands and held it out. 'Are ye sure about that?'

'Aye, ah'm are.'

'How many teeth then?'

'Ten.'

The wee man snorted. 'Ten times ten more like. Pull the string, sonny, slip in your hand an' count.'

'He – he has no arithmetic,' said Clare apprehensively.

'Well,' said the wee man, 'just tell me how sharp they are.'

The creature in the bag stirred. It uttered not a sound but dabbed and dunted upon the inside of the canvas. Clare noticed that the drawstring was of thick, hard leather, pulled tight. She glanced up at Frederick who gave her a wink and whispered into her ear, 'The boy will come to no harm, believe me.'

With forefinger and thumb the little man tugged the drawstring loose and shook the bag vigorously. On toe tip William tried to see inside but the owner would have none of that. He lifted the bag up. 'One hand in. Are ye brave enough, sonny?'

The little man's hands were scarred, some scars wrinkled, others freshly pimpled with blood. There were darker, bruised wounds too. If it had not been for Frederick's reassurances she would have snatched William up and beat an immediate retreat into the street.

The joke was wearing thin and Frederick was keen enough to sense it. 'No, Cluny, put your snake away before it does damage.'

'S-snake!' Willy stiffened and leaned into the tall man's thighs, one hand, very little now, curling upward in search of adult protection.

Frederick said, 'You, Miss Kelso, would you not care to put your hand into Cluny's bag to see if you can make the serpent spit?'

'No, sir, I would not,' said Clare. 'Even although I'm sure it's no serpent in there, just a poor chicken.'

'I fear we have been rumbled, Cluny.' Frederick laughed.

'Aye, Mr Striker, I fear we have,' said the wee man and

tucking the bag under his arm again walked off towards the portico without a word of farewell.

William's eyes followed him, and the bag, every step of the way into the street. 'S-s-snake!' he hissed, under his breath.

Clare said, 'I see no amusement in teasing such a wee lad, Mr Striker.'

'It will do him no harm,' Frederick said. 'I suspect that, like his father, he suffers from a severe lack of imagination. Why are you here on such a bitter day as this?'

'To buy meat.'

'Too chilly for Mrs Purves, I suppose.'

'Yes, her constitution is not—'

'Do not tell your mistress that you saw me here,' Frederick interrupted.

'Why should I not?'

'Because I ask it of you.'

'What if a certain small person should mention it?'

'A certain small person is probably too ashamed of himself to mention it,' Frederick said.

Clare looked down at William who, white faced, had turned his cheek to her apron and gripped her hand with both fists.

'Well, Mr Striker, you may be right,' she said.

'Will *you* keep my secret?'

'If I can, without telling an outright lie.'

'That's a good enough answer, Clare,' Frederick said. 'Off with you then. Do not keep the Purveses waiting for their supper.'

'Will you call at Purves's Land again?'

'Of course,' Frederick said, 'but not for some weeks. Even the pleasure, the extreme pleasure, of meeting you again, Miss Kelso, cannot stay me from my business.'

'I understand.'

'I am glad that you do,' Frederick said.

Clare dropped a half-curtsey and firming William's grip in her own, said, 'I'll bid you good day then, Mr Striker.'

He paused, touched his hat, bowed. 'Are you, perhaps, acquainted with Lady Sinclair?'

'I am acquainted with her reputation,' Clare surprised herself by saying.

'Indeed!'

'I have seen her from a distance about the town.'

'Ah, but have you ever visited Sinclairs' Land, say with your mistress?'

'No, Mr Striker, I have not had that pleasure.'

'Would you like to?'

'Mr Striker, I'm a nursery-maid, not a gay lady.'

'Only,' said Frederick, 'because the Purveses will not admit it. You are, in fact, more of a lady than most of the women in this town.'

'What—?'

'My word on it,' he said.

He touched her lips lightly with his ungloved forefinger as if to silence her protestation then, with another discreet bow, turned and hurried off to join his odd companion. Puzzled, Clare stared after him. She saw the men meet, laugh, and then go off together, arms linked like brothers.

'S-s-s-snake?' hissed Willy, shuddering.

'No. Chicken,' Clare told him and with less patience than the boy was used to, led him quickly along the aisle between the carcasses.

In genteel society dancing had long been regarded as part of polite education. Schools of steps, assemblies and seasonal balls were nothing new. Theory and practice were somewhat different animals, however, particularly in the west of Scotland. In olden days the balls had been wild affairs, memories of which could still bring a glint to the eyes of wheezy old gentlemen and faded ladies and set their feet tap-tapping as if ranting pipe and trembling string still thrummed beneath their wrinkles and black bombazine.

Old Mrs Purves had often told Clare how her father had been a subscriber to the building of the Assembly Hall, that gatherings in those days were at five and that all the men were gallants and all the ladies gay as campions. Of less selective memory, old Mr Purves had a different tale to tell, of young men crowded dourly at one end of the ballroom, young ladies shyly at the other and no commerce at all between the genders until the Master of Ceremonies flung three or four couples on to the floor and forced them on Pain of Death to walk the Minuet.

Mr Andrew had first encountered Edwina at a dancing party. He had been dressed as a Jacky Tar and had danced a very lively and intricate Hornpipe which, so he said, had wrung rapturous applause from all the girls present. Mistress Edwina had another opinion on that event: 'What a damned fool he looked in his big bonnet and shrunk smock, red as a turkeycock, thumping about. Monsieur Polignac, *my* dancing master, had nothing but disdain for the clumsy Hornpipe. He taught us proper steps.'

'What sort of steps, mum?' Clare would say. 'Can you recall them?'

'As well as I recall how to breathe,' Edwina would say and, if she was in a jolly mood, would take Clare's hand and lead her through the patterns one by one.

Later, when she had moments to spare, Clare would bow and dip and side-step in time to a glamorous music that she carried in her head, and imagine that one day she too might have a handsome gentleman to turn her about.

Clare told nobody of her morning meeting with Mr Striker. It seemed that Master William had been temporarily robbed of his pithe by the encounter. In fact, he would not venture alone into yard or garden in case he met again 'the mannie wi' the snake', a piece of nonsense that his mother and father put down to childish fantasy and too much pork at supper.

Clare could not help but think of Mr Striker, of his flattering remark that she was a lady in all but name, his half-promise that one day she might enter the Sinclairs' mansion by the front door and be treated as an equal by Sir John and Lady Betté. She did not dare confess her ambitions to the other servants, of course, for they would have mocked her and thought her ridiculous. Nevertheless Clare considered it wise to prepare herself for the eventuality by pumping Elsie Gollan for information on the inhabitants of Sinclairs' Land who were, it seemed, both despised and admired at one and the same time.

Apparently Lady Betté was not willing to concede that she had passed her prime, could no longer stand up with the cream of the crop, her own daughters included, and have gentlemen leaping five-barred gates to pay their devoirs to her. Sir John did not seem to object to his wife's philanderings provided she did not dandle with anyone of consequence. He had her all to himself for most of the summer when the family resided in the Sinclairs' estate at Wyvercroft in darkest Ayrshire where, it was rumoured, the old boy made his wife pay for the licence she had enjoyed in town all winter. Lady Betté was clearly not cowed by her diminutive husband nor was her *joie d'esprit* bruised by his nameless punishments. As soon as the last sheaf was gathered from the rigs of Wyvercroft and the fieldhands hanselled with ale and porter, back she bounced to Glasgow, eager for the season and fresh conquests.

As a daughter of one of the Plantation Princes, Betté had inherited not only a tidy portion of Papa's money but also his disposition to wassail. What she unfortunately lacked was a male's inalienable right to indulge freely in vices or any trace of the *hauteur* that had kept her father more or less on Virtue's straight and narrow path. She had, alas, also inherited her Papa's breadth and height, his equine features and large mouth. She was blonde as wheat, though, and clear of complexion, so that paint and powder kept her youthful and her bosom, a wonder in itself, distracted critical gaze from the gentle decay above.

Edwina Purves was dreadfully envious of Lady Betté's liberal attitudes. Edwina fondly imagined that if she had not been stuck with such a dour clod of a husband she too might have shared the pleasures that kept Betté young. As it was, a few mild flirtations, including the one with Mr Striker, were as close as Edwina dared come to playing with fire.

The first word that filtered down to Purves's Land about a St Valentine's Ball at Sinclairs' Land derived from a most unusual source – a letter from the Purveses of Moorfoot, a rusticated clan that dwelled in a tumbledown castle in the hinterlands of Lanarkshire. The Moorfoot Purveses' eldest daughter, Frances, had, it seemed, been invited to attend Lady Betté Sinclair's grand ball at the Mansion and would she, Edwina, put up with a guest for a week or two and see to it that Miss Frances was properly accoutred and attended for the occasion? Nothing to that. Young women may have felt lost in country seats but they were seldom totally forgotten. What stuck like a fishbone in Edwina's

throat was the fact that news of the ball had come in from
the country, and the even more distressing fact that Andrew and she had not received an invitation.

'Where is it?' Edwina had screamed. 'Where is our
card?'

'Dearest, I have no idea,' Andrew had answered with a
lack of concern that drove Edwina into a fury.

'Are we not going? Are we being slighted? What have
you been up to, sir?'

'Nothing, madam.'

'Why then have we not been invited when this – your
cousin, I mean, has been?'

'I'm afraid you'll have to ask Lady Betté to answer that
question.'

'How *can* I? How can I possibly—'

'Perhaps,' Andrew had said, placatingly, 'it's a dance for
young folk only. Before you fly into a fizz, Edwina, I
suggest that you first enquire among your friends to discover how many of them have received cards of invitation.'

'Ah! Yes.'

Answer: all of them.

Upwards of one hundred, the cream of Glasgow's rank
and fashion and a number of lesser mortals too, already
had gilt-edged cards adorning their mantelshelves or
propped alluringly on dressing-tables. Only the banking
Purveses, it seemed, had been ignored.

Edwina could not take tea anywhere, in town, suburb or
distant village, without the subject of the Sinclair's ball
being raised. And then eyebrows and then embarrassed
silences, a clearing of throats and a swift change in the
direction of conversation. Spurned and rejected, Edwina
came down with a persistent megrim that in spite of
purgings and bleedings kept her confined to Purves's

Land. Headache saved her the humiliation of having to confess that, for reasons unknown, she and her family had been left out of the season's most prestigious social event. Her condition and her temper were not helped by the shoal of letters that came up from Moorfoot, brimful of questions, instructions, anticipations.

Though old Mr Purves had declined to purchase an out-of-town estate, he had acquired, furlong by furlong, certain fields along the city's borders. What these were and what they yielded in rents and tithings were matters that Mr Purves kept strictly to himself. He saw no reason to surrender to his daughter-in-law's blandishments to move to the country. He had been born in this tenement, had no taste for travel and preferred a pavement under his feet to mud and straw. His surviving brother Jamie, on the other hand, had never liked town life and had sunk his inheritance into the purchase of a castle, some clay fields and a small but thriving tannery. Jamie was now on to his third wife. Something in the air of Moorfoot, or the reek from the tannery lum perhaps, had carried off two spouses, and the brood of mainly female children who sprawled through the castle's halls were never quite sure to what line they properly belonged or who they might be calling Mother next.

William and Jamie were in no way estranged but they were not given to sentimental gestures like letter-writing or regular visiting. Month upon month would go by without communication between the families. Daughters, however, were daughters the whole world over and the prospect of visiting Uncle Purves and Cousin Andrew in the city had become for the little Moorfoot maids a symbol of maturity and independence. Husbands of quality were to be found in Glasgow. Better mates by far than the sons of the peapods who were paraded in Lanarkshire's marriage markets. Frances was the forerunner of what Edwina feared would become a stream of provincial bumpkins, all chattering and fluttering about Purves's Land. She would have had less objection to chaperoning some ardent rustic maiden, of course, if she, Edwina, had been invited to the Sinclairs' ball too.

Letters seemed to imply that Lady Betté was an intimate of the Moorfoot Purveses though in actual fact none of the inhabitants of the castle had ever clapped eyes on her. Andrew had been down to Moorfoot to shoot now and then, when he was younger, and was ruthlessly interrogated by his irate wife about those excursions.

'Who is she? This Frances?'

'I think, if I recall, that she is the ravishingly pretty one,' Andrew answered. 'Although, I must confess, they all looked much the same to me last time I visited. All dark as Egyptians. All my uncle's wives have been dark-haired. Peggy is no exception. She's expecting again, by the way.'

'At her age? Disgusting!' from Edwina.

Clare obtained information from her master in a more cautious and persuasive manner. 'Is Miss Frances coming alone to Glasgow?' she asked on one of the infrequent occasions when she had Andrew to herself.

'I expect she'll have maids with her. Where we shall put them all I really cannot say,' Andrew answered. 'Perhaps I should have Bob run out the chaise and trot down to fetch them. That would be the thing to do, would it not Clare?'

'Yes – if the mistress agrees.'

Andrew was silent for a moment then said, 'No. I do believe I'll leave it to my uncle to supply transportation.'

Clare said, 'If Mrs Purves isn't going to the ball, who will chaperone Miss Frances?'

Andrew frowned. 'You might well ask.'

Clare said, 'Will Mr Striker be there?'

'Where?'

'At Lady Betté's.'

Andrew was seated by the fire in the study parlour, vest unbuttoned, wig laid on the floor beside him, a copy of *The Mercury* open on his lap. It was late into the evening and the children were asleep. Clare had brought him a glass of spiced wine and a dish of macaroons, for which he had a fondness. He nibbled at the edges of one of the almond cakes before he answered. 'I wouldn't be at all surprised.' He pushed the rest of the macaroon into his mouth. 'Why do you ask?'

'I – I just—'

'Sit.'

'Beg your pardon, sir?'

'Sit down, Clare.'

He glanced towards the door then shifted a quilted footstool with his toe and nodded at it. Clare hesitated then, gathering in her skirts, obeyed. She seated herself at Mr Andrew's feet like a pupil before a master and, after a hesitation, accepted the glass he offered her. She drank a little wine and handed the glass back, watched him nurse it awkwardly, turning it between finger and thumb.

'Clare,' he said, at length, 'I have noticed how you look at Mr Striker and, indeed, how he looks at you. Do you see a husband in him, is that it?'

'Oh, no, Mr Andrew. I cannot possibly think of Mr Striker in those terms. He's too far above me.'

'Not so far, not nearly so far as you might imagine,' Andrew told her. 'He has a certain amount of money. And will have more before the next year is out unless I'm mistaken. But he is a common enough man. There would

be nothing in him – or in you – to prevent a marriage.'
Andrew twirled the long-stemmed glass again, not meeting
Clare's eye. 'Except that I do not believe that it is marriage
that Frederick Striker has in mind.'

'I do not know what you mean, Mr Andrew.'

'Oh, I think you do.' He set the glass on to a side table
and took Clare's hand. 'You are, you know, an exceedingly
attractive young woman. I am often asked about you. By
men of better stamp than Frederick Striker. I have nothing
against the fellow personally. In fact we are involved in a
business venture together. I just do not think that he would
be a suitable husband for you, Clare. Candidly I would not
want to see you wasted upon him.'

Clare flushed with annoyance and excitement. Only
recently had it begun to dawn upon her that, because of
her looks, she might be able to pull herself out of Purves's
Land, out of the servant class. It was, after all, her father's
idleness and profligacy not his breeding that had condemned the family to near-impoverishment and denied
her entry to more respectable society.

As if he had forgotten it, Andrew was still holding her
hand. She looked up into his face and detected a softness
there that she had not often remarked before.

'I told your mother years ago that I would take care of
you and, thus, I am obliged to speak to you frankly now. I
trust that you will not take it amiss.' Not daring to speak,
her thoughts whirling, she shook her head. Andrew went
on, 'For, though you are neither my sister nor my cousin, I
do regard you as more than a servant. Besides, you should
have some advantage out of our kinship.'

Clare was suddenly eager to discover the names of the
other gentlemen who had asked after her, what compliments had been paid. She felt, though, that such questions

would display conceit and that, for all his good intentions towards her, Mr Andrew would not give the best of answers.

Andrew was saying, 'A good marriage can be arranged for you, Clare, I'm sure. Not on the instant, of course, but when you feel that you are ready to leave us and assume the responsibilities of a household and a husband.'

'What sort of a man might I hope for, Mr Andrew?' Clare said, and heard herself add, 'A man like you, perhaps?'

He released her hand at once and sat back in the chair. 'Well, no. I am, after all, married.'

'And we are kin, are we not?'

'Hardly, hardly,' Andrew said. 'Kinship would not be an issue. What I meant – what I mean – is that it will not do to reach too high in your aspirations.'

'How high shall I reach, Mr Andrew?'

She realised that she had embarrassed him but had also pleased him. For the first time that she could remember she tasted the pleasure of manipulation. Awareness of her attraction was the last thing in the world that Andrew had intended to instil but the deed had been done and there could be no undoing of it now. He blustered and shrugged. 'Oh, I cannot say. A soldier, perhaps, or a tradesman of standing. If only we had a cashier in the bank who was young and unmarried.'

Hiding her disappointment at the failure of Mr Andrew's imagination, Clare got to her feet. 'I must get back to the nursery.'

'Yes, yes. You had better.'

She did not moon over strong-thighed young men as Jinty and Maddy did, nor did she mope for a husband as did Pym, picking and sorting through chance acquaintances as if they were oranges on a stall. Until recently, she had not even thought of herself as desirable, though Elsie Gollan had once told her that she would make a fine mistress for a laird and might climb into a golden bed by that ladder. What Andrew had done was sharpen Clare's sense of value to a point that came perilously close to conceit. A year ago, a month ago, she would never have done what she did now.

In lieu of a curtsey, she dipped her head and kissed Andrew quickly upon the brow. 'I'm glad you're not my brother, sir,' she said and then, before he could recover from his surprise, turned and left the study in a swirl of skirts and petticoats.

It was warm in the nursery. The Purveses were not niggardly with fuel and the fire had been banked up and sprinkled with a little damp sand to keep it restful and restrained throughout the night. Outside, cold air pressed against the tenement's wooden walls and creaked on the slating. Hair unbound, Maddy lay on her back in the cot by the wall. William had crept in beside the girl again. He was cuddled up to her, his cheek, flushed with heat, pressed to her small, conical breast as if he was listening to her heartbeat. Dorothea and Margaret were asleep too in their separate cots but her conversation with Mr Andrew had left Clare wide awake. She seated herself on the nursing chair before the fire, took off her shoes and stockings and, with skirts hitched up, extended her bare legs and studied them critically.

By some lights she might be considered too thin. She was certainly no plump-kneed country wench who, like a mare, would be thought ideal for breeding; no more was she bony and angular like Pym or all knobby like Maddy. She had shape, shape and smoothness, and her skin in the firelight looked soft as pink satin. Some merchants and burgesses stared at her as if they were stripping her with their eyes. Even Mr Shenkin and Mr McCoull would look at her, quills wistfully poised, as if something in her appearance had taken them by surprise.

Her brother Davy had been considered handsome, with the same fair colouring and piercing blue eyes as she had. Ross was more like his father, swarthy and muscular. Mother had once told her that her father's mother had been a beauty who, though she had died young, had had more beaux trailing after her than any crown princess in Europe. However it came about, by whatever channel, Clare knew that what Mr Andrew had told her was true. She was not destined to languish on kitchen stairs or wither in a nursery, bent crooked from caddying ashes and water buckets and other people's children. She deserved, and would have, better.

She rose from the chair and took off her apron, dress and petticoats. Clad only in her shift she felt as weightless as a reflection in a looking-glass. She raised her arms and, without a sound, executed the first steps of the Minuet that Edwina had taught her.

In the window, tinted by firelight, she caught a glimpse of herself. No powdered hairpiece, no silk gown, no fine lawn or French lace was needed to improve her. Even in a cotton shift, bare-armed, bare-legged, she was good enough for any man and, on a bridal night, would surely make him forget that she lacked lands and policies, titles and deeds or a dowry of cold, hard cash.

It was accepted by civic authorities that, in course of time, the new Glasgow would be erected around the great road that ran south from the Old Bridge and, to ease that end, the Parish of Gorbals had lately been disjoined from neighbouring Govan. It was also believed that Gorbals' current guddle of weavers, tailors, nailers, gunsmiths, maltmen and rogues would be gradually incorporated into larger programmes of expansion and progress. Some cynics supposed otherwise. They saw in the feuing of old farmsteads and the building of new streets not progress at all but an opportunity for fifty thousand brand new victims to be plied with beer and whisky, cheated at cards, fleeced at dice and generally lured into degradation by Gorbals' gamblers, publicans and whores.

Cluny Martin had no fear for his moral welfare. He had been in worse places than Gorbals and survived. He was not a resident of the parish nor even one of its regular visitors. His beat was to the west of the city, around the inns and farms that sprawled down river from Anderston to Cardross and, in season, beyond. Besides, he did not come alone across the Brig that cold January evening. He had for protection the company of a gentleman, a tall gentleman who, as well as having money in his purse, kept a dagger in his boot and carried a malacca cane with a swagger that suggested he knew how to use it.

Among the sports who assembled in the barn at the back of the Neptune tavern, a long, low, ramshackle hostelry west of the village, were several who knew Cluny both by sight and repute. Apart from a nod, however, they gave no signal of recognition. Mr Frederick Striker they knew not at all for none there had much to do with gentlemen outside of gambling circles. Frederick had been careful to steer clear of those since certain unfortunate incidents in the Northern counties of England had somewhat marred his welcomes and tarred his reputation. Gorbals in January,

though, was safe enough for a fellow of sporting inclinations who, up to that hour, had not shown his mug at a
cockfight in Scotland and, win or lose, would not do so
again this side of Martinmas.

What made the January main at the Neptune worthy of
Frederick's attention was the fact that Lord Drumfin had
brought out his splendid birds to match against any scruffy
old bundle of feathers that local breeders cared to pitch into
the pit for a pound or two.

Arthur Nye, Lord Drumfin, was the most famous, most
fanatical cockfighting man in the whole of Scotland. At his
country seat at Kennart he had not one but three pits. The
best of them had been built into the ballroom of Kennart
House at a cost, it was said, of four hundred pounds.
Kennart had become the site of notorious week-long
mains, with squires and earls and even viscounts travelling
three and four hundred miles to match birds and squander
fortunes there.

Drumfin was a large, fresh-faced fellow with bulldog
dewlaps, merry eyes and a hearty laugh. He was always
cheerful, never down and, at sixty-eight, was more active
and energetic than most men half his age, in the Parliament
House and out of it. It was said that it was blood kept the
old boy young, the blood of gamebirds mingled with the
blood of the criminals that his judgments sent to the
gallows. When he was not arrayed in the splendid garb
of a High Court judge, the laird of Drumfin sported suits of
plain russet broadcloth and a huge dusty wig of ginger hair
that hung about his jowls like a cockerel's wattles.

When Drumfin travelled to Edinburgh for the court
sessions the best of the birds went with him. And when he
went upon the Circuit in spring and autumn he was
invariably accompanied by a feeder, a trainer and a selec-

tion of gamebirds of the second water just in case a battle or two might be squeezed between the business and pomp of the assizes. The calling of the January main at the Neptune was all Drumfin's doing. In the cold season he could not find opponents readily and, on vacation, he needed the stimulation that only battles could provide to warm his wintry blood. It mattered not to Drumfin that his best birds had to be left at home. A local main against inferior feathers provided a good opportunity to test the mettle of fresh youngsters and grind a last guinea or two out of faithful old warriors who deserved to die gasping in the pit and not of boredom in the fair green close, unmourned even by their harem of hens.

Perhaps what Lord Drumfin really enjoyed was the celestial spirit of anarchy that hung over a cockfight. In spite of the Articles of the Match that were drawn up, read to and signed by all participants, somehow the fight reflected the spirit of Scots law as practised at certain assizes.

Tom Powers, landlord of the Neptune, was the titular opponent of Lord Drumfin. It was he who put up the stake for the match at forty pounds on the odd battle. Landlord Tom was no owner or breeder. Nine gamecocks had therefore to be found to match against Drumfin's birds. Word of mouth soon brought the amateur fancy clamouring to Tom's door, clutching birds and guineas and to bet on each battle, beak to beak.

Cluny had been at the inn the previous afternoon for the ceremony of weighing. Drumfin's best handler and feeder had acted as the laird's agents. The birds had been balanced to the ounce and schedule of battles drawn. No wagers had been made, however, for Drumfin would not allocate that pleasure even to trusted minions and liked to

look a man dead in the eye before he rooked him of his
money. It was seven winters now since Drumfin had lost a
January main but the amateurs did not think of that or
calculate the odds against them. Each had faith in the bird
that he had reared and trained, eager to participate against
pure bred blackbreasts and Kennart birchins. It was worth
risking a year's wages just for the chance of beating a laird.

The noise in the barn was deafening by the time Frederick and Cluny arrived. Smoke, thick as whale fat,
grasped the throat. By the hearth at the rear of the building
three hefty farmers were warming a rooster at the flames
and crooning to it, while another pair were giving a last clip
to an arrogant red. On the flagstones close by the door two
young weavers, hardly more than boys, were chanting in
pig-Latin over a puny wee Dun and sprinkling it with holy
water from a tiny glass vial. Drumfin's birds, caged not
bagged, were ranged on a trestle table in the least draughty
corner, guarded and cossetted by a trainer and feeder and
viewed by the hundred or so gamblers, the *cognoscenti*, who
had come from far and wide to wager on the events.

Cluny found a quiet spot behind the benches and an oval
table littered with pewter mugs and empty pie-dishes.
Kneeling, half hidden by the table's edge, he unfastened
the drawstring and gave the canvas bag a wee shake. Out
popped the bird's head, already trimmed bald for the
battle. The eye was mean. The beak, cut too, opened
and closed as if to say, 'What's this? What's all this?'

'Here we are in the Gorbals, Satan,' Cluny muttered, his
lip dangerously close to the bird's beak. 'What do ye think
o'it then?' Satan answered with a swift, blurry snap at his
master's nose but, pinned by two fingers round his gizzard,
missed by a whisker. 'Ah, so you're hungry, are ye, son?'
Cluny dug his free hand into his pocket and brought out a

pinch of mixed grains and herbs that the bald-headed little monster pecked from his palm along with three or four spots of fresh blood.

'Is he ready?' Frederick asked.

'Primed like a pistol.'

'How many can he take?'

'Take them all, b'God, so he will.'

'I've heard that Drumfin will not fight a bird against its weight.'

'Aye, I've heard that too,' Cluny said. 'But his lordship made the rules so his lordship can change them if he wishes. I'll put ma bonnie wee Satan up against an alligator if Drumfin has one wi' feathers on it.'

With a jab of his elbow Cluny knocked Satan's head down into the bag and tugged the string tight again. He glanced up at Frederick. 'He'll not know who you are, will he? Drumfin, I mean.'

'No, Cluny,' Frederick said. 'I hold no gamebirds, so as far as the laird's concerned I'm a man invisible. When will the battles begin?'

'Soon.'

'And when does Satan fight?'

'Third.'

'And fourth?'

Cluny sat back on his heels, the bag resting in his lap. He looked up at Frederick, grinned, winked and said, 'The old accumulator will turn up trumps, sir, never fear.'

'To the tune of two hundred pounds, Cluny?'

'To the tune o' two thousand, if you have the nerve.'

Darkness had fallen and torches were lit before Drumfin was ready to take his seat on the quilted bench that Tom Powers had upholstered to accommodate the noble bottom. With turn of the tide the wind had risen. It whistled among the barn's rafters and scraped through the thatch and made the gamebirds restive and even more ready for the fray.

Lengthy preliminary rituals had worn on Frederick's nerves. He had calmed himself with sips of gin from a flask and had watched Drumfin as a hawk watches a mouse. Ironically he might have introduced himself to the noble lord, dropped a name or two and been invited to share the quilted bench. But anonymity was more important than comfort or prestige and Frederick had no wish to blow a month of plotting and preparation. This was to be no random flutter. He had come to the January main for the specific purpose of acquiring rush capital. He had first seen Satan fight in a Welsh main in Rutherglen and again at an All Hallows' fair at Cardross. There, on the Clyde shore, the little grey gamecock, weighing hardly more than three pounds, had destroyed four rivals in half an hour and when pulled off with hardly a scratch had been spunky enough to take on four more. Pickings from stakes and wagers at country pits were too scant for Frederick's needs. It was not until he heard of the match at Gorbals that he had sought out and cultivated Cluny Martin and purchased himself a share of Satan.

Frederick felt that he was due a stroke from fortune. His luck had been running ill for years now. He had counted on his sister's inheritance from Arthur Bates to solve his problems. But Bates' money, farmland, everything had vanished into a swamp of litigation when Bates' children had challenged not only the validity of the will but the legitimacy of the marriage and even the manner of the old man's death. Since then Frederick had scratched for cargo fees and purchase prices, worked off loans with expensive borrowings, never quite able to catch up with himself or make the one killing that would pay ransom for all his industry and sufferings.

Once more his grand schemes and elaborate plots had come down to a wager. His dreams of palaces and private fleets rested now on the speed and cunning of a scruffy grey bird stuffed into a canvas bag. From the night's match Frederick required a clear sixty pounds in profit. Drumfin would give no better odds than evens against an untried bird in the first battle but Cluny had assured Frederick that the noble lord would not shirk a match on the bye to follow. And even a third if Satan won.

'Did Drumfin inspect our bird?'

'Aye. He laughed at it.'

'I trust he will laugh the other way before the night's out,' Frederick said.

'Depend upon it,' Cluny said. 'Give me the money now, sir, unless you've had a change o'heart an' wish to slap it on his palm yourself.'

'No, as arranged.' With a motion so swift as to be almost invisible Frederick Striker transferred the calfskin purse from his to Cluny's pocket.

'What's here?'

'Twenty pounds.'

'Five are mine?' Cluny asked.

'Yes.'

'Drumfin has some fine birds, no doubt o'that.'

'What are you saying to me, man, that we will lose?'

'Nah, nah,' said Cluny Martin. 'Show our Satan a russet feather an' he'll fly wi'out fear.'

'Twice?'

'Three times,' said Cluny.

The masters of the match, Drumfin and Tom Powers,

sat on opposite sides of the pit. The main's official umpire, the Teller of the Law, stood just inside the knee-high wooden ring. The first battle was called and setters-to stepped through the gate and allowed the Teller to inspect the sharp steel gaffles that were fastened with waxed thread to the birds' spurs. Wagers were being made among the crowd, most of them directly with Lord Drumfin who, though he had an agent with him, slapped each man's hand with his own to signify a bond.

The gamecocks were held forward beak to beak, allowed to take a preliminary peck at each other while still held in the setters' hands and were then lowered down to feint and parry and, at length, buckle-to in a whir of wings and feathers. Frederick was drawn to the pit's edge. Nobody gave him a second glance. All eyes were on the pit, on the combatants, who rose and flew and fell back, separating only when no wound had been inflicted, no advantage gained. As had happened before at cockfights, Frederick experienced a moment or two of strange sadness, of awe at the realisation that the creatures had no knowledge of what fates rested upon their efforts. Instinct alone drove them. They fought because Nature had endowed them with a hatred of their own kind and a pride that would take them to the point of death.

The first battle ended not in death but defeat after a good, lively twenty minutes. The second battle, swift and gory, lasted only seven or eight minutes. It terminated in the demise of a grey-breasted bird whose first fight was also his last. The owners, the pig-Latin boys, were humiliated by their bird's bad showing, paid their debts and swept out of the barn, leaving the tattered remains to be scooped up by Drumfin's setter and thrown on to the midden.

Drumfin was elated. 'By God in Heaven,' he shouted. 'I

have found a champion here, I fancy. Do you see, he's hardly winded, that young Flounce of mine. Tell you what, I'll set him again, on the bye, in just half an hour if there are takers.'

The sporting gentlemen had been too impressed with Flounce's performance, however, to rush into rash wagers. They watched and muttered as the Spanish cock named Flounce was handed by the setter to his lordship who stroked the striking neck and head and blew tobacco fumes upon him to cool him down.

'Well? Well? What do ye say to all this, Tom Powers? Is there not a man among you who has a bird to match my Flounce?' Drumfin shouted.

'I'll match him,' Cluny Martin said.

'What? Is the weight equal?'

'One ounce is the difference,' said Cluny calmly, 'in my bird's favour. I'll bleed him till he's even if ye like, sir.'

Drumfin laughed heartily, shook his head. 'No, no, mannie. There's no need for such generosity. On the bye, off the card, in half an hour?'

Drumfin had played right into their hands. Frederick slid the silver flask from his pocket and nipped a mouthful of gin to moisten his dry lips.

Cluny called out, 'I'll put my bird in the ring twice, your lordship, to make it fair. But only if you'll dress the odds.'

Drumfin was no longer laughing. Cluny stepped into the pit with Satan in his hands. He held the bird towards Flounce and the pair struck at each other, cruckled and crawed with frantic vigour. The fancy stamped on the floor of the barn, chanting, 'Match. Match. Match.'

'What odds, mannie?' said Drumfin.

'Twenty against a hundred an' fifty. On three.'

'Explain.'

'If my bird falls or refuses the count in any battle then your lordship wins. If my bird takes the next two on the card an' your Spanish cock as well then I'm in for one hundred and fifty pounds.'

For the law lord, there was almost as much pleasure in negotiation as in the fight itself. He cried out in delight. 'This is madness. This barbered sparrow you're holding will never survive three bouts.'

'Perhaps not, sir,' Cluny agreed. 'But maybe he will. Do we have a match on those terms, your lordship?'

Frederick pressed his knees against the woodwork. Drumfin hesitated. He was quietly searching the crowd with his eyes, looking for the accomplice, the patron. When at length the learned judge's gaze rested upon him, Frederick could not resist. He nodded and received a curt nod from Lord Drumfin in return.

'Aye,' Drumfin announced. 'We have a match,' and the crowd, who loved anything bold and unusual, went wild.

Satan's first victory was achieved in seconds, not minutes. He did not fence with the handsome russet that was put against him. There was no parry and *sneck* of beaks, no jockeying for advantage. The little dusty-grey bird hardly seemed to move at all. He rose in a blur of feathers, hooked his gaffles into the russet gizzard, dragged the bantam down on to the sand. It was done so quickly and efficiently that the crowd were quite stunned. They screamed at Drumfin's bird to get up and fight, to show heart but the poor creature was done for. Satan, his work accomplished, crouched passively to wait for it to breathe its last, which did not take long. Drumfin was not well pleased. There had been nothing for him to admire in the fight. The ruthlessness of the little grey bird struck no chord in his lordship. He felt cheated at having paid good money for no sport at all.

Cluny squatted over Satan, holding him firmly to the floor of the pit. 'Next up, sir?'

Drumfin's second bird fared little better than the first. After three or four raking assaults it retreated and, for all the skill of his lordship's setter, could not be made to fight again. It was counted out and removed to have its cowardly neck wrung on the spot behind the benches.

Frederick felt better. His luck was on the turn at long last. He watched the scramble of the hoi-poi to wager on the grey mongrel against Drumfin's Flounce. Drumfin leaned over the barrier and snarled, 'Well, is he fit for one more?'

'For a dozen more, your lordship,' Cluny answered confidently.

Drumfin threw his coat open, hooked his thumbs into the waist of his breeks. His fatness no longer seemed jolly and his heartiness had gone. He had assumed the air of a man who could without compunction order a hanging on naught but a scrap of evidence.

He called across the pit, 'You, sir. I say, sir, do you own this fiend?'

'No, Lord Drumfin,' Frederick answered. 'I do not.'

'You have the purse, though?'

'I have my own purse, sir. What of it?'

'The one and a half hundred stands, of course, but what do you say, sir, to a wager of one hundred more?'

'Tell me your terms,' said Frederick.

'One hundred on evens that my Flounce will not be pinked.'

Frederick leaned forward and whispered, 'Cluny?'

Cluny answered, 'Satan will spiflicate that damned struttin' parrot, never fear.'

'What's wrong, sir?' Lord Drumfin called out. 'Do you not have the belly for it? Or do you not have the purse?'

'I have both, sir,' Frederick lied. 'There is, however, a wager still upon the table.'

'Rabbit droppings!'

All the money that Frederick had loose in the world was already wagered. If Drumfin demanded to be shown the colour of his gold then he would be shamed and reduced. And he would lose the original stake too, for such were the laws of the game.

Smirking, Drumfin was dangling a kidskin purse between finger and thumb, tolling it at Frederick like a little bell. Two hundred pounds. Enough to pay the pirates in Liverpool twice over. Frederick felt a fingernail of fear scratch at his heart. He did not know exactly what would be done to him if he welched on a wager here in Neptune but he had seen what had happened to defaulters elsewhere; tarred and feathered, stripped and beaten, once perfunctorily hanged. Not for an instant did he suppose that Drumfin would be lenient enough simply to address the matter to law. His lordship's reputation was fearsome and Frederick knew only too well that punishment would be immediate and complete.

The fear itself was exciting, the thrill of recklessness the most absolute emotion in the world.

'Done, sir,' he heard himself cry.

'Hah!' Drumfin shouted, seated himself upon the quilted bench and with a snap of his fingers, summoned the Spanish gamecock to be brought again to the ring.

It came as no surprise to Eunice Striker Bates when her brother crept into her bedroom in dead of night and laid himself across the quilted counterpane. She wakened on the instant. Though newly out of sleep she was not frightened by the sound of the man in her chamber. She knew exactly who it would be and what he would require of her at this ungodly hour. In spite of the intense cold in the unfired room she turned down the clothes and drew Frederick's great, sad, shaggy head on to her bosom. His ear was like a chip of ice against her flesh. His hands on her bare shoulders made her flinch. Nevertheless she held him tightly, let him shiver, sigh, groan like some gigantic baby that the Lord had foisted upon her to succour and to tend. She was four years younger than her brother but she had the same flat, clacking sort of voice, tidied by an accent they had practised together after their escape from the Charity House.

She said, 'What is it, Frederick? Tell me, dearest, what ails you?'

'I lost it.'

'What? The twenty pounds?'

'Yes.'

'Dear God!'

He kneed his way closer, rested his upper body, complete with burningly cold buttons, against her chest. Frederick was no weakling when it came to confessions. He did not weep. It was not her forgiveness he sought, or her sympathy, but her collusion.

She said, 'I thought the bird was certain.'

'I went too far.'

'How far?'

'Three battles.'

She could smell greasy smoke on his clothing, mud too and, so sharp were her senses, gin and tobacco and even, she thought, chicken scurf.

Frederick said, 'It was the third that did for me. The bird put up a damned fine show. I wasn't cheated.'

'Nonetheless, you lost?'

'Yes.' Frederick shifted position once more. 'I am in debt to Lord Drumfin too now.'

A pause: 'How much?'

'A century.'

As if it mattered: 'Pounds or guineas?'

'Pounds, Scots.'

Another pause, then, 'Did you give him your mark?'

Frederick uttered the soft barking laugh that turned some women to water. It was one of a crop of moody little gestures that he could, when he wished, accumulate into fatal charm. Eunice had not been blessed with that gift. She had to make up by directness what she lacked in persuasion.

'No, dearest, I did not even drop my name.'

Eunice said, 'How did you get away?'

'As soon as the cause was obviously lost,' Frederick said, 'I legged it out of the pit and across the open fields. I did not risk the bridge but borrowed a boat from the shore above the Herd's House.'

'I do not know where that is,' Eunice said. 'What of the other fellow, the cocker?'

'He was hot on my heels when I quit the village. I'm sure he would make a good escape too.'

Frederick folded his long legs and sat cross-kneed, heavy as a cathedral gargoyle in the centre of the bed. He linked his arms around his shins and hugged them instead of her, which was a considerable relief to Eunice. She groped for the counterpane and covered her breast and shoulders with it. 'This man, Drumfin, will surely hunt you down.'

Frederick said, 'It is not my intention to forget the debt, merely to defer payment until such times as a ship comes in.'

'But you did not explain that to him, did you?'

'It was hardly the time or place for rational conversation.'

'He will find you, you know.'

'Not if I can help it,' Frederick said, flatly. 'The question is, my dearest, what now?'

Eunice did not answer at once. Frederick waited with patience born of experience, knowing that she would be arranging possibilities in her mind.

Eunice sighed. The villa reeked of lath and plaster, varnish and limewash. The dust of construction had hardly settled yet and when spring rains came in earnest the unfinished drains would add more odours to the pot pourri of smells that drifted in from the fields.

The downstairs parlour was furnished with a few pieces that Frederick had managed to spirit away from Addison's Edge before Arthur Bates' relatives created such a furore that he'd had to abandon his claim on Eunice's behalf. The rest of the villa's rooms were so barren and bleak that rats had not even sniffed them out yet. Apart from a family of fieldmice under the kitchen floorboards, there was a strange lack of the stealthy scratching and scraping that spoke of long tenancy and turned a house into a proper home. Eunice would lie in the night and stare at the ceiling beams, missing not the companionship of Arthur, who had been old and dreary even when she married him, but that of the bats and bees, martins and mites that had made the Shropshire farmhouse seem so alive.

Very softly, Frederick prompted her. 'Money must be found, Eunice. The finding of money is our first priority.'

'Was it not always?' Eunice said.

She did not have to be as direct with Frederick as she was with other people. She did not share his coiling deviousness or his utter lack of regard for the consequences of his actions. What had happened in Shropshire, at Addison's Edge, had frightened her beyond measure. She had willingly signed away her claim to the farm and its policies on condition that Arthur's heirs drop their examination of the marriage and the circumstances of her widowhood.

She said, 'Why will you not tell me why you need so much money, Frederick? What sort of commerce takes you so often to England?'

'It's not something that you should bother your head with,' Frederick told her.

She said, 'Has it to do with Addison's Edge?'

'What? Oh, is that what you think? No, no, Eunice, I have seen to it that all of *that* is squared away.'

'Will you not tell me?'

'There is no *need* to tell you.'

Frederick removed and discarded his hat and wig and, stretching, groped for the tinderbox. It would be an hour or more, Eunice guessed, before her brother would talk himself out and allow her to snuggle beneath the sheets and try to rediscover a patch of warmth in the sagging straw mattress. If they had had a servant she would have been able to ring a bell and summon tea and toast, have a fire lighted or a warming pan brought up from the kitchen as she had been able to do at Addison's Edge. For all his faults, Arthur Bates had not been mean. Frederick, though, had a prejudice against resident domestics. He claimed that they could not at present afford the pittance that would employ a day maid. Eunice wondered what her brother's fine friends would think if they could see how meagerly he lived.

Flint struck sparks and flame pricked the shavings in the tinderbox. Eunice found the end of a wax taper and, leaning from the bed, lit it and lifted it to the wick of a tallow candle. She did not flinch when Frederick put one long-fingered hand about her waist and lightly bussed her neck. Gestures of affection from her brother were commonplace, echoes of intimacies forged when they were both too young to know that society frowned upon such things. Since then they had sought comfort from each other in the old manner by exchanging hugs and kisses, bound less by passion than by secrets shared.

Over her round bare shoulder Frederick watched the candle splutter and flame run long and fluid along the wick. Eunice inclined her head and let her hair brush his cheek. She knew only too well how the candle's slanting rays picked out the pits and pustules that neglect and disease had etched into her flesh. Her face was strong, broad – and ugly. In contrast her figure was that of a Juno, ripe enough to tempt any man who could endure her scarred countenance.

'Perhaps,' Frederick said, 'you should marry again.'

Eunice ground out the taper, snapped shut the lid of the tinderbox. 'What! Do you intend to mate me with another farmer so decrepit that he can do nothing but paw me for his satisfaction?'

Frederick said, 'Glasgow is a stern city, my dearest. I have no doubt that you would create a stir in its society if only you would—'

'Say it. Say, "show your face".'

'Has it not dawned on you, Eunice, that I have made ingress to the finest houses in Glasgow? I am made welcome by a class of person by whom we were once shunned and despised.'

'That is because you are a man.'

'Do you recall how we used to huddle in the closet and

enumerate all the things that we would wrest from the world?' Frederick smiled and raised his hands in supplication as if fulfillment might fall from the ceiling like manna from heaven. 'Silver plate, a carriage and pair, servants in livery. Do you not remember, Eunice, all the things we thought we wanted when we were shut up in that cold, dark closet?'

'All the things *you* wanted,' Eunice said. 'God help me! I have listened to you for thirty years, Frederick, and I am listening still.'

Frederick slid an arm about her shoulders, leaned back with her upon the bolster. 'At least we have clean beds, a candle, food in our belly. And we have prospects, Eunice, high prospects.'

'You told me that selfsame thing when you consigned me to a marriage with Arthur Bates.'

'Ah, but this would be a different arrangement.'

'You mean one that will not get us hanged?'

Frederick paid no attention to the question. He continued, 'If you must know, Eunice, I have cultivated the friendship of a banking family.'

'Yes, the Purveses.'

'The son is eager to make an individual mark. He has guaranteed me certain sums in credit to purchase cargoes for import and resale. We have brought in one or two quite profitably already.'

'What sort of cargoes?'

Again Frederick ignored the question. 'However, Purves is a cautious fellow and will not advance me cash or credit on the full sums. He insists that I pay my share.'

'Do you not bank with him?'

'Indeed, indeed I do,' Frederick said. 'But I dare not empty all of my account with Purves and Purves or

Andrew will smell fish. Do you see? I must have cash to bring in the next cargo. When that is done Purves will be more trusting. His greed will get the better of his judgment and all will be plain sailing.'

'Meanwhile you need cash to buy this cargo?' Eunice said.

'No, it's already purchased. I need cash to have it shipped.'

'Does Purves believe that you are rich?' Eunice said.

'Well-to-do, if not rich.'

'What of your other friends, will they not advance you money?'

'What other friends?'

'Your powdered friends, the Sinclair woman, for example.'

'Betté is merely an iron in the fire, a feather on the water,' Frederick said. 'I only put myself through society's hoops for you, Eunice, not for any pleasure it gives me.'

'For me?'

'Husbands *are* to be found this far north, you know.'

'No, Frederick. I won't consort with bankers and lords. I might be fit to be a farmer's wife but I am not fit to grace the dancing floor. You are the one with all the charm. Why must I be sold and traded for advancement? Why must I be a wife again?'

'To become a widow, of course.'

'No!' Furiously she flung the counterpane aside and swung from the bed. She stood trembling, her back to him. Candlelight outlined the shape of her body through the transparent folds of her gown. In that pose, face hidden, black hair tumbling, all her charms voluptuously displayed, he could have found a husband for her at the drop of a glove. She pivoted, dug her fists into the mattress and thrust her face close to his. 'No!' she shouted. 'No!'

Frederick sighed and said, placatingly. 'Naturally, my dearest, I will force you to do nothing that does not suit.'

'Why do *you* not find a wife, Frederick?'

'Beg pardon?'

'Why do *you* not profit from your connections? Why do *you* not marry a wealthy widow or a daughter of one of your noble acquaintances, one with a settlement worth having?'

'Good prospects do not grow on bushes, Eunice.'

'Do they not flourish in drawing-rooms, Frederick? Are none to be found in Sinclairs' Land, for instance?'

'No rich widows that I can think of, alas.'

'Only adultresses?'

'Eunice! Really!'

'For profit instead of pleasure, Frederick, why do you not do what you do best?'

'And what might that be?'

'Seduce somebody.'

Frederick frowned, drew up his knees to his chin again and crouched into a tight, brooding ball, just as he had done when they were children locked in dank closets and airless cellars. At length he cocked his head and, with a little smile that was both boyish and rapacious, said, 'You know, Eunice, you may have a point.'

3

The Country Cousin

From the moment that Edwina clapped eyes on Frances Purves she knew that the girl would bring nothing but trouble.

Andrew's memory of his cousin was clearly flawed. The child was singularly unprepossessing. The little heart-shaped face that Edwina dimly recalled from the last family gathering had become swollen with conceit. The girl's figure was no longer dainty and had gained in breadth what it lacked in height. In fact, the impression that Frances gave as she entered the hall of Purves's Land was of a little unbroken mare decked in ribbons and flounces and hooped with a pair of baggy panniers that had gone out of fashion years ago.

Fran clutched the bumrolls to her hips, charged up the staircase and flung herself upon her aunt. She nuzzled her grotesquely painted face into Edwina's breast and left a smear of rouge that not even turpentine would remove. When the girl raised her lips to be kissed her frizzled hair smelled like horse-hoof and crackled like brown paper.

'Auntie, aw, Auntie, I miss him already,' Fran cried and, with the presumption of youth that assumes the whole world to be conversant with its troubles, burst into snorting tears.

With as much solicitude as she could muster – which wasn't much – Edwina said, 'What's all this? Who do you miss? Do you miss your father, is that it?'

'Naw, not Daddy – Iain.'

'Who, pray, is Iain?'

'Ma lover,' said Frances, indignant that such a salient fact should not have been broadcast by handbill and cryer round every close in Glasgow.

'Your *what*?'

'Ma lover. Ma swain.'

'What swine are you talking about?' said Edwina.

'Swain. Swain, lover, intended, betrothed.'

'Ah!'

'He couldn't come wi' me.'

'Why ever not?' said Edwina.

'He wasn't asked.'

'Oh,' said Edwina, feeling decidedly better. 'How awful for you. And how dreadfully remiss of Lady Betté not to invite your lover to the ball.'

'Ain't it, though,' said Frances.

Edwina steered her tearful guest upstairs to make way for the three caddies who had staggered round from the chaise with a mountain of luggage.

'Iain is no' as ton as we are, but,' Fran said.

Edwina had forgotten how trying a bumpkin accent could be. She had not yet acquired the knack of translating it into plain English. She was also discomfited by the girl's penchant for touching and kissing, demonstrative behaviour that she found less than appealing. She disengaged Fran's arm from her waist and led the girl to the first floor room that had been swept and polished for her occupancy. She opened the door, gave the girl a nudge to ease the vastly padded hips through the narrow aperture then signalled to the caddies to bring in the luggage.

The room, not the best in the house by a long chalk, leaned out over Saltmarket Lane at a steep angle. One tiny bottle-glass window opened to a prospect of nothing more glamorous than a crumbling gable and four reeking chimney pots. The bed was clean, however, and Edwina had found a miniature dresser, a steady chair and an upright cupboard for furnishing.

'Very nice,' said Fran, with more manners than conviction. 'Where's the dressing-room, but?'

'Ah!' said Edwina. 'Do you have a dressing-room at home?'

'Aye. One for me. An' one for Tilda.'

'Tilda?'

'Ma lady's-maid.'

Edwina peered at the pile of bandboxes and valises that the caddies had dumped upon the floor as if she expected the maid servant to pop out of one of them.

'Where is Tilda?' she enquired.

'No' here.'

'Why ever not?'

'She's on the pod,' Frances said.

'Pardon?'

'Got a pea in the pod,' Frances said.

'Oh! Pregnant!' Edwina exclaimed. 'How nice! Does her husband work on your father's estate?'

Fran gave her relative a quick disparaging glance. 'Husband? Tilda hasn't got a husband. Tilda thinks it might be the mannie who works at the mill who stuck it there or maybe the tinker-johnnie who came through at the back o'last harvest. If you ask me, but,' Fran smirked, 'it was Daddy.'

Edwina fluttered her mittened hands, cleared her throat, opened her lips but could find no suitable comment to make.

Fran said, 'Well, Auntie, where *is* ma dressing-room?

And where's ma maid? Daddy said you'd have a maid for me.'

Edwina's patience with this knowing little ingrate evaporated. She had just sufficient control not to shout but there was steel enough in her voice to cause Fran to purse her lips and plump down upon the side of the bed in a sulk.

'First,' said Edwina, 'I am not your aunt. I am wife to your cousin, no more than that. You may call me Mrs Purves or you may call me Edwina but you will *not* address me as Aunt in future. Do you understand?'

Fran glowered, and nodded.

'Second,' Edwina went on, 'Purves's Land is not some rambling barn like Moorfoot Castle. It's a town house and, as you should have been taught, town houses in Glasgow are exceedingly expensive to purchase and maintain.'

'You mean there's no dressing-room?'

'None that can be spared.'

'What about ma dresses?'

'I will see to it that you have hanging hooks and the use of one of the linen presses at the end of the passage,' Edwina said. 'That is a minor inconvenience in the scheme of things, Frances, and one that you will simply have to endure.'

'Aye,' Fran agreed. 'But I will need t'have a maid.'

Though she had no concern at all for the girl's personal welfare Edwina did not want to be charged with neglect of her obligations. After listening to Frances' chatter she was rather afraid that the child might run wild and be vulnerable to the predations of certain urban sophisticates who could scent knowing innocence and rustic money at three leagues. It wasn't a maid Fran Purves needed but a guardian.

At first Edwina thought of Pym. But she had a fondness for Pym and did not wish to sacrifice her own comforts for the sake of a child who would probably not appreciate it. Next she thought of Maddy but Maddy was too young and too wild to be made responsible for the guest's behaviour.

'Well,' Frances said impatiently, 'am I t'get a maid or not, but?'

Thus harried, Edwina pulled open the bedroom door and yelled down the passageway, 'Clare.'

Tea was formally served in the Purveses' drawing-room about two hours after Fran's arrival. Andrew and his father, as well as old Mrs Purves, were obliged out of politeness to attend the ceremonial. They listened with varying degrees of shock to the young visitor's uninhibited revelations about life and love in Jamie's household and her anticipations of the pleasures of marriage to Mr Iain Russell who, it transpired, had already proved his virility by fathering several bairns on servants and fieldhands but not, Fran was quick to add, on her Tilda.

If old Mr Purves was dismayed by the dismemberment of his brother's reputation he gave no sign of it and remained pleasant and amiable towards his garrulous niece. Andrew, it seemed, was a little more prudish and could not sit still in the face of such an uncouth monologue. After one cup of tea he offered his excuses and left the drawing-room to seek out Clare.

Clare was in the guest's bedroom, engaged in shaking out Miss Purves's petticoats and gowns, hanging them on whalebone straighteners and on hooks in the cupboard. Andrew glanced along the passage, closed the bedroom door and beckoned Clare to him.

'What can you do, Clare?' he whispered.

'About Miss Purves?'

'Uh-hmmm.'

'She's not awfully polished, is she?'

'She talks too much,' Andrew said. 'Too freely.'

'Can you not have a quiet word with her?' Clare suggested.

'I wouldn't know what to say to such a dreadful wee Hottentot. She wasn't like that last time we met. On the other hand, when they are all together, the Moorfoot clan, perhaps one does not notice their eccentricities.'

'Perhaps Mr Purves could—'

'Actually, my father seems to find a peculiar charm in Fran's forwardness. He's sitting at the tea-table as if entranced by her.'

'I expect he's more used to "the old ways",' Clare said.

'I don't know what to do with her,' Andrew said. 'I could find more civilised company in a waterside tavern.'

Clare was tempted to inform Mr Andrew that he did not know the half of it. For an hour before tea she had been regaled with tales of Moorfoot that would bring blushes to anybody's cheeks. She, however, had not had the benefit of a sheltered upbringing and remembered only too well the barbarity of the penny squires that rode into Greenock town on market days. It had also occurred to Clare that her father had been tarred with the same brush as the Moorfoot Purveses, that a coarse, vulgar streak ran through the family like a knot in oak.

'What I'd like you to do, Clare, is to knock off the corners. Give my dear cousin a city shine, as it were.'

'I doubt if she'll attend to me, Mr Andrew,' Clare said. 'The truth is, I do not think she even wants to be in Glasgow. I think she'd rather be at home with her – her gentleman.'

'Gentleman! Iain Russell is only after Frances' dower money.'

'How can you be sure?'

'I can read between the lines of what Frances told us at tea,' Andrew said. 'Her darlin' Iain is nothing but an arboreal ne'er-do-well. Lanarkshire is full of them, youngest sons of youngest sons. I suspect Uncle Jamie engineered an invitation to the Sinclairs' ball just to get Frances away from Russell for a time, and to put her in the way of finding a more suitable husband.'

'At Lady Betté's?'

'A fashionable ball is really little more than a marriage mart, you know.'

'Would it be impertinent of me to ask how much dower money will go with Miss Frances when she is wed?' Clare said.

'Five thousand pounds, I believe.'

'God in Heaven! Sorry, Mr Andrew, I did not mean to swear.'

'It's enough to make a saint swear,' said Andrew. 'Behind his whiskers, though, Uncle Jamie is dashed shrewd. He knows the only way he'll be rid of the burden of his daughters is to gilt them in good Scots pounds. The only way Frances could sweep a man off his feet unaided would be to hurl herself at him from a stepladder.'

Clare laughed and Andrew too had a wry little smile upon his face at the image he had devised.

'I'll do what I can, Mr Andrew,' Clare said. 'But who will take care of the children if I'm to spend so much time with our visitor?'

'Maddy will attend to them,' Andrew said. 'Come to think of it, perhaps we should treat you as Frances' companion rather than her maid. I don't see why not. You are, after all, related to her too, after a fashion.'

'How will Mrs Purves take to that suggestion?'

'Phooh! At the moment Mrs Purves will take to any suggestion that will keep Frances out of her way. Would you object to being my cousin's companion, Clare, for as long as she remains with us?'

'No, Mr Andrew, I wouldn't object at all.'

'In that case you may sup with the family and dine with us too – if we don't have other company.'

Clare paused. 'And the ball, Mr Andrew? Will I be obliged to accompany Miss Frances to Lady Betté's?'

'You'll go with her, of course.'

'Into the ballroom?'

'We'll have to see about that,' Andrew said and, giving her cheek a little pat, added, 'Good girl, Clare. I don't know what we'd do without you.'

Much to Clare's surprise, acting as companion to Frances Purves proved to be much less exacting than she had supposed it would be. Stripped of her heavy velvets, hairpiece and appalling panniers Fran was revealed as a timid girl whose loudness hid not conceit but insecurity. She was intelligent enough to realise that out of the rude circle of Lanarkshire society she was nothing but a plain, broad-hipped, unsophisticated country girl whose relatives looked down their snoots at her. Bragging was her defence. But after the candle had been snuffed out in the bedroom that first night Clare discovered a different Fran, a child who snuffled into the bolster and cried not for her lover but for her Mama and her sisters, someone who needed reassurance and a dependable friend.

At heart Frances Purves was pure putty, eager to be

shaped into the likeness of a lady. Within a day of arrival she had come to hold Clare in a kind of esteem that was somewhat embarrassing.

'I am only a servant in the house, Miss Frances.'

'Naw, you're a kinswoman. An' you're my companion,' Fran would protest. 'Servants don't have good manners like you. Besides, Cousin Andrew told me all about you. He told me I was to listen to you. He fair likes you, does Cousin Andrew. Has he never tried t'dandle you?'

Blushing, Clare rebuked the country girl for her lack of modesty and advised her to count to twenty before she spoke her mind in future.

'Everybody knows fine well what men an' women do,' Fran protested. She was seated on the bed watching Clare dextrously snip an excess of braid from the bodice of a day-dress.

Clare said, 'Perhaps. But that doesn't mean you can discuss the subject in public. In any case, well-brought-up young ladies are not supposed to know about such things, not until after they're married.'

'If it's "those things" you're talkin' about,' said Frances, 'I've seen—'

'Enough!' said Clare.

Clare Kelso and Frances Purves were almost of an age Clare's competence and style as well as her prettiness made her seem not older but wiser. It was not long until Fran treated her as if she was a sister and came to rely on her completely for instruction in the social graces. Fran, however, was not the only one to be changed by the relationship. Clare could not resist playing to the hilt her role as mentor to the country lass and soon discovered in the contrasts between them just how different she, Clare Kelso, was from the average member of the kitchen crew, and how much better.

Purveses, male and female, were glad enough to sacrifice
Clare on the altar of Peace and Quiet. They had never been
stuffy in domestic arrangements, saw no harm in Fran
being taken under Clare Kelso's wing. Elsie Gollan, Maddy and the other servants were scandalised, however, and
muttered rebelliously about Clare's elevation. If they had
had their way, they would have had her pilloried for her
presumption.

Clare's beneficial influence upon the little Moorfoot
barbarian was swift to show effect. Fran became more
discreet and cultured and her table manners improved to
the point where she no longer poured ale upon her breakfast porridge, ate cheese from her fists or wiped her mouth
in her sleeve. Miracle of miracles, she even ceased to
discourse upon the mating habits of the denizens of Moorfoot. If it had not been for Edwina's seething anger that
such a wretch should have been invited to Lady Betté's ball
when she had not, the woman might have taken pleasure in
the girl's progress and have trotted her out to tea with ladies
of good-breeding. Edwina was not the stoical or forgiving
sort, though. When an invitation to the ball still failed to
turn up she remained closeted in her bedroom with only
Pym for company and hissed about the cuckoo in the nest
and drank more negus than was good for her liver or her
spleen.

Clare had extracted from Frances an answer to the
question that Edwina was too proud to ask. Why had
Frances been favoured with an invitation when she, Edwina, had not? The reason was simple. John Sinclair and
Jamie Purves, together at a shooting match, had fallen to
discussing the tribulations of having so many daughters to
fend for. Whisky had oiled the confidences and Sir Johnnie
had left with a promise 'to see Purves right'. Lady Betté's

gracious invitation had followed within a month, and Jamie had driven himself out of the coverts long enough to arrange Fran's sojourn in Glasgow mainly, as Andrew had surmised, to get her away from the idiot Iain Russell who kept his brains in his breeks. Lady Betté, therefore, had never set eyes on Miss Frances Purves. But that did not matter. There would be plenty of eligible young men at the ball. One extra heiress would simply add a little more stock to the broth as far as Lady Betté was concerned.

What Frances did not know, and was consequently unable to impart to Clare, was the reason why Edwina had been snubbed by the Sinclairs. Neither of the girls could have guessed that Lady Betté was a little under the influence of Mr Frederick Striker and, while she would not lend him money, she was not above joining him in mischief. It was, in fact, Frederick who had persuaded her ladyship to delay the sending of an invitation to the Purveses. The pair would pause in their strenuous embraces and chuckle together at the news that Edwina had not been seen at a well-bred tea-table for weeks and was probably locked in her bedroom sulking and fizzing at that very moment.

'Oh, I would not like to be in Andrew's shoes,' Frederick would say.

And Lady Betté, laying her hand where it should not be, would say, 'But would you not like to be in Andrew's bed?'

'God, no!'

'I think you lie, Frederick.'

'I lie only with you, Betté.'

'That is surely not the truth?'

'I lie only with you but I *lie* with everyone.'

'Devil!'

After brief debate Andrew and his father decided that

Frances was presentable enough to accompany the family to church. Indeed, it was felt that a dose of the preaching of the ill-named Mr Brimston might do the girl good. The minister of St Matthew's was a great one for ranting against sins of the flesh. It was hoped that his sermon might awaken in Frances a sense of guilt about her corporeal predilections and, if Brimston was in really good form, scare the wits out of her as well. Frances was well used to Sabbath church parades, which were so much part of country life. Besides, she was keen to see and be seen by Glasgow's gentry. Kirk she regarded as a platform for airs and graces; attendance there might be followed, by an invitation to take dinner at the home of some lady who had sons to spare.

Clare walked up High Street to St Matthew's Old Parish Church by Fran's side but when she reached the vestibule she hesitated, uncertain of her place. Andrew put a hand on her arm and murmured in her ear, 'Come with us today, Clare. There's room in the family pew,' then, to her surprise, guided her into the body of the kirk.

As a rule Clare sat with the servants in the gallery. She had never been downstairs before. She was surprised at the changed perspectives. Mr Brimston's pulpit seemed to loom over the masters' pews, frowning ominously at the padded seats upon which the titled and landed classes planted their bottoms whenever they were forced to pass a Sunday in town. From upstairs the kirk looked much less intimidating than it did at this level. Somehow the lightness and airiness of the gallery and its distance from the pulpit separated you from Mr Brimston's godly wrath, as if servants were souls not worth the bother of saving.

Clare felt stiff and awkward at this public elevation of her position within the family. She was known by sight to many of the congregation and to almost all the servants upstairs. She imagined that she could hear a malign buzz of disapproval from the gallery. But to the uninformed eye, she reassured herself, she would be quite indistinguishable from any middling-quality girl who occupied a shoulder-high pew in the nave. True, she wore one of Edwina's cast-off dresses, but she had repaired, cleaned and pressed it carefully and it looked as good as new upon her neat-waisted figure. She wore leather shoes with stone buckles that she had bought from a packman last year, and a blue cloak with a snood, a triangular hat and clean, undarned gloves. Sneaking glances this way and that, she compared herself favourably with the ungainly wives and daughters of trading families, women whom no amount of money would ever transform into ladies.

Fran fidgeted on one side of Clare and on the other Mr Andrew wriggled and knocked his elbow against the partition that seemed to have been inserted between the pews to increase the torment of the sermons or more probably to keep the worshippers awake. Clare tilted her chin. The kissing strings of her hat tightened as she angled her head discreetly this way and that. She let her glance stray to folk she recognised, to men who had bowed and discoursed with her on her walks abroad with William. She felt a strange small thrill at being here with the Purveses, the fine hairs on the nape of her neck rising in response to it.

'Good morning, Miss Kelso,' Frederick whispered from the pew directly behind her. 'I am pleased to see you out and about upon such a beautiful morning.'

Andrew glanced round quickly. 'Striker? Is that you?'

'Indeed, Purves, it is.'

Frederick had somehow managed to infiltrate the bench bought and paid for by Albert Shaw, a grain merchant from Jamaica Street. He was obviously no trespasser, however, for he sat comfortably between Shaw's two half-grown sons and their mother.

Andrew muttered, 'I thought you were in Liverpool?'

'I am only just returned,' Frederick explained.

When he inclined his head towards Andrew his wig brushed Clare's cheek and made her shiver.

'Did all go according to –' Andrew began. But at that moment the side door from the vestry was flung open and in charged Mr Brimston, a great black-bound Bible extended in one hand, like the head of an enemy claimed in battle.

Conversation died instantly as the minister marched to his favourite spot before the Communion table and swung to confront the flock of sinners that in the course of the morning he would shear like so many sheep. 'GOD,' he shouted, 'BE WITH US IN THE SEASON OF OUR DEPRAVITY AND REDEEM US FROM CONGRESS WITH DEMONS OF THE FLESH.'

Mr Striker touched Clare's shoulder, then sat back while Mr Brimston, already red in tooth and claw, clumped up the steps to the pulpit to begin the first of his long harangues.

Neither of the two young Shaws caught Fran's fancy during the course of the dinner that the Purveses laid on after Mr Brimston had finally released them. To her chagrin, Clare was pointedly not invited to join the guests in the dining-room, and ate in the nursery with Maddy and the children. After the guests had departed, about a quarter past four, it did not take Fran long to seek out Clare and persuade her to dress again for a stroll upon the Green before the sun went down. Hardly had the girls left the gate of the coachyard before Fran launched into a long account of what she imagined had taken place over pickles and cold mutton.

'He touched me, Clare. I swear Mr Striker touched me.'

Clare tried not to show her annoyance. 'Accidentally?'

'He placed his hand on ma knee, above ma knee,' Fran said, 'wi' stealth, wi' purpose.'

She clung to Clare as if they were sisters from a good house or a brace of ladies of the town bent on defying the civil edict that prohibited them from being seen on the streets on Sundays.

'Mr Striker would not be so forgetful of his manners as to touch you in full view of everyone. I think you are mistaken, Miss Frances.'

'I am not mistaken. He got fair carried awa' wi' me, I tell you.'

'What did Mrs Shaw have to say to that?'

'Mrs Shaw? What's it got to do wi' her?'

Clare had no notion what sort of relationship existed between the Englishman and the prim little wife of the grain merchant but she was irritated at Fran's suggestion that Frederick had been smitten by her, by a rustic.

'I have heard,' Clare lied, 'that Mr Striker and Mrs Shaw are *very* close friends. In fact, I believe I have heard that Mr Striker has many *very* close friends among the married ladies in the town.'

'Aye, I wouldn't doubt it.' Fran hugged Clare closer, almost tripping over her feet in her excitement. 'I've seen his likes before.'

'Oh! Where?'

'After the hunt,' Fran said. 'Seen them wi' their breeks down too up in the coppice an' behind the kennels.'

'Mr Striker is *not* one of your Moorfoot oafs.'

'What is he then? Tell me what he is,' Frances said, 'since you seem t'know him so damned well.'

The strength of her feelings, her rashness, surprised Clare. It took a moment to recognise what they signified. Three or four deep breaths calmed her. She sought Fran's hand again and patted it. 'I'm sorry, Miss Frances. I had no right to speak to you like that.'

Fran, however, had not been offended. Her voice when she spoke was full of conspiratorial glee. 'By God, you've a fancy for that man yoursel'. Here now, tell me, has he ever tried t'dandle you?'

That very forenoon Mr Brimston had railed loud and long against the evils of fornication. He had extolled the virtues of chaste Christian marriage and accentuated the need for women to be modest within marriage as well as out of it. Clare had heard too much kitchen talk to be deceived by the minister's idealism. Girls like Jinty and Maddy, women like Elsie Gollan, might clatter on about a man's prospects, his income, his manners, his gentility but what really fascinated them and consumed their attention was how he would perform in the bedchamber, an aspect of wedlock that was, she believed, of even more importance to men.

Twice now the country girl had asked her that same question and she answered Fran as she had before, indignantly. 'He most certainly has not.'

'I'll wager he's thought about it, but.'

'How can you possibly guess what goes on in the mind of such a person as Mr Striker? Why, you hardly know him.'

'I can see it in his eyes.'

Clare believed that she was being drawn into this distasteful conversation quite against her will, yet she did not resist. 'And what special mark tells you what a man desires?'

'Huh! I thought you were supposed t'be sophisticated,' Fran said. 'Do you not even know how t'tell when a man's heated, when he hungers for you?'

'No, I do not,' Clare said. 'I suppose you'll be telling me next that Mr Striker is mad with desire for *you*.'

'No' just for me.' Fran grinned. 'For you too. God, Clare, I reckon that man could take on the pair of us one after the other an' never a pause for breath.'

Displaying more anger than she really felt, Clare tore her arm from Fran's grasp. 'How dare you talk of Mr Striker in that disgusting manner?'

Fran was not daunted, not contrite. She laughed and pursued her companion with quick little steps as Clare hastened out of the mouth of the lane and headed towards the sward of public land that flanked the riverside. 'Wait, Clare, wait for me.'

'Not if you're going to talk like that,' Clare snapped.

Sabbath air was cool and clean-tasting for ropeworks and brewhouses gave out no smoke and the forges of the little manufactories were cold at the week's end. Fisher nets draped the sagging poles that divided the Green from the river and a herd of cows was ambling towards a milking byre at the back of the cottages, idly watched by five or six urchins and a man with a whippet on a leash. The trees and little houses that surrounded the Green were etched against clear evening light and two small wherries, sails burnt-pink in the setting sun, glided between shoals and sandbars on the water's glassy edge. Clare felt anger drain from her. She slowed her step and let Frances catch up with her.

The girl hesitated, gently took Clare's arm again and said, 'What's wrong, Clare? Do you think he could be the man for you, is that it?'

'I – I do find him attractive, yes.'

'There you are then.'

'I'm only a nursery-maid. I've no dowry, no prospects. Mr Striker will be after something better.'

'He's no' genteel, Clare. Maybe he has got some money an' would like more, but he's no' titled landowner. Edwina says his house is just rented.' Fran drew herself closer. 'If you ask me Edwina fancies him too.'

'I know it,' Clare said.

Fran giggled. 'Can you imagine it? Can you imagine Mr Striker rollin' about wi' Auntie Edwina? Her lyin' there like a heifer, kickin' her legs in the air an' lecturin' him about his manners while he was servin' her?'

Clare chuckled. Taking that as a signal of truce Fran clasped her companion's arm more tightly and together the girls turned back towards the houses of the town just as a thin, chill little wind drifted off the river, stirred the trees' bare boughs and darkened the wherries' sails.

Fran said, 'He'll be at Lady Betté's for St Valentine's.'

'How do you know?'

'He told me.'

'He told you rather a lot, didn't he?'

'Is he one o' Lady Betté's pet rams?'

'I've heard gossip,' said Clare. 'But it may not be true.'

'It'll be true,' Fran said. 'Still, we can see for ourselves how the land lies on the night o' the ball.'

'I won't see much from the servants' hall.'

'You'll be upstairs wi' us. I'll make sure o' it.'

'Us?'

'Edwina an' me.'

'What!' Clare exclaimed. 'Has she received an invitation, after all?'

'At dinnertime. Handed to her by no less a personage

than your Mr Striker. It had been an oversight, an error
that she hadn't had it before.'

'Edwina would be pleased.'

'Fair puffed up.'

'Will Mr Andrew be there too?'

'Aye, of course he will,' said Frances. 'Him, her, me an'
you.'

They crossed the cobbled causeway that linked the foot
of the green to the tail end of Saltmarket Street and, under
the shadows of the buildings, felt the stealthy cold of the
winter night take possession of them. For a time they said
nothing. It was not until they reached the gate in the lane
behind Purves's Land that Fran checked Clare and drew
her to a halt.

'Have you ever done it?' the country girl asked.

Clare did not pretend that she did not know what the
question meant. She inspected Fran's rough, rouge-red-
dened cheeks, the nose that showed too much nostril, and
the round, enquiring eyes that exhibited no eagerness or
guile but just a reflection of her own secret fears.

She shook her head. 'Have you?'

'No,' Frances said. 'Never.'

'What about Iain Russell?'

'All talk.'

'Oh!'

'I – I want to do it,' Fran said. 'But I don't want to either,
if you understand what I mean.'

'Perfectly.'

'You too?'

'Yes,' Clare admitted. 'Me too.'

Strictly speaking, Eunice was at liberty to walk out in the
city's broad streets at any time, to strike up acquaintance

with any person, woman or man, that she pleased; Frederick put no restrictions upon her in that respect. Such freedom was not easily exercised, however, for it was not just liberty to take the air that Eunice craved but social congress, a circle of friends, welcoming voices, things not easily acquired by a woman on her own.

In spite of her upbringing – an insane father, a drunken mother and, latterly, the demeaning regimes of the Doncaster Charity House – Eunice was not lacking in social graces. She had been allowed to retain much of the booty from the relationships that Frederick had arranged for her and from her short-lived marriage to Arthur Bates. She had pretty dresses, shoes, hats and trinkets enough to put on a highly respectable front to the world when opportunity was offered. It was typical of Frederick to burden them with trunks and chests and boxes of apparel. No matter how desperate their situation had become, not so much as a glove had ever been sold. Fine feathers, Frederick told her, made fine birds. Quality clothing was not a luxury but a necessity, part and parcel of their stock-in-trade.

Eunice loved her brother dearly. She would never forget how he had stood by her, how he had fulfilled promises made on bended knees in the grassland behind the Charity House, how he had returned for her as soon as he could with the vow that one day he would make her rich. Paradoxically, Eunice also hated her brother. She could not forget how he had used and spoiled her, how deception had become fraud, fraud had become theft, one crime tangled with another until she could no longer separate truths from lies, right from wrong. At one time or another Frederick had been – or had pretended to be – lawyer, preacher, doctor, wool merchant, and the owner of a plantation in the Caribbees. He had played the roles with such conviction that Eunice herself had begun to believe in them. Gradually she had become blind to the direction in which Frederick's deceptions were leading her. Until it was too late. Until Mr Bates lay dying, then dead.

She had assumed it would stop there, with land and a farmstead to parley into another, more suitable marriage, one that would see her settled and finally discharged of her debt to Frederick. But that promise too had proved false. Soon they were in flight again, to Dublin, to Liverpool, then on to the pretty little cathedral city in Scotland where Frederick rapidly recovered his optimism and became, in imagination if not in fact, a wealthy merchant trader.

In no time at all Frederick had infiltrated himself into Glasgow's best society. Eunice knew by experience that he would eventually coax her out of hiding. He would introduce her to some fellow that he had picked out for her, some man with money or influence over money. And she would be expected to behave as Frederick had taught her to behave, winsomely but without scruple. The courtship would be clandestine. Not for Eunice the gaiety of the dancing floor, meetings over teacakes, the pleasure of concerts or family picnics. She was a creature of darkness, kept out of the light. She would be brought forth only when Frederick desired power over some person whose influence, Frederick would convince her, would make them rich at last.

Sunday: bells.

What church would take her in, though? At what altar could Eunice Striker Bates present herself to be washed clean of her sins by the blood of the Lamb?

Sunday: without worship or healing.

She was a prisoner in a new villa on the outskirts of an alien city. She could do nothing but wait for Frederick to come and pull her out, shake her as if she was a loose dress from the hamper in the corner.

Frederick had departed early. He had looked very smart in his best blue suit and buckle shoes. Though she thought it cold, Frederick had refused to spoil his splendid appearance by wearing a greatcoat. Eunice had not gone out on to the path to wave him farewell. She had not the stomach for it.

Church held no salvation for Frederick's soul. He would smile, bow, shake a paw, kiss a lady's fingers, touch the pulse on her wrist, be invited to dinner, to tea, to sup somewhere. He would make his rounds, always ready to extend himself, alert as a jay to explore and examine opportunities, ready to snatch any advantage that might bring him profit or position.

Eunice would pass the Sabbath as she passed every day.

Prepare food.

Clean house.

Since the affair at Addison's Edge when the testimony of domestics very nearly got them hanged Frederick had turned against servants. There was not much to do about the house, he said. She could do it well enough without interference.

Sunday: Eunice's rituals had grown elaborate and prolonged over the months. She swept the empty rooms, washed the kitchen's stone floor. Cleaned grates, lit fires, scrubbed pots, polished pans. She changed bed linen. She gutted fish or trimmed beef. Peeled apples, steeped raisins, kneaded dough, churned butter. Made ready a supper that Frederick might not come home to eat.

Sunday or not, when all was done she would be weary enough to shape an act of worship that she had devised for herself in the bare upstairs bedroom with the window, rain or shine, flung open to the sky.

Bible. Chair. Cushion.

She needed no text.

In fact she did not dare to open the Bible for fear that there would be illuminated before her upon the page some line or verse from whose random condemnation she could not escape. She left the black leather binding sealed with its tapes and held the Holy Book in both hands as if to wring from it a blind and generalised salvation. Back to the window, she knelt upon the cushion and rested her elbows and brow upon the edge of the chair. In this posture she would struggle to pray. She would mutter, moan, clutch the Bible ever tighter in her fists as she sought to infiltrate the Mansions of the Lord, as Frederick did the mansions of the rich.

At first she had prayed for ten minutes, then it was a quarter of an hour, half an hour, an hour by the clock. Now she remained motionless on her knees for a time without time, hour upon hour, until the chair edge left a bruise upon her brow, her knees swelled and her patience induced the strange phenomenon that had first manifest itself on Christmas Eve and had recurred several times since.

Old wounds upon her back and buttocks would begin to smart and itch. She would experience a sly oozing of blood, its sticky presence on her garments. The first time it had happened she had been terrified. Now she wondered at it as a sign she could not interpret, but a sign, nonetheless. It moved her to joyous panic, drove her to her feet, forced her to hobble into Frederick's bedroom where, tearing off her garments, she would gape at the reflection of her body in the cheval glass, see the old dead wormcast scars outlined by pinpricks of fresh blood, bright red blood that would sting and begin to dry as soon as she exposed them to light.

She had not told Frederick of this happening. She did not understand it yet. He would not understand it at all.

The wounds had been dormant for over twenty years, mere traces on the surface of her skin, pale hairless ghosts of past pain, past sufferings. It was her father who had put the whip to her. In the year after her mother had been found dead, her father would beat Eunice mercilessly and often. Frederick would be locked into the low cupboard under the staircase. From there he would watch through a crack as his sister's face was thrust into the lap of the latest slattern his father had taken up with, her shift peeled down into a puddle of cloth about her ankles and the man cursing, would slash and flail with a length of tarred and knotted rope at the child's sparse flesh.

No reason was ever advanced for the punishments. Giving pain gave pleasure to Ronald Striker and diverted him from his own despair. Those were reasons enough. Only Frederick knew how Eunice had acquired the scars upon her body. When some other man would glimpse her naked back or feel with ardent fingertips the blemishes upon her round flesh, Eunice would do what Frederick had told her to do. She would hood her lids and smile, let the fellow believe that she had once revelled in a perversity whose pleasures he was too dull or too timid to comprehend.

All of that was far in the past, distant and dusty. She should be thankful that she had found respite here in the suburb of Grahamston, in Frederick's new villa. She should have felt secure. Unencumbered by the guilt that she carried with her like clothes in a basket, she desperately wanted to belong here.

She prayed for release, for a sign.

And – on Sundays – bled.

Today the bleeding was light. The threads of blood were gone almost as soon as she exposed them to the air. With curious interest and very little fear, she continued to study herself in the long mirror in the clear, promising light of the spring afternoon.

Boom. Boom. Boom. The sound reverberated like thunder through the secluded house. Eunice was filled with terrible dread. She leapt back guiltily from the mirror and hauled up her clothes. It could not be Frederick. Frederick had his own special latchkey. She fumbled with tapes, laces, buttons. Who knew she was here? Who knew she was alone here?

Boom. Boom. Boom.

She could not bring herself to leave the upstairs room. She could not descend the stairs and fling open the house door. She was irrationally afraid of what would confront her in the winey rays of the afternoon sun. She sank to her knees before the cheval glass, pressed her fists to her breasts and prayed again.

Long minutes passed like lead. There was no more knocking, no sound of footsteps or whispered voices. No scratch of tools upon the window frame. At length Eunice opened her eyes, rose and stole across the landing to the room that overlooked the garden at the front. She did not have to move close to the window. Through the coarse glass the horseman on the road was obvious. The horse was a huge grey gelding, straggle-maned and rough-saddled. The man too was huge. He had an unshaven chin and greasy locks not hidden by his broad-brimmed hat. Blue canvas jacket, baggy breeks and thigh-length boots gave him the appearance of a sailor but no cutlass, only a short dagger, hung in the scabbard at his belt. Silent as a shadow, Eunice watched the stranger drag on the reins and make the horse prance round and round. He scowled up at the house. Raising himself in the iron stirrups, he gathered black saliva into his mouth and spat furiously upon the gate, to leave his trace as dogs do. Then he galloped off towards Glasgow in a cloud of wintry dust.

Eunice waited ten minutes before she went down into the hall and stood behind the door. She was tempted to unlock it and step on to the path to assure herself that nothing worse than a gob of tobacco juice had been left for her brother to find, but she could not bring herself to leave the shelter of the house.

Instead she climbed back upstairs to Frederick's room, opened the door of a cupboard that hid behind the cheval glass and took out the stone bottle of Holland gin that her brother kept among his snuffpots and tobacco pipes.

She uncorked the bottle with her teeth. She spat the cork on to the floor and, holding the dumpy vessel in both hands, drank from the neck in greedy gulps.

Down her spine and across her buttocks the withered wounds were smarting again, stinging and smarting as if they, not she, recalled the reason for her punishments and had determined to hurt her anew.

From the moment that Edwina received the invitation from Striker's hand all was sweetness and light in Purves's Land. It did not seem to occur to her that she had been the butt of a malicious jest. She accepted Mr Striker's explanation for the delay readily enough and his apology on behalf of the Sinclairs. It was as if the plain white card had had written upon it a recipe for youthfulness which instantly erased the woes of matrimony and motherhood and transformed Edwina into a carefree girl again, without a thought in her head but ribbands and flounces and beaux.

Tea was served and whisked away before Andrew or his father could catch a second cup from the silver pot. Frances, and Clare with her, were spirited away to Edwina's dressing-room to admire the gowns and the fabrics that Edwina had purchased but had not had made up.

Pym, a sallow-skinned woman some six or seven years older than Clare, was not best pleased at having to share her mistress's joviality with interlopers. She hid her peevishness behind a display of excessive attention as Edwina scuttled hither and thither with this gown and that bolt of cloth, fretting as if she was being arrayed for a bridal night and not just a ball at Sinclairs' Land.

Andrew, in search of supper, popped his head round the door at one point. His intrusion was greeted with such shrieks that he might have been a bandit invading a seraglio and not the provider of all the fashionable largesse. He retreated at once, went off to drink claret with his father and casually enquire of his manservant Peter-Pierre what suit he should have cleaned for the glittering occasion.

'Men!' said Frances, much into the spirit of the thing.

'Men, indeed!' Edwina agreed. She even went so far as to pinch her cousin-by-marriage's fat cheek before she turned her attention once more to the handglass that Pym held up for her.

Before the rude interruption by her husband Edwina had been in process of trying on wigs and hairpieces from her collection, while Clare experimented with ribbon, thread, needle and a heron plume.

'No souls, men,' Edwina went on. 'No understanding of the price we ladies must pay for our beauty.'

'Aye, it's a right struggle,' Frances said gravely. 'But if you don't put yourself through it they'll look at you as if you was just wallpaper.'

Clare handed the improvised hairpiece to Pym who settled it solemnly on Edwina's head and primped at the shoulder curls.

Edwina said, 'Did you see from whose hand my invitation came? Did you notice how he engaged my attention?'

'Mr Striker, are you meanin'?'

'Who but?' Edwina knocked the hairpiece backwards for Pym to catch as a cricketer will catch a ball. 'Now there is a man of infinite sensibilities. In Mr Striker I'm sure that a lady might uncover a rare combination of ardour and discretion.'

'What lady?' said Frances.

'Why,' said Edwina, 'any lady in whom the gentleman in question saw the light of hidden charms.'

'You, but?' Fran might have uttered a hoot of best Lanarkshire laughter if Clare had not tapped her ankle in warning. 'But, Auntie, you're already married.'

'My dear, what a simpleton you are,' Edwina said. 'It's not a *wife* that Mr Striker wants at the present time.'

'What is it then?'

Pym held another hairpiece above her mistress's head and did some light titivation of the thinning hair on Edwina's crown before she lowered the ornament into place.

'Love,' said Edwina. 'It's love that Mr Striker seeks.'

'Like Iain?'

'No,' sharply delivered, 'not like Iain.'

'What about Cousin Andrew?'

'Not like him either, not in the least part.'

Frances opened her mouth to press on with questioning but Clare thought it prudent to intervene. 'The plume's quite appealing, mum, but perhaps a little too tall.'

'Yes, perhaps,' said Edwina. 'Of course, I have the

bearing for height. Add shoulder curls and I think I might have found something pretty for the barber to work upon. Pym, your opinion if you please.'

'Not graceful enough for you,' Pym said tactfully and before her mistress could begin to add and subtract from the hideous hairpiece quickly replaced it with a neat little wig *à la Grèque*.

The casualness with which Sir John Sinclair guarded his wife's honour puzzled and disturbed Frederick more than a little. Sometimes he felt that Johnnie was almost colluding in the affair, tacitly encouraging Betté to cuckold him right under his very nose. Man of the world though he was, Frederick found something unpleasantly perverse in Sinclair's negligence. It made him uneasy, though not sufficiently uneasy to deny himself any of the golden opportunities for stolen love-making that old Sinclair, by accident or design, seemed determined to push his way. It was dashed peculiar, though, to take tea at five o'clock with the family, to watch Sir John don hat and coat and toddle off to visit friends at the club, to observe the daughters flitter away upstairs and then, with butter hardly dry upon his lips, to have Betté lock the door of the gilded drawing-room, and pounce.

Now and then Frederick felt that he was being cheated of the purer pleasures of seduction, of persuasion, refusal, recantation, yielding. He also felt reduced by the urgency of Betté's demands upon him and by the hasty nature of their couplings. He could not, of course, accuse Betté of indifference – she was a fountainhead of passion – but when the sally was over she would have her clothing arranged and hair pinned almost before he had risen unsteadily to his feet, exhausted but oddly unsatisfied.

There were times when he wished that Betté would permit him simple flirtatious discourse and deny him that larger favour; and thus restore some value to the granting of it.

On that particular Sunday he had tried to stay Betté a little. He had news to impart, the tale of what had happened in the Captains' Bank and what he had discovered there. But Betté would have none of it. She was fired by her customary animal passion. To his consternation he had been unable to keep pace with her demands and had, at the last, disappointed her. Afterwards, he declined supper and a hand at whist and, about half past eight o'clock, limped dejectedly home to Grahamston.

To his surprise the villa was in total darkness.

Fumbling for his key, Frederick quickly inserted it in the latch-lock, turned it and pushed upon the door, only to find that it had been barred from within. 'Eunice,' he called out. 'Eunice, open the door. It's only me, only Frederick.'

It did not occur to him that harm might have befallen her. He assumed that she was in one of her temperamental moods. The moods had become more frequent since they had taken possession of the suburban house. It was not that she did not want to live there. She had fallen in love with the villa the moment she had clapped eyes on it, because of its seclusion. He could sense her presence behind the door. 'Eunice, let me in this instant.'

'Are you alone?'

'Yes, damn it, of course I'm alone.'

The long bar clanked as she lifted it from its sockets. The door opened an inch. He caught a glimpse of her dark eyes peering at him from the aperture.

'Dearest, what is it? What's wrong?'

She admitted him to the hallway which, like the rest of the house, was without light. She moved swiftly behind him to replace the iron bar. She wore only a flimsy gown though the house was as cold as a tomb. When he groped for her arm he found her flesh icy, each hair stiff and bristling like frosty grass. She leaned her shoulder against him.

Softly, Frederick said, 'Something's happened.'

'A man came today.'

'Man? What man? What did he want here?'

'I did not admit him. He went off in a temper.'

Frederick's throat had become suddenly clogged. He swallowed. 'Small fellow, dressed like a horse-coper?'

'Big,' said Eunice. 'Huge. He rode a grey gelding. By his apparel he might have been a seaman.'

Frederick sucked air through his teeth. He had half-expected a visit from Cluny Martin, who would have had some justification for squirming and squabbling a little. But Cluny did not know where he lived. The man that Eunice had described, however, was also known to him and represented a much greater threat to his person and to his plans than did the little cocker. He regretted his initial reaction. Eunice had guessed the truth, that he knew the man who had frightened her. He took her arm, guided her through the darkness to the parlour where he lit first a candle and then the kindled fire.

'Who is he?' Eunice asked.

Frederick was shocked by her appearance. She was ghastly pale and seemed thinner, pared down. In the first moment after his arrival she had been dependent upon him but now she had regained her strength and was, or seemed to be, practical and persistent. She said, 'You must tell me who he is and what he wants here. He spat upon the gate, you know.'

'Oh!' Involuntarily Frederick wiped his hand upon his thigh, then stooped to the grate and blew into the twigs

below the small coals. 'He'd have done you no harm,
Eunice.'

'Who *is* he?'

'His name is Harding, Brock Harding.'

'Is he from Shropshire?'

'What?' Frederick spun round on his heels. 'God in
Heaven, Eunice, is that why he frightened you? You
thought he came from Addison's Edge? No, he's from –
not far away. He called to see me on a matter of business, I
expect.'

'In a violent rage?'

'Perhaps he was annoyed because I was not at home.'

'How did he know where to find you?'

'I make no secret of where I live,' Frederick said. 'By the
by, Harding isn't a sailorman. He's a blacksmith.'

'Lord Drumfin's blacksmith?'

'What a fiery imagination you have, Eunice,' Frederick
said, trying to jolly her out of it. 'Why must you always
imagine the worst? Harding has no connection whatsoever
with the noble Drumfin who is, I believe, presently lording
it over the court in Edinburgh.'

'You owe him money.'

'I have written to Drumfin,' Frederick lied. 'I have
promised to pay him by summer quarter-day. He will
be satisfied with that.'

'Who then is the man on the horse?' Eunice demanded.
'Do you owe him money too?'

'Not exactly,' Frederick said. 'I owe money to his
brother. For a cargo. Harding merely wants to know when
the money will be paid so that the cargo might be delivered.'

'A blacksmith who is also a trader?' Eunice said.

'He's a local agent for the shippers, that's all.'

Frederick was becoming snappish. He hated any form of interrogation, particularly questions from Eunice to whom he found it difficult to lie.

Eunice said, 'Can you not pay him?'

Frederick said, 'I am, as you know, short of the readies at this present juncture.'

'What is the cargo?'

He hesitated. He could never be sure what Eunice knew about the nature of business and what she did not.

'Salt.'

'Is there money in salt, Frederick?'

'Oh, yes.'

Strangely, his blunt answers seemed to appease Eunice. Stepping past him she plucked a dish from the mantel and lit a stump of tallow from the tall candle. Tonight her face was more mask-like than ever. The blemishes on her complexion were livid and profuse. Frederick could not bear to look at her and, seeming casual, turned away to warm his hands at the spluttering fire.

'Supper?' Eunice's commonplace question surprised him.

'If you please,' said Frederick.

She retreated silently down the half-step into the pitch black kitchen but left behind her a faint whiff upon the air, an odour that Frederick, sniffing, soon identified as Holland gin.

'Oh, God!' he murmured and then, gathering his charm about him like a cloak, followed Eunice's tiny light down the half-step into the gloom.

4

At Lady Betté's

━━━━━◆◆━━━━━

It was a bad week for serious business in the Captains'
Bank. Who had time to concentrate on trade when one's
womenfolk had gone barking mad? Out in the city the
interests of the ladies held sway. Here were a scurrying of
maid servants, a striding about of valets, a last-minute
gallop of seamstresses, tailors and barbers. There were
carriages and trunks, caddies and footmen, gleeful inn-
keepers, cooks having tantrums and wine merchants a gala
day, until one might have supposed that the whole of
Glasgow was going to Lady Betté Sinclair's ball and not
just a privileged hundred or so from the upper and middle
ranks.

In the matter of personal loans, however, Purves &
Purves did well. Things were brisk through Monday
and Tuesday and picked up to breakneck pace by Thursday forenoon. Quantities of fresh ink had to be mixed,
quills cut, ledger paper trimmed as gentlemen or their
agents queued up to borrow against the cost of being
fashionable. Little bits of profit quickly accumulated into
handsome reading, however. When the doors had been
locked and lamps lit and the clerks were sucking their
bunioned thumbs, old Mr Purves purred over the tallies of
interest that would come his way and wished that dear
Lady Betté would give a ball every month in the year.

There were, mark you, penalties to be paid for the bank's

spratling profits. Upstairs, the Purves household was no different from half a hundred others about town. What with Edwina changing her mind every six minutes and Mr Andrew, even Mr Andrew, having to dig deep into his savings to pay for the miles of fabric and trimmings that littered his lady's dressing-room. For a goodly portion of each day old Mr Purves found himself alone at the helm. What Andrew was up to during his extended absences remained a mystery. But his father had an inkling that Vanity, call it Pride if you prefer, had taken his son by the throat too and that Andrew might have a sartorial surprise to spring upon the girls come Friday.

If much of the hurly-burly was, in the female aspect, made as an oblation to Venus it was some grumpy old Norse god who decided to remind the socialites that February was his month and that gay, pastoral frolics were best left until leaves were on trees and not plastered on to turbans with stitching and gauze. In the course of Friday morning dark clouds massed over the Clyde and, about the time of the Tolbooth chimes, released a sleety flurry that had girls shrieking in horror and, when snow came hard on sleet's coat-tails, dissolved them into tears of frustrated rage. 'Ruined. My muslin will be ruined. You must find me a sedan.'

'My dear you will never fit into a sedan, not in those hoops.'

'Hire a carriage.'

'Not a carriage to be had.'

'A canopy then.'

'Dreadfully sorry.'

'A cape, in blue, to match my shoes. Oh, my kidskins will be in shreds before I reach Buchanan Street.'

'You may borrow my hessians if you wish.'

'What!'

'I jest.'

'Oh, you jest, do you? With real India muslin at thirty-six shillings the yard you have the audacity to jest.'

'Tell you what, I'll hire Lombardi's balloon, howzat!'

'Ooooooooooooh!'

By the time the last forkful of dinner had been gulped down and suggestions of a civilized tea rejected, the sullen clouds had dispersed and left the evening clear and cold with a crisp layer of snow to marl the muddy thoroughfares and rendered the pavé passable. Cold did not matter. Cold was good. Cold starched fabrics, shined the eyes, rouged the cheeks and pinched away tiny wrinklets on the throat that paint and lace could not quite disguise. The ladies breathed again.

Sinclairs' Land, aloof in the upper reaches of Buchanan Street, had discreetly absorbed the columns of tradesmen who, like ants, carried in vast quantities of wine and spirits, gross boxes of candles, confections, oyster barrels and a ton of more robust comestibles all to the hammer and scrape of the carpenters who were building the musicians' dais and erecting the trestles from which supper would be served.

By the time the first carriages and sedans began to wend west from the High Street and north from the Stockwell the mansion, ablaze with light, glistened against the starry sky like a gigantic sugarcake. Four stout grooms, brought up from Wyvercroft, kept traffic flowing through the gates and along the short gravelled drive. Soon the steps below the house's open doors were mobbed by gay ladies, gentlemen and servants. And the strains of an overture floated like incense from within to quicken your pulse and make your heart trip as you came up the street and caught sight of the stately pediments. Once you were inside the vast tee-shaped hallway, you were sucked with other guests and servants into an exhilarating free-for-all in which not even the stuffiest old gent could quite maintain his dignity.

Separation of sexes and classes took place with all the decorum of a cattle auction. Apartments for cloaks lay one way, dressing-rooms another, certain 'offices' were set apart down a long interior passageway which could not be navigated by ladies in hoops without a certain heavy listing to starboard or port. Maids, footmen, valets and other lackeys were given firm instructions not to wander but were, with the best intentions, whirled away and lost, and found again, dragged by the cuff to mirrored niches or the dressing-rooms to help Madam change her shoes or Miss to garter her stockings or on toe-tip to puff powder over the Honourable's wig.

Mr Andrew had excelled himself in providing a stylish mode of transport for his entourage. With three well-dressed women and a servant to cater for he had rejected the use of the Purveses' carriage, unless the weather was bad. Instead he had hired a team of footmen to support a tassled canopy of painted buckram over the heads of his womenfolk. He had told Edwina that as she was his Cleopatra, and as he could not find a barge to sail along Ingram Street, he had plumped instead for a queenly canopy to protect her complexion from the moonlight. In fact Edwina's white and silver satin gown was so trained and padded that a whisper of wind from the wrong direction might have carried her off like a kite.

Frances exemplified the beauties of simplicity in a gown of pale mauve with a minimum of boning and padding. Her hair had been kept natural, lightly curled over pearls. Clare had been short of time and had only three pounds to spend, plus an extra guinea that Mr Andrew had slipped her. She had made the best of her figure in a striped muslin and a coiffeur dressed backward and low but without the sausage curls that Edwina's barber had tried to foist upon her. Even Pym was nicely dressed, for in the servants' hall below the ballroom, there would be reels and capers and courtship jigs too, and she had put a whole year's wages on her back.

It was, however, Mr Andrew who astonished them all. He had rejected Frenchified fashion in favour of a blue-green coat, buff waistcoat and breeches, and an expensive new back wig. The breeks did the trick. Their line was as smooth as gannet-skin and showed off Mr Andrew's flat stomach and muscular thighs dramatically. He looked so handsome and imperious as he lounged in the hallway of Sinclairs' Land awaiting the reappearance of his wife and cousin from the dressing-rooms, that it was all Clare could do to stammer out her question. 'Am – am I to go with Pym or am I to come upstairs with Miss Frances, sir?'

'Are you not dressed for the dancing floor, Clare?'

'I – I think I am, Mr Andrew.'

'Well, we must not waste all that beauty on knaves and varlets, must we?' Andrew said. 'This is not the royal court you know, Clare. There will be no inspection. Stay with Miss Frances.'

'I hardly know how to dance.'

'Then you will be in the best of company,' said Andrew.

On her return from attending her mistress Pym was not well pleased at being handed Clare's cloak and the plush bag that contained her outdoor shoes but with Mr Andrew standing by she could not voice her objections.

Arm in arm with Frances, Clare ascended the crowded staircase that led to the ballroom. Anxiety knotted in her stomach when she saw that a major domo in magnificent silk livery stood by the doorway to announce each of the guests to the company. All around her were Glasgow's well-to-do citizens. She was acutely aware that she was nothing but an interloper in whose veins the blood of the Purveses ran very thin indeed. Somehow she imagined that an odour of servility clung to her and that the high-bridged, hairy-nostrilled major domo would be sure to sniff it out and would refuse her admission to the glittering room over which he stood guard. She clung to Frances as to a lifeline.

Frances was also nervous, a little awed by the grandeur that opened like a vista before them. She had to clear her throat before she could whisper their names to the major domo.

'MISS FRANCES PURVES.'

Fran gave a giggle and little dip to acknowledge the volume of the announcement.

'MISS CLARE KELSO.'

Guests assembled within the ballroom were far too self-absorbed to be listening, though the mention of a Lord This or Lady That would have had heads turning. Almost unnoticed the girls moved forward into the huge, mirrored ballroom. The flow carried them towards a long side table upon which glittered a hundred long-stemmed glasses into which a batallion of young footmen were pouring champagne. A glass was handed to Clare's juggling hands, which already held a fan and a reticule, and she was drawn on towards a reception line at the end of which Sir John and Lady Betté waited to greet their guests.

'I'm Frances Purves, frae Moorfoot.'

'Why of course you are, my dear. How brave of you to make such an arduous journey to be with us tonight.'

'I've been stayin' wi' my cousin.'

'Indeed! And who might that be?'

'Andrew, the banker.'

If Lady Betté appeared vague, behind her husband's apple-cheeked smile was calculation as he sized up each guest to see what use he might make of them in the course of the evening.

'Miss Kelso, Clare Kelso.'

'How pretty you look, my dear. Does she not look pretty, John?'

The host's eyes were upon her, his hand touching hers.

'Why, yes, a veritable rose.' Clare juggled the glass as the man stooped and kissed the back of her wrist. 'So pretty, so fresh.'

'She's my cousin too,' Frances said, though no enquiry regarding Clare had come from either Sinclair. 'She lives in Purves's Land all the time.'

'Does she?' said Sir John. 'Gracious! How fortunate Andrew is to have two such flowers to tend and water.'

'Uh?' said Frances but Clare, with a shuffle, had pushed her on to make room on the line and to release herself from Johnnie Sinclair's sticky scrutiny.

Fran paused to sip bubbles from her glass. 'God, am I no' glad that's over. Now we can get down to enjoyin' ourselves.' She glanced about her. 'Where are the men?'

'There, I think,' said Clare.

Males, young and old, had separated themselves from the women and posed in groups about the base of the musicians' dais. They seemed determined to impress rather than be impressed and paid not the slightest heed to the flock of females who occupied the gilded chairs beneath the long windows. It was, Clare thought, like two armies casually massed for battle and only in need of a trumpet to begin hostilities. As if reading her companion's

thoughts, Fran said, 'Bit of a damp rag so far, don't
y'think?'

'It hasn't started yet,' Clare said.

'Aye, well, it's high time it did.' Fran raised her glass
ostentatiously, downed the contents in a swallow, and
coughed. 'Conviviality, that's what we need here. I tell
you, if this was Lanark the roof beams would be ringin' by
this time.'

Clare sipped champagne in the hope that its efferves-
cence might reawaken in her the excitement that had
dwindled away these past few minutes.

'Do you not know anybody?' Fran asked.

'Not a soul,' Clare answered.

'Here, I hope we're no' goin' to be wallflowers.'

'Perhaps I shouldn't have accompanied you.'

'Huh! It might be better fun downstairs.'

The depressing lull after arrival did not last long. Soon
strains of music from the dais ceased and Madame Celestial stepped forward in a billow of spotted muslin to call the
guests forward for the Grand March and Minuet. The
orchestra was conducted by a little Italian gentleman with a
dragonfly moustache who whipped his musicians into a
rousing *fortissimo* as soon as Madame had finished her
announcement.

The girls watched husbands dutifully separate themselves from the stags, saunter across the waxed and polished floor, side-step the first splashes of grease from the
high-hung chandeliers, and present themselves to their
wives. Bachelors tugged at their waistcoats, smoothed
the cloth of their breeches and adjusted their wigs. The
more gauche among them even buffed the toes of their
shoes against their calves as if a last polish might secure
them the girl of their dreams. In spite of apparent indif-

ference each unattached gentleman had already studied the covey of ladies and by discreet enquiry from friends and rivals had ascertained who was who and what was what in terms of pedigree and income. Targets had been set, bows drawn and at a second word from Madame Celestial and a sweep of her little jewelled claws there was a sudden tidal surge from the base of the dais and a pitter-patter of eager heels as the stags shed dignity in pursuit of opportunity and headed *en bloc* for the hinds.

Caught with a half-empty glass in her hand Clare was at a loss what to do with it until a young footman plucked it from her fingers and whisked it away on a silver tray.

'Frances, what is a Grand March?' Clare whispered.

'You just toddle about hand in hand with some man,' Frances answered, adding anxiously. 'God, we're goin' to be left on the shelf.'

'I thought there were cards, tickets for each dance.'

'Only at assemblies, no' at a private ball,' Fran hissed again. 'Pick me. Anybody, pick me.'

'May I have the pleasure of escorting you on the Grand Parade?' Clare and Frances spun round immediately.

Frederick Striker looked dashing in a suit of snuff-coloured velvet worn over a frilled shirt. His hair was set *au naturel* and the forelock bobbed impudently when he bowed.

'Which one o' us do you want?' Frances asked.

There was no hesitation on Frederick's part. 'Why you, of course.'

Taking the country cousin on his arm, Frederick stepped on to the dancing floor and left Clare all alone.

Mr Walter Malabar, though hardly more than a boy, had all the self assurance of a libertine. He was not the only young man to offer his arm to the prettiest girl in the room but he was probably the most pushing and certainly the most garrulous. He chattered on and on about his family connections, scholastic achievements and prospects. Just who he supposed Clare to be was a matter that was not resolved during the progress of the Grand March and Minuet.

Mr Malabar was no better acquainted with the steps of the dances than was Clare. He lagged a beat behind the rest of the company and let Clare follow as best she could. If he had kept his mouth shut Clare might have been more impressed by him, for he was fair-haired and handsome and had the most perfect set of small white teeth that Clare had ever seen. She was relieved, however, when March and Minuet were over and Mr Malabar left her to scoot off to boast to his chums how much he had impressed James Purves's daughter, she who was worth five thousand at the altar and was pretty as a lily to boot.

Clare, of course, was no stranger to many of the burgesses present. Word was soon out that the beauty was just some lowly relative of the Purveses who had been brought to the ball out of charity. In another sort of house, at another sort of ball, Clare might have been ostracised. But not here. Lady Betté was too vulgar and too energetic a hostess to allow that to happen or for the evening to fall victim to propriety.

Grand March and Minuet were the first and last concessions to formality. Madame Celestial and the Italian conductor had been hired less for their class than their adaptability. Metaphorically the orchestra loosed its stays and neckties and played, albeit from music books, the country dances with which the vast majority of the guests had been reared. Trains and hoops, breeks applied tight as varnish over walnuts, were sore encumbrances to dignity at first but fustian in Glasgow was never more than skin deep and a sense of the ridiculous even nearer the surface than that. Soon everyone, with a few exceptions, was having fun. It was just as well that Sir John had had his mansion constructed by certificated builders for by half-past ten o'clock that Friday night the vaulted roof rang, the floor shook and windows vibrated in their frames with the birl and bellow of uninhibited merrymaking, fuelled by bumpers of rum punch and cups of ruby wine.

Clare's pleasure was spoiled only by the fact that she could not attract the attention of Mr Frederick Striker. He seemed to have forgotten his promise entirely, to have set his cap instead at Fran. The hostess was not at all put out by being ignored by her current lover. Edwina, on the other hand, was furious, and evinced palpable ill-will in that direction. She did everything in her power to magnetise Frederick, but he was no more than passing polite to her and spent more time between dances in conversation with Andrew than he did with Andrew's wife.

Mr Walter Malabar fell, literally, at the first hurdle. Three lanes into Strip the Willow down he went and limped away with a buckled ankle to find his Mama to dry his tears.

Next to pay tentative court to Clare Kelso was Mr Ninian Murray, a fine young man, son of a famous physician and destined to follow his father into medicine. Unlike Walter Malabar, however, Mr Murray was very shy. He had little to say to Clare and left her with a bow as soon as the dance was over as if, somehow, he had been trying her out and had found her wanting in all but beauty. There were others too, several of them, but even the most pleasant and vigorous could not engage Clare's full attention. From the corner of her eye she watched Frederick dance with Fran and experienced a hurt that ruined the excitement of her first excursion into society's upper circle.

Only when Mr Andrew deigned to dance with her did her mood lighten. He held her firmly, brows twitching as he concentrated on the figures, hands clapping to the beat of the timpany. When it was over Clare thanked him for his kindness. He would have none of it and turned her gratitude back upon her, neatly.

For an instant Clare sensed in Andrew a loneliness and disappointment similar to her own. She was tempted to stay with him, to touch his hand casually to indicate that she understood his feelings, if not the reason for them. Edwina, however, was crying out for her husband to fetch her another glass of wine, displaying such voluble possessiveness that Andrew had little option but to attend her. At that moment Madame Celestial, to the accompaniment of cheers from the younger gentlemen, announced that supper was being served in the long gallery.

Clare was close to the doors and, for reasons other than greed, was tempted to go at once in search of a plate of cold meats and a dish of confections. She was unsure, however, whether ladies required gentlemen to lead them in that line too and she loitered, feeling foolish, while the younger element made a beeline for the doors.

'Clare?'

Frederick called out to her. Her heart beat faster as she watched him approach, yet there was in her breast a cold lump like a swallow of water straight from the pump on a winter's morning. Her first words to him were, 'Where is Miss Frances?'

He was already guiding her towards the doors. 'Popped downstairs.'

'Will she not expect you to wait for her?'

'If she does,' Frederick said, 'I'm afraid she'll be doomed to disappointment.'

'I don't want to—'

'To eat supper? I'm sure that you do.'

'Well, if—'

'And after we have eaten our fill we will dance together.'

Clare said, 'What if I have promised myself to others?'

'Have you?'

She paused. 'No.'

Frederick laughed, steered her along a passageway lit by candles in gilded ramshorns and into a long gallery in which tables were set out in line.

On scores of silver dishes were smoked meats and fishes, fowls roasted golden brown, boiled eggs sprinkled with herbs, ripe cheeses and flans of fruits of all kinds, dried, glazed and fresh. Tan-coloured portraits of Sir John's ancient ancestors peered down approvingly at the lavish spread and one murky gent with a foaming brown beared seemed almost ready to lean out of the frame to spear a scallop with his sword. What with the crackling log fire and the tapers, the deep, darting shadows, Clare felt as if she had been carried off to some remote highland stronghold far from Glasgow's cheery streets. She stood close to Frederick while he ladled food on to plates, shouldered his way through the rabble of voracious young folk to secure a dish of pickled oysters and finally persuaded a footman to yield up a full but uncorked bottle of claret and two wine glasses.

Shepherding Clare before him, Frederick carried the booty out of the gallery by a small side door and along another short, dark passageway to a small room at the mansion's rear where, for some reason, candles and a fire had also been lighted. Clare hesitated at the sight of a canopied, four-poster bed. 'Mr Striker I–'

'Is it not a relief to escape from the monkey house? Here we may sup in perfect peace.'

'What about Miss Frances?'

'Oh, I doubt if she'll find us here.'

Clare said, 'I am not sure, sir, that this is a respectable arrangement.'

'True,' Frederick conceded. 'But one usually leaves respectability at the stoup in Sinclairs' Land.'

He put plates and glasses carefully on to a hexagonal table and pulled the loosened cork from the claret bottle with his teeth.

'Is this Lady Betté's bedroom?' Clare asked.

'God, no. Betté sleeps upstairs, in a French bed with a quilted headboard and short legs that end in lion's paws.'

'How do you know such a thing?'

Frederick did not respond. He handed her a claret glass and gave her a glance that was both quizzical and speculative. She decided, prudently, not to press him for an answer. He dabbed up a pickled oyster on the end of a fork, held his lace handkerchief below Clare's chin and laid the soft, sharp, slippery thing on her tongue. She had eaten fresh oysters often before. They were no great delicacy in the height of summer but at this season they seemed so, and she savoured the feel of the flesh in her mouth as well as its sharp salty tang. Frederick fed her another.

The suddenness with which she had replaced Frances as the object of Frederick Striker's attentions did not disturb Clare in the least. She was elated at being here with him and too wrapped up in the pleasure of the moment to harbour suspicion.

'More?' he said.

'Please.'

He fed her again.

Clare sat very still, knees pressed together, body upright in the straight-backed chair. She felt cool now that the perspiration of exertion had dried. She watched Frederick swallow three oysters in rapid succession then dab at his lips with his handkerchief.

'One more, Clare?'

She shook her head, sipped at the strong wine and observed how expertly Frederick broke up a breast of cold cooked chicken and popped the tender pieces into his mouth. He ate heartily but without gluttony and hardly took his eyes from her while he did so. The compliment came as no surprise. 'You are very beautiful, Clare Kelso.'

'Thank you, sir.' Oddly, it was Fran who had taught her how to accept flattery, to take it as if it were due.

'I know so little about you, Clare.'

'I know even less about you, Mr Striker.'

'Do you know that my name is Frederick?'

'Oh, yes.'

'Let me hear it from your lips.'

'Frederick.'

'Are you, as Frances informs me, a full cousin to Andrew Purves?'

'No, Frances is wrong. I'm only a cousin germane.'

'What of your family?'

'They are all dead, except my brothers who are at sea.'

'Do you hear word of them?'

'No, not for many years.'

'How sad,' said Frederick. 'So the Purveses are all the relatives you have left, in effect?'

'Yes,' Clare said. 'If you wish to hear me say it, Mr

Striker, I am but distant kin, a poor relative. I have none of the advantages of family, as does Miss Frances.'

'Why do you put yourself down?'

'Because I am down,' Clare said. 'I am where God put me, and grateful enough to be no worse off.'

'Do you not feel that you deserve better?'

'I do not know what I deserve,' said Clare.

She had no defence against his questions. She found she enjoyed talking about herself, that her modesty, like the civility of the average Glaswegian, was only skin deep. Frederick sat back, put the plate on his lap, broke and ate a wedge of hard cheese over it. 'What do you know of me?'

Clare was caught a little off guard. She had been thinking of herself and how she might react to him. Now Frederick had deftly reversed the position. The conversational game was more complicated than she had imagined. 'Only – only what I have heard by rumour.'

'And what have you heard – by rumour?'

She had become heated again, without cause, for the fire was no furnace and the air in the room was cool. Frederick gave her assistance. He said, 'Have you, for instance, heard that I am more than a platonic friend to Betté Sinclair?'

Startled by his directness, Clare blurted out, 'Are you?'

'Have you heard that I am not to be trusted?'

'No. I have not heard that.'

He laughed. 'Well, I'm not.'

'Pardon?'

'I am susceptible to beautiful women. I freely admit it,' Frederick said. 'When I meet a truly beautiful woman I wish to know her as well as decency will allow.'

'To – to what end, Mr Striker?'

'For friendship's sake.'

Clare suffered a qualm of doubt, a faint suspicion that he

had spoken these words before, used the lines to discover without delay what it was that a woman expected of him. Clare pushed her plate to one side. 'Married women too, Mr Striker?'

'Come now, I thought you were going to call me Frederick?'

She would not be deterred. 'Married women?'

'If you mean a married woman like Mr Andrew's wife, my answer would be No.'

Clare had failed to realise just how tense she had become until a log dropped in the grate, and she started. The free nature of the conversation was exciting and dangerous, quite different from the clumsy *doubles entendres* with which Peter-Pierre or Coachman Bob tried their hands at seduction. She cursed herself for flirting with Frederick Striker, for partnering him in what was obviously a mating dance. But she could not stop now. She heard herself say, 'Do you not find Miss Frances to your liking?'

'Frances is very much to my liking.'

'In that case why are you not feeding her pickled oysters instead of me?'

Frederick gave a little shrug. 'It seems that I am not to *her* liking.'

'Oh.'

'I expect she will tell you why she dislikes me when you two are together and alone. Is that not how it is with girls who share a bed? Do they not confess all, share each with the other all the tremulous secrets of their hearts?'

'I do not share a bed with anyone,' Clare said.

'Even so, will you not defend me against her calumnies?'

'What?'

'Will you not speak up for me when your cousin miscalls me?'

'Fran is not my cousin,' Clare said. 'I am, for your information, her maid not her confidante.'

'If the subject does come up, how will you speak of me?'

'I will tell her that I found you to be a perfect gentleman,' Clare said, adding, 'who knows how to serve oysters.'

'A ready wit, I see,' Frederick said. 'Do you also, like Miss Frances, have a blunt tongue? Come now, I cannot believe that you do not snuggle together under the covers in this cold wintry weather. Tell me what you will talk of tonight.'

Clare got to her feet. 'I think I hear the orchestra strikin' up again.'

Frederick rose too. 'Have I offended you?'

'No, Mr Striker, but—'

'Would this offend you, Clare?'

He did not touch her with his long-fingered hands but leaned across the hexagonal table and kissed her on the cheek. He straightened, watching her intently.

Clare stammered, 'I – we – must go now.'

'Are you afraid of me, Clare?'

'No, sir, I am not.'

In her confusion she began to gather together the forks, glasses and plates. Frederick stopped her with a hand laid gently on her arm. 'No need for that.'

'Oh, I'm – I'm sorry.'

Saying nothing, he placed his fingers over her trembling hand, led her out of the bedroom and back along the passageway to join the dancers in the ballroom once more.

Dizzy from a reel and purple as a damson, Frances slumped down on a chair by Clare's side.

'Where did he take you?' she asked, without preamble.

'Who do you mean?'

'Och, don't play the innocent wi' me, Clare. Mr Striker. Where did he take you at the supper hour?'

It was the first opportunity that the girls had had for a word together, for Frederick had danced every dance with Clare and had not left her side until nature had called him away. Frances had not been slow to seize the chance. She had torn herself from limping Walter Malabar and, busily fanning herself, had hurried to corner Clare.

'To a quiet room,' Clare said.

'Oh-hoh!'

'I'm sorry if I came between you,' Clare said. 'It wasn't exactly my fault.'

'Aye, I know it wasn't,' Fran grinned and tapped her companion's kneecap with her folded fan. 'If it was anybody's fault it was mine.'

'Frederick told me you had rejected him.'

'After a fashion, I did.'

'But why? Do you not like him?'

'I like him fine,' Frances said. 'But I think he likes you better. Anyway there was no point in encouragin' him. I'll be awa' back home to Moorfoot on Monday.'

'Moorfoot isn't the back of beyond. Frederick might have entered into a correspondence with you. Might have visited.'

'My Daddy would have a thousand fits if Mr Striker strolled into our hall wi' marriage on his mind. My Daddy would see through Frederick Striker as if he was a glass window.'

'See through – I don't understand.'

'Never mind,' said Frances. 'It's no' me Mr Striker is really taken with. All the time we were dancin' all he talked about was you.'

'Frances! Really?' said Clare. 'Surely not?'

'Sure as sugar. Cross ma heart an' cut ma throat.'

'I'm sorry.'

'Sorry because he prefers you to me?' Frances said. 'It's no' your fault you were born wi' a pretty face. Besides,' she grinned and winked, 'I don't think you're sorry at all.'

Frederick's appearance at the doorway put paid to the girls' conversation. He paused for a word with Lady Betté then, laughing heartily at something the woman had said, exchanged a remark or two with Andrew, nodded to Edwina in passing and came on down the length of the ballroom. The girls watched. There was an air of gaiety in Frederick that Clare had not detected before. She wondered if he had become expansive because of her. Wondered if what Frances had told her was, even in part, true. She was impatient for Frederick to return to her, to take her arm, to dance with her.

She got to her feet, looked down at Frances. 'You're right,' she said, 'I'm not in the least sorry,' and then glided off to meet Frederick who, seeing her, raised his hand and greeted her with a beaming smile.

By one o'clock Edwina could take no more. She was mad at Clare Kelso for robbing her of the opportunity to flirt with the most attractive man in the room. She had been all but ignored by Frederick, salt rubbed in the wound by snide and sidling questions about the beautiful girl who seemed to have captivated the Englishman. Edwina hated having to explain that Clare Kelso was no visitor to Glasgow but had been a member of her household for the past six years or so. She was pushed to define Clare's relationship to her and say why the girl had been brought to the ball.

Andrew, it seemed, found Edwina's euphemisms and prevarications amusing. 'Stop smirking,' she'd told him.

'Our family's reputation may be damaged because of this whim of yours to allow Kelso to pretend she's one of us.'

'Nonsense!' Andrew had retorted and had swung her harder than the reel demanded. He had caught her again, stiffly. 'This is not the Provost's Ball, Edwina. There are precious few genuine snobs in this company. The family's reputation, such as it is, will be quite untarnished.'

'As for Mr Striker—'

'Yes?'

'Oh, be quiet!' Edwina had told her husband and had pushed herself away from him several beats ahead of the step.

By one o'clock Edwina was ready to quit not just the ballroom but the whole conclave of Glasgow society. She declared that she had a megrim and wanted to go home. She ordered Andrew to fetch the girls at once. The ball was far from over. In the past hour the music had become wilder, the dances less anglified. Betté Sinclair's daughters had thrown gentility to the winds and were hooching and birling like sonsy young witches. To Edwina's jaundiced eye the scene was more suited to a barn than a ballroom. When it became apparent that Andrew was not going to leap to do her bidding, Edwina left the glittering room on her own and flounced downstairs to find Pym and Peter-Pierre and tell them to make ready to depart, with or without the rest of the Purves party.

There was nobody in the hall except a weary footman who was packed off against his will to unearth the servants. Edwina hung about the hallway, twiddling her thumbs and listening to the skirl of pipes and muffled yells from the servants' hall. She was still there, waiting, when Andrew came clipping down the grand staircase, alone.

'Where is she? I mean, where are they?'

'Saying goodbye to our hosts,' Andrew answered. 'I'll arrange for the canopy to be erected. It might take a few minutes, for I suspect that the footmen will have been at the ale too.'

'I am not leaving here without them.'

'The footmen?'

'You fool!'

'If you mean the girls,' said Andrew, quite calmly, 'they will join us at the gates.'

'Who is she with?'

'The Malabar boy.'

'Kelso, I mean.'

'You know perfectly well who Clare is with. She's been in his company all evening since supper.'

'Frederick Striker.'

Andrew studied his wife with peculiar intensity as if, just for a second, he was about to blow up and lose his temper with her. He did not, however. He nodded passively and turned to watch Peter-Pierre drag a giggling Pym along the corridor from the servants' hall.

'Are you sober, Pierre?' Andrew asked.

'Shobersh a judge, shur,' Peter-Pierre replied, after which dressing and departure became a débâcle that claimed all Edwina's attention and temporarily deflected her pique.

Only when she emerged from the dressing-room with her cloak fastened and her slippers, reticule and fan in the plush bag did Clare realise how fortunate she was to have an escort who was not half seas over drunk. She had been oblivious to the tippling that had been going on in the side rooms until she encountered a gang of less youthful guests reeling about the hall, to the shame of their wives and daughters and the amusement of the servants who were in little better shape themselves. Frederick, though, was as sober and upright as a pine tree in the midst of the brawl that seemed to have developed on stairs and steps and along the driveway.

He sized up the situation, took Clare's arm and whispered, 'We'll go out by another route.'

'But the Purveses are waiting at the gate.'

'You will be with them directly, I promise.'

Clare had already grown used to surrendering to Frederick's will. She let herself be led down another long dark corridor which ended in a door that opened into a walled garden on the mansion's south gable. Odours of fresh earth and evergreen enveloped her. Little furry, flame-shaped firs and the naked boughs of fruit trees were outlined against the glow of flambeaux from the street beyond the walls.

Frederick drew her along a flagged path to an iron gate in a garden arch. From there Clare could just make out the Purveses, all of them clamouring to instruct the hired footmen in the art of erecting a canopy, while Pym and Peter-Pierre gleefully danced a jig about them, with never a thought for tomorrow's inevitable retribution.

'There they are,' Clare said.

'And here we are,' said Frederick.

Before Clare could protest, he'd pulled her to him, tugged down her hood and kissed her mouth. They were screened by the angle of the wall, but the noise of the revellers seemed uncomfortably close in those first few seconds of embrace.

Clare was too taken aback to resist. Frederick put an arm about her waist and elevated her until her toes were hardly touching the ground. He kissed her again, his coat and her cloak wrapped about their bodies like wings. Knee and thigh pressed insistently against the front of Clare's body. Even through a gown and petticoats she felt their hardness. She groaned gently, and gasped for breath. Frederick released her. He said nothing and sought no more from her. Taking her hand, he unlatched the iron gate and led her, in a daze, over the zig-zag flagstones that crossed the mansion's lawn.

Clare was deaf to the rumpus from the house, the hoarse clatter of horses and coachmen from Buchanan Street. She could still feel the warmth of Frederick's mouth against her lips, the pressure of his thigh against her stomach. A step or two short of the gates Frederick stopped her. He bowed, kissed her wrist and murmured, 'Goodnight, my darling.' Then he handed her over to Frances who had been delivered there by a more conventional route by the injured Mr Malabar.

For the Purveses it was not a dignified exit. Footmen stumbled and cursed, torches smoked, the canopy flapped like a loose sail. Pym and Peter-Pierre refused to walk in a column and capered hither and thither, arm-in-arm. Holding her skirts with one hand Fran clasped Clare's arm and led her on ahead of the great, daft, ostentatious canvas, ahead of Andrew and Edwina who were valiantly trying to keep covered and yet avoid the tossing tassles and listing poles.

'What a night that was' Fran whispered, hugging Clare to her. 'I'll never forget the Sinclairs' ball as long as I live.'

Fran required no agreement from her companion but when the country girl gave an exuberant skip Clare was moved to follow suit. Step-in-step the girls skipped to the street corner where they paused to look back at the sugarcake mansion, at the man and boy who had lingered at the gates to wave them a farewell.

'*Au revoir. Au revoir*, Walter.' Frances shook her shoe-bag in the air. 'Write to me at Moorfoot.'

Clare said nothing, however, and did not respond when Frederick waved to her. In spite of the hot and novel sensations that clamoured within her, she did not know where she stood yet or what, if any, Frederick Striker's intentions might be in the dull and wistful days ahead.

5

A Sister in the City

On Monday morning Frances left Purves's Land to return home to Moorfoot. The departure was a tearful occasion for both girls and Clare's immediate restoration to the nursery came as a rude shock to her new-found sense of importance. Nothing, in fact, was quite the same after the ball, and the daily routine seemed unbearably tedious and trivial. Clare missed Frances' companionship and also the status that the country girl's visit had conferred upon her. Most of all, she missed having a friend to whom she could talk freely of her feelings towards Frederick Striker.

To Clare's profound disappointment she heard not a word from Mr Striker in the weeks after the ball. She had nothing, therefore, to cling to as winter trudged into spring, nothing but the memory of his kisses and his caress. She had hoped for more.

Happy memories were not enough to compensate for Edwina's harsh treatment or the servants' malicious invective. Even Peter-Pierre, who had once had a soft spot for Clare, had spurned her in favour of Pym who, Clare guessed, was sneaking out of the house at nights to lie with him in the stable loft. For a time Clare almost regretted that she had not surrendered to Peter-Pierre, for at least she would have had a present friend, a shoulder to lean on and somebody to help fill the hollow in her heart. She turned for consolation to the banking clerks.

Mr Shenkin in particular had always been fond of Clare and Clare exploited that fondness now with a degree of calculation. She was too desperate to suffer guilt over her manipulation of the gentle little clerk. She treated him to tea and almond biscuits, to special glimpses of her ankles when she scaled the stepladder to fetch down a ledger for him from the high shelf, though all to what purpose even Clare was unsure. She supposed that she required to discover yet more about Frederick and that the clerks were the only people who could help her do so. Clare was unaware, however, that Mr Shenkin had been something of a ladies' man before his marriage and that he remembered enough of female wiles to twig what Clare was up to. It would not have flattered the girl to learn that what Mr Shenkin felt for her was sympathy not desire.

Mr Shenkin's desk companions were decidedly amused by the changed behaviour of the beautiful young girl whom they had fostered from childhood to womanhood. There was much conjecture among the three as to what had taken place to awaken self-awareness in Clare and to release in her such a sudden surge of female guile. Mr Rossmore, who had come within an ace of being a guest at Sinclairs' Land, had friends in high places and considered himself sufficiently well informed to pronounce, 'Striker's at the back of it. He danced with Clare all night, I'm told.'

'No *savoir faire*, that chap,' said McCoull. 'One just has to look at him to spot a wrong 'un.'

'I'm not so sure he is a wrong 'un,' said Mr Rossmore.

'Do you think Striker went so far as to —' Judiciously Mr Shenkin left the sentence unfinished.

'Lord, no,' said Mr Rossmore, emphatically. 'Mr Andrew would not have permitted it. If he had thought that Clare was in moral danger he'd have intervened in a trice.'

'Personally,' said Mr McCoull, 'I lay the blame on the unsettling influence of that Moorfoot girl.'

'Only nature is to blame, I fear.' Mr Rossmore had grown daughters of his own to confirm his opinion. 'What Clare needs is a husband to look after and to look after her. Pity you already have a wife, Shenkin.'

'Yes, tell me,' said Mr McCoull, 'is Bea in good health?'

'Stop, I beg you,' said Mr Shenkin. 'Clare is young enough to be my daughter. I feel sorry for her, that's all.'

Always sensitive to delicate situations, Mr Rossmore tapped McCoull's sleeve to prevent further teasing. He said, 'What do you think Clare wants from us?'

Mr Shenkin said, 'To find out more about Frederick Striker.'

'We'd all like to find out more about Frederick Striker, would we not?' said Mr McCoull.

'What have you told Clare so far?'

'Very little. What more *can* I tell her?'

'You could tell her about the removal of the ledger,' Mr McCoull suggested. 'You could tell her that Mr Andrew is engaged in some *very* private transactions with her friend the Englishman.'

'Nothing suspicious in removing a ledger,' said Mr Rossmore. 'Old Mr Purves has always certain favoured clients off the records. It's simply a means of protecting delicate negotiations on the trading front.'

'Negotiations about what, though?' said Mr McCoull.

Mr Rossmore avoided giving an answer. 'I doubt if such dry commercial matters would interest Clare. I suspect she wishes to discover his place of residence which, it is reasonable to assume, Mr Striker has so far kept to himself.'

'We can give her that tidbit of information, can we not?' said Mr Shenkin.

'Confidential information?' said Mr Rossmore.

'Oh, what harm can it do?' said Mr McCoull. 'Striker lives with his sister.'

'We have only his word on that,' said Mr Rossmore. 'The woman with whom Striker resides has not been brought out yet. To the best of my knowledge, she has not even been seen in the streets with him.'

'Come now, Mr Rossmore, surely you do not infer that the woman is not his sister?'

Mr Rossmore was somewhat given to theatrical gestures. He put his hand over his eyes. 'See nothing, hear nothing, pay no tithe.'

'There is no evidence to suggest that Striker is other than a merchant trader,' said Mr Shenkin. 'I certainly do not wish to see Clare hurt. On the other hand Frederick Striker might prove to be just the chap for her.'

'Let *him* prove it,' said Mr Rossmore.

'Yes,' said Mr McCoull. 'Two Irish cargoes do not constitute a grand adventure in trade.'

'From little acorns –' said Mr Shenkin, lamely.

'Why has Mr Andrew taken him out of the ledger?' said Mr McCoull. 'What's Mr Andrew up to, I'd like to know.'

Mr Rossmore leaned over the teacups. 'Spendthrift wife.'

'What! Mistress Edwina?'

'The only wife he's got, more's the pity,' said Mr Rossmore. 'It's my opinion that she would have herself elevated out of Purves's Land, taken to a place on the hill.'

'Old Mr William would never stand for that. This is the ancestral pile, after all,' said Mr Shenkin.

'Ambition in a woman is very difficult to stifle,' said Mr McCoull, whose own wife was not temperamentally so very different from the lady upstairs.

'Be all this as it may,' said Mr Shenkin, 'how does it help Clare?'

'Yes, we had better tell her something,' said Mr McCoull, 'before she bares all to Mr Shenkin's wondering eyes, what!'

'Oh, please,' said Mr Shenkin in a pained voice.

As the three gentlemen contemplated the problem Mr Shenkin took out his snuffbox and offered it around. Each of the men took a pinch and reached for their handkerchiefs. One gigantic sneeze seemed to do the trick for Mr McCoull who announced inspiration with a loud, 'Ah-hah!'

'What ever is the matter?' said Mr Rossmore.

'The Duck Club.'

'What about the Duck Club?'

'Why do we not invite Striker to the Duck Club?'

'In the month of March? Ain't no ducks about in the month of March,' said Mr Shenkin.

'No, but we could give him early notice,' Mr Rossmore seemed taken with the idea. 'The first club meeting will be the Saturday after Easter Day, unless I miss my guess.'

'But what shall we do with him?' said Mr Shenkin.

'Feed him like a lord, pour him a libation or two,' said Mr McCoull, 'and assess his merits and his intentions. Three of us should manage a reasonable judgment between us, should we not?'

'Sound idea,' said Mr Rossmore. 'There may be somebody at the Linden Tree, a club member, who will recognise our Englishman. Striker cannot, after all, have lived his life in a glass bowl.'

'How will this help Clare?' said Mr Shenkin.

'That remains to be seen,' said Mr Rossmore. 'Mark

you, I'm still not convinced that we should be playing at matchmaker for a mere servant girl.'

'But finding out more about Frederick Striker might be awfully interesting, for whatever cause,' said Mr McCoull.

'Indeed, it might,' Mr Rossmore agreed.

'Who will extend the invitation?'

'I will,' said Mr Rossmore.

'Perhaps we should ask Mr Andrew's permission first.'

'Why? Mr Andrew is not a member of the Duck Club.'

'Did he not attend the Fair Supper the year before last?' said Mr McCoull.

'Yes, but only as Jack Grigson's guest.'

'I'm not sure I care for this,' said Mr Shenkin.

'It was your concern for Clare Kelso that started it, if I may remind you,' said Mr McCoull.

'There's no harm in asking Striker to eat roast duck with us, nothing in the least improper,' said Mr Rossmore. 'Yes, I'll drop him a line of invitation soon. Moresby will take it out to Grahamston.'

'How soon?'

'Very soon,' Mr Rossmore promised and with that shooed his clerks back to their quills.

After the night of the ball at Betté Sinclair's mansion Frederick Striker had been so moody that Eunice was afraid to talk to him. She sensed that some new worry troubled his mind, some fresh complication in an already complicated scheme of things. It was almost a relief when, come Monday, he suddenly announced that he had pressing business in Ireland and would be leaving to catch a boat from Greenock that very afternoon.

Eunice packed his valise. She noted that he took only his second-best suit. She received from him five pounds to keep her fed in his absence, and kissed him on his cold, distracted cheek before he hurried down the garden path to climb into a hired fly. Her relief at being rid of him was short-lived, however, for he had not been gone out of the house for an hour before boredom, and with it anxiety, came in upon her again.

In the thatched farmhouse at Addison's Edge she had never been bored. She had had butter to churn, hens to feed, argumentative servants and fieldhands to keep in order, and Arthur Bates, old though he might be, to provide conversation and company of a sort. She'd even had a little pianoforte that Arthur had bought for her. When she was down in spirit she would sit before its keyboard and pick out airs remembered from her time in the Charity House and hymn tunes from the church.

Arthur had been much taken with her musical talent and had promised, come autumn, to employ a proper teacher to travel from Shrewsbury to instruct her in correct fingering and the reading of printed music. That promise, like most other promises made to her, had not been fulfilled. Arthur had fallen ill and died before it could be made good.

She thought often of the little upright instrument, how the hours would fly while she was seated at it, of rainbows in the farmstead's bottle-glass windows and the shadows of swifts darting across her vision like notes of melody made visible. Sometimes she would sit at the kitchen table in the Grahamston villa and dab her fingertips against the scrubbed wood, trying to restore the fleeting happiness that she had known at Addison's Edge and to shut out guilt and fear.

On Sunday Eunice dressed herself soberly and went alone to the Church of the Redeemer, a shed behind the timber yards. Here a strange, frowned-upon sect held their

services. Eunice was tolerated, not welcomed, by the
swart-clad men and women, who saw in her perhaps
elements of sins beyond redemption. She was not invited
to anyone's home for dinner or for tea, and walked back to
Grahamston by the long route to eat pickled beef and cold
boiled potato all by herself in the villa's kitchen.

That night she stripped and bathed and prayed, bled a
little. She wrapped her body in a linen sheet tight as a
shroud and stood by the upstairs window, looking out over
the moonlit fields and stark hedgerows, waiting for ghosts
to keep her company. She had not enough fancy to conjure
up shades of the dead nor was she weak enough to
persuade them to appear, to transform her little fears to
terror and thus relieve the paralysing monotony of her
solitary vigils.

Monday brought another week.

And that week passed.

Catkins on the willow turned full and fat. Daffodil
sheaths swelled and split into buds. The weather was fair
and foul by turns, sunshine mingled with squalls of rain.

Frederick had been gone almost a fortnight before the
snow came. Moist, warm showers of flakes fell and lay and
melted all in the space of an hour. The showers left Argyll
Street glossy with mud and turned the water in the sweet
well at the kitchen door a clear brown like apple cider.

Eunice had taken a great notion for broth. She had
braved the snow showers that morning to tramp into
Glasgow to buy soft green new-season leeks, turnip, pulses
and a meaty ham bone. She had dressed in her amber
velvet and had coiled up her hair in Dutch braids. When
she returned she was too lazy, and too hungry, to change
again. She covered the dress with an apron, dolloped water
into the big black pot and put it over the fire flame while she

steeped the pulses. The walk to and from market had sharpened her appetite. She had had no breakfast to speak of and it would be a while before the broth was ready. She poured herself a mug of ale, set out a quarter of an oat loaf, a dish of butter and the last of the marmalade. She had just sat down to eat when the front door knocker clacked, made her jump and snatch up a carving knife from the table.

Holding the blade before her Eunice crept from the kitchen into the hallway and pressed herself against the wall by the side of the door. The rapping was crisp not thunderous.

'Who – who is there?'

'Letter for Mr Striker.'

Eunice transferred the knife to her left hand, tugged at the bolts and opened the door a quarter of an inch. 'Yes?' she said, warily.

The man was about thirty-four or five. He was dressed in black velvet, buckled breeches and white stockings. He wore a rather old-fashioned tricorn over natural hair that was pulled into a cue and fastened with black ribbon. He smiled and held up a sealed letter. 'For Mr Striker?'

'He – he is –' Eunice found herself tongue-tied.

'Your master's not at home, lass?'

'No.'

'Your mistress then?'

Beyond the messenger Eunice could see another man at the gate. He was older, shabbier in dress, and was armed with one of the long ebony sticks that some city porters carried as a badge of rank.

'Who is the letter from?' Eunice asked.

'Mr Rossmore of the Captains' Bank.'

'And who are you?'

'I am Andrew Purves, ma'am.'

Eunice let out her breath. She allowed the door to swing open of its own accord. 'Will you not come in, Mr Purves?' she said and, with the carving knife hidden behind her back, ushered the unexpected guest into her empty house.

As far as Maddy was concerned, Master William Purves was the cock of the walk. She did not deliberately set out to spoil him, it was just that she was too young to know how to combat his manipulative moods. One minute Willy would be strutting, arrogant and insufferable, the next he would be clinging, the next after that he would be up to some devilment that poor Maddy could not predict and therefore could not prevent. In the evening he would come to her, all coy and timid and polite, and beg to be allowed to sleep in her bed. She could never find it in her heart to refuse him, no matter how wicked he had been during the day. Maddy liked having the boy cuddled beside her. It reminded her of the time when she had lived at home and shared a big shuck mattress with her brothers and sister and how they would fight like ferrets for shares of the blanket and how they would sleep wrapped in each other's legs and arms, like one creature and not five separate. For that reason too Maddy could not say no to William, not on any account.

Dorothea was another matter. Maddy could not stand the prissy little brat and made no allowances for the child's tender years. Though Maddy was forbidden to administer physical punishment to the children, she would take Dorothea into a corner and slap her legs or tug her ringlets for no reason at all, just to see her cry. Maddy hated the tiny pursed pink expression that Dorothea wore when she held back tears, and saw not courage but stubborn defiance in it.

William was well aware of the torments his sister had to endure at Maddy's hands. He offered no fraternal defence. In fact, he rather enjoyed the show. He would stand quiet and watchful and smug while Maddy slapped and tugged, would wait for the shriek that would tell him that Dorothea had been broken at last, as girls deserved to be broken. Not like him, not like a man who could fight back, and did. Later, when Dorothea had crept into a corner behind the cupboard to snivel into her sleeves, William would taunt her for her weakness, tell her how wicked she was to annoy poor Maddy and what Mama would do to her if ever Mama found out. Then he would scramble up on to Maddy's knee, kiss her nicely and lay his head upon her breast.

Things had grown worse in this respect while Clare had been away from the nursery. On her return she was dimly aware that something was wrong. At first she had too much on her mind to pay close attention to the children. Gradually, however, she became aware of new allegiances, of subtle changes in Dorothea's behaviour. From being an open and loving little girl Dorothea seemed to have become sly and surly.

Clare kept a weather eye on Dorothea. She inspected her daily for spots and rashes that might give warning of illness. She was even concerned enough to consult a volume on domestic medicine that Mr Andrew had bought for her, and on the book's recommendation to purchase a stock of simple remedies that she kept locked in the high cupboard in the dresser. Later Clare was to wish that she had confided her apprehensions to Mr Andrew, but by that time it was too late.

Also eager for news of Frederick Striker, Edwina had invited several of the town's more informed and genteel

ladies to take tea with her at four o'clock in the afternoon.
As was the way, Edwina's pleasure engendered near panic
in the kitchen, for Elsie Gollan was resentful of the mistress's intrusions into her domain and maids and boys felt
the lash of Elsie's tongue all that long day.

Mr Andrew had prudently taken himself off on business.
Old Mr Purves had sought refuge in the office behind the
banking hall until it was time for his dinner appointment at
the Exchange. He went off at the trot at noon and left Mr
Rossmore in charge. Clare wisely kept the children out of
sight and warned them well against playing in the passageways or getting under the feet of the servants. Some of
Edwina's nervous irritability, however, seemed to perme-
ate the nursery like pollen blown on the wind. Master
William rampaged about wilfully, baby cried, Maddy
cursed and Dorothea, as if she sensed what was to come,
clung pettishly to Clare's skirts.

'What is it? What is wrong with you, Dorothea?'

The little girl shook her head while William, behind
Clare's back, pulled hideous faces.

Maddy was sent to fetch dinner on a tray from the
kitchen. It was meagre fare today, vastly unappealing to
William, to whom cheese and oatmeal dumplings were no
substitute for meat. He slouched in his chair at table,
paddled his spoon in the dish, wiped mealy fingers on
Maddy's hair, flicked sauce at his baby sister, and when
none of that gained him enough attention suddenly and
deliberately deposited one of the round dumplings on to
the floor.

It was now quite late in the afternoon, a slender hour
or so before the first of the lady guests was due to arrive.
Tea things were being laid out in the drawing-room and
old Mrs Purves was being carefully dressed by her maid,

Lowther, who was old too and very patient. Edwina, shut away in her dressing-room with Pym, had just reached a final frantic state of indecision over the combining of hairpiece and gown. Below, in the banking hall, Mr Rossmore had finished his dinner and had been obliged to unlock the building's front door with his own key since Moresby – blast the fellow! – seemed to have got lost on the road to Grahamston. Mr Rossmore had just wiped the scowl from his face to greet Mr Anderson, a progressive weaver who had come to plead for a loan to buy a new double-tread loom, when yelling broke out upstairs.

'What have you done with that dumpling?' Clare said.

'Ate it,' Willy answered.

'No, you did not. Do not lie to me. Where is it?'

Maddy was feeding baby who, since she had acquired teeth, was happy to have a gravy spoon to gnaw upon and was mumbling and dribbling and quite oblivious to the tensions around her. Maddy had witnessed the fate of the dumpling but as William's ally she would not betray him.

Dorothea, however, had no such scruple. She leaned against Clare and tapped Clare's ankle with the toe of her slipper.

'What?'

Clare glanced down beneath the hang of the tablecloth and saw at once the spray of soggy oatmeal that the rejected dumpling had left in its wake. 'William,' she said grimly, 'Pick it up.'

'Nah!'

'*Pick it up this instant.*'

'Nah!'

Clare rose and snatched at the insolent little boy. William, however, was too quick for her. Yelling as if he was being murdered, he ran for the door.

With unerring instinct for the damage that it would do, Willy hurled himself out of the nursery and up the staircase to his mother's room, screaming all the while, '*Mama, Mama, Mama, Maaaaaa-maaaaaah!*'

Below, Mr Shenkin's hand poised over a page of compound reckoning and his nib dripped a blob of ink among the figures. 'Damn!' he exploded and raised an exasperated first towards the ceiling. Weaver Anderson, who had been explaining how with the new loom two apprentices could do the work of four, paused and politely pretended not to hear the rumpus, while Mr Rossmore, frowning, muttered some platitude about lack of discipline and cursed under his breath at the necessity of having to apologise to a weaver at all.

'*Maaaaaa-maaaaaah!*'

With Clare in hot pursuit, William burst through the door of Edwina's dressing-room. Edwina had just begun the delicate process of lowering her gown over an assemblage of undergarments. Being partly powdered and painted she had slipped a bag of fine muslin over her head and her features were so obscured by it that Willy was for an instant confused. He paused, then charged. At the moment that William hurled himself at his Mama and glued himself to her with sticky fingers, down slithered the tea-gown. Edwina screamed. Pym tried to beat the boy away with a whale-bone stiffener and Clare, with little Dorothea clinging to her skirts, reached out to rescue Willy from the jaws of death.

'Mama, Mama,' William sobbed. 'She hitted me.'

Edwina tore the muslin from her head, dislodging her hairpiece in the process. 'What!' she shouted. 'Who?'

'She did.' William pointed accusingly at Clare. 'I dropped a puddin' by accident an' she hitted me on the head.'

'I did nothing of the kind,' Clare said, hotly. 'He would not eat his dinner and deliberately threw it on the floor.'

In her present frame of mind Edwina would have taken her son's word against the world's even if he had claimed that his pudding had been stolen by a passing giraffe. She said, 'Did you *see* him throw his dinner on the floor, Kelso?'

The question was so unexpected that it caught her off guard. Clare later regretted her honesty. 'No, but I saw—'

Edwina said, '*Did* you hit him?'

'No, I never lifted a finger to—'

'She hitted me,' William growled.

'She did not,' said Dorothea. 'Clare did not hit him, Mama.'

'*What* did you say?'

'Clare did not hit William. He's telling fibs.'

The other four persons in the room, William included, stared in amazement at the little girl for several silent seconds, then Edwina exploded. 'How dare you address me? How dare you speak to me without permission? You little tattletale.' Edwina leaned forward. 'It was *you* who threw the dinner on the floor, not poor William.'

'No,' Clare said. 'She doesn't know what—'

William leapt away as Edwina, in a whirl of silks, grabbed at her daughter, snagged her in the crook of her arm and dragged the child off her feet. Dorothea made no attempt to struggle and escape. Pinned against her mother's padded. hip, she hung as mute and limp as a corn doll.

'Please, mum,' Clare pleaded. 'She's done nothing to deserve a whipping.'

'I say she has,' Edwina snapped. 'And I am her mother.'

Unbidden, Pym had plucked a silver-backed hair brush from the dressing table. She slapped it down into Edwina's groping palm. There was nothing Clare could do to temper Edwina Purves's assault upon the child. The act had no link with justice. Betrayed by her brother, Dorothea had become a convenient scapegoat for Edwina's frustrations and ill-will. She glimpsed frilly petticoats, thin, soft bare calves and thighs and then, just as Edwina delivered the first blow, swung round and left the dressing-room.

She did not abandon Dorothea completely, however. She was brave enough to stand directly outside the dressing-room door. Her hands were rigidly clasped, nails biting into palms, as the beating continued, on and on. Dorothea's cries quickly changed to gulping sobs and then to breath-catching shrieks which, like flint drawn over glass, raised fine hairs on Clare's neck and set her teeth on edge. And then they ceased. Clare waited, counting, silently counting her heartbeats: five, six, seven, eight, nine . . . fifteen . . . eighteen . . . twenty.

It was Edwina who eventually jerked the door open. The unsightly hairpiece was gone. Her mousey hair was spiky with perspiration and her cheeks glowed as if the exercise had been pleasurable and invigorating. The hair brush remained clutched in her hand, embossed silver smeared with blood, bristles tinted pink. Behind Edwina, Clare could make out Pym. She was grim and tight-lipped and white as a sheet. Pressed tight against Pym's apron, William was whey-faced too. He stared, eyes round as platters, at his sister, who lay motionless upon the floor.

'Take her away,' said Edwina, dismissively. 'Take them both away, out of my sight.'

'Yes, Mrs Purves,' Clare said, through her teeth.

She knelt, lifted the unconscious child and carried her out of Edwina's dressing-room into the passageway, while William, for once struck dumb, followed meekly on.

'In God's name, man, where have you been until this hour?'

Tom Moresby put his ebony stick in the wrought-iron rack behind the door and hung his leather satchel from the brass hook above it. 'Deliverin' your letter, Mr Rossmore.'

'Four hours to cover the mile to Grahamston and back?' Mr Rossmore went on. 'Have you been squandering time in a dram shop, Moresby?'

'Och, no, Mr Rossmore, that I have not.'

Tom Moresby could lie with a perfectly straight face. He had, in fact, spent over two hours pleasantly ensconced at a table in Denny Howe's tavern near the Clyde Street rope-works, where he had partaken of a dish of strong cheese and onions washed down with two drams of Ferintosh whisky. He had paid for his dinner with the two shillings that Mr Andrew had tipped him in recognition of his loyalty. It was there in Denny Howe's that Mr Andrew had picked him up after his, Mr Andrew's, visit to Frederick Striker's sister was over. And it was there that the master and he had devised the lie that would keep them both out of hot water.

'What delayed you then?' said Mr Rossmore.

'Mr Striker was not in residence.'

Mr Rossmore, frowning sternly, waited for the rest of the explanation. Moresby's reputation as a man economical with words was to his advantage now, as was his unblemished record as sober servant of the bank. 'Well, I'm waiting.'

'I gave the letter over to the lady o' the house.'

'And?'

'She did not see fit to open it.'

'Good God, Moresby, is that all you have to tell us?'

'What more would ye like, sir?'

Mr Rossmore had had, by his lights, a hard afternoon. He had finally decided to advance Weaver Anderson thirty pounds at a four per cent rate of interest and he was concerned that old Mr Purves, who avoided truck with woollen trades as a rule, might criticise him for it.

'Perhaps a wee bit more information about the lady of the house would not go amiss, Moresby,' suggested Mr McCoull who, with Mr Shenkin, had joined the pair by Mr Rossmore's desk.

'Mrs Bates will see to it that Mr Striker gets the letter as soon as he returns to his domicile,' said Tom Moresby.

'Mrs Bates?'

'His sister, a widow.'

'Did the sister happen to tell you where Mr Striker was at this time?' said Mr McCoull.

Moresby shrugged. 'Why would she be confidin' in me?'

'Or when he would be liable to return?'

Moresby shook his head.

Mr Rossmore said, 'The acquisition of this mountain of news did not surely consume your attention for half of an afternoon, Moresby. I'll swear I smell spirits on your breath.'

'She fetched me in, fed me an' ga'd me a dram.'

'Which you did not, of course, refuse?'

'It would ha' been impolite, Mr Rossmore.'

'So,' said Mr McCoull, 'you were privileged to enter the inner sanctum, were you?'

'Inner sanctum?' Moresby tugged on the gloves that he had just removed. 'I was at Grahamston, sir, no' the kirk.'

'I mean, inside Frederick Striker's house,' said Mr McCoull, patiently. 'So, what was it like?'

'It was like – like – just a house.'

Thus it went on for another five or six minutes, with Moresby becoming more stupidly evasive and his inquisitors more frustrated. It might have gone on longer if Mr Andrew Purves had not sauntered into the hall and, by his appearance, sent Messrs McCoull and Shenkin scuttling back to their desks.

'Quiet afternoon, I see, Mr Rossmore,' said Andrew.

'Quiet enough, sir,' Mr Rossmore lied.

'Good, that's good,' Mr Andrew said and, not quite meeting Tom Moresby's eye, drifted into the back office and quietly closed the door.

It would not have been true to say that Andrew Purves had been swept off his feet by Eunice Striker Bates. He had, however, been much taken not only with her appearance but with her bearing and fortitude. In addition, his opinion of Frederick had been somewhat softened around the edges by certain facts that Eunice Bates had unwittingly revealed in the course of their long conversation over bread, cheese and hot gin punch.

Andrew had been deliberately polite, and cautious to a fault. The last thing he'd wanted was to give Mrs Bates the impression that he was prying or, as noon came and went, to take advantage of the rapport that seemed to have sprung up between them.

'Why have we not seen you before?' he'd asked, at length.

'Frederick thinks it would be indiscreet.'

'Why ever would he think that?'

'I am not out of mourning yet.'

'If I may enquire without giving offence,' Andrew had said, 'how long is it since Mr Bates passed on?'

'Almost a twelve month.'

'After a long illness?'

'No, a brief illness,' Eunice had said. 'A brief illness to end a brief marriage.'

'And yet you are still mourning?'

'I have nothing else to do,' Eunice had answered, with a little gesture of her shoulders that took all trace of self-pity out of her statement.

Now, back in Purves's Land, Andrew loitered by the office window, stared out at sunlight dappled on cobbles and the smoky facades of tenements in Saltmarket Street, and thought of Eunice Striker Bates. Hands in pockets, he rocked on the balls of his feet and hummed a tune to himself at the recollection of how she looked when she smiled, how the scars on her face seemed to fade and become marks of character, not blemishes at all. He had been there, contentedly mooning, for a good ten minutes before sounds of laughter from the apartment upstairs disturbed his reverie.

The laughter had a braying note, definitely female. Andrew groaned a little. He had quite forgotten that Edwina had invited ladies in to tea: Mrs Hornbeam, Mrs Dewar and the two Miss Pratts. Why had the names stuck? Over the years of marriage to Edwina he had acquired the knack of taking in fewer and fewer of the inconsequentialities that made up almost the whole of his wife's conversation.

Sometimes he wished that he was more like his father, more sociable and 'clubbable', so that he could escape to the Lodge or the Hodge Podge Club. Beefsteak, a jug of claret and a wag with his peers was all that his father

seemed to demand out of life. Andrew did not share his
father's bonhomie, or his shallowness. What was more
important, he did not share his father's unambitious attitude to the banking business. What truly bothered him was
that neither his father nor his wife ever saw fit to enquire
what he desired out of life. It was simply assumed by the
family that Andrew would quietly follow the Purves's line
of discretion and acuity in domestic as well as business
matters. Was he regarded as too dull a dog to notice, for
instance, how secretive and selfish his father had become
or how Edwina flirted with every unattached male who
came within her ambit?

Now, damn it, he was supposed to go upstairs and
present himself to the ladies. His presence was required.
He must knock and enter, smile graciously, bow, shake a
lace paw or two, decline tea. Having thus demonstrated
uxorious loyalty and perfect obedience he would be politely requested to depart so that Edwina might garner
compliments about him and, by inference, about the
qualities required of her to hold such a fine stolid fellow
in thrall, in marriage.

Andrew spun round from the window as a second gust
of laughter came down from upstairs. He clenched his fists
in his pocket and uttered a long, harsh groan of self-
disgust. Perhaps his father and his wife were right. Perhaps
he had nothing to give to the world except the image that
had been chosen for him – dour, honourable, decent,
devoted young Mr Andrew, son, husband and father.

Hating himself for his resignation, he trudged upstairs to
do his duty.

Clare heard Andrew pass the door of the nursery, heard
laughter in the drawing-room abruptly cease. When it

came again it was of a different kidney, decorous and light, brittle as table crystal: women pretending to be ladies to impress a gentleman.

Queen of the tea-table, Edwina would be wreathed in little dimpled smiles, sweet as seed cake. Below the cloth the hems of her dress would still carry traces of the vinegar that had been used to remove bloodstains. She would not boast to the ladies how she had recently flogged her four-year-old daughter into a state of insensibility or invite anecdotes from her friends to illustrate their propensity to inflict similar cruelties upon servants and children. Edwina would not have to strain to be nice. The episode, the beating would have been put right out of her thoughts now that she was being admired and pandered to. It would sully her conscience not one whit, not now or later.

Clare knelt by the cot. She held Dorothea's hand and inspected the child's pupils, two thin dark slits between puffy lids. The opiate that she had administered had been tardy in taking effect. She listened gravely to the child's ragged breathing which, now and then, would have a catch in it, a sob or gasp, and the hand that Clare held would tremble as if with palsy.

The bristles had marked Dorothea badly. They had scratched and torn open the delicate skin of her thighs and buttocks. The silverwork had left great blotchy weals that would soon turn to painful bruises. Clare had done her best with remedies from the medicine cupboard. She had bathed Dorothea's poor, hot little body in lukewarm water tinted with essence of marigold and hyssop. She had wrapped Dorothea in a clean linen sheet and tucked her below a warm woollen blanket with a pan at her feet. She had slipped between her lips a half-measure of poppy mixture to help her find rest from pain, to forget in sleep the ravages of shock.

Nursing the little patient had kept Clare from flying into blind rage. She had seen Dorothea smacked before. Once or twice she had even recommended to Mr Andrew that the little girl be punished or that William be taken over his knee to impose discipline or impart a lesson in obedience. But it had been done out of necessity, the need regretted. Edwina's outburst had been violent and cruel and its wilfulness, its disregard for truth had sickened Clare and infuriated her almost beyond measure.

Clare had locked William into the small closet-like room. The boy at least showed some signs of guilt. He was aware that he had behaved badly. He had uttered not a word in mitigation but had gone dolefully into the room and seated himself meekly on the side of the cot. On Clare's instruction Maddy had wrapped the baby up warmly, strapped her against her body with a shawl and had taken her out of doors for an airing before the sun went down.

Clare had had to be rid of them, to have them out of her sight, to be left alone with the injured child, in case she lost control and in fury said and did things that she might later have cause to regret.

She did not hear Mr Andrew quit the drawing-room. She was startled by his knock upon the nursery door. She knew at once who it was, however. Nobody else in the household was ever considerate enough to give warning of entry.

'Ah, Clare, you're here,' Mr Andrew said.

'Yes, as you see.'

He approached the cot, then frowned. 'What's wrong with Dorothea? Is she ailing?'

'She – no, Mr Andrew, she was punished by your wife.'

He came closer, stood by Clare's side and leaned forward to inspect the child. 'She's exceedingly flushed, is she all right?'

'I'll see to it that she's well taken care of,' Clare said.

Andrew placed his knuckles gently upon the child's brow and his frown deepened. 'She's sweating.'

'I administered a sleeping draught.'

'Indeed? Was that wise?'

'She was very distressed.'

'And in pain, no doubt.'

'Great pain,' Clare said.

'What in Heaven's name did Dorothea do to merit such a punishment? She's not as a rule a wicked child.'

Clare hesitated. She could hardly now recall how it had all started, the petty incident with the dumpling. Cause seemed to have become disconnected from effect in the course of the past hour. Haltingly, Clare explained something of what had happened.

'My wife – what – beat her?' Andrew said.

Still kneeling by the cot and not trusting herself to speak again, Clare nodded.

Andrew said, 'Beat her with what?'

'I – I wasn't in the room, sir.'

'Clare! With what?'

'A hair brush.'

'Good God!'

It was all Clare could do not to blurt out the whole cruel story and shout accusations against Edwina Purves. She bit her lip hard. Andrew rested a hand upon her shoulder and said, 'I think I understand.'

Clare said, 'Dorothea didn't deserve such punishment.'

'No. I am sure she did not,' Andrew said. 'Where's William?'

Clare indicated the closet room. 'In there.'

'Is he also being punished?'

'William wasn't whipped.'

'In spite of the fact that it was his mischief that started all the trouble?' Andrew asked.

It was not loyalty to William that prevented Clare from answering but uncertainty as to what Mr Andrew truly felt for his children. She was unsure of the nature of masculine affection. She had been made responsible for the care of this man's children and yet she could not protect them against this man's wife. She wondered how Andrew would have reacted if Edwina had beaten her instead of little Dorothea.

She said, 'It's so unfair.'

'Aye, many things in life are, Clare.' Andrew had both hands upon her shoulders now and for a moment he rested his body against hers before he stepped back. 'Will you let William out for supper?'

'If you wish it, Mr Andrew.'

'Yes,' he said. 'I think I do wish it.'

He cocked his head as if he could hear something other than the prattling laughter of the women in the drawing-room, something sweeter and infinitely more soothing.

For a moment it seemed to Clare that he was about to confide in her, then changed his mind. Denying the impulse, he gave a shake of the head and turned towards the door.

'Take care of Dorothea,' he said, 'until I get back.'

'When will that be, sir?'

'Before supper.'

Edwina had kept on the gown she had worn for the tea-taking party. It lent her a certain regal pomposity at the supper table when she straightened her shoulders, looked down her nose, and said, 'What's this?'

'This,' Andrew informed her, 'is your son William.'

'What's he doing here?'

'He has come to eat supper.'

'What? At our table?'

'Would you have him sup with the hogs, like the Prodigal?'

'Do not be ridiculous, Andrew.'

'Father, do you object to sharing table with William?'

'Not if he behaves himself, no.'

'Mother?'

'What, what's that you're saying?'

'William will be supping with us from now on, Mother.'

'For why?'

'To learn better manners.'

After a pause, Edwina said, 'What ploy is this, Andrew? Having children sup at one's table is just not done. William's place is in the nursery.'

'His place, from now on, is here.'

'Oh, is it? Well, I for one will not put up with—'

'Oh, you will, Edwina. Indeed you will.'

'Have I no say—'

'Only if you wish to starve between dinner and breakfast.'

'Is this because –' said Edwina, flushing.

'Because?'

'She deserved it,' Edwina snapped.

William had been specially dressed for the occasion in a close-fitting coat and tight little trousers, face scrubbed, hair combed. Not one whimper of complaint had come from the boy during the torture of being washed and dressed, for his father had been in the nursery to observe the process, arms folded and an expression on his face that not even William dared defy.

'What?' said old Mrs Purves, who had not been informed of the afternoon's scandal, 'What does who deserve?'

'Nothing, Mama,' Andrew said.

'Where's my broth, then?'

'It will be served presently, my dear,' said old Mr Purves who, unlike his wife, had more than an inkling of what had taken place and was intrigued to observe how his son was dealing with it.

To Edwina, Andrew said, 'Did she deserve to be beaten insensible?'

Edwina retorted, 'Andrew, I'll not be treated as if—'

Andrew said, 'Be still.' His voice was so dangerously calm that it cut off, at least temporarily, Edwina's protestations. 'Father, will you be good enough to ring the bell so that we may sup like civilised human beings?'

Obediently old Mr Purves lifted and shook the brass-tongued handbell. The dining-room door opened at once and Jinty and Bab, both inordinately clean and tidy, carried in the covered silver dishes in which Mr Andrew had instructed Elsie Gollan to serve the meal. One entrée dish was placed in the centre of the table and another, smaller vessel was set down before Master William.

'Is that my broth at last?' said old Mrs Purves.

'No, dear, you had your broth at dinner-time.'

'What is it then?'

Old Mrs Purves reached out to pluck the cover from the entrée dish, but Andrew forestalled her by lightly smacking her thin wrist. 'Ah-ah, Mother! Not yet.'

'What, what, what's going on?' the old woman protested. 'Why am I not being allowed to eat?'

'First we must give thanks to the Lord. Is that not right, Andrew?' said the old man, getting into the swing of things.

'Yes, Father. Will you do the honours, please?'

Bowing his head, old Mr Purves mumbled a few words of gratitude for food and family, an act of grace and piety not usual in the household. On conclusion of the grace, Andrew released his mother's wrist and said, 'Now.'

The old woman lifted the silver cover from the serving dish and let out into the room the aroma of a rich beef stew.

William's head lifted from his chest, his nose twitched, his eyes glittered. He resettled himself upon the firm cushion that had been put upon the chair to raise him, and snatched at his spoon. Without comment, Andrew placed one hand on his son's chest to restrain him and with the other hoisted away the lid from the small dish to expose a glutinous mess of oatmeal and coagulated cheese.

'What, in God's name, is that?' Edwina said.

'Tell your mother what it is, William.'

'Dumplin'.'

'Tell your mother what you are going to do with it.'

'Eat it,' William said, and doggedly began to spoon the grimy grey substance into his mouth.

'Tell your mother what it tastes like, William.'

'Ex'lent. Ex'lent. Hmmmmmm!'

Whereupon Edwina, hands to her face, fled from the table and the room, leaving the Purveses to enjoy their rich beef stew in more or less peace and harmony.

No man was quite certain how Mother McNab defied both Science and Nature and brought forward by a good six weeks the first hatch of ducklings on the Bunhouse pond. It was a tragic year indeed, though, when Glasgow's gastronomes went hungry into May and the tall tale that Mother

McNab sat on the eggs herself was, among the more gullible, readily swallowed. However the old dear did it, the Saturday after Easter saw notice put about that the first crop of swimmers was due for martyrdom in Mrs McNab's kitchens, and men to whom good eating and serious drinking were no novelty set out about half past two of the afternoon to wend their way westward to the village of Partick and the famous Linden Tree inn.

Mr Frederick Striker declared, not once but several times, that there was no place on earth he would rather be than out on the poop deck of the Linden Tree with three such noble fellows as Rossmore, Shenkin and McCoull. He had been tardy in replying to Mr Rossmore's invitation only because he had been delayed upon business much longer than he had anticipated.

'Where?' came the innocent enough question.

'Oh, in distant fields less agreeable than the banks of the Kelvin,' came the innocent enough answer.

Recently there had been much buying and selling of private land around the Yorkhill and Kelvinhaugh and the setting of the Clyde shores with whin and stobs to firm them and deepen the channels. But Partick village was much as it had always been, a spotting of white cottages inhabited by millers, bakers, maltsters, salmon fishers and ferrymen, a green eden for city dwellers, complete with a ruined castle and a canvas-sailed windmill to add to its olde worlde appeal.

The Linden Tree inn was no thatched hovel, however. It was a three-storied wooden building that showed the inclinations as well as the handiwork of the ship's crafts-men who had constructed it some forty years ago. From a distance it resembled some great mastless galleon hung on a sloping slipway above the Bunhouse dam. All brown and black, with lead-paned windows and two railed decks set astern, like main and poop, it provided airy views of the Kelvin's confluence with the Clyde. All around were grass-lands, thick at this season with daffodils, and trees in bud and tender leaf, including the huge old fissured lime that gave the inn its appellation.

Frederick drank from the beaker of cold punch that was served to all gentlemen upon their arrival. He drew in an ostentatious breath of country air, let it out as slowly as if it was tobacco smoke and sighed contentedly. He had good reason to be contented. He had found a generous patron at last, safe away from Glasgow, had paid for and released the cargo just before it spoiled. He had even seen it through its various passages safe to port and had collected in his hand the payment for it which he had taken south at once to buy another untaxed load.

It was not just the success of his venture into commerce that brightened Frederick Striker's mood and lightened his heart. He had rising within him the sap of spring, the stuff of the lover. One wooing had gone well in its preliminaries. Now if the three endearing, naive bank clerks had aught to do with it, it seemed the other would go even better.

Frederick did not let them spar for long. They were no dashed good at it in any case, and might never have got around to the point of the invitation at all if left to their own devices. He sat back, beaming, lifted the pewter beaker and held it before him. 'Let us drink to spring, gentlemen.'

'Spring!'

'Spring!'

'And to the ladies,' said Frederick.

'Ladies?'

'One lady in particular,' Frederick said.

'Oh, and to whom might you refer, Mr Striker?' Rossmore said, with what he thought was a casual lift of an eyebrow.

'Why, your Miss Kelso, of course.'

'Well – ah – she's hardly "our" Miss Kelso.'

'I thought you knew her well?'

'We do.'

'Let's drink to Clare, then,' Frederick persisted, hiding his amusement at the little glares and glances that greeted his directness. 'To the fairest flower on all Clydeside. What do you say, gentlemen. Clare?'

'Clare!'

'Clare!'

Frederick drank, then said, 'I wonder if the young lady in question would be flattered by our toast to her?'

'Oh, she would, she would,' said Shenkin, who winced and bit his lip when McCoull kicked his shin under the table.

'Why,' said Rossmore, still thinking himself sly, 'would you drink to a mere servant girl, Mr Striker, if one might be so bold as to enquire?'

'Servant girl? Is Clare not kin to Andrew Purves? I thought—'

'Kin? Yes. Quite! Yes, of course,' Rossmore corrected himself. 'She *is* kin – of a sort.'

'German cousin,' said McCoull.

'He means "cousin germane,",' said Rossmore.

'Do you like her, Mr Striker?' said Shenkin.

'It would be a dull dog indeed who did not take to Miss Kelso,' Frederick answered. 'I am a man of the world, gentlemen. I have travelled far and wide. I have seen the women of Holland,' he lied, 'of Spain and France too. I have consorted, shall we say, with fair colleens in Ireland and raven-haired Welsh girls but I have never, ever seen any girl to compare in grace and delicacy with your Miss Kelso.'

'You *do* like her then?' said Shenkin who seemed more delighted than dismayed by the panegyric to the female sex and saw nothing sinister in it.

'Do you not all like her?'

'Yes, quite, indeed.'

'To Clare then?'

'Clare, to Clare.'

They touched pewter, sat about in an uncomfortable silence.

Frederick knew that he had them where he wanted them. Inwardly he crowed at the realisation that he had enlisted, without any effort, three allies to assist him in his campaign. They would have loved to have asked him if his intentions were 'honourable' but they did not know how to put the question, how to define the concept of honour except by a marriage vow and wedding ring. He despised them for their provincial mentality, and attitudes shaped not by choice but by the habit of timidity.

It was a perfect day and a perfect place to think of Clare and he knew that each of his companions was thinking of her too, in much the same way as he was. It came as a shock to him when, out of the blue, McCoull asked, 'How is your sister?'

'What?'

'Your sister, Mrs Bates?' said Rossmore.

'What do you know of my sister?'

'She it was who took in my invitation.'

'I thought a porter delivered it?' said Frederick.

'A porter did,' said McCoull.

Frederick said, 'So you have not met my sister?'

'That pleasure still awaits us,' Rossmore said.

Frederick glanced from one to the other. Rossmore's slabcheeked, well-fed features gave nothing away; no more did the bony McCoull or the swarthy Shenkin. At mention of Eunice, the linking of her name with Clare's, some of his buoyancy of mood diminished.

'Perhaps Mrs Bates would care to take tea with my wife some afternoon?' said Rossmore.

Frederick did not answer at once. He stared out over the river then let his gaze scan the other diners, a dozen or so gathered at four long tables in the inn's upper room. They were all hearty, all drinking, all tucking into their rations of crisp golden-brown duck. He wondered what it would be like to have no cares in the world. Dull, he decided, tedious to the point of madness.

'No,' Frederick said, lowering his voice. 'My sister is still in mourning and is not up to meeting people just yet. When she is more settled perhaps.'

'Not widowed long?' said McCoull.

Of the three interfering clerks Frederick was most wary of Rossmore, but he liked McCoull least. There was something of the weasel in the gaunt man who would, Frederick felt sure, be a treacherous sort of friend if ever one was foolish enough to be drawn into friendship with him.

'No, not long.'

'Sad for a happy marriage to end in death,' said Shenkin.

'Sad, but inevitable,' said Rossmore.

Little pinpricks of sweat had come out on Frederick's palms. He was suddenly, oppressively uncertain of them. Were they more informed than he had given them credit for? Had they somehow learned of his troubles at Addison's Edge? If so, how did they intend to apply the information? What damage could they do to him and what would it cost to buy their silence?

'We were just saying,' Shenkin told him, 'only last week, how essential is the state of wedlock to a woman's happiness.'

'Yes?' Frederick asked.

'We were talking about Clare Kelso at the time, I believe,' McCoull said. 'Is that not right, Mr Rossmore?'

'Quite right, Mr McCoull.'

'We were speculating on what sort of fellow she might marry,' said Shenkin.

Frederick grinned. He had been wrong to suspect them of dark motives. They were just clumsy matchmakers concerned about the girl's future.

He said, 'And what conclusion did you reach?'

'Oh, it was mere speculation,' said Rossmore. 'It isn't up to us to reach conclusions.'

He noticed a kitchen lass emerge from the head of the broad staircase, bearing an enormous tray laden with dishes, and knew that soon they would fall to eating. He could not resist one last barbed question, designed to shock the stuffy little clerks.

'Does she sleep with a servant?'

'What?' said Shenkin.

Rossmore said, 'No, sir, Clare Kelso does not sleep with servants. She is a woman of some education, you know.'

'Does that mean she is pure?' said Frederick.

'Pure as driven snow,' Rossmore stated.

His accomplices nodded enthusiastically and Frederick, enveloped suddenly in the rich aroma of sage and onion stuffing, said 'Aaah!'

It was late in the April evening before Frederick returned to Grahamston. Rossmore and his clerks had sent a boy to find a hired carriage for they had eaten and drunk far more than was good for them and the prospect of a long walk back to town did not appeal. Frederick had turned down the offer of a ride, had thanked the three profusely for their generous hospitality and, tight about the middle but clear-headed, had set off on foot to walk the miles home.

Succulent though the duck had been and picturesque the surroundings, he had been too much on his guard to mark the dinner down as a complete success. The accountant and clerks were nosey as moles and would have wheedled secrets out of him if he had been careless. They were curious about his business with Andrew, about his origins, his prospects, his sister, and concerned about his 'intentions' towards their delectable little protégé, Clare Kelso.

At least the afternoon had served one valuable purpose. From the clerks he had learned that Clare Kelso had no dowry, no secret inheritance that would fall to her on marriage. The shedding of that fond illusion had clarified Frederick's mind considerably, had made his motives as pure and unsullied as Clare Kelso's virtue. He whistled as his dinner slipped down and increased his stride to cover the distance from Partick village to the suburb of Grahamston in just over half an hour.

The villa looked as it if had been painted in oil colours. Shrubs were frivolous with leaf, the trees umbrageous, the broad road no longer clabbered with mud but dusty, the evening air sprinkled with spiralling clouds of gnats. He reached his house and opened the wicket and went up the path to the door. Still whistling, Frederick opened the lock with his latchkey and stepped into the sunlit hall. 'Eunice. I'm home, dearest.'

The air of the house too was still, criss-crossed by shafts of light that defined the textures of the atmosphere –

drifting vapour from a kettle, a dusty shimmer by the parlour door, a whiff of coal fumes and, suspended in radiance on the stairs, a faint and puzzling blue-grey haze.

Frederick sniffed. 'Eunice?'

She came around the corner of the staircase from the bedroom landing. She was neat as a glove, her hair pinned up, the material of her dress gaudy and gorgeous in spilling light. She paused, smiling, then moved down towards him, parting that puzzling haze before her as if it was gauze. Frederick sniffed again.

She was close to him now. He could smell spice from her garment, the slight sharp sting of Holland gin, the familiar musk of her body. But around all was wrapped that other smell, one not at all difficult for his sharpened senses to identify.

'Who's been here?' he said.

Dress whispering, she placed her hand on his shoulder and lifted herself up on the toe of one slipper like a dancer in the ballet.

'Why, nobody.'

'Do not lie to me, Eunice.'

'Nobody, silly.'

She kissed him softly upon the cheek. He caught her shoulders, turned her to face him and stared into her eyes. They were blank as new parchment, mystifyingly uninformative. He felt a strange crimp of panic and, if she had not been his sister, might have shaken the truth out of her. 'A man has been here,' Frederick said. 'I smell his pipe.'

'Gin,' she said. 'I took a little taste of your gin, Frederick. That's what you smell.'

'Tobacco smoke,' Frederick said.

'Imagination,' Eunice told him and, laughing without sound, glided languidly off into the parlour's sunlit haze.

6

The Linden Tree

Traffic between Edwina Purves and Miss Clare Kelso was restricted to essential communications, carried for the most part by intermediaries. Neither Clare nor her mistress wished to have anything to do with the other. If and when they encountered each other, the only greeting exchanged between them was a frosty nod; yet, somehow, the balance of the relationship was no longer weighted in Edwina's favour, a fact that Clare perceived only gradually as March gave way to April's lengthening days.

Young Master William continued to sup with his elders and betters and the nightly task of preparing him to look like a little man was added to the other burdens of the nursery staff. In August, like it or not, Master William would be enrolled at the Academy's day school. In preparation for that great event Clare had been told to give the boy instruction in the rudiments of reading, writing and counting.

Clare, however, was more concerned with Dorothea. The little girl had become indrawn since her beating. Her body had healed quickly enough but she had been disturbed in her behaviour by the incident and had sunk into a phase of mute dependency.

Willy did not like one bit the fact that he had been relegated from the position of power to which his gender and his age had entitled him. He resented the attention that Clare gave to his sister but he was astute enough to keep his mouth shut and to pretend to behave. Family supper was a torment. The flannel of his trousers itched, the jacket was restricting, the polished shoes hurt his ankles, and he hated, hated being scrubbed and combed. Most of all, though, he detested the turbid atmosphere in the dining-room and the fact that his parents and grandparents behaved as if he was not there at all. They talked among themselves, did not address him except to reprimand him for some minor breach of manners or to urge – nay, demand – that he ate every last scrap of whatever dish emerged from under the silver lid, and pronounce it good.

Willy's only audible howl of complaint came when he was forced to the slate. No more the freedom to ramble and make mischief, to discover or invent a hundred ways of passing time from breakfast to dinner, dinner to supper. He was suddenly, dismayingly, a scholar, bum glued to a hard wooden stool, elbows to a hard wooden table, eyes to the big cards and printed pages that Clare had set out for the lesson or to the heavy oblong slate upon which he was expected to copy the unwieldy curves and straights that formed real writing.

All bad enough, all enough to cause rebellion in the breast of a boy less wilful than William. When Dorothea was brought to share his teaching table, however, that was the last straw.

'What's *she* doing here?'

'Learning,' Clare told him.

'She's a *girl*!' Willy exclaimed, incredulously.

'I know it,' Clare said. 'What's more, she's a good girl.'

Dorothea, meanwhile, sat meek as milk on the stool by Clare's side. She wore a little bonnet and apron and had already begun to demonstrate superior manual dexterity by copying a large letter A in chalk upon a hand slate.

'*No*,' Willy cried and repeated, 'she's a *girl*. I'll not be taught along wi' a *girl*. 'Specially *her*.'

He scrambled to his feet, stool toppling noisily. His petulant outburst was treated with such calm disdain by Clare and so completely ignored by his sister that Willy's control was swamped. He broke into a war dance of such violence and volume that the floor shook and the table rattled and Maddy took the baby into the little closet room out of harm's way.

Dorothea fashioned a nice round letter B, gently blew chalk dust from her fingers and slipped the slate to one side for Clare's approval. 'Well done, Dorothea,' Clare said. Master William stamped, whirled, punched the air, kicked at the cot, hopped and ranted and foamed. 'Now, let's try the letter C,' Clare said. 'At this rate, Dorothea, you'll have your alphabet in no time at all.'

The girl had difficulty with E and G but was guided by Clare's hand upon her own and had got along as far as the sturdy letter K before William, exhausted by his lack of success in attracting attention, fell upon the floor. He was still there when, some five or six minutes later, his father quietly opened the door of the nursery and stepped into the room. Andrew did nothing, said nothing. He put no question to Clare and offered no reprimand to his son. He simply stood by the door with his arms loosely folded, and waited.

Head buried in his arms, cheek to the boards, William did not appear to have noticed his father's presence. But, after a spell, he crawled on to his knees, flexed his elbows and raised himself to a standing position. His face was scarlet and tear-stained and his nose ran.

'Do you not have a handkerchief, William?' Andrew said.

Truculently, the boy shook his head.

'A gentleman should always carry a handkerchief,' said Andrew and, with a whisking motion, tossed his own to William who caught it and, with bruising vigour, wiped his runny nose. Meanwhile Andrew had come forward to the scholars' table and leaned over his daughter's shoulder, 'Why, that is excellent work, Dorothea. I could hardly do as well myself.'

'Clare helpt me, Papa.'

'I wonder,' Andrew said, 'if I would prove as able a teacher as Clare – for a little while.' He lifted Dorothea, seated himself precariously upon the stool and lowered his daughter on to his lap. He lifted the block of chalk with finnicky distaste and transferred it to Dorothea's eager fingers. Then he glanced up at Clare.

'You have a caller, Clare,' Andrew said.

'Beg pardon, sir?'

'A visitor. He has asked leave to have conversation with you. He's downstairs in the banking hall. You may take a half-hour but, if you will, please return in time for dinner.'

'A caller? Who?'

'Mr Striker.'

Flustered, Clare rose and said, 'Frederick – Mr Striker? Are you – I mean, are you sure it's me he wants to see?'

'He asked for you by name.'

'What – what should I do?'

'Dust the chalk from your gown,' Andrew said, 'and go, before he changes his mind.'

The nosegay of spring flowers had come from the basket of the old woman who occupied a stance at the corner of the Trongate piazza. Clare recognised the dyed-blue thread and distinctively large bow that she had watched the old

woman fashion many and many a time. It was the nosegay
upon which Clare concentrated her attention as she
crossed from the foot of the stairs to the chair by the door
where Mr Striker waited, like a hopeful client. He got to his
feet as she approached. His hands were ungloved and he
held the flowers passively, cradled across his fingers. He
showed no nerves and no embarrassment at the public
situation. The posy was his declaration of honourable
intent.

Mr Shenkin peeped over the tops of his spectacles and
Mr McCoull half turned away, pretending to be busily
engaged in wiping his quill with a leather. Only Mr
Rossmore had the temerity to watch Clare's reaction to
the giving of the gift.

Frederick wore a suit that Clare had never seen him
wear before. It reeked of money, was not gaudy or out of
taste for a morning visit, every string and button in
perfect place. She felt like a dowd, ugly and ill-kempt,
by comparison. He offered her the nosegay. She accepted it.

Although Clare did not glance at Mr Rossmore or the
clerks she had the strange feeling that they were not at all
surprised and that only civility kept them from breaking
into spontaneous applause.

'I have asked permission to speak with you alone,'
Frederick said. 'Andrew, as your master and guardian,
has granted me a half-hour. Will you walk out with me,
Clare?'

'I am not dressed for walking out, Mr Striker.'

Before Frederick could interpret Clare's declaration as a
refusal and a tiff develop out of nothing, Mr Shenkin
prompted in a stage whisper, 'The garden, Clare, the
garden.'

Clare said, 'Perhaps, since it is fine, you would care to join me in the garden for a little while, sir?'

'By all means,' said Frederick.

How his manner had changed from that first time. Gone was the insinuating brashness. He was modest now without being shy. She could not credit that this same man had swept her into his arms and kissed her mouth only a matter of weeks ago. He was as respectful and tentative a suitor as she could have wished for.

'This way, Mr Striker.' Holding the flowers in both hands at a level with her breast, she led the gentleman across the banking hall towards the doorway beneath the stairs. As she turned she saw that Mr McCoull was grinning and nodding at Mr Shenkin, who made a little circle with fingers and thumb as if, somehow, this was their triumph and not hers.

She did not feel remotely triumphant. Oddly, she felt very little in those first minutes of meeting. What she had longed for had, it seemed, come to pass. Frederick had come to court her and, if all went well, his courtship might end in marriage.

Clare opened the low door in the rear of the tenement and allowed Mr Striker to pass through before her.

The garden at the rear of Purves's Land was not stately like that of the Sinclairs. To the left a long L-shaped corner contained drying greens and a narrow strip of black earth where Lowther, old Mrs Purves's maid, had persuaded a few flowers and herbs to grow. Behind a mortared stone wall alive with ivy leaf lay several plots where vegetables were cultivated. At the garden's end privets massed into an impenetrable hedge and against them, in shade, was a rustic bench placed there years ago when old Mrs Purves had been young enough to enjoy sunshine. The family seldom came out here now and the garden, without being untidy, had a sad, neglected air. An odour of weeds and of the middens over the wall rendered it, on that late April morning, less than a perfect eden, and the number of small windows that looked down into it made it no place for a private tryst.

To those servants who peeked from the little windows the sight of Clare Kelso's *tête-a-tête* with the town's hero added salt to communal wounds. The couple settled on the mossy bench with Clare Kelso prim and straight at one end and Mr Frederick Striker, one long leg stretched out, inclined towards her as if she was a Medusa who had turned him right to stone.

Jinty pushed Nancy out of the way. Elsie Gollan boxed both sets of lugs with a wooden spoon to make room for her head and shoulders at the glass.

'What's happenin'?'

'Nothin'. They're talkin'.'

'What about?'

'Huh! You can guess what about.'

'Is he touchin' her?'

'No, not yet.'

'Is she lookin' into his eyes?'

'I canna quite see for the pea trellis.'

'Try the laundry window.'

'Aye, there's a notion.'

'Wait. It's got no view at all.'

'Ach, damn! What's he doin' now?'

'He's got her hand.'

'Is she no' lookin' at him yet?'

'Aye. Aye, she is. God, the bitch is givin' him licks wi' those blue eyes o' hers.'

'I wonder if she's watchin' from above?'

'The mistress? Aye, I wonder if she is.'

'Pym'll have told her.'

'Look, look, he's strokin' her.'

'Her what?'

'Her hand.'

'What's he sayin'? God, I wish we could hear what he's sayin' to her.'

Wild pigeons came down in company with three or four white doves from the roof of the mill across the backs in Low Green and crooned on the walltop above the ivy. A breeze from the river stirred the privet, swirled dust and brown leaves across the garden, disarranged Clare's hair round the fringe of her cap. Tenderly, long-fingered Mr Striker brushed the fine blonde strands back into place.

Behind the downstairs window, Nancy clutched Jinty by the thigh and shivered deliciously, Elsie Gollan ground her horse teeth and slapped the spoon against the wooden frame.

In the alcove of the little bow window that protruded from the nursery upstairs, Mr Andrew looked down upon the scene and stroked his chin thoughtfully; while one floor above him Pym hovered uncertainly by the window of her mistress's dressing-room and wondered what effect the news that Mr Striker was engaged in courting Kelso in plain sight would have on the megrim that had sent Edwina crawling back to bed.

For a quarter of an hour Clare was oblivious to the tenement and its threatening windows. She looked at her slippers, at the moss-green stones, at the posy in her hands. Only now and then would she glance up at her suitor, meet his gaze and glance away again. At length she rose. Mr Striker tried to detain her but she shook her head. She gestured towards the house and when he reached for her

Jessica Stirling

hand, stepped back, not in alarm or dismay but with flirtatious insistence that it was time to go. Faces disappeared from the windows as Frederick Striker escorted Clare back into the tenement. Somewhere in the depths of the kitchen passageways, short of the door to the banking hall, perhaps he kissed her.

Moments later Frederick came striding through the banking hall, beaming, his hat spinning on his forefinger. 'Good-day to you, gentlemen, good-day, good-day.' He paused at the door and bowed. 'My humble thanks for all that you have done.' And then, tapping hat to head, he left.

Mr McCoull, risen from his stool, leaned on the desk to watch Mr Striker pass the window. 'I wonder what passed between them to put him in such a jolly mood.'

'We shall have to ask Clare,' said Mr Shenkin.

'Nonetheless,' said Mr McCoull, 'there goes a happy man.'

'Hmmm!' said Mr Rossmore. 'A man in love, I'd say.'

Composed and calm, except for a spot of colour on each cheekbone, Clare entered the nursery. William and Dorothea looked up from the work table and Maddy, with Margaret on her knee, gave her a penetrating stare from a chair by the fire.

Mr Andrew had not abandoned his post as tutor. He leaned against the window, legs extended and crossed at the ankles, arms folded.

'I–I trust I haven't missed dinner?' Clare said.

'No,' Andrew said. 'I expect dinner isn't quite ready yet.' He stirred, pushed himself upright. 'However, I have some business to conduct before then so, if you will excuse me, I will make myself scarce.'

'Mr Andrew?'

'Yes, Clare.'

'May – may I have a half day off?'

'That, I believe, is your entitlement.'

'I've never asked before.'

'I know.'

'I never had anywhere to go before.'

'But now you do?'

'Yes, sir.'

'Any particular day?'

'To suit the household, sir.'

Andrew frowned and gave the matter of a suitable afternoon serious consideration. 'Friday?'

Clare dropped him a little curtsey. 'Thank you.'

'How will you let him know?' Andrew asked.

'I shall write to him,' Clare said.

Again Andrew frowned, again hesitated. 'Give the letter to Moresby. He'll see that it is safely delivered. One thing, Clare, are you sure that Mr Striker will be in town at the week's end?'

'I'm sure.'

'How do you know?'

'He told me so,' said Clare.

Infatuation? No, infatuation was not possible between two people in their situation and with their diverse experiences of life. The ornate kettle on its stand, the silver cream jug and sugar bowl, the very shape of the tongs seemed to emanate an aura of formality and decorum that, happily, kept rough, unpolished passions at bay.

'What did your wife have to say to it?' Eunice asked.

Andrew answered, 'Curiously – or perhaps not so curiously – nobody in the house has had the temerity to tell her yet.'

'Not even her maid?'

'Pym? No, Pym is the soul of discretion when it comes to saving her neck. Besides, I do believe that Edwina's confidante has found a confidential companion of her own.'

'Oh! Who might that be?'

'My valet, Peter-Pierre.'

'Peter-Pierre? Is he French?'

'He is no more French than I am,' said Andrew. 'He came to us as a very young boy, sent down from Fifeshire. My father did have a French servant in those days and young Peter decided he wanted to change his nationality. He began by changing his name but never quite managed to get the pronunciation right.'

'Peter – ah – Pierre?'

'Exactly.'

'And he is, you say, the intimate of your wife's maid?'

'Since the night of the Sinclairs' ball,' Andrew said.

'What will you do if a pregnancy results?'

'What I have done with servants before,' Andrew said. 'I will put her out for a week or two and will find fostering for the baby close at hand if, that is, Pym wishes to remain in our service.'

'What, however, if Monsieur Pierre wishes to marry her?'

'In that case, they must both leave. My father will not have married persons on the staff of the household.'

'Why not?'

Andrew shook his head and shrugged. 'Tradition, I suppose, or too many squabbles.'

'How unusual.'

'Perhaps.'

'In my house –' Eunice Bates hesitated then continued in a little rush as if to get it over with, '– my house in

Shropshire, most of the servants were married, one to the other. I personally found it convenient and settling. Very settling.'

'That, of course, was a farm,' Andrew said, 'was it not?'

'Yes.' She had decided not to say more but could not help herself. 'A very pretty farm. It wrenched my heart to have to leave it.'

'Was it required of you,' Andrew said, 'by sentiment or, if you will pardon me, by Frederick?'

'By law,' said Eunice. 'The documents of the will were not adequate and Arthur's children threatened to put them to the court.'

'Surely, though, your husband's *will* would be clear in the matter and the court would have found for you, in substance at least.'

'Frederick said that was not worth the test. I was glad to be away from them, if not from Addison's Edge.' She had not intended to reveal such detail, not even to this man, especially not to this man. It was done now, however, and she could not retract it. She said, 'I would be obliged, Mr Purves, if you would not discuss the matter with Frederick or tell him that I spoke of it.'

'I will discuss nothing that passes between us, Mrs Bates,' Andrew assured her. 'How, indeed, can I do so without confessing that we have met and are – are on the way to becoming friends. At least, I hope that is the case.'

She poured tea briskly. 'That is the case.'

'In turn,' Andrew said, 'you must not give Frederick the least sign or hint that you know where he has been this afternoon or who accompanied him.'

'I do *not* know where he has been.'

'No, that's true.'

'Where will he take her?'

'Walking?' Andrew said. 'Boating on the river? I'm afraid I do not know what lovers do these days.'

Eunice laughed. 'Come now, Mr Purves, I cannot believe that.'

Andrew cleared his throat. 'In terms of peregrination, I mean.'

'Peregrination?' said Eunice, who knew perfectly well what the word meant. 'What an odd way of putting it.'

'Stepping out,' said Andrew. 'If your brother's courtship takes root, do you suppose that he will bring Clare here?'

Eunice shook her head. 'How can he? I am always at home.'

'To meet you, I mean?'

'Not unless Frederick believes that it will be valuable to the progress of –' Eunice stopped. 'You are concerned for this girl, are you not? Do you care for her?'

'I care for all my servants.'

'And kinfolk too?'

'Naturally.'

'But do you not care for Miss Kelso particularly?'

Andrew sighed. He was drawn by Eunice Bates' directness but now and then found it disconcerting.

'I made a promise to her mother, once, that I would look after the child,' Andrew said.

'She brought no money of her own, though?'

'Not a penny.'

'She must, in that case, be very beautiful.'

'She is,' said Andrew then, realising his churlishness in praising one woman to another, added apologetically, 'She's very young, of course.'

'Inside, in our hearts, we are all young,' said Eunice.

'I sometimes doubt that about myself.'

'Men are different, perhaps,' Eunice said, without sarcasm.

'Responsibility does it.' Andrew nodded like an old owl. 'Too much of it, too soon thrust upon us.'

'Dear, dear!' said Eunice. 'How grave and solemn this conversation is becoming.'

'Yes,' said Andrew, gravely.

'More tea?'

'Thank you, no,' Andrew said. 'I must go soon.'

'How soon?'

'Oh – soon.'

'Will you call upon me again?'

'With your permission.'

'That you have, Mr Purves,' Eunice said. 'An hour's notice and I will be ready to receive you. At any time.'

'You're most gracious, Mrs Bates,' Andrew said and, because it was on his mind, tactlessly added, 'It will be a way of keeping an eye on Clare.'

'Yes,' said Eunice thinly. 'And on Frederick?'

'Quite!'

Clare was not entirely a fool. She did not imagine that Frederick would conduct himself like a po-faced elder. What she recalled of their previous meetings gave her cause to be wary of him, and of herself. What she recalled most vividly were his hands upon her waist, his arms about her, the pressure of his lips upon her own. The sweet phrases that he had lavished upon her during their conversation in the garden at Purves's Land had been measured against an attraction that could not be disguised by flowery language.

Clare was both frightened and fascinated by the implicit promise that she would be lured into loving him. She had a need to please. With Frederick she could not take admiration for granted. He had consorted with women high-born and low and she would surely be judged against them. If she could make him love her then she could make him change. Perhaps, she told herself, all that he required from a wife were qualities that she already possessed, without being aware of them. If she was true and obedient to Frederick, would he not be true and obedient to her?

On that first afternoon he collected her from the door of the bank at half past one o'clock, and led her out of Glasgow and along the river road to the Linden Tree where, he said, they would take dinner together.

The day was dry but cloudy and still as a curtain. The first explosions of May blossom seemed to hang over the hedgerows as if timelessly suspended. In fields and gardens labourers stooped to sprouting rows and there were cries of lambs from private flocks and of calves from the spring drop and smells of horses and brewing and sawn wood. Further along the route, the musty odour of a flour mill grinding out the last of the winter's store of grain tickled Clare's nostrils. There were no ducklings to be had at the Linden Tree on Friday afternoon but roast beef and freshly caught fish made admirable fare. The lower room of the eating house was surprisingly crowded, with ladies as well as gentlemen munching their way into the afternoon in an atmosphere of contentment rather than conviviality.

Frederick was gay and charming. He told her about escapades with English lords and ladies, about hunting on horse-back and the breakfasts that were served before the field went out and the huge suppers that were served afterwards. He spoke of country fairs, of gamblers, of fast mail coaches, London's coffee houses, pleasure gardens and theatres. He painted a picture of a life packed with exciting experiences and when he asked her to tell him about herself, Clare found her life shoddy by comparison.

Frederick refused to let Clare sit silent. He extracted from her much about her father, mother, her Greenock childhood. When those subjects were exhausted he guided her into indiscreet revelations about what went on behind the wooden walls of Purves's Land. Dinner merged into tea-taking, the afternoon into evening. Cloud lifted and the banks of the Kelvin were bathed in soft light, the grass like velvet, the trees like lace.

Frederick paid the table and escorted Clare out on to the walk that ran from the Linden Tree to the river. When she asked him what hour it was he told her, to her amazement, that it was after six o'clock and that soon he must take her home. but first he must show her the vista of the Clyde.

In the feathery shadow of the linden tree he kissed her. If there were people about Clare was unaware of them. She had become separated, not just from the landscape of the Kelvinside but from the Purveses, from the tenement in town, from everything that she was and had been up to that moment.

Frederick rested his shoulders against the tree, stretched his legs and drew Clare between them, crushing her skirts with his thighs. He kissed her, tenderly at first and then with passion. He whispered that he could not resist her, had no defence against her beauty, wanted her more than he had ever wanted any woman. His hand moved caressingly over her breast.

If it had been dark Clare might have given herself to him then and there. She burned with strange sensation and the longer and more intimately Frederick touched her the more consuming that sensation became. Her need reflected Frederick's need of her. He transformed her from being a servant, a kinswoman employed under sufferance. She believed that Frederick would change her further, print upon her a brand new pattern of his own design; all because he loved her and wanted her. And in those few minutes under the linden tree Clare loved him in return.

When he released her, she could hear his breath, not a confidential whisper now but a dry, gasping sob. Perspiration on his brow, a trembling hand pressed against the tree bark; 'God,' he groaned and, for a moment, closed his eyes.

'Frederick, are you unwell?'

'No, no, my love.' He clasped her waist, plucked her clean off the earth and swung her out of the shadow of the linden tree. 'Do you not realise what's happening?'

'I—'

'Do you not feel it too?'

'Frederick, I—'

'You do, I know you do.' He placed both hands upon her shoulders as if to stop the afternoon from spinning, to hold them steady at its still centre. 'I'm desperately in love with you, Clare. I am your slave, your captive.'

The sensation within her had become fluid and ran like honey across a warmed spoon. This was not the same man who had flirted with her that October afternoon in Mr Purves's office. He was as changed, as new as she was.

'Your captive, Clare,' said Frederick again.

'And I yours,' she answered him.

Fifteen weeks for Cluny Martin was a positive lifetime. He could not believe that a busy man like Lord Drumfin would be able to keep before him for all that while a wee matter of an unpaid gambling debt. Besides, strictly speaking, Cluny was no welcher. He had put up his stake before the matches, and if he'd had to leg it afterwards it was only done in the heat of the moment and to avoid awkward questions about his connection with Mr Striker.

Cluny might not have had too much brain but he was not daft enough to linger in the vicinity of Glasgow. He had, in fact, taken himself on a long visit to his cousin who lived in a croft in an isolated glen near Loch Sloy in distant Argyllshire.

His cousin had gamebirds, quite a flock of two-year-olds. Being an amiable fellow, he was willing to trust Cluny to finish their training and to take the best, four in all, off on the rounds of the spring fairs and markets to scratch up a little money for the pair of them. Fortunately, Cluny had not wagered all his capital on poor Satan and had a grubstake put aside to start him off again. So, with the four best birds in wicker cages slung on poles over his shoulders, Cluny had come down to Luss, then on to Dumbarton town to play the gentleman's game again – and hardly a passing thought for Frederick Striker, Lord Drumfin or the events of that January night in the Neptune.

What Cluny did not know, what none of his rustic acquaintances were willing to tell him, was that Lord Drumfin was not the sort of man to treat the loss of a wager by default lightly. As soon as the spring season started, two robust young cockers from Kennart were out and about in search of Cluny Martin, and his patron, with a bag of jingle on offer to any man or woman who could point a finger in the right direction.

The right direction turned out to be a Friday fair in Garbutt, a village on the banks of the Clyde estuary, which had for many years drawn out the fancy for a flat race and a main of gamebirds to follow it.

Garbutt's pit was built into the side of a sandy slope that

rose up from the water's edge south of the village. Broom-covered hillocks provided good vantage for the hundred or so gamblers that attended. Tarry torches hoisted on stobs would light the scene after nightfall for with thirty battles on the card, and a beercart, a dram-seller's stall and women peddling crabmeat buns and bowls of soup, the event might well run on until morning or the following midday.

Cluny presented three birds at lower weights. He won each battle comfortably, soon had forty pounds Scots distributed about his person and was feeling fat and confident. Leaving the cages in charge of a responsible young lad for a moment or two, he climbed up the sandy hillock and into the broom bushes to relieve himself.

And that was the last that anyone ever saw of little Cluny Martin.

In dawn light his gamebirds were spirited away by the responsible lad and duly found their way into ovens and soup pots in and around Garbutt. No enquiries as to Cluny's fate were voiced by those of the fancy who knew him. His cousin assumed that Cluny had run true to form and had hove off with the four birds and all the winnings. In due course, the cousin supposed, when times were hard, Cluny would turn up again at the door of the croft near Loch Sloy. But he never did.

Only Lord Drumfin and his henchmen knew for sure what had happened to little Cluny Martin. And they, of course, were not disposed to reveal under what sod on Kennart's broad acres the body had been buried or what Cluny had told them just minutes before he died.

Frederick had arrived at Sinclairs' Land late in the evening, too late for Sir Johnnie to be bothered taking himself out.

Besides, there were other guests for supper that night. It was well after eleven o'clock before Frederick found himself alone at a little card table with his friend and lover and, over a desultory game of piquet, was subjected to a murmured interrogation that did not please him at all. 'Have you not found your heiress yet, Frederick?'

'None suitable, Betté.'

'The Purves girl, no?'

Startled, Frederick fumbled his cards and glanced guiltily across the drawing-room towards the gathering by the fire-place. He leaned forward, 'What do you know of that? Was I spied at the Linden Tree?'

'The Linden Tree? How on earth did you manage to get her to the Linden Tree?' Betté picked up and restored to him the cards that he had dropped.

'I asked permission. She was allowed to come.'

'I see. So the girl is back in Glasgow?'

'Beg your pardon?'

'Staying with the bankers again?'

'What Purves girl are we discussing?'

'The heiress, of course. Proud Jamie's daughter.'

'Ah!'

Lady Betté cocked her head and, with her painted eyelids lowered suspiciously, said, 'What other girl is there?'

'None, none,' said Frederick, hastily.

The progress of the card game ceased. 'So it *was* the Purves girl that you entertained at the Linden Tree, was it?' Betté said.

Frederick hesitated. He could not be sure that the cunning vixen did not already know the truth and was trying to expose him in a lie. He had no need to be ashamed of what he had done so far, or of his eventual intention.

Betté would surely applaud his initiative, be agog for details of his assault upon innocence. Nonetheless, Frederick found himself momentarily tongue-tied. He hemmed and hawed and picked at the scattered cards as if to read a fortune there.

'Or was it the other one?' said Betté. 'The beautiful servant?'

'Uh – yes, perhaps.'

Her ladyship's lip wrinkled in disgust. 'No appointments there, Frederick, no material advantage. She may be a jewel to look upon but she is worthless otherwise. Did Purves tell you differently?'

'Purves is looking for a husband for her.'

'The fool!' said Lady Betté. 'He would do better to take her for his mistress. That, I suspect, is what the po-faced Andrew really wants.'

'He feels responsible for her because of some deathbed promise to her mother, I believe.'

Betté was somehow put out by the news. 'Why do you pursue the servant and neglect the heiress?'

'Pursuing one does not preclude catching the other.'

'If you think that then *you* are the fool, Frederick.'

'I do not see why I should not enjoy a toy.'

'You have me to enjoy, have you not?'

'Ah,' said Frederick, smoothly, 'but you are not a toy, dear Betté.'

'No, I am not,' Betté Sinclair said. 'Not your toy at any rate. What, pray, do you suppose that you are to me?'

'What?'

Johnnie Sinclair was watching them from his stance by the fireplace. He had a daughter on a couch on either side of him, flanked by two other young women, daughters of a burgess who, with his new young wife, had been flattered to be invited to take supper with the great Sinclair. Johnnie could converse with half his attention and a quarter of his brain and his eye was upon the card table fifteen or twenty paces distant. He was full of admiration for the manner in which his wife discarded lovers, not simply tossing them aside but tearing them in halves and quarters first.

'You have never loved me, Frederick,' Betté Sinclair showed him her plump, aristocratic profile in a pout.

'What! I've loved you until I've ached—'

'In the loins, but not in the heart.'

'Heart?'

'Here.' Betté lightly pressed a forefinger to her breast. 'Here is where the heart is, Frederick, a fact of anatomy that seems to have escaped you.'

'What is this?' Frederick scowled. 'What is going on?'

'Did you not know that I loved you?'

'Love? No, I did not realise that – that *that* was involved.'

'To you it was stolen pleasure. To me it was much, much more.'

Frederick crouched over the table, his long chin almost touching Betté's bosom. 'Are you telling me that you loved me?' he hissed.

By way of answer Lady Betté delivered a sigh that was a masterpiece of ambiguity.

'Oh, no, you didn't,' Frederick said, in dismay. 'You did not love me in that manner. Surely?'

'How utterly without feeling you are, Mr Striker,' said Lady Betté, haughtily. 'Now that you have found another *toy* I suppose that you will reject me without qualm.'

'Betté, for God's sake!'

'Very well, sir, if that is to be my lot, I will be gracious enough to accept it.'

'Your lot? Betté – your ladyship – I had no notion that the nature of the attraction between us had altered, that you had become romantically inclined.'

'Love, Frederick, love is something that you will never understand. It isn't in you to give or to receive it.' She rose and looked down at the man. He stared up at her, open-mouthed, as if she had suddenly grown not horns but wings. 'I regret only that I did not see it before.'

Flabbergasted, completely deceived by her performance, Frederick unfolded himself from the chair. When he reached across the card table to grasp her arm, Betté drew sharply away. 'I must ask you *not* to visit me at Wyvercroft.'

'I never do, never have.'

At that moment Sir John called out, 'What's all the fuss, Striker? Have you caught her cheatin'? Shouldn't worry. She does it all the time.'

To Frederick, Betté whispered, 'I will be gone from Glasgow by Wednesday and you may, without conscience, put my suffering out of your mind. We will not, sir, meet again.'

Frederick whispered, 'But what have I done?'

'You have broken my heart, Mr Striker.'

'Betté – your ladyship – I had no idea—'

'Leave, if you please. Discreetly.'

Frederick had no option but to obey. He had a feeling that he was being dismissed not just from Betté Sinclair's company but from her circle and that he would not be permitted to enter it again on any pretext. He mumbled his farewell to Sir John and the company and left the big drawing-room at once. He did not look back.

If he had he might have caught the glance that Betté Sinclair exchanged with her husband, a wry smile tucked like a dimple at the corner of her mouth in response to Johnnie's wink.

'Is Mr Striker going, my dear?'

'Mr Striker has gone,' said Betté, leaving Johnnie curious as to whom she would fasten on next.

Eunice said, 'You are very pensive tonight, Frederick. Is business not going well?'

'What?' He looked up from the teacup. 'No, business is going exceeding well.'

'What ails you then?'

'Nothing,' he said, flatly. 'Absolutely not a thing.'

'What did you do today?'

He put down the teacup and rubbed his eyes. A frugal candle lit the kitchen and the house, his house, seemed particularly shabby after the brilliance of Sinclairs' Land.

'I walked in the city.'

'All afternoon?'

'What do you suppose I did, Eunice?'

'If I knew, I would not be obliged to ask.'

'I visited my banker.'

'Andrew Purves?'

'Yes – Andrew Purves.'

'This afternoon?'

'Yes – this afternoon.'

'Did you dine with him?'

Frederick squinted. Did Eunice too know where he had been and who he had been with? God, the perfidy of women, the throttling smallness of Glasgow. A man could not relieve himself without the whole town knowing of it.

He said, 'I dined at the Tontine, with other gentlemen, not Purves.'

Eunice had a fine bone china cup, relic of a set which had

been destroyed one piece at a time. She so liked its shape and delicacy that she took her drink from it at every opportunity. He wondered, vaguely, if she sipped gin from it too when he was not around to stay her.

Eunice said, 'Did you sup at the Tontine too?'

'I supped with the Sinclairs.'

'And how *is* Lady Betté?'

'She – they leave for the country on Wednesday.'

'Who will you find to give you supper then?'

'Eunice, what the devil's wrong with you?'

She placed the oval rim of the bone china cup against her nether lip and held it there, as if she intended to play the vessel like a flute.

'Why are you angry with me?' Frederick said.

'I'm not.'

He hated it when she stared at him with her luminous brown eyes, when she fell silent in the midst of conversation. He could not rid himself of the haunting suspicion that she could on occasion read his thoughts.

'Why are you looking at me like that?' he said.

'Like what?'

'Eunice—'

She clinked the cup into its saucer. The motion of her arm stirred the candle flame and made shadows flicker in the corners of the kitchen. She wore a deep cut gown and her skin was incredibly, almost unwholesomely, pale. She had a little cap on her head but it did not hide the fact that she had trimmed her hair short. He would have asked her the reason for it, via a compliment, but he was afraid that even that comment would somehow give offence.

'What has happened to your plan, Frederick?'

'Plan? Which particular plan?'

'To find yourself a wealthy wife?'

Ah! So that was it! She had been brooding on remarks and casual promises made months ago. He really must find her a profitable companion soon, if only to take her mind off his affairs. Ironically he was well on the way down the long stony road to betrothal, if she had but known it.

'Would you not prefer me to find you a wealthy husband?' Frederick said.

Eunice said, 'An aged, one-legged sea captain, perhaps, or a consumptive saltmaster to take me off your hands?'

'Eunice, I do not want you "off my hands". I am your brother. It is my duty to take care of you.'

'I am beginning to think, dearest, that I am better off taking care of myself.'

Now what had riled her? Frederick's hurt at being abruptly and inexplicably cast off by Betté Sinclair had jolted his confidence to a point where he saw in Eunice, even Eunice, threat to his various schemes. He had not forgotten that strange whiff of pipe smoke but could not believe that she would deceive him by taking a lover that he had not selected, one from whom no profit could be derived.

His own immediate situation was not parallel. He was a man – and thank God for it – and was entitled to fiddle his own tunes. He could have done without these distractions tonight. He had the progress of his pursuit of Clare Kelso to consider. The practical aspects of commencing an affair with an engaged servant were already proving difficult and he required a calm state of mind to solve them satisfactorily.

'How would you do that,' he said, 'other than by making a suitable marriage?'

Eunice seemed about to give him a pointed answer, changed her mind and shrugged. 'Yes, Frederick.'

'Yes, Frederick – what?'

'Marriage must always be "suitable", must it not?'

'In our circumstances, yes.'

'For both of us?'

'Of course, for both of us,' said Frederick.

'Do you promise?'

He had no clear idea of what discontents were nibbling at her brain or what she meant by extracting vague promises from him on a score that did not yet concern her. He was too unsettled to argue or, for once, to probe. He swallowed the dregs of lukewarm tea then, forcing a smile, patted her arm and said, 'Yes, Eunice dear, I promise.'

To which his sister answered, 'Good!'

At which particular point in the courtship Clare became convinced that Frederick really *did* intend to marry her remained unclear. It was certainly early, before their first love-making. Perhaps as early as that first Friday when, in a wonderfully romantic haze, she returned to the nursery in Purves's Land to complete the last of the day's duties.

Six or eight weeks before, Clare might have been tempted to blurt out an account of her adventure to Maddy, to share with the younger girl the thrill of her wooing by the handsome and charming Mr Striker. But the thrashing of Dorothea had changed all that. Clare was not inclined to share with anyone, least of all a servant, the hopes that Frederick had roused in her. Whenever it was that she decided that Frederick truly loved her, that decision became of less moment than Clare's realisation that she would yield to him as soon as he asked it of her. There was enough of her father's fiery passion in her nature to override her mother's legacy of common sense. She was

eager to become Frederick's lover, however separate that
issue might be from becoming his wife.

The following morning, Mr Andrew asked her if she had
enjoyed herself. Clare answered unequivocally that she
had. When Mr Shenkin, Mr Rossmore and Mr McCoull
sounded her out on the progress of her romance, she told
them more or less the truth. She did not try to hide from
her friends how attracted she was to Mr Striker.

Caution and reserve were not quite thrown to the winds,
however, until a Friday towards the end of the month. By
then she had been three times out with him to the Linden
Tree and once, for a couple of hours stolen from the
evening, for a walk upon the Green. Frederick always
made a point of seeking Andrew's permission before
wafting Clare away from the tenement, as if somehow
he was engaging Andrew as a conspirator in seduction.

Private rooms in public places were legion throughout
the city. Mother McNab kept three on the upper floor of
the Linden Tree. Members of the Duck Club knew of
them. The more worldly of that number had even used
them on occasion, either for some prolonged carousal or,
individually, for satisfying appetites enhanced but not
appeased by stuffing and roast duckling. Sea-captains
would have felt at home in the cabin-like room with its
oak panels, low oak beams, a fire imprisoned behind an
iron grid and the bed hidden out of sight by a curtain,
windows that admitted no outward view except to the sky
and the topmost branches of the linden tree, and none
inward at all.

Clare feigned innocence of Frederick's purpose in ush-
ering her up the steep, gallows-like staircase at the rear of
the building, quickly into the private room. Cold cuts and
salads awaited them on the oval table. Crystal glasses,

sparkling wines chilled in bottles driven into a tub of cracked ice. The fire smouldered in knurled red knobs behind a curved iron lattice.

Clare could hardly bring herself to eat, though she drank several glasses of sparkling wine, icy cold and refreshing to her dry mouth. The bolt on the inside of the door had not been shot but sense told her that none of Mother McNab's serving lassies would dare to disturb them.

'Are you not hungry, Clare?' Frederick asked.

'No.'

It was still early and when she listened hard she could hear laughter from the dining rooms below.

She had chosen to wear a plain open robe, the best cast-off that had ever come her way from Edwina in the days before Edwina had fallen out with her. She had preserved the gown carefully, had repaired and altered it to suit pictures of fashion in one of Edwina's books of prints. She had spent much of her wage on replacing the ribbons that fastened the bodice and on a fine diaphanous neckerchief which was swathed about her shoulders and bunched in front of her *décolletage*.

It was that item of her clothing that Frederick chose to remove first. He stood by her side and a little behind her and kissed her just below the ear. She shivered, did not resist.

'You are warm, Clare,' he murmured.

'Yes.'

'Will you allow me?'

'Yes.'

For an instant, she felt too small to cope with him and, just as his fingers began to pluck at the button, she put up her hand and touched his wrist. He paused. She could feel him stiffen.

He said, 'Do you not want us to be comfortable?'

She said, 'Yes,' put her hand back down into her lap, turned her head this way and that and let him tease the neckerchief from about her throat and breast.

He kissed her again, upon the nape.

'I love you with all my heart, Clare Kelso,' Frederick said, cheek against her shoulder. 'Tell me that I may nurture hope that you will love me too, one day?'

'I do, Frederick. Oh, you know I do. I love you now.'

'Will you consent, Clare, my dearest?'

'Consent?'

'To let me show you how much I love you?'

'Yes,' she said, quickly.

He slipped his right arm about her waist, pulled her head into the crook of his left arm and kissed her firmly upon the mouth. She felt his lips part and his tongue part her lips. That first, unexpected intimacy shocked her. He drew her up from the chair without releasing her, his tongue slipping and darting into her mouth, moist and hot. She closed her eyes. The kiss seemed to go on and on until she could barely breathe. When he pulled back she gasped and clung to him as if he had rescued her from drowning. He waited, holding her, until she recovered her breath, then he put his finger to the point of her chin and tilted her head up.

Greedy now for the sensations that open lips and fluttering tongues stirred in her, Clare opened her mouth invitingly. He kissed her again. He ran his hands over her back, down to the waist of the bodice and into the folds of the gown, stroking the fabric as if he was shaping it to her limbs. He brought up the front of her body against his and, gripping her tightly, lifted her on to toe-tip. Kneading her hips with both hands, he rubbed himself against her.

Clare uttered a voluptuous little cry, cried again when he let her go. He did not, however, break the vital contact between them but drew her by the hand around the oval table and, reaching out one long-fingered hand, shot the bolt at the top of the wooden door. He spun her around, like some mad step in a dance, and jerked open the curtain that screened the bed.

Spotless white linen sheets, bolsters and pillows, a tight coverlet of patterned wool: Clare opened her mouth, not to take his kiss now but to deny him, to deny herself. No sound came forth. Moving easily Frederick seated himself upon the bed, spread his long legs and, lightly holding her by the fingertips, guided her into the vee between his thighs as he had done before, against the linden tree.

Sunlight and the trembling shadows of the leaves of the linden tree stained varnished panels and the umber folds of the drapes. She had always supposed that darkness and stealth would mark the night of her marriage, that her faceless husband would be as fearful and as solemn as she. Daylight, birdsong, laughter faint below, Frederick's infinite patience, her own unanticipated desires made fears pale away. For a second or two, she seemed almost to be standing curiously apart from herself.

Frederick held her for a long time, doing nothing, as if allowing her time to protest, to withdraw, to tear herself away. When she could stand his passivity no longer she leaned forward and kissed him full upon the mouth. She felt his thighs tighten, clench about her, his hands curl beneath her gown, stroking softly upwards until he found the tops of her stockings and her unclad flesh. He set her a half pace back from him and, keeping one hand upon her, furled up her garments one by one. He nodded and pressed her to hold the gatherings, pinched and bundled in her fist, while he caressed and fondled and at length kissed the soft contour of her stomach.

'I love you, Clare, I love you,' he murmured.

She did not dare to doubt his word.

She whispered, 'Yes, Frederick, yes.'

Still brushing her with his mouth, he reached down to undo the drawstring of his tight, buff-coloured breeches then, released, pulled Clare hard against him and rolled her beneath him on to the bed.

From that day visitations to Purves's Land became more frequent, Frederick's requests for a share of 'Cousin Clare's' time more persuasive. To each of them Andrew acceded without demur for he had learned from Eunice that Frederick had talked seriously of marriage plans and had even gone so far as to spend money on furnishing the empty rooms in the Grahamston villa. As yet, Frederick had not revealed the name of his intended bride to his sister but, Eunice said, it was typical of Frederick to play his cards close to his chest.

The Sinclairs had gone off to Wyvercroft for the summer and Frederick, it seemed, had lost interest in cultivating other well-to-do ladies about town and bestowing upon them the pleasure of his company. He was at home for much of the day, every day in the week, except on those occasions when he called at Purves's Land to escort his lady-love out to dine or to walk for an hour or two upon the banks of the Clyde. Andrew could no longer toddle casually along to Grahamston of an afternoon and be sure of finding a welcome and a dish of tea awaiting him. Eunice and he had to undertake the most furtive sort of arrangements just to meet at all and, because of it, the easy unstrained nature of their relationship began to change.

Andrew had always regarded himself as an honourable fellow, bred to straight dealing. Now, however, thanks to

Frederick Striker, he had one foot, if not two, caught in a tangle of fraud and deception, in machinations which, to his chagrin, he found not only profitable but also stimulating. He could not deny that Frederick's shifty schemes had brought home the bacon. Initially he had been lured into financing the Englishman's trading ventures out of a vague desire to acquire money of his own, to present to Edwina the country estate that she professed would make her happy. Recently, however, Andrew had come to regard the accumulating nest-egg in a more selfish light: an attitude that hardened him to Edwina's constant pettiness and complaints and that enabled him to keep her, but without bullying, firmly in her place.

'He is courting her, is he not?' Edwina would say.

'Of course he is.'

'Such a man! Tut!'

'Do you wish to chaperone her, Edwina?'

'Certainly not. She is a servant and deserves no better.'

'I received the impression that once upon a time you found Mr Striker interesting and attractive.'

'I have changed my mind,' Edwina would say.

'Because he courts one of our servants?'

'I've heard things about Mr Striker,' Edwina would say. 'You would not be so keen on foisting Kelso on to him if you had heard half the things I've heard about that so-called gentleman.'

'Do you wish Clare to stay with us for ever?'

'What?'

'I would have no objection. She more than earns her keep. She tutors the children very patiently and thus saves me the expense of hiring a professional scholar.'

'The children will not be with us for ever,' Edwina would point out.

'Unless we have more.'

Silence greeted this remark.

The spectre of another pregnancy never failed to smother Edwina's muddled discontents. Her first-born was present before her every night at supper, glowering and fidgeting, and her domination from a distance of her family had been teased away from her by Andrew's interference. He was often in the nursery, and now and then took Dorothea out to make rounds with him or take the air upon the Green, as if she was fifteen and not five years old. The incongruous sight of a respected adult male with a girl child clinging to his hand struck Edwina as not just eccentric but socially heinous. She said nothing, though. She had just enough native wit to realise that in these past weeks Andrew had gained strength and confidence and that her power over him had, in consequence, waned.

Clare was unaware of the subtle strife that marred the Purveses' domestic harmony. She had no idea that her master was gravitating towards the state of bliss that so thoroughly possessed her. She had read of men mated to opium and the exotic waking dreams it induced. She had witnessed men to whom the imbibing of wines and spirits was all that that gave point to their lives. But never before had she understood the true nature of addiction, how much it demanded, how much it gave in return.

It was not love strengthened by chastity and repression that gripped Clare's soul in a vice, but love-making of the most physical and uninhibited kind. All modesty was burned away by her hunger for Frederick and there was no more talk, no more thought, of marriage, only of where and when they might next be together. Hardly had the gate of the yard closed behind them than Frederick's hands were upon Clare's body, her mouth fastened greedily upon his. Every darkened close, every deserted lane coaxed them to linger and pander to their desire so that, by the time they discovered a quiet spot among the bushes by the river or pattered upstairs to the room above the Linden Tree, they were both in such a swelter of passion that the first of their several unions was accomplished with an almost savage ferocity and selfishness, and a depth of satisfaction that was in itself like the action of a drug upon the girl.

All Clare could think of as she fed Dorothea, dressed William, nursed baby Margaret, was when she would next be alone with Frederick. When she sat primly in the servants' gallery in kirk on Sunday and heard Mr Brimston's rant against temptations of the flesh, she experienced no qualm of guilt but only a full, bruised, cloying sensation at the memory of her last long rendezvous with Frederick.

It was on the last day of May that Frederick told her he would have to leave her for a time. It was no longer possible to delay business that had already been delayed longer than was wise. No, alas, he could not take her with him. Travel was too expensive. Besides, he required to have all his wits about him to conduct his transactions and, if she were there, he would be depleted of strength in mind and body.

They were lying naked, tangled and dewed with perspiration, in bed in the Linden Tree. Clare had her fingers twined in his hair, holding him as if in fear that he would vanish before her eyes. The day was humid, sunlight filtered by a strange vaporous cloud that was hardly cloud at all.

Clare wept at his words, clung to him desperately, suddenly filled with doubts and forebodings. The very prospect of separation brought dread, a fear that the magical element of coupling was all that held him to her, and that when he was gone he would not return. He pressed her body against his, crushing her flanks and breasts, cupping her waist with one hand, her neck with the other while great sobs shook her and she repeated his name, like a charm, again and again and again.

'Two weeks or three, Clare, dearest,' Frederick consoled her. 'You must be brave. If you are brave I will bring you a length of fine Irish lawn. How would you like that?'

'No, I do not want you to go, Frederick.'

'I have no choice, darling girl. Would that I were rich, like Andrew Purves, or had rents and tithes to live on like Johnnie Sinclair. But I must earn my living, Clare, and, as I am a trader I must attend to my cargoes.'

'Where will you be?'

'Here, there.'

'In England?'

'Yes.'

'How will I live without you?'

'Keep yourself busy. The time will pass. I'll be back before you know it.'

'No, no. It will be an eternity, Frederick.'

He separated himself from her, their skins sticky in the heat, leaned and lightly kissed the points of her breasts, then lifted her and sat her squarely before him, cross-legged like a tailor. For an instant, just an instant, he reminded her of Andrew. His concern, his tenderness had that same quality of reluctant male practicality. Her doubts and dismalness began to diminish, but not her pain.

'It will not be easy for me either, Clare,' he told her. 'I would prefer to stay here, exactly here, in this room with you for evermore.'

'If we were mar—'

He kissed her again, her mouth this time, three, four, five dabbing kisses. 'Tell me that you love me, Clare Kelso.'

'Oh, I do, I do, Frederick. With all my heart.'

He sat back on his heels and stared at her, perplexed.

He said, 'You are *so* beautiful, my dearest, the envy of angels as you are now. I will think of you every minute of every hour, I promise you.'

'You will forget me.'

'How can I?' He stroked her wet cheeks and ran his fingertips across her parted lips. 'Clare?'

'Yes, darling.'

'Lie down.'

Eunice was ready for him when he arrived. She knew of his coming. He had thoughtfully had a note delivered by Moresby, whose loyalty was unquestioned and whose discretion did not have to be bought, merely rewarded now and then with the price of a dram of good malt whisky. She wore a gown of lilac and purple that showed her figure wonderfully. She admitted him with a smile of such warmth and welcome that Andrew hesitated in the villa's hallway.

'Madam?' he asked, tentatively.

'I am pleased to see you,' she said.

The house was full of the smells of cooking, redolent of spices, odours of new wood and leather and that good rich fustiness of new carpeting or dyed rug. In the parlour were an inlaid table and a handsome secretaire-cabinet in satin-wood, a carved settee with tapestry upholstery and three matching chairs which proved to be more comfortable than they looked. New wax candles blazed in a silver candelabra and the fire crackled brightly.

'How do you like it?' Eunice asked.

'I like it well.' Andrew ran a hand along the inlay of the table and involuntarily calculated what the furnishings had cost Striker. 'Frederick has done well by you, Eunice.'

'There's more,' Eunice said, 'in the dining-room.'

'Ah!'

'Where we will sup, shortly.'

'Ah, yes! Good!'

'The feathering of the nest is not for my benefit entirely,' Eunice said. 'Though Frederick has not told me so in as many words, I believe that he intends to marry before the year is out.'

'I wonder,' said Andrew, 'who his bride will be.'

'I thought that you might be able to enlighten me.'

Andrew shrugged. He walked about the room. The furnishings were too ornate for his taste, precisely, and made the room cramped in a way that he did not like. Nonetheless, he felt a peculiar worm of envy within him at all this newness, at the prospect of Striker settled here with Clare, and with Eunice too.

He could imagine himself seated upon the settee with Clare on one side of him and Eunice upon the other, bathed in the light of the fire and in the warmth of their love. Contrast with the shabby rabble of Purves's Land was, for a moment, acute.

'It is my cousin, I expect,' Andrew said.

'The servant girl?'

'Yes.'

'Is she pleasant?'

'Very pleasant,' said Andrew.

'Is she biddable?'

He found her question puzzling and paused before answering it, 'She will be obedient to him – but she has a mind of her own too.'

'Why is he doing it?' Eunice said. 'Why is he marrying a woman with no money?'

'I expect he is in love with her.'

'I gather she is beautiful.'

'Exceptionally so.'

Eunice nodded and Andrew, who had seated himself carefully upon one of the brand new chairs, felt discomfited by the sadness that had replaced her smile. He longed to reach out his hand to her to offer comfort, as he would have offered it to Clare, then realised that Eunice did not need that sort of comfort at all. He glimpsed, at that instant, the depth of hurt in her and the strength that she had acquired to heal and hide her dark and secret wounds. She lifted her hands and touched her hair. Her face was marbled with firelight and in that uncontrived pose she looked statuesque, almost, Andrew thought, magnificent. Daunted, he found nothing to say.

'I will be her housekeeper,' Eunice said. 'Is that not the role of dependent sisters?'

'Perhaps Frederick will employ servants now that he has something for them to do.'

'I do not mind being housekeeper. I would rather be housekeeper to my brother than wife to a man I did not love.'

'Even if your brother has a wife too?'

Eunice stiffened. 'What do you mean, sir?'

Startled, Andrew said, 'I–I mean nothing, nothing at all, Mrs Bates. It was only a passing remark.'

She was in one humour and out of it as swiftly as cloud billowing shadows over a cornfield. He got awkwardly and uncertainly to his feet. Before he could extend further apology, however, Eunice was smiling again. 'You must excuse me, Mr Purves. I have pigeon-pie in the oven and I am uncommonly nervous over its fate. With your permission I will leave you alone with the sherry decanter, there, for four or five minutes.'

Andrew bowed. 'Of course.'

She served the supper with her own hand. The brown soup was as fine as any Andrew had ever tasted and better by far than anything that Elsie Gollan was capable of producing. Turbot was followed by the pie, succulent but not heavy, and then a fairy feast of jellies, creams and sweetmeats, all washed down with hock and a ruby burgundy.

Frederick's parsimony with the domestic purse seemed to have been no more than temporary. The purchase of the items of supper would have cost a pretty penny and Andrew was gratified to realise that Striker's promise of high yield had not been a hollow boast. He knew perfectly well where Striker was and what his next illicit cargo would fetch but did not raise the subject, did not mention Frederick at all during the course of supper or even afterwards.

The weather was too mild for such a fire. The house had become stuffy and stiflingly hot. Port and tea, on top of the wines, made Andrew's head spin a little and he asked Eunice if he might open a window to take a breath of air.

'Is it a fine night, Andrew?'

'Aye, it is.'

'Is there light?'

'Bright moonlight and no cloud.'

'Shall we walk out-of-doors for a turn?'

He was well aware that it was approaching midnight, that he should return home with excuses at the ready but, still dizzy, he suddenly abandoned himself to impulse and said, 'Why should we not?'

They were too far west for the Watch to challenge them. Grahamston was quiet as moonlight itself, save for the cry of hunting owls and the desolate yelp of a vixen in the coppices behind St Enoch's burn. Eunice wore a riding coat with braided lapels and a pinched waist, a feathered hat. She looked, Andrew thought, as dashing as a highwayman. It was necessary for her to take his arm. It was the first time that contact between them had been close and sustained. Even through layers of clothing he could feel warmth, her body's heat.

The moon rode high, silvering roadways and lanes, the gardens bright as day. Eunice was no stroller, not even at night. She led him away from the stark shape of the Grahamston tollhouse, walking briskly, led him down a narrow rutted lane between hedges towards the river. Andrew was happy to go with her. His head had cleared as soon as he had tasted the clear mild summer's night air and he felt sharply alive now. There was nobody abroad to see them, to remark on his companion and their midnight promenade. It was as if he walked with a phantom. The analogy pleased him for he knew that the phantom was benign. She held his arm to her, neither tightly nor tensely, and they walked step-in-step, with their heads up and not a soul to hinder them.

It was only when they came out of the shadows of the hedges that Andrew realised where she was leading him. He had been to this part of the river shore before, though not for many a day. Here, years since, his old nurse had brought him to sip the water from Ninian's well, and to make a wish.

He could almost believe that old Nurse Todd, dead for a decade, would be waiting for them, seated on the worn wooden step that led to the cradle of the well.

Over the years the well, in drying, had lost its power and its attraction. He supposed that old folk might still sip from the stone basin, cupping rainwater in their hands, mumbling for a miracle to cure their aches and pains. Children too might play about the stamped ground and, if the story had been passed down to them, might dare each other to climb the step and tickle the shallow puddle, and taste, and make a wish. None of his wishes, that he could recall, had ever come true and, latterly, he could not think of anything to wish for at all. He felt vaguely foolish, with this flat-voiced English woman on his arm, the Clyde lit by silent silver, buried disappointments in his heart raised and revived by recognition and adult ruefulness.

'Do you know where we are, sir?' Eunice asked.

'Indeed I do.'

He did not ask how she had heard of the magical old well or if she knew of its powers. He assumed that she did. He judged her to be that kind of woman, phlegmatic but also fanciful. He did not scorn her for such inconsistencies for they were also part of his secret nature, if mixed in different densities.

'Shall we make a wish?' Eunice said.

'If it suits you, Mrs Bates, please do.'

'Oh, Andrew, do not be so stiff,' Eunice said. 'Have you never made a wish here before?'

'Not since I came out of short frocks,' he lied. 'I have a vague recollection of my nurse bringing me here.'

'If two people wish together,' Eunice told him, 'the power of the spirit of the well is doubled – or so it's said.'

'By whom is it said?'

'Everyone.'

'How did *you* discover Ninian's well?' Andrew asked. 'Who told you of it?'

'There's one near every town,' said Eunice. 'I did not
have to be told of it. Will you not play the little game, Mr
Purves, just to please me?'

She had stepped on to the wooden stoup and leaned the
small of her back against the salt-stained moss of the cradle
stone. The well had no shape now. It had been weathered
back to something primitive. In the circumstances, Andrew
did not feel inclined to risk it, or anything. Eunice's
position, one shoe extended, the greatcoat thrown open,
her strong arms beckoning, touched in him some nerve of
dread that was not in the slightest childish.

'It's silliness, Eunice.'

'For me. Please.'

He laughed in embarrassed surrender. 'In payment for
the excellent supper, and if you must have it so,' he said,
'I'll accommodate you. I do not believe in this nonsense,
you understand.'

She moved to one side and he scrambled up beside her.
He steadied her, and himself, with a hand on her waist and
let her rub shoulders with him as she peeled off her kidskin
glove and pushed up her left sleeve. She held the glove in
her mouth and, muffled, asked, 'Are you ready?'

'Yes.'

He placed his hand into the shallow basin until his
knuckles touched water. Damp moss fringed the aperture.
There was no flow, and yet the water was cold. He let his
hand slip down into it until it was submerged, palm
uppermost. He felt rather than saw ripples as Eunice
too dipped her hand below the surface and touched his
fingertips with hers.

Turning his head, he looked up and away from her. He
stared down river, down the frosted ribbon of moonlit
water that straggled between the haughs of Stobcross and

the wind-mills of Deansfield, shores beaded with the bright white roofs of crofts and farms, steeples and stark mansions, none of which showed lantern or candle.

Eunice's hand closed, her fingers twined with his. She brought his hand up, well water trapped in the cup formed by their palms. 'Drink, Andrew,' she said. 'And make your wish.'

He cleared his throat and glanced down. Swiftly he dipped his head and sipped with his lips from the water there, touching her skin as he did so. The water, curiously, was not stale at all. He let it trickle over his tongue and resisted the temptation to wipe his mouth when it was done.

'Yes?'

'Yes.'

'You did not close your eyes,' Eunice said.

'No,' Andrew said. 'Now you.'

She closed her eyes and put her face down. Her hair draped her cheek and bobbed. He felt her lips upon the water, upon the mound at the base of his thumb. She came half up, eyes still closed, and sighed. He saw moonlight cling to her wetted lips and her cheeks smooth as alabaster in the nacreous light. She opened her eyes, blinked, and looked at him solemnly. He no longer felt like a fool. Her fingers were still linked with his and if he had wished at another time, he might wish not for a wonder or a petty thing but just for the moment that had already come to pass to come his way again.

'Amusing,' Eunice said. It was not a question.

'Yes.'

He gave her his handkerchief to dry her hand. Then he took her arm and walked her back between the hedges to the villa's wicket gate where, wishes notwithstanding, he left her, to float home alone along the moonlit road to Purves's Land.

In the course of the weeks that followed the excursion to the wishing well, Mr Andrew Purves and Mrs Eunice Striker Bates met frequently but with no lessening of discretion and no increase in intimacy.

There were times when Andrew thought that the closest Eunice and he were ever going to get was that touch of hands underwater. However licentiously his brethren in the city might choose to behave was up to them. He could never forget that he was both a married man and a gentleman, and he would not take advantage of a lonely widow, beyond encouraging her friendship. What Edwina thought of her husband's absences Andrew neither knew nor cared. She was his wife but not the keeper of his conscience. He had done – so far – no wrong.

Frederick stayed away. Two weeks extended into three, three into a month. May became June and June passed into July and there was no indication when Frederick intended to return.

Eunice received two letters, written three weeks apart, both long upon the road. One came from Liverpool, another from Belfast. Both were short to the point of being curt and gave no clue as to what business delayed her brother.

Andrew, on the other hand, had one long letter from his partner. From what was written between the lines he deduced that Frederick was riding with the cargoes to take advantage of the summer's trade and the crying need for salt among cattlemen and fisherfolk.

Andrew did not tell Eunice that he had heard from Frederick. He did not tell Clare either. Andrew, in fact, became secretive in his ways and only his quiet and cultivated manner prevented him seeming furtive. Old Mr Purves guessed that his lad was up to something. He suspected not a woman but a deal in business and was not, for that reason, distressed enough to interfere. Andrew was still conscientious, still devoted to bank matters, still the master of the household. What time he stole from finance and domestic duties was due to him and old Mr Purves did not grudge it.

Clare, on the other hand, had gone into a decline. Pining for her sweetheart day and night, she said little, not even to her friends in the banking hall. She was pale and melancholy and obviously depressed by Frederick's neglect and by the fact that he had not seen fit to write to her.

'Have you heard from him, Mr Andrew?'

'No, Clare, I'm sorry.'

'Have you heard nothing of him at all?'

'Not a word, Clare, not a word.'

Clare kept out of the kitchens. Given chance, Elsie Gollan would gloat and chortle and tease her and she was too emotional not to be hurt by jibes or to hold back tears. When she was alone, however, she wept a great deal. She had just enough sense and control not to blubber when Maddy was within earshot or to give the slightest hint of emotional turmoil to the children. She spent more time at the table, teaching William and Dorothea, than was entirely good for them, and in June's hot, hot spell would not take them out until an hour before supper when the air had cooled somewhat and the glare of the sun had been reduced by evening shadows.

In the fat of the summer season, Glasgow was hopping with countrymen and women. Small fairs and markets, almost every weekday, attracted showmen and packmen and freaks, buyers and sellers of produce creamed from river to sea, from garden, field and meadow. Even the rain, when it came, was not cold but warm. It sprinkled grain crops and soft fruit bushes and plumped up the fruit in the orchards that, just a minute ago it seemed, had been foaming with blossom. It would have been a good time if only Frederick had been there to touch her, love her, bring the whole ripening canvas of young summer alive. Without him Purves's Land was stifling and sticky, the town full of dust, noise and stenches that made Clare queasy and, even after the rain came, often quite nauseous.

Now, more than ever before, she felt isolated. Sometimes, very late at night, she cried into her pillow, not for Frederick but for her mother. Things were happening in and around her that she did not fully understand, subtle changes that frightened her and added to her growing anxiety over Frederick's long silence and the waste of the passing summer. At length her worries drove her, sensibly, to act, to seek counsel not from Mr Rossmore or the clerks, not from Mr Andrew, and certainly not from Edwina, but from a woman who did not know her well enough to point an accusing finger and tell her what a fool she'd been.

Eunice had all but abandoned her sessions of self-tormenting prayer. Now and then she would fish out the Bible, drag a chair into position, drop a cushion on to the floor, would kneel, bow her head and try to concentrate on guilts past and present, on penance, forgiveness and healing. She felt more foolish on her knees than she had done dipping a hand in Ninian's well. Frowning, she would try to regain the intensity of her belief, the desperation that had caused her to reach upward, and inward too, to pluck away pain.

After a third ineffectual attempt to focus her mind on suffering, she frowned ruefully, rose and put the cushion back on the chair and the chair in a corner and the Bible back in the cabinet by the bed.

Nothing had happened. Nothing would happen. She did not bleed, would not bleed again. On her back all traces of the fine white scars had finally gone. Even the terrible pitting on her cheeks seemed to have closed since the sun came out and meadows greened. When she knelt before the open casement all she could hear was larksong, not thunder. When she gazed across the fields she saw only grazing cattle and flocks of fat sheep, not grey wraiths or strange riders come to punish and destroy. When the bell above the lintel jangled or there was a knock upon the post she did not cower and hide but ran happily to open the door, sure that it would be Andrew, her friend, or at worst old Moresby, his messenger. It always was – until that warm, wet, pastel-tinted Friday afternoon when the person on the step was a bedraggled stranger.

'Who are you?' Eunice asked.

'My name is Kelso, mum. Clare Kelso.'

'What do you want here?'

'I need to see Frederick. Mr Striker, I mean.'

'Did he tell you he lived here?'

'No, I discovered the house from Mr Rossmore's book,' the girl said. 'Do you – do you not know who I am?'

Eunice said, 'Yes, I know who you are. But what you have not explained is why you are here.'

'Because I'm expecting a child,' the girl said.

'Come in,' said Eunice and ushered the beautiful creature into her tidy hall.

7

An Ear to the Door

———◆◆◆———

The ramshackle tenement hung precariously over a horse dealer's yard, its stairs thick with midden soil and, with the evening humid after rain, clouded about with midges and black flies. Broods of children mooched around the stable doors and others girned in the rooms off the passageway along which the midwife guided Clare. In one of the foetid chambers a baby shrieked like a herring-gull but the woman paid it not the slightest heed. She waved her elephantine arms to stir the fog of woodsmoke and cooking grease that hung in the passageway and when she had found the right door, opened it and pushed Clare quickly into the room before her.

Droplets of sweat beaded the woman's swollen cheeks and her enormous sagging breasts hung like breadfruit in the collar of her dirty cotton shift. Her hands were slippery upon Clare's flesh when, with the girl lying upon sacking on bare floorboards, she lifted Clare's skirts and petticoats for a perfunctory examination. Through the broken casement Clare could look out across the upper end of High Street to the College Gardens and glimpse the buttresses of the cathedral tinted pink in sultry evening light. She pressed her lips together and tried to close her nostrils to the stink of the woman's body, but she gagged and winced at the hideous intimacies that seemed so remote from the sensual pleasures that she had enjoyed with Frederick not so long ago.

The woman's voice was thick as chocolate, smoothed by passage through many fat chins. She asked for money, five shillings, before she would put the questions that would confirm as fact Clare's guess that she was seven or eight weeks pregnant. Clare paid the sum, exact, from her purse and, lifted from the sacking, stood abashed and sick with worry before the woman who, like a soothsayer, held such expert knowledge of the future.

The woman enquired about the father. She supposed, she said, that it would be some randy son of the household or even the master himself who had put the bairn there. Clare neither confirmed nor denied it and gave away nothing beyond details needed to fix the duration of the pregnancy and to allow the woman to calculate when the infant would be born.

February: the name of the wintry month revealed there in the stifling heat of July carried Clare's thoughts to a scene of firelit comfort, to a wool-wrapped haven in a house that Frederick would rent for them to share. She shivered at the realisation that marriage to Frederick was now inevitable.

'Are ye wantin' rid o' it?' the woman asked.

Clare stiffened, shouted, 'No.'

The midwife seemed amused, was not offended by the girl's vehemence.

'Am I well?' Clare said. 'Can I carry a term?'

'Och, aye, you seem healthy enough t'me, lassie, if a wee bit on the skinny side,' the woman told her. 'Listen, if you're wantin' my services when the time comes, send somebody here for t'fetch me. I'm never very far away.'

Clare promised to consider it.

She left the tenement hurriedly and walked back downhill to Purves's Land in a kind of dream.

All the bubbling passion that had been in her had been stifled by other emotions. She walked with one hand upon her stomach, as if she could already feel her child, Frederick's child, stir and kick within her.

The worst part was surely behind her.

Innocently, she assumed that Frederick would love her all the more for the sake of the baby, as well as for herself.

Andrew said, sadly, 'Is there no doubt that Clare is telling the truth?'

'None at all, I fear,' Eunice answered. 'She swears that she has been with no other man but my brother.'

'Oh for sure, on that score,' Andrew said. 'Frederick has been wooing her determinedly, as you know. The question now is, will he marry her?'

'She's very beautiful, certainly.'

'What do you mean by that?' Andrew said.

'She has no money, no dowry and no prospects of an inheritance.'

'That could be remedied, I suppose.'

'You would put a price on her?' said Eunice.

'If necessary, yes.'

'Does she mean so much to you, Andrew?'

'She is my kin, Eunice.'

'I have told her that she may come here.'

'What, for the birth?'

'For whatever she needs.'

'But if Frederick –' Andrew paused, shook his head.

Eunice said, 'You must not tell her that you are aware of her condition. If she comes here again I will suggest that she informs you. But until she chooses to do so Andrew – say nothing.'

'Because she will guess who revealed her secret?'

Eunice said, 'She is little more than a child, Andrew. In the months ahead she will need to have about her folk that she can trust.'

'Us, do you mean? Both of us?'

'Yes,' Eunice said. 'Separately at first and then, if it falls that way, together.'

Andrew looked at her for a long moment then asked, 'What about Frederick? Can she not trust Frederick? Will she not be able to depend upon Frederick?'

'That,' said Eunice, frowning, 'remains to be seen.'

Mornings were the worst times. Return of summer's heat did not help and Clare could not bring herself to eat anything much before noon. It was all she could do to serve porridge to the children. The sight of cooked fish or a dish of buttered eggs drove her out of the nursery to retch into a towel in the closet.

She consulted the book on medicines that Mr Andrew had given her. She found much information there concerning her condition. She was fearful of the recommended substances, however, lest she take the wrong dose and damage her child. Finally she slipped out one Saturday evening, as late as she dared, hurried to the Apothecaries' Hall in Virginia Street and, with her shawl pulled over her head, presented herself at the counter and enquired of the old man on duty what 'her friend' might do to help the sickness.

The deception was of no avail. The old man knew her by sight, as he knew almost every servant and dame in the heart of the city, and Clare had been to the Hall often enough to be fixed in the old man's memory.

'Aye, and who will it be this time?' he said.

'Sir?' Clare kept her head turned away from the four great flares that lit the high, musky room.

The old man was the principal druggist. He was dressed in a strange brown apron that came up to his neck and a plain white shirt crimped at his wrists by black garters. He was very old indeed. The bones of his skull showed through skin as thin and brittle as parchment and his wig, an old pompey, seemed to be supported only by his ears.

'Pay no heed, pay no heed,' he said with just the wisp of a smile. 'Let me say that if it is somebody of your disposition, young lady, then I would grind a special powder to take away the sickness. If, on the other hand, it was some great sanguinary lump, I would dispense another sort of powder entirely.'

'She – she is not unlike me.'

'In that case – wait.'

The room was shelved on three walls, floor to ceiling, and row upon row of blue glass jars, each neatly labelled, glinted in the flare-light. Five or six plaster busts glowered down from on high and a portion of a skeleton, minus the bones of one arm and a leg below the knee, dangled from a hook in the cavity beyond which lay the laboratory. Of that deeply mysterious room Clare could see little, only the breast of a water tub taller than a man, a brick fireplace upon which simmered two large copper pots, and a small tow-headed boy, buried in an apron, who was keeling away at a something in a marble basin. Boards of sale were nailed to the Hall's supporting pillars, advertising recipes for this and that disorder, most to do with the bladder, the complexion or the bowels. Clare tried not to read them, even the words induced in her a sense of frailness and a queasy closing in her throat.

The old man returned. He carried under his arm a china mixing bowl which contained a coarse grey-greenish combination of herbs. He tipped the material into a scale, shook out the grains that clung to the bowl, fiddled with tiny brass weights and then, with one hand, fashioned a funnel of paper from a quire on the countertop. He poured the herbal into the funnel from the scoop of the scale, sealed the paper top with a lick and a spit, and handed it over to Clare.

'One shilling.'

Clare had the coins in her hand. She had thought it might be more, much more. Some of the children's remedies that she had bought had cost her up to four shillings. She put down the coin which the old man transferred to a drawer.

'A pinch between finger and thumb before bed and again on rising. Wash it down with clean water, and you will be as right as my glove in no time.' He cocked his head, and held the pompey in place with his fingertips. 'This bairn, was it bred in sorrow?'

'No,' Clare said. 'I believe it was bred in love.'

'That being the case, it will be carried and delivered safe and sound.' He winked, almost. 'Take my word on it. Love is a medicine that never fails.'

Whatever potency love had it was not to be compared to the herbal. Within a day the sickness had gone and Clare felt as well as she had ever done. She was filled with a kind of elation that superceded her fear that Frederick had gone for ever and shame at the thought that sooner or later she would have to confess her sin to Mr Andrew, as Frederick's sister had advised her to do. Much as she had appreciated Mrs Bates' comfort and advice, however, Clare did not follow her suggestion; nor did she visit the handsome new villa in Grahamston again.

She had no need.

Well again, she'd rediscovered patience and went patiently about her duties in the nursery, sure and certain that when Frederick came home he would marry her and take her away as his wife.

What Frederick had brought her, stoutly bound in oiled canvas and laid flat on the draycart that had transported it from the quay, was an object that Eunice had long desired. There were other bundles too pushed in beside a long box and a wicker hamper. Frederick himself, in a new emerald green suit, was seated on the board with the driver, a valise on his knee and a new white hat trimmed with a red cockade raised in his hand in welcome.

Eunice, and half the labourers in Grahamston, heard Frederick coming. He instructed the carter to toot upon his dented horn, to sound something that a huntsman might just have recognised as the call 'A View'.

The view that Eunice had from the villa's upstairs window, then from the garden gate did not chime well with her grim mood. Not even Frederick's smacking kisses or the wild ebullience of his manner could erase her apprehension and her fear of the fall that was due.

It was the wrong time for accusation. Not only Frederick's mood but even the weather and hour of the day mitigated against Eunice's desire to challenge and inform her brother of the burden of responsibility that awaited him. She had been halfway through baking a batch of griddle scones in the hope that Andrew would manage to drop by that afternoon. Her brow was sticky, her hands floury. She held them away from Frederick's fine new suit as he kissed and hugged her. Eunice reminded herself to hang a quilted bedspread at the upstairs window, to signal to Andrew that Frederick had returned.

The carriers unloaded cargo from the dray.

'Do you see what I have brought?' Frederick cried. 'Treasures from the Orient my dearest. Well, not quite the Orient, but the best that money could buy in Liverpool.'

It was, as she had guessed, a pianoforte, a beautiful instrument with keys of solid ivory and a delicate inlay across the top of the board. There was a long padded bench to match it and a carved wooden music-holder to stand on top, all in place in the window bay of the parlour before Frederick chased away the carriers and, with a flourish, admitted her. So great was Frederick's pleasure in the gift that for the moment, Eunice could do nothing other than feign amazement and delight.

'It may be a little slack in the wires after its sea voyage.' Frederick kissed her and nudged her towards the bench. 'But I will find a musician to put it back in tune. Do you like it, Eunice?'

'It's quite beautiful.'

'Play for me.'

'What now? Like this?'

'Yes, play that tune you used to play to Arthur Bates. What was it – "The Maid of Malton"?'

Eunice wiped her fingers carefully on her apron, then took it off and draped it over a chair. Ten weeks ago, she would have been thrilled to have a pianoforte in the house, would have smothered Frederick with gratitude. Now, however, guilt and suspicion ruined her pleasure and she seated herself stiffly on the bench and contemplated the keyboard bleakly and without confidence.

'Play, play for me. Oh, we'll make the house ring with fine music and jolly songs.' Frederick leaned against her, a

hand on her shoulder. 'Go on, Eunice. You haven't forgotten the melody, have you?'

'No, Frederick, I haven't forgotten.'

She touched the keys without the damper, heard little
hammers click and strings sing and felt soft vibrations in
the polished wood and through the ivory blocks. Looking
down, she picked out the tune with her right hand then
added in the bass with her left. It came back to her at once:
'The Maid of Malton.'

When Frederick's lips touched her neck in an affectionate and admiring kiss, she could almost for a moment
imagine that it was Arthur there. She stopped abruptly.

'Go on, go on,' Frederick urged.

She gave a little shake of her shoulders to break the
contact of his hands, turned on the bench, looked up at him
and said flatly, 'The Kelso girl is expecting a child, your
child, Frederick.'

'Ah?' He stepped involuntarily back from her, hands
raised, limp at the wrists like a fop's. 'Ah!'

'Is that all you can find to say?'

'Who, may I ask, imparted this – this pearl of information?'

'The girl herself. She came here in search of you. I gather
that you did not write to her in the course of your travels.'

'I had no leisure to write, besides –' He shrugged. 'Do
you think she is telling the truth?'

'I do.'

Frederick stepped back again, found just enough space
between the crowded sticks of furniture to pace.

Eunice said, 'Do you deny that the child is yours?'

'No, oh no,' Frederick said. 'No, that, I fear, is not in
contention. If Kelso is indeed expecting, then I am un-
doubtedly the father.'

'She thinks you intend to marry her,' Eunice said. 'She believes you made her a promise.'

Frederick linked his long fingers and cracked his knuckle-joints. 'Has she informed Andrew Purves of the – the occurrence?'

'No.'

'How can you be sure?'

Eunice paused, cautiously. 'I have the girl's word on it.'

Frederick went to the window, looked out at the ragged grass and untrimmed privet hedge, at the dusty street. He ceased cracking his knuckles and stroked his chin instead.

'What will you do, Frederick?'

'I will discuss the matter with Purves.'

'Should you not first discuss the matter with the girl?'

'No. With Purves.'

'When?'

'Immediately.'

Members of the high-styled fraternity who had first sub-scribed to the establishment of the Tontine Coffee House – 107 numbered 'lives' in all – were no constipated aristo-crats but persons whose interests soared above the buying and selling of sugar, tobacco and lengths of long lawn to take in literature, the fine arts, and, of course, fair quan-tities of salacious gossip. The long, wide, lofty room was split by massive Doric pillars and lit by a domed skylight as well as side windows of Venetian glass. The *beaux esprits*, who had paid good money for the privilege, were not, however, averse to sharing the club with strangers. To this end they had provided 'boxes', or partitioned cubicles, where a visiting gentleman might find privacy to sip his Turkish, peruse the newspapers or engage in amicable discussion. In one such box Mr Andrew Purves met Mr

Frederick Striker a quarter of an hour after a note had been delivered into Andrew's hand at the bank and barely one hour after Frederick had rolled into Grahamston to the ebullient echoes of the carrier's horn.

Frederick had supplied himself with a pot of strong coffee which he sipped from a handless cup. He had been taking tobacco too and the air in the cubicle was thick with fumes.

'Andrew.' Frederick rose and cast aside the issue of *The Times* that he had snaffled from the racks. He shook Purves's hand, then seated himself again at the brass-topped table. 'How decent of you to join me at such a short notice. Will you have a cup?'

'I thank you, no. I am dining in half an hour.'

Frederick smiled. 'That being the case, I will not waste time in idle conversation.' He reached below the table, lifted up the new valise and put it down on the brass. '*Voilà!*'

'What is that, if I may ask?'

'The bag is a gift. Handsome, is it not? Made especially for you, Andrew, by a craftsman in Dublin town.'

'Thank you, Frederick.'

'Within,' Frederick went on, 'are banknotes. Ten pounds and twenty pounds on each, drawn from the Bank of Scotland. Reputable enough, I believe?'

'To what total value?'

'Two hundred and ten pounds.' Frederick beamed. 'Are you not pleased with the return of your investment?'

Andrew did not reach out for the valise. He was seated ramrod straight on the chair, arms folded. Dulled by August heat, the atmosphere held wraiths of tobacco smoke and a faint bumble-bee hum of conversation from the long room above the partitions.

'Very pleased,' Andrew said. 'How many cargoes did you run?'

'Four in all.'

'And the excisemen gave you no trouble?'

'Not a bit of it.'

'You have been gone from Glasgow a considerable period of time to attend to the loading and sale of just four cargoes.'

'I had other things to do, as well. I bought furniture.'

'To feather your nest, Frederick?'

Frederick paused. He reached down, lifted the dish of coffee and drank the black liquid in a swallow. He dabbed his lips with his handkerchief while Andrew Purves, grim as Charon, waited without a prompting word.

Frederick said, 'I gather that *you* have news for *me*?'

'Do I?'

'Come along now,' Frederick said, sudden sharpness in his tone. 'Do not beat about the bush. I can tell from your manner that you do not approve of – of something. What?'

'Clare Kelso—'

'My intended?'

'Is she your intended?'

'Of course.'

'Clare Kelso is pregnant.'

'It would be strange,' said Frederick, 'if she were not.'

'What the devil do you mean?'

'Pregnancy is a natural result of coupling.'

'So you admit it?'

'What is there to admit?' said Frederick. 'The girl was as eager as I was for union.'

'She was also a virgin.'

'You're behaving like her father, sir, not her master.'

'I do not think of myself as her master.'

'Oh?' said Frederick. 'How do you think of yourself?'

'As her guardian,' Andrew said. 'I do not wish to see her damaged.'

'Damaged? What an odd word to use,' said Frederick. 'I take it that Clare has told you of her condition and has made her wishes known to you.'

Andrew flushed and stammered. 'No, we have yet to discuss the matter of her desires, or her future.'

'How do you know of the pregnancy then, if Clare did not tell you? Your wife Edwina, is she perhaps in Clare's confidence?'

'I heard from – from another source.'

'Gossiping servants! What a bugbear!' said Frederick with a note of sarcasm.

'The point is—'

'The point is, sir, that I will marry her,' said Frederick. 'We may make our arrangements on that premise.'

'Arrangements?'

'I am not taking her with nothing, sir.'

'You took her in the full knowledge of her position.'

'That position has changed.'

'Good God!' Andrew exclaimed. 'Have you no honour?'

'Not a shred.'

'What do you want from me?'

'Credit.'

'You already have credit.'

'Credit – without interest,' Frederick said.

'How much credit?'

'One thousand pounds.'

'Impossible.'

'How so?' said Frederick. 'Are you not a presiding partner?'

'Of course I am.'

'Finance me privately then, if you do not trust me to repay a bank loan.'

'Am I, by chance, being blackmailed?'

'Certainly not,' said Frederick.

'What if I say that I will not do it?'

'Clare will become your problem.'

'I am willing to keep her, and her child.'

'Will she, though, be willing to stay?' Frederick said.

'She will have little choice in the matter.'

'She is in love with me, Andrew,' Frederick pointed out. 'In your eyes, she may be a fool for it but the fact is that she loves me. Anything less than marriage will wound her sorely.'

'It *is* blackmail.'

'It is an arrangement, sir. No more, no less than I would ask of you if Clare Kelso was your sister, or your daughter.'

'Except that she is pregnant.'

Frederick wrapped his long fingers around the coffee cup and brought it to his mouth. 'How does that alter things?'

Andrew studied him with revulsion tinged by a certain admiration for the fellow's audacity. It was obvious from the return in the valise that the illicit and untaxed cargoes of rock salt that were finding their way from Cheshire quarries to Ireland and thence into Scotland were bringing Frederick high profits. Striker might invest his own gains in the purchase of further cargoes now, Andrew guessed, but Striker would not risk losing all to confiscation by the King's men or to a storm in the Irish channel. He preferred to work on credit.

Frederick said, 'No, Andrew, young Miss Kelso would not be the first servant to bring an unwelcome addition to the Purves household, would she? Confess it, you have dealt with this situation before.'

'Clare is different.'

'Because she is educated and beautiful?' said Frederick. 'What difference does that make? She is a female without title or dowry. As the father of her brat, I might pay you a few shillings or a sum down, wash my hands of the whole affair and trust to your sense of decency and honour to see to the child's welfare, and the poor mother's too. That's how it is usually done, is it not?'

'How different will it be for Clare if I agree to your request for credit without interest?'

'It will be, for Clare, the difference between paradise and purgatory,' said Frederick. 'I will attend her quite openly at your house. I will publicly declare my intention to marry her and will do so. I will stand before God in the ceremony and both Clare and the child will then have my name. She will live in Grahamston with me, bear me more children, and be happy as the day is long.'

'And your sister?'

'Eunice will put up no complaint,' said Frederick. 'In fact, I have a feeling that my sister will not go too long without a husband of her own.'

'Indeed?' said Andrew.

'Eunice is *my* responsibility, however,' said Frederick. 'For the time being, Clare is yours.'

'What of your other women, sir?'

For a split second Frederick's self-assurance wavered. He glanced up quickly from filling his cup and a blot of coffee tippled from the spout of the pot on to the brass table.

'Other women?'

'That multitude of female friends and admirers that you have cultivated here in Glasgow?'

'Betté, old Betté, do you mean?' Frederick was easy

again, dismissive. 'Oh, she has served her purpose. The others too. Do you not believe me when I declare myself in love with Clare?'

'But not enough in love to take her as she is?'

Frederick sighed. 'Enough in love to wish to give her a comfortable home and a modicum of security. If she was your daughter—'

'I have a daughter,' Andrew said. 'Two, in fact.'

'You force me into conceit, Andrew: I am worth a tidy sum on the marriage market. There is no escaping that fact. I will be worth even more by summer's end. With application I might have my pick of half a dozen young heiresses.'

'Most of whom would be instantly disowned.'

'You do not care for me, sir, do you?'

'Not a great deal, sir, no.'

'I am, however, the husband that Clare desires.'

'I regret to say that you are,' Andrew admitted.

'I am her first choice, her first offer.'

'Yes.'

'Enough of this unseemly haggling,' Frederick said. 'I'm not asking you to *give* me money. You will be paid back every single penny, I promise you. And you will have the satisfaction of knowing that you have brought happiness to your cousin. May I also remind you that I did not conduct the courtship in secret, that you encouraged me and gave me your permission?'

'Yes, yes.' Andrew had not been unaware of his part in fostering the affair.

Frederick wiped fingers and palm on the waistcoat of his gaudy green suit and extended his right hand across the table. 'Do we have the terms of a bargain, sir?'

Andrew hesitated. All sorts of other fantastical deals and

trades were spinning in his thoughts, brokerage on his own behalf as well as Clare's. He could, there and then, have risen and left, kept Clare in her misery for himself. He could also, there and then, have negotiated with Frederick for his sister, not as wife but as mistress. He felt suddenly demeaned, less by Striker's mendacity than by his own libidinous desires.

Abruptly, he stuck out his hand and shook the Englishman's long, dry fingers.

'Is it done, sir?' said Frederick Striker.

'It is,' said Andrew Purves.

Clare had no intimation that she had been bargained for and bought. Andrew doubted if she would have been flattered either by his generosity or by the extravagant price he'd had to pay to be rid of her. The first Clare knew of Frederick's return was when the door of the nursery creaked open and he put his head around it, finger to his lips to silence Maddy and the children who had seen him first.

Clare had spent the morning at the table with William and Dorothea and was in process of putting away school-books and slates into a pine chest. It was William's stillness and Dorothea's perplexed frown that caught her attention but just as she swung round Frederick caught at her and swung her from her feet. She gave an involuntary squeal of astonishment that quickly changed to delight as he rained kisses upon her brow and cheeks and, setting her lightly down, kissed her mouth until she had no breath at all left.

'Will I take the children out?' said Maddy.

'No,' Frederick answered.

'Aye,' said William, who had recognised the man with the snake and, though he had matured considerably these past months, still nurtured a lurking fear that he would be consumed by a serpent.

Frederick, however, had no eyes for the Purves children or for Maddy. He gripped Clare by the shoulders and studied her flushed features with gravity. 'Put on your best gown, my dearest. We will just be in time to take dinner at the Tree.'

'My – my duties—'

'Damn your duties. Besides, I have Andrew's permission to take you away.'

'Are you sure, Frederick?'

'What's wrong with you, Clare?' Frederick demanded in mock anger. 'Do you not want to accompany me on an excursion? Do you have another beau waiting in the wings?'

'No, Frederick, no.'

'Come along then.' He laughed, slipped a hand into the folds of her dress, gave her flank a squeeze and whispered, 'I'm famished.'

Two hours later Clare lay upon the bed in the upstairs room in the Linden Tree with Frederick, his first hunger satisfied, naked by her side. He had paid dearly for the use of the room, which had been reserved for another gentleman, but his desire had been such that he would have paid ten times over to be, thus, alone with her.

At first Clare had been afraid that love-making would damage the child within her. Frederick, however, confessed that he had learned of Clare's condition from his good sister Eunice, and had assured Clare that there was no danger in answering the demands of passionate nature at this stage. He had had her half-undressed even before the maid brought in dinner on a tray.

The fact of her pregnancy seemed to have changed nothing in their relationship. Now that he lay by her in the humid chamber, feeding her fragments of cold duckling bitten from the bone, tenderly stroking her round stomach, the fatalism that had sustained her broke forth and she clung to him and burst into an unexpected flood of tears.

'Now, now, my darling lass,' Frederick consoled her. 'This is no occasion for weeping.' He patted her back with his unoccupied hand and discreetly dropped the duck bone behind him on to the floor. 'Did you not trust me to return?'

'I–I thought when you did – did not write that you had forgotten me.'

'If I had known what a momentous event had occurred I *would* have written. I'd have found a dove, or a dolphin, to carry the letter to you, post-haste.'

'Did your sister not inform you of my condition?'

'I was travelling, you see. Knocking about from inn to inn. Eunice did not know where I was. Damn it, I hardly knew myself from day to day.'

'Where – where did you travel to?'

'Now,' Frederick went on, as if the question had not been asked, 'I am home. Now I am with my own true love and all will be well between us, will it not, Clare dearest?'

Clare lay back against the bolster and wiped her wet cheeks with the heel of her hand. There was a certain greasiness everywhere because of the duck, and the heavy odour of cooking rose in the still thundery air. No fire burned in the grate today, thank God, for she felt weighted and weak with the increase in heat in the atmosphere. Frederick's love-making had been too swift to satisfy her but when he put his hand upon her again and kissed her swelling breasts, she sighed and gave a final sob that made her tummy leap against his hand.

'Ah-hah!' Frederick put his ear to her stomach and, smiling broadly, murmured, 'Are you in there, my son? Can you feel Daddy?'

'It's too early, I think,' Clare said.

It had grown quite dark in the room, darker still in the curtained alcove where the bed was. Frederick seemed vague and indistinct above her, except for his touch. He stirred, eased his hip and thigh against her, slid an arm beneath the small of her back and raised her against him.

She could feel the hair on his body prickle against her flesh, the dark stubble on his chin scrape her breasts. She was not ready for him yet. She felt that Frederick was somehow less real than he had been, as if their sinfulness had been rendered casual by the act of conception.

Even when Frederick straddled her, stooped and massive in the confines of the alcove, she felt that he was less real than the seed in her body and that the man had become but an essence of other things.

'Did he propose to marry you?' Cameron Adams interrupted. *'When was that promise made?'*

Clare shook her head. 'Later, days later.'

'Were you glad or sorry?'

'I was relieved, I suppose.'

'Naturally,' Cameron Adams said. 'But then there were many things that you did not understand about Frederick Striker, were there not? Things that emerged and became known to you only long after they'd happened.'

'Many things,' Clare admitted.

Cameron found it difficult to reconcile the woman seated on the prison cot before him with the foolish girl who had fallen for such an obvious seducer. Of course, he had never understood women and the attraction that roguishness held for them. At what point, he wondered, had the girl recognised her lover for false, detected in him not mere cunning but ineluctable evil?

He said, 'Striker promised marriage but he did not keep his promise? What did Andrew Purves, having paid one thousand pounds, as it were, have to say about that?'

'Andrew paid only five hundred. He refused to sign to Frederick the second line of credit until the day of our marriage.'

'A day that never came,' Cameron said.

'I thought it would,' Clare gave a little sad tut of annoyance at her own naivety. 'I believed Frederick when he told me that we would marry when he returned from his next excursion in the winter of the year.'

'In the interim,' said Cameron Adams, 'you continued to visit the upper room at the Linden Tree?'

'No, never again,' Clare said. 'He took me to his house.'

'With his sister present?'

'He sent her out,' Clare said. 'No, he did not have to send Eunice away. She went quite willingly. It was all arranged, as to a schedule.'

'Friday afternoons?'

'And Sundays too sometimes.'

'What did your mistress, Edwina Purves, have to say to all of this?'

'She was ill-pleased.'

'What did she do?'

'Nothing,' Clare said. 'There was nothing she could do. She crowed over me, when Frederick was not about, and told me to my face that he would never marry me, that my child would be born a bastard whether I liked it or not.'

'Yes.' Cameron nodded. 'Purves and the sister? What did you know of that relationship?'

'At the time, not a thing,' Clare said. 'Eunice confided in me at a later date.'

'Will she speak for you at your trial?'

'She has said that she will.'

'Is she Andrew Purves's lover?'

'She says that she is not. She claims to be a close friend, but not a mistress.'

Cameron kept his doubts on that score to himself. He had known that Eunice Striker Bates would speak on behalf of his client but he was now beginning to doubt the wisdom of pressing her to appear, in opening that book of secrets to the interrogation of the Advocate Depute.

Unprompted, Clare went on, 'She is in love with him. Eunice with Andrew. I think she would have been closer to me even than she was if it was not for that.'

'Do you mean that she would have pressed her brother to marry you?'

'No, Eunice had no more power over Frederick than I had. He is not a man who could be pressed to do anything that did not suit him.' Clare hesitated. 'He cared about my baby, though.'

'Wait,' Cameron said. 'Before we come to the baby you must tell me about that autumn and winter and the reason why nobody, not Eunice, not Andrew, not you, nailed Striker to a marriage date.'

'He came and went as suited him,' Clare said. 'I hung on his promise.'

'Because you were in love with him?'

'That is the reason, yes.'

'He was not, however, in love with you?'

'I believe that he was – for a time.'

'Are you still in love with Frederick Striker, Clare?'

She did not answer, made no sound, no involuntary gesture that would indicate a base to her behaviour, add reason to her illogical desire to protect and defend Striker even now.

Cameron said, 'Can you not answer?'

She said, 'I heard something that I was not supposed to hear. After that, I had a sense that Frederick would not marry me. I became reconciled in the knowledge that Frederick was not free to do as he wished. I did not quite give up hope.'

'When did this incident take place?'

'In December. On a Sunday afternoon two or three weeks before Christmas.'

'Where?'

'At Frederick's house.'

'Was Eunice present?'

'No. She had, as usual, gone out.'

'To allow you to be with him?'

Clare said, 'We were no longer together in that way. I was into my seventh month and was becoming large. He did not want it of me. He seemed content to have me with him, and was attentive to me in every way.'

'Yet you were not his wife?'

'No, I was not his wife.'

'And you continued to live, as before, in Purves's Land?'

'I had my duties there. My size did not interfere with my ability, though Mr Andrew forbade me to carry water pails or hods of coal. William had gone up to school, to the Academy. He had become quite adult and he was more pleasant to me than ever before. He no longer took supper with the family but had a tray all to himself, and the closet room to himself too. I helped him with his books as best I could.'

'And marriage?'

'Promised finally for New Year.'

'On a given date?'

'The first day of January, after Frederick returned from his last journey of the year. In time for me to spend the final weeks of my confinement in his house.'

'But something happened to prevent it?'

'Yes.'

'What?'

'I heard something I should not have heard.'

'Will you tell me what it was?' Cameron asked.

'If you wish,' Clare answered.

She lay upon the bed in the upstairs room with a woollen shawl drawn up over her knees as far as the mound of her stomach. She seemed larger than she really was, her dainty figure distorted by the high-riding position of the baby within her. She did not feel unwell. She had been back to the Apothecaries' Hall on two occasions and had received from the aged dispenser there sympathetic advice and several potions made from herbal extractions which had alleviated the personal indispositions associated with the carrying of a child. She was not ill but weary, weary and impatient, snappish with Frederick who, that particular afternoon, seemed distant and distracted. He was not short with her but firm in his suggestion that she would do well to rest. He had lighted the fire in the upper room, had given her tea and a milk biscuit before escorting her upstairs. He had not, however, sat with her but had gone downstairs again without delay.

Clare had been acquainted with Frederick now for fourteen months, the ball at Sinclairs' Land had taken place less than a year ago, yet she felt sometimes that Frederick had been with her always. It was odd how central he had become to her, how everything in her life revolved around him, yet how little she really knew of him and how infrequently they were together. Hardly had he returned from one trip to the south than he was off on another, coming home for a week or ten days before packing his valises and setting off again for destinations that remained, to Eunice as well as Clare, vague in the extreme. In the months of her pregnancy she saw more of Eunice than she did of Frederick and often felt closer to the woman than to the man.

Friday afternoons were spent with Eunice, seldom with Frederick. There was never anyone else present, no visitors from town, no callers, no friendly faces at the tea table before the fire in the parlour. Most oddly there were no servants, not even a day maid; a rare omission for a household as well-to-do as Frederick's.

On those few afternoons in October and early November when Frederick was at home Eunice went off without apparent reluctance and did not return until dusk or after, passive and pleasant, but without tales to tell. Now, in the gloom of December, she went off without a bidding, though Frederick had told her there was no need to go at all.

Clare had been lying down for a half hour or so. Lulled by the heat of the fire, she had dozed off. Later she calculated that it was about three o'clock when the voices awakened her. She had not heard anyone admitted to the house and had no idea how long the men had been present in the parlour. It was probable that she would not have wakened at all, would have remained oblivious to the parlour meeting, if one voice had not been raised in anger.

'Damn me, Striker, do you not know what this means?'

Clare jerked out of light sleep. She was instantly awake. She put her hands across her stomach and sat up.

She heard the same voice shout, 'Drumfin can do any-thin' he wishes. You should have told us that Drumfin was your enemy.'

She heard Frederick answer meekly, too low to catch.

'Have you not paid him?' came the next shouted question.

Another voice, urgent but feeble, hissed at the speaker to be quiet. For a long moment silence hovered in the room below.

Outside the casement the sky was already dark with cold rain-cloud and the gathering of dusk. She wondered if Eunice had returned, if she was still dutifully walking Glasgow's Sabbath streets. Clare did not know what prompted her to slip from the bed and steal to the bedroom door. She opened it with excessive care, cocked her head and listened intently. She could hear odd words in medley, a single phrase separate from the rest. But not nearly enough to appease the keen curiosity that had come upon her. She shed her slippers and crept to the head of the stairs. Keeping in the shadow, she rested her stomach gently against the varnished rail.

Out of the parlour, amplified by the stairwell, the voices became audible. 'Aye, Striker, whatever you may say, Drumfin *can* come down upon us and bring the excisemen to Quinn's door.'

'Look, Brock, I'll pay him,' Frederick said. 'I promise I'll pay him and that will appease him.'

'It's too damned late to pay him an' hope to get away wi' it,' the man named Brock answered. 'Drumfin can squash us flat as fleas if he so chooses.'

'It is a mystery to me why he has not done so,' said the man with the feeble voice. 'Oh, God, God! I should never have listened to you, Brock Harding. I'm too old to go to jail.'

'Whining about it will serve no purpose, Quinn,' Frederick said. 'You were happy enough to join us when all was calm. Now you must brace up and see it through, like the rest of us.'

'I did nothing,' said the old man. 'I stole nothing.'

'You stole from the King's purse,' said Frederick. 'Pray, do not come all pious with me now, sir. You've been pilfering guineas from the taxman for years, like every saltmaster who was ever born.'

'But not by the ship's load, not on this scale.'

'No, nor makin' profits on this scale, either,' Brock said.

Frederick said, 'How can you be sure that it is Drumfin? The agent you caught may not have told you the truth.'

'Aye, but he did,' said Brock. 'He told us all about your wager at the Gorbals cockpit, an' about Martin.'

'Where is he now, this agent of Drumfin?'

'With the fishes,' said Brock.

'Best place for him, I suppose,' said Frederick. 'Did he happen to mention what happened to Martin?'

'Dead an' buried, what was left of him.'

'Look,' Frederick said, 'it is, I confess, a shock to discover that we are threatened by a lord, particularly a law lord. Drumfin has not caught us yet, however, and we have little or nothing in transit.'

'Only the store,' said Quinn. 'If the excisemen find the store, all will be up with me.'

'Sell it,' said Frederick. 'Sell all of it and shift it by night. We will close our shop in Ladybrook until such times as—'

'What do you say?' Brock demanded. 'I've spent the best part of three years setting up the routes. Now, because of your stupidity, Striker, you expect me to close them down?'

'There are other saltmasters, other pans,' said Frederick.

'Are you cutting me out?' said the old man plaintively.

'Better to cut out than cut up,' said Brock.

'How can I sell my salt? Who will take such a stack from me? How can we move the loads without danger of being seen?'

'I can arrange all of that, Quinn,' Brock said. 'But I'll want recompense for my trouble.'

'How much?' said Frederick.

'I take the risk. I take the price.'

'What, all of it?'

'Aye, every last penny.'

'But I paid for the load,' said Frederick. 'I have money invested in—'

'You're lucky I haven't killed you,' said Brock. 'I could cut you off, Striker, just as easy as I cut off Drumfin's lackey. It would be the simplest thing for me to do.'

Frederick's flat voice made talk of killing seem unemotional and he appeared less disturbed by the bully's threats than by the loss of revenue from the illegal enterprise.

Silence for a half-minute or so. Clare could hear the old man moaning and mumbling to himself, but Frederick said nothing. She was frightened by what had been revealed of Frederick's so-called 'business' ventures which, she gathered, had to do with contraband cargoes and involved dealings with cut-throats and murderers.

At length, Frederick said, 'No, Brock, I do not think that you will dispose of me.'

'What's to stop me?'

'A letter in a box in a safe place.' Frederick added, 'Not here.'

'Damn your letter, Striker. I'm not afraid o' words.'

'A letter in which names are named, dates and places too.'

'What the devil do you mean?'

'A letter to the Sheriff of the County of Ayr, to be delivered in the event of my premature demise.'

If Clare had not been awake already she would have been roused now surely by the roar of a furious shout that escaped Brock's throat. 'I'll tear this house apart. I'll find your damned letter, damned if I won't. Then I'll see you off, Striker.'

'A foolish move, sir,' said Frederick calmly. 'Oh, I agree that Drumfin may make things hot for me. Even if I pay him now, he has lost face. And that will never do for a law lord. Like so many of his ilk, face is all he has. But Drumfin can do little or nothing to you, Brock, or to Quinn, provided—'

'Provided we toe your line, ah?' Brock interrupted.

'May I remind you,' Frederick said, 'that *I* sought *you* out. You may have set up the routes, but I conceived the whole scheme and, what's more, financed it.'

'And ruined it,' put in the old man.

'I will pay Drumfin what is his due on that foolish debt,' said Frederick. 'I will even pay him interest. That might stay his hand until . . .' He hesitated. '. . . until I marry.'

'Marry?' Brock cried. 'What does marriage have to do with it?'

'Marry and obtain unlimited credit,' Frederick said.

Clare stifled a gasp. Her hands closed on the rail and, for an instant, she felt giddy.

'Hoh, so you're marrying money, are you?' Brock said. 'Who is this unfortunate lass?'

'That's my secret,' said Frederick. 'The relevant issue is that we will be able to finance new routes, come summer.'

'Without me?' bleated the old man. Neither Frederick nor his accomplice deigned to reassure him.

Brock laughed. 'Aye, you're a clever one, Striker, I'll say that for you. You've insured yourself against every even-tuality. But what if this heiress will not marry you, after all?'

'She will. It is all but arranged.'

Brock said, 'So, do I get my winter's feed from Quinn's store or do I not, man?'

'Yes, but I want it out and away by the beginning of the week. And be damned careful in the doing of it.'

'Be careful yourself,' said Brock. 'I may not be as inclined as I was to remove you from the face of the earth, Striker, but I doubt if the promise of an inheritance will appease a man like Lord Drumfin. Keep your head low below the bulwarks, would be my advice.'

'Advice I intend to take,' said Frederick.

'What about me, what about me?' piped up the old man.

'You have nothing much to fear,' said Frederick.

'My money? My profit? My share?'

'You have had your share, Quinn, and it is done,' said Frederick.

'What will I do now, though?'

'Go back to your saltpans, an' be glad you're still alive to do so,' Brock said. 'Count your pennies, pleasure your wife and, if you value your life, say not a word to anyone.'

Some minutes later the men left.

Clare had shaken off giddiness and crouched behind the rail to catch sight of them.

It was dark in the hall, however, and Frederick did not deem it necessary to light them out with a lantern. Clare had only the rays from the parlour fire to give her glimpse of Brock who was, as she had imagined him, so brutally large that he had to stoop his head beneath the lintel of the door to make his exit. The old man was not quite so decrepit as his voice suggested. He was of middle height but stringy. He wore, as far as Clare could make out, rusty old pantaloons and a padded, many-pocketed coat and had a long thin muffler, like a grey worm, wound round and round his throat. He lingered in the hall, anxiously hopping from one foot to the other as if he had something desperate to say to Frederick before departure. Frederick, though, would have none of it and elbowed him out of the open door into the gloom of the December evening, without ceremony or heart.

There were no farewells.

Frederick closed the door immediately, spun on his heel and stared up the staircase into the shadows of the landing.

Clare retreated in panic. Holding her skirts around her she crept back into the unlighted bedroom. She barely had time to throw herself upon the bed and, panting, settle her limbs and close her eyes before Frederick thrust open the door. She made herself yawn, stir, open her eyes slowly.

'Darling, is that you?' she said, sitting up a little.

'How long have you been awake?'

'Just now. I thought – did I hear voices?'

'What did you hear?'

He was by the bed now, bent over her. His eyes seemed yellowed by the light and when he stretched out a hand to stroke her hair it was all Clare could do not to flinch.

'Is it Eunice? Has Eunice come home?'

'No, an acquaintance, just an acquaintance dropped by,' Frederick said.

She met his gaze without blinking. She could not love him at that moment, not with all his lies buzzing like black flies in her mind, yet she had sense enough to deceive him, to yawn again, then smile. 'I thought I dreamed it.'

'Perhaps you did.'

'The man?'

'Gone now.' Frederick eased himself on to the bed by her side, took her in his arms and rocked her soothingly. 'Gone now, all gone.'

'Never to return?' said Clare.

'What?'

'Listen, I hear someone at the door.'

Frederick stiffened and leaned away from her. Releasing her he listened tensely to the sounds from the hall below.

'Eunice, I expect,' said Clare.

'I'll just make sure, shall I?' he said, anxiously.

And Clare, straight-faced, said, 'Do.'

Clare left Grahamston soon after Eunice returned. She said little to Frederick as he walked her back to Purves's Land and noticed nothing definite or final in his parting kiss. She was anxious to be rid of him, to put behind her the afternoon's confusions. And she was eager to find Andrew and ask him outright if he intended to pay Frederick to marry her. The Purveses were entertaining the Shaws to supper, however, and Clare had no opportunity to speak with her master alone.

At a little after ten o'clock the following morning Clare was summoned to the office of the banking hall where, to her utter astonishment, she found not only Andrew but also Eunice.

'What are you doing here?' Clare blurted out.

Breakfast cups and plates were set on a side table and Eunice, elegantly dressed, was seated on a chair by the desk with a teacup and saucer balanced on her lap.

Until that instant Clare had been blissfully unaware that Andrew and Eunice were acquainted. 'Do you know who this is, Mr Andrew?' she asked, rather foolishly. 'This lady is Frederick's sister.'

Clad in sober grey suiting, his neat 'working wig' square on his head, Andrew stood behind the desk. 'Yes,' he said. 'I know.' He did not seem to know what to say next, however, and it was left to Eunice to break the news.

'Frederick's gone,' the woman said.

Panic clutched at Clare, memories of the conversation she had overheard yesterday, talk of murder and revenge. 'Vanished?'

'Not exactly,' said Andrew. 'Frederick left a letter which Mrs Bates was good enough to deliver to me personally.'

'Is there no letter for me?' said Clare.

Eunice glanced at Andrew who shook his head. 'No, Clare, I'm sorry. No letter for you.'

The letter on Andrew's desk was long. Even from the middle of the room Clare could make out Frederick's upright script upon the sheets. She was tempted to step forward and pick up the letter, but before she could act Andrew swept the pages into a drawer.

Clare said, 'He isn't coming back, is he?'

Again Eunice and Andrew exchanged glances. 'Frederick has left very particular instructions regarding your welfare,' Eunice said. 'He has asked that Andrew and I take care of you until such time as he returns to Glasgow. However it may appear, Clare, I do not think that my brother has abandoned you.'

'Will he not be here to marry me?' Clare said.

'I have doubts on that score,' said Andrew.

Eunice was more direct and forthright. 'No.'

The news did not affect Clare as she expected it would. She was strangely relieved to be rid of the burden of pretence. She was fortunate to have friends at all, allies who would not desert her. What she really deserved was to be thrown out to fend for herself, but Andrew would not let that happen. Her brain remained clear as a crystal but her legs somehow let her down and she groped for a chair and seated herself upon it before she could show weakness.

Eunice was at her side instantly. 'Are you unwell, Clare?'

'Tea, give her tea,' Andrew suggested.

Clare brushed their solicitude aside. 'I'm perfectly well, thank you. I do not require tea. I require only to be told what will become of me and my child when it is born.'

'You'll come to my house for the confinement,' said Eunice. 'After the infant is born and you are recovered you will return to service here in Purves's Land.'

'Are those Frederick's orders?' Clare said.

'Something of the sort,' said Eunice.

Clare said, 'And what of my baby? Will you take it?'

'I cannot,' said Eunice.

'Cannot or will not?'

'Clare,' said Andrew, with just the faintest note of warning. 'You must be content with the plans that have been made for you. No harm will come to your child, I assure you.'

'Provision will be made,' said Eunice. 'The baby will be put out to foster parents.'

'No.'

'Close by,' said Andrew, 'in Glasgow. You'll be able to visit, see to the child's raising. And when she – or he – is old enough I will find a place for it here.'

'As what?' Clare said. 'A stable boy, a kitchen drudge? Is that what Frederick wants for his son? Well, it's not what I want.'

'You have no choice in the matter,' Eunice informed her.

To Eunice Clare said, 'Frederick has deserted you too, has he not?'

Eunice appeared to lose patience. She flung her hand

out in a gesture of contempt. 'You do not know my brother as I do or you would not be so damnably keen to become his wife. Was that why you gave in to him – to better yourself?'

'I loved him. I imagined that he loved me,' Clare said, without a trace of self-pity. 'What's more, I do not think that he has deserted me. I think he has gone into hiding and that, when all's well, he will come back for me.'

'Gone into hiding?' said Eunice.

Andrew said, 'Clare, what makes you suppose that Frederick is in hiding? What has he told you?'

'He told her nothing,' Eunice stated. 'Frederick does not confide in her.'

'Yesterday,' Clare said, 'when you were out, Eunice, two men came to the house.'

It was Eunice Bates' turn to be startled. She had gone around the desk to stand near Andrew and, in the instant after Clare spoke, put out her hand to find support from the man's arm. 'What men?'

'Oh, did Frederick not tell you? Did Frederick not *confide* in you?'

Clare's anger was not destructive. She felt icy cold and sensed that, for the moment, she had the upper hand. She drew in two or three deep breaths. There was a line of discomfort across the top of her stomach this morning, not painful but cramping, as if her child had hitched itself higher within her. She eased herself on to the chair again and, leaning back, pressed the base of her spine against the upright. She looked up at the woman and the man with something approaching defiance.

'Clare, please,' said Andrew. 'You must tell us what you saw.'

'Two men,' Clare said. 'I do not know their names. I

could hear almost nothing of what was said. I was asleep in the upstairs bedroom when they arrived.'

'What *did* you hear?' Eunice said.

'Raised voices. Angry voices,' Clare said.

'Did you make out what they were saying?'

'No, I could not hear them clearly.'

'Did you see them, even a glimpse?'

'How could I see them? I was afraid to leave the bedroom,' said Clare.

'How do you know that there were but two of them?' Eunice Bates asked.

'I *think* there were only two,' Clare said. 'They made a great fuss as they were leaving.'

'And then?'

'Frederick came up to me at once. He was agitated, greatly agitated.'

'What did he tell you?' said Eunice.

'Only that he had had an argument with a friend, and that I must not worry my head about it.' Truth was much more malleable than Clare had ever supposed. Perhaps she had learned the knack of bending it from Frederick. 'He kneeled by the bed and told me that he loved me. He made me promise that I would not think badly of him.'

'What did you take that to mean, Clare?' said Andrew.

'I do not know. I know only that I was afraid for him.'

She felt guilty at lying to Andrew, who had always been a kind and generous master, but the feeling was snuffed out suddenly when she saw how Eunice clung to Andrew's arm and realised, at that moment, that she had been a victim of their deception too.

Armed with her own secrets Clare felt stronger than ever before. She answered their anxious questions with apparent candour but told them nothing of what she had learned.

After a time she got to her feet and tugged down the wings
of the unstayed bodice that rode lightly on the summit of
her belly.

'That,' she said, 'is all I can tell you.'

'What do you intend to do, Clare?' said Andrew.

'I will do what I have been ordered to do.'

'Good,' said Andrew. 'Sensible. And for the best.'

'You see, I know that Frederick will come back for me
and will marry me just as soon as circumstances allow,'
Clare said.

Eunice frowned. 'Do you truly believe that?'

And Clare, lying glibly, answered, 'Yes.'

8

The Irish Trade

———————————

Christmas for Clare was a lonely time, dreams of love and comfort lost in animosity and anxiety. On New Year's Day she joined the servants in the kitchen to partake of the feast that Andrew's bounty provided. She did justice to the goose, the venison, the buttermilk puddings but did not unite with the others in their raucous hilarity. She endured the coarse wit of Elsie Gollan and her crew only until the meal was over and slipped away before beer kegs were tapped and serious drinking began. She could not bear the servants' maudlin sentimentality and the vicious streak that liquor brought out in them, and lay upstairs, alone, firm in her resolve that she would never condemn her child to a life of servitude in that strident community below stairs.

The Purveses had prudently gone out to dinner at the Shaws and would remain away until long after dark. Andrew and his father would be first home to crack the whip and clear a path through the human debris. How Eunice celebrated the New Year Clare had no clue. She supposed that she might have obtained permission to visit the widow, might have sat like an equal at table with her or played melodies upon the pianoforte and discussed what dark adventures Frederick had been forced to endure because of malice and misunderstandings. But Clare had a feeling that Eunice would not be alone the whole day long and guessed that Andrew would somehow find

time to call upon her and offer his own brand of consolation.

To her surprise Clare received a New Year letter from
Frances Purves. The hand, like the girl, was nervous and
energetic and difficult to interpret. It seemed that Frances
had learned of Clare's plight and was offering now to speak
to her father with a view to taking Clare into service at
Moorfoot. Two more mouths to feed, Frances wrote
ingenuously, would make no difference to her Daddy.
And when Mr Malabar finally concluded his wooing
and married her then she, Clare, might come along to live
in Edinburgh and keep house for them.

Clare was touched by the girl's concern. She replied at
once, thanking her for her generosity but turning the offer
down. Though she told Frances that she expected Mr
Striker to return to Glasgow at any time, she did not believe
it, and she was not disappointed when no letter came in
greeting from the south.

January went out in icicles and black frosts.

As her time approached Clare grew heavy and clumsy
and possessed of the gloomy notion that she would not
survive labour. During the final weeks she drew deep into
herself and was almost indifferent to what became of her by
the time Andrew instructed her to pack her belongings and
had Moresby drive her out to Grahamston.

Eunice welcomed her warmly, without any sign of
disaffection or annoyance that Clare had not called upon
her. She helped Clare to a chair by the fire and showed her
the shower of little gifts that she had purchased for the
infant; tiny mutches with lace borders, long muslin frocks,
flannel petticoats and even, rather prematurely, a coral
gumstick. Sight of the objects suddenly blessed her child
with life, made a person out of it, and Clare was overcome.

She wept in Eunice's arms, took strength from the woman, and from a sense of Frederick's presence in the house as well.

That evening Andrew brought round a midwife, a small, chubby, cheerful woman named Grant. She took Clare upstairs and examined her, smiling and crooning away as if Clare was a child and not a mother-to-be, and then went downstairs to report to Andrew, supposing him, perhaps, to be the father. Ten or fifteen minutes later Andrew climbed the stairs and brought Clare the information that all was in place and as it should be and that Mrs Grant would be on hand just as soon as labour pains commenced.

Later Eunice brought her broth and brown bread and sat with her while she ate.

'What will you call the child?' Eunice asked.

'If it's a girl I will call her by my mother's name.'

'And if it's a boy – after your father?'

'No, I'll call him Frederick.'

'Oh, he would be flattered, I'm sure,' Eunice said. 'But perhaps, in the circumstances, it would be better not to place that burden on the bairn.'

'Burden?'

'Do not call him after my brother.'

'Perhaps I should call him Andrew?'

'That,' said Eunice, 'would be even less tactful.'

'Ah!' Clare exclaimed. 'I begin to see what you mean. What name would you choose?'

Eunice gave a little grunt, smiled and took away the bowl and spoon. She placed them on the shelf by the fire, stooped and stirred the coals with an iron poker. She looked broad and matronly in wide skirts and apron and the envy that had marked Clare's attitude to the woman of late smoothed away. She could not grudge Eunice Andrew's friendship. Eunice was so different from the shrill, self-centred Edwina, so much more like Andrew.

Before she could prevent herself, Clare said, 'Could I not stay here – afterwards?'

Eunice glanced round then rose. She still held the poker, its blunt tip smoking with tarry granules, and she was smiling no more. 'I would take you in, Clare, if I dared. But there is less here than you perceive. I'm nothing without my brother's protection. This house, for instance – if the rent is not paid then I will be thrown out of it.'

'Oh, no, surely not.' Clare propped herself awkwardly on her elbow. 'Frederick would not—'

'He has done it before,' Eunice said. 'Frederick is my brother and it is my duty to love him and do his bidding but I cannot predict what he will do next. Frederick is not like Andrew. Frederick is not like any man I have ever met, Clare.'

'No, nor I.'

Eunice set the poker down upon the stones of the hearth and kneeled upon the plain boards, the fire blazing at her back.

'Frederick has no feeling. He is empty, here.' Eunice touched her breast. 'Here, Frederick has only a hollow, an emptiness.' Eunice shook her head, sadly. 'It's not because of Frederick that I cannot take you and your baby in. It's because of me. We're of the same blood, Frederick and I. When the time comes again, and I'm certain that it will, I will do what he asks of me, even though I know it to be wrong.'

Clare said, 'I don't understand.'

'Andrew Purves is the man to adhere to, Clare. Andrew will not let you down. He will see to it that you never go hungry, that you never go cold. Yes, he will see to it that your child is brought up decently and securely.'

'But he will not love it as Frederick will.'

'Frederick loves nothing,' Eunice said, then scrambled to her feet again, laughed and clapped her hands together. 'Listen, I have a name for you. Oh, yes, a fine name for a small boy Peterkin.'

'Peterkin?'

'When he grows up he can be called Peter.'

'The manservant at Purves's Land is called that.'

'You offered me a choice, Clare,' Eunice said. 'And I like that name for the memories it brings me.'

'Happy memories?' said Clare.

'He was my first love. In London. Peterkin Brown.'

'Was he a pretty fellow, pleasant and witty?' Clare said.

'All of these things,' said Eunice. 'He lived in the room below the roof of our first lodging in London. I was sixteen years old and even more ugly than I am now. But that did not seem to matter to Peterkin. He had no money, hardly enough to feed himself, but he wrote me poems and would sing me songs. He would stand at the top of the stairs when he knew that Frederick had gone out, and he would sing to me. Oh, he sang so gently, so sweetly.'

'How old was he?'

'Nineteen,' said Eunice.

'Did he really love you?'

'Yes.'

'Why did he not marry you?'

'I told you, he had no money.'

'What difference—'

'All the difference. To Frederick, all the difference in the world. Besides,' Eunice had come close to the bed now, leaned her hip against the pillow and let her hand, as if casually, touch Clare's. 'He was so full of life, my Peterkin.

I was wildly in love with him. I have never been in love with anyone like that since.'

'What became of him, do you know?'

'He died.' Eunice shrugged as if to apologise for sentiments that were stale to all but her. 'He had run away from home and come to London to live out his last months. He knew that he was dying, that he would not last out the summer. And yet he loved me, sang to me so sweetly from the top of the stairs.'

'Were you there when he—'

'No, I had gone on by then.'

'On where?'

'To another man,' said Eunice.

Tentatively Clare laced her fingers with Eunice's for a moment and then removed her hand and placed it across her stomach. She said, 'Will Frederick remember that name, Peterkin Brown?'

'Frederick forgets nothing,' said Eunice.

'In that case I *will* call my child Peterkin,' Clare said.

'If it's a boy,' Eunice said.

'It will be,' said Clare.

Labour began with church bells on Sunday forenoon and ended in the dead, cold darkness of Monday morning at around a quarter past two o'clock. Only latterly was there great pain and all-consuming effort, but the calm and practical ministrations of both Midwife Grant and Eunice Bates saw Clare safely delivered of a boy child, healthy and complete in all respects. He was dipped in cold water, washed in warm, then given a quarter-spoonful of malt whisky to clear obstructions from his throat and mouth and to settle his stomach. He was handed to Clare wrapped not in a woman's shift, as was the custom, but in one of

Frederick's best linen shirts. He lay among the folds and frills with blue eyes open and his little pink features, not in the least pusillanimous, puckered slightly as he contemplated his mother for the first time.

Mrs Grant stayed until morning, ate her share of the rich cheese that Andrew had brought to maintain tradition, and drank two mugs of ale that had been laid in to revive and sustain the new mother. That done, she was duly paid and, to Eunice's delight, departed back to her cottage in Anderston.

Eunice had attended births before, had helped to care for newborn infants too. But this case was different. This infant was so close and dear to her that when she laid him down in his wicker basket and tucked the sheets and blankets about him she experienced such a wave of emotion that she could not help but weep. If she had been of a less practical disposition she might, in those early days, have come to regard the child as her own, but common sense prevailed upon Eunice and she contented herself with nursing and petting the newborn while Clare gathered her strength through sleep.

Andrew called on Monday afternoon. He made avuncular noises over the tiny mite, handselled the crib with a silver crown piece, congratulated Clare, and then went downstairs to eat the dinner that Eunice had prepared for him. Much later that evening, Messrs Shenkin and McCoull took the liberty of calling unannounced. They spent a good half-hour in adoration of their protégé's offspring, drank a glass of gin-and-water to Peterkin's health and tactfully made no mention at all of the absent father.

Mr Rossmore came next morning. He dropped off a gift of baby clothes and a silver half-crown, told Clare how well she looked, complained mildly about the daft name she had chosen for her son then, rather surprisingly, kissed the wee soul smack on the brow before hurrying off about his business.

Kindness and generosity surrounded Clare and her son for the first few days after the birth. Behind the warmth, however, lay the intractable fact that she would soon be separated from her son. Eunice would not take him. Andrew could not. Edwina had put her foot down very firmly at Andrew's tentative suggestion that Clare's child might be raised in the nursery at Purves's Land. Edwina reacted as if bastardy was a catching condition like scrofula or consumption and Kelso's infant would imperil the health and welfare of her own small brood. A week to the day after Peterkin put in his appearance, Andrew arrived with Moresby in a hired chaise.

Mother, child and baskets of belongings were brought downstairs and put into the chaise and, with Eunice watching tearfully from the doorway, were driven towards a foster home that Andrew had vetted, approved and paid for in advance.

Cameron Adams said, 'The home of Mrs Handyside, I presume.'

Clare answered, 'Yes, in Tobago Street in Caltoun.'

'Far from Purves's Land?'

'Too far for my liking,' Clare said. 'In distance, however, I could walk there in a half-hour.'

'Since your child remained with the Handyside woman for the next ten months,' Cameron said, 'I take it that the foster house was not dirty or disreputable and that the child was not ill-treated there.'

'Oh, no, quite to the contrary,' Clare informed him. 'The cottage was in open land, with fields and gardens and trees

about it. And it was as clean as could be. I never had any fault to find with what Andrew Purves found for Peterkin. He was put to a good wet nurse too, until his weaning began.'

'Did you not give him suckle after those first days?'

'No. My milk was drawn, and he took from another breast.'

'You were, though, free to visit him?'

'Indeed, on two afternoons in each week,' Clare answered. 'Friday from one until six o'clock, and for some hours on Sunday afternoon.'

'Better, I suppose, than losing him completely.'

Cameron watched her in the candlelight but she gave him no sign of bitterness or resentment. She lifted her shoulders and sighed. 'I missed him sore at nights. But, aye, I was still his mother, and he knew me.'

Cameron said, 'What of his father? What of Frederick Striker? Was no word at all of his whereabouts forthcoming at this period?'

'No, nobody knew where he had gone to.'

'How did Mrs Bates survive; for cash, I mean?'

'I do not know,' said Clare. 'I'm sure, though, that she did not have correspondence with Frederick. He did not know that he had become a father.'

'Did Mrs Bates visit the child at Handyside's?'

'Yes, once or twice each week.'

'When you were present?'

'No, at other times.'

'Do you think that Eunice Bates would have liked the child for herself?' Cameron asked.

'She was attentive to him, loving even, but she had no proper position to offer me and she could not take Peterkin from me. Mr Andrew would not have allowed it.'

'In case somebody – folk in general, Edwina Purves in particular – suspected that he had fathered the babe?'

'*I do not think that was the reason.*'

'*Did he continue to consort with Eunice Bates?*'

'*I believe so.*'

'*So,*' Cameron Adams said, *drawing his greatcoat about his cold flanks, 'so – the child was being well taken care of at the cottage in Caltoun, you returned to your duties at Purves's Land, and Frederick Striker remained* in absentia?'

'*Yes.*'

'*How long did this situation pertain?*'

'*Until April's ending.*'

'*When Frederick returned to Glasgow?*'

'*Yes.*'

'*To marry you, Clare?*'

'*No. Not to marry me.*'

'*But were you not worth one thousand pounds Scots to him? That was a fair bridal price for a man like Striker to grab at, was it not?*'

'*He no longer seemed interested in me or in Andrew's money,*' Clare said.

'*Why?*'

'*He had better fish to be fried.*'

'*In that case why did he come back at all?*'

'*To see Peterkin.*'

'*Indeed?*'

'*To make sure that a child had been born and was living,*' Clare said. '*And to take Eunice away with him.*'

'*Ah!*' said Cameron Adams. '*To take her where?*'

'*To Ireland.*'

'*For what purpose?*'

'*To use as bait,*' said Clare.

Eunice would not have been flattered to learn that in a winter spent in exile Frederick missed her more than he missed his little Scottish mistress. He had not forgotten Clare Kelso – far from it – but her pregnancy had imposed upon him certain obligations which, having little to do with the gaining of *real* money, Frederick preferred to avoid both in thought and in deed. He had not intended to stay away from Glasgow for so long but the pleasure of travel somehow caught up with him. What had begun as a flight from the vengeance of Lord Drumfin soon became an end in itself, an end that led with surprising alacrity to the possibility of new beginnings.

Armed with enough hard cash to substantiate his claim to be a wealthy merchant, Frederick easily found access to Liverpool's rough-and-tumble society and, with equal ease, to the gaming clubs and coffee-houses in which London manners were imitated. He was careful to steer clear of harbour taverns where he might by ill chance run into Brock Harding's sea-captain brother. Salt had been good to Frederick, no doubt of that. None of his other ventures had ever paid quite so handsomely in such a short space of time. With reluctance Frederick put prudence on the scale against profitability and, without fixing himself to a final decision, elected to sit snug as a bug in Liverpool for a month or two in hope that the wind would blow Thomas Gabriel Geary, Irish landowner and counsellor-at-law, back his way again.

On the surface, Thomas Gabriel Geary was as dry and grim a stick as one would meet at any ecclesiastical gathering. It wasn't, however, Protestant faith that brought the gentleman off his estates near Dublin two or three times a year but a love of gambling and women. In summer Geary would head for London like a bee to pollen, but in spring a landfall at Liverpool was enough to satisfy his appetite for travel and dissipation.

Gabriel Geary did not look in the least like a rake. He was thin, upright, stern, even mournful in countenance.

Frederick had never once seen Geary smile, not even when he cleared the board at Hazard or triumphed with one of the svelte young wives at the so-called Nuns' Club in Sydenham Street. It was not Gabriel's sparkling personality that attracted Frederick. What spurred him to cultivate the Irish landowner was mention of a daughter, an only child, who, now that she was of age, would soon be brought forth to shine upon the world in the hope of finding a husband more reputable and upright than her father.

In mid-summer of the previous year Frederick had at long last got to meet *la belle Irlandaise*. She was then a child of fifteen, with a figure like a Grecian nymph, a Dublin education, and the key to an estate of £1,000 a year plus above £20,000 in ready money. Marianne was apparently without thorn. Frederick was touched by her trust in him, a stranger, and just a mite puzzled by her father's willingness to allow him to play suitor and companion to such a jewel. There was, of course, an Aunt Florence in attendance, a formidable woman, sister to Gabriel's deceased wife.

Frederick was far too downy a bird to go hard at little Marianne. He kept his passion to a flicker, carved her name on a tree, requested a lock of her hair, wrote her tender notes. On the whole, he impressed himself so thoroughly upon her in the course of a fortnight that the child had no eyes for any of the other gallants that waved in her direction.

Gabriel Geary doted on the girl. He had grown accustomed to spoiling her. When, out of earshot of the formidable Aunt, she confessed to father that she was irrevocably drawn to Mr Frederick Striker, the grim and ageing Gabriel was put at once into a quandary, heart and habit set to wrestle with head. What swayed Geary to foster the *possibility* of a nuptial agreement between Mr Striker and his daughter was Mr Striker's apparent reformation and the splash of money he made at Eastertime.

To Frederick's disappointment, that Easter Marianne had been left behind in Dublin but he quickly realised that this was a ploy on Geary's part to determine not only Frederick's seriousness of purpose but also his worth.

For a fortnight Frederick steered clear of the Nuns' Club, though he did not eschew the gaming tables where, on most evenings, he accompanied the solemn Mr Geary to assist him in throwing good money after bad. He breakfasted with Gabriel, took dinner with him, walked upon the quays and rode out through the picturesque countryside in the fine weather that blessed the season. He spoke of his admiration for Marianne, of his 'concern' for her. He made known his awareness of her youth and delicate sensibilities, hinted that he had entirely given up 'impure' pleasures. And, in due course, he happened to mention his handsome widowed sister, Eunice, who kept house for him in Scotland.

On the very last evening of Gabriel Geary's holiday, after an excellent run at the tables, a good supper and several bottles of claret, the Irish gentleman put forward the invitation that Frederick had anxiously awaited.

'Come to Dublin, Frederick. Come to Kildrennan and stay awhile with us.'

'How generous, Gabriel. I confess that I will be glad to have an opportunity to consort with your charming daughter in her natural habitat. What month will suit?'

'June, sir,' said Gabriel Geary. 'And bring your sister. If she's willing.'

'I'm sure she will be,' Frederick said.

'Go where?' said Eunice.

'To Ireland. To Kildrennan, near Dublin.'

'For what purpose, Frederick?'

'To visit a friend of mine.'

'I do not want to go to Ireland,' said Eunice.

'But you must, Eunice.'

'Why must I?'

'Because I have made a promise.'

'To whom?'

'My friend, Mr Gabriel Geary.'

'And to his wife?'

'He has no wife. He is a gentleman upon whom much tragedy has been visited.'

'In addition, do you mean, to meeting with you?' said Eunice.

Frederick had arrived in a hired fly. He had appeared, totally unannounced, out of soft late-April darkness. Eunice had been newly in bed and was too sleepy to be attentive to sounds on the road outside. The first she had known of her brother's return had been the scratch of his key in the latch and the familiar, dreaded voice calling out her name. Her first inclination had been to throw herself out of the bed and to escape via the casement into the fields. As she heard him bounding upstairs, her heart beat faster and faster and there was a terror in her of what he would say when he saw her, of what news had reached out to that unknown place where he had hidden himself throughout winter and spring.

An hour, a half-hour earlier and he would have found

her with Andrew, and it was that realisation that caused her such fear and, in smaller measure, a habitual pang of guilt.

She did not rise, did not panic. She lifted herself on the pillow, as if she had been deep, dead asleep, and prepared herself for whatever Frederick might bring with him when he burst exuberantly into the room.

At first it had been all Darlings and Dearests and a torrent of regrets that he had not found time to write to her, a thousand expressions of delight at seeing her so well and still so beautiful. She had allowed him to hug her, kiss her, and had responded with just enough control to quell his suspicions that she had been anything other than faithful to his wishes and loyal to his commands.

Frederick seated himself on the bed and endeavoured to put an arm round her. Cajolingly, he said, 'Gabriel is a very pleasant gentleman, Eunice, mature and sensible.'

'And rich?'

'Comfortably off,' said Frederick. 'A counsellor-at-law with estates worth two or three thousand pounds a year.'

'And a family?'

'A daughter.'

Eunice said, 'Will we have to murder her too?'

Frederick swung his feet to the floor. 'Eunice, in God's name, what are you saying?'

Eunice bit her lip and drew away from him. She folded her knees beneath the sheets and linked her arms about them, unintentionally adopting one of Frederick's favourite poses.

She said quietly, 'Have you not made a promise to someone else, Frederick?'

'What? Who?'

'To Clare.'

'Devil take it!' Frederick cried and raised his hands

upward like a priest. 'In my excitement at seeing you, dearest, I had quite forgotten about poor Clare. How is she? Has she been delivered?'

'Yes. You have a son, Frederick.'

The information stopped him, even him. It dammed his rush of enthusiasm for the latest profitable escapade. He frowned, not in annoyance but in bewilderment, as if news of fatherhood had been wholly unexpected. 'A son, d'you say? Well, that is something extraordinary, is it not?'

'Considering that you left her in her seventh month, Frederick,' said Eunice, 'it is not in the least extraordinary.'

'Is she well, is the child well?'

'Both thriving.'

Frederick smiled, then laughed. 'I say – a son!'

Eunice said, 'A bastard.'

'Oh, that can be easily remedied.' Frederick chuckled, rolled round on to the bed and kissed his sister before she could pull away. 'I will give her my name as soon as possible.'

Eunice knew him too well. She was not taken in.

Frederick stroked her cheek with his fingertips. 'Is that what has you pouting, dearest? The fact that I have not fulfilled my obligation to the little servant girl? I take it that she has been taken care of by Andrew Purves, as I suggested?'

'Yes, we have all three been taken care of by Mr Purves.'

'All three? You too?'

'You did not leave me enough money. Mr Purves was kind enough to make an advance against your account to keep me in bread and fuel.'

'I see, I see. Well – that's fine,' said Frederick. 'For a moment I misunderstood. I thought you meant that he—'

Eunice interrupted. 'The child has been fostered. Put out to a good woman in the Caltoun district.'

'Do you visit?'

'Of course.'

'Is he like me? Is he a darling? Yes, we must visit together.'

'Perhaps you would do well to call upon Clare first,' said Eunice. 'Particularly if you intend to arrange a marriage with her.'

'Yes, yes,' said Frederick. 'That must be done, done with all haste. Before we leave for Ireland.'

'We?' said Eunice.

'You and I,' said Frederick. 'I should have realised that you would be concerned about the servant girl. It's your kind nature, Eunice. Why, did you suppose that I would leave her or my child without adequate provision for the future?'

'I take it, Frederick, that you do intend to leave them here in Glasgow.'

'Such a long journey would not be good for an infant,' Frederick said. 'Besides, I do not know that Clare would wish to be separated from him. By the by, what's his name?'

'Peterkin.'

Frederick frowned again. 'Odd, damned odd sort of name. Have I not heard it before somewhere?'

'Perhaps you have,' said Eunice. 'So, you will marry Clare, and then go?'

'A promise is a promise,' said Frederick. 'Besides, Gabriel Geary has no kinfolk and no connections in Scotland. It will be perfectly safe, I assure you.'

'Will it?' said Eunice. 'Do they not hang you for murder in Ireland?'

'What's this talk of murder, Eunice? How morbid you are sometimes,' said Frederick. 'Very well, I will let you in to my secret. I have a bride awaiting me in Kildrennan. Gabriel Geary's daughter, head over heels in love with me and willing, if I read the signs, to become my wife at first asking.'

'Why do you need me then?' Eunice said.

'To support my cause,' said Frederick. 'Geary's no fool, Eunice. He is doubtful of my integrity. I need you to charm him, convince him that we Strikers are—'

Eunice could hold her tongue no longer. 'Do I understand that you intend to marry Clare Kelso here and then abscond immediately to another marriage in Ireland?'

'Why not?' said Frederick. 'I will clear this house, take the five hundred pounds that Andrew Purves is willing to pay to give Kelso's child a name, then we – you and I – will be off, to be heard of no more in this godforsaken country.'

'*This* is your plan?'

'Indeed it is, Eunice. This time it cannot fail.'

'A bigamous marriage?'

'Better than no marriage at all,' said Frederick.

'And will you simply give up your child?'

'There will be other children, Eunice. Mine and – perhaps – yours.'

'How long have you known this girl, this Geary?'

'Marianne? About a year?'

'I see,' said Eunice.

'Do you also see the advantages?'

'Oh, yes, Frederick. The "advantages" are all too obvious.'

'What do you say, then? Shall we fold our tents, Eunice, seek peace and sanctuary in a new land?'

'For the last time?'

'Absolutely the very last time. Now, what do you say?'

'Let me sleep on it,' Eunice answered, to appease him and give herself time to think.

'None of this plotting could have been known to you at the time, Clare?' Cameron Adams said. *'When did you learn of it and from whom?'*

'From Eunice,' Clare said. *'Later.'*

'How much later? In what month?'

'I do not recall.'

'I believe that you do recall. I believe you recall everything that happened and the sequence in which it fell. Why will you not be frank with me, Clare? What are you hiding?'

'I am hiding nothing, sir.'

Cameron Adams said, *'Striker did not marry you?'*

'No, he did not.'

'Did he call upon you, see you?'

'Yes.'

'But he did not propose to marry you?'

'He asked me to wait.'

'Again?' said Cameron. *'What answer did you give him?'*

'I said that I would be pleased to wait.'

'Are you a fool, Clare? Is that what you would have us all believe?' Cameron said, testily. *'No, you're not a fool. Even on our short acquaintance I know that you have brains in your head. Why did you not press Striker to fulfil his promise? Did you not think of your child and its future?'*

'I was no longer sure that I wanted to marry Frederick.'

'Indeed?' Cameron exclaimed. *'And when did this sea-change in your affections occur?'*

'About that time.'

'The early summer of last year?'

The girl nodded. Cameron peered at her. Her manner had changed. It was not fatigue but slyness that caused her head to *droop, her gaze to slip away from his. He hesitated, then put it to her with brutal candour. 'You did not kill Peterkin: Frederick Striker did.'*

'No, it was an accident.'

'I cannot lay that nonsense before a jury,' *Cameron got to his feet and strode about the table, three or four paces back and forth.* 'Do you want to hang, Clare Kelso? Do you feel that you deserve to die?'

'No, Mr Adams.'

'Do you feel that you have nothing to live for now that your son is dead? Is that it?' *he said, quite angrily.*

'I do have something to live for.'

'Why then will you not tell me the whole truth?'

'I have told you what I can.'

She had pulled up the blanket to cover her and keep her warm. It was the cold, dead heart of the night now. The town lay silent as a graveyard outside the Tolbooth's walls. The candles were down to fretted stumps and, impatiently, Cameron blew two of them out to preserve the wicks that remained and, in the gathered gloom, seated himself upon the stool again.

'Did Striker call to visit the child?'

'No, not on that occasion.'

'Are you certain, Clare?'

'Mrs Handyside would have told me if he had been there.'

Cameron said, 'He did, however, call upon you?'

'I told you that he did.'

'Did you not urge him to call with you to see Peterkin?'

'I did. But he was reluctant.'

'Why was he reluctant.'

'He had very little time.'

'God! No time to see his son!' *Cameron exclaimed.* 'What did he do with his precious time then?'

'He took me to the Linden Tree.'

Cameron's head slumped, his shoulders sagged. He let out a groan. 'How often?'

'Three times.'

'And he had – he made –'

Clare nodded.

'Perhaps you are a fool, Clare Kelso.' Cameron sighed. 'What if he had left you pregnant for a second time?'

She said nothing, merely shrugged. But she was watching him again, and again he had that sense that he had snatched at the truth but had somehow missed it, that it had gone slithering away from him like a ball of mercury pulverised into a hundred particles.

Cameron said, 'Where is Striker now? Is he hiding in Ireland.'

'I do not know where he is.'

'How can you be sure that he did not marry the Irish heiress?'

'I am sure that he did not.'

Cameron said, 'Eunice Bates did not accompany him to Ireland last summer, I take it?'

'No, Frederick went alone.'

'To woo this other girl?'

Clare raised her shoulders, shook her head.

'So,' Cameron Adams said, 'Striker came, then left again, and his sister did not accompany him. I presume there was, by this time, a scarcity of money?'

'Yes.'

'Striker gave you nothing?'

'A few pounds – and some French lace.'

'How long did Frederick remain in Glasgow?'

'Two weeks,' said Clare. 'Twelve days, to be exact.'

'And then went where – to Ireland?'

'I cannot be sure where he went.'

'*Was he angry at Eunice?*'

'*Very angry.*'

'*Did Purves take care of her needs?*'

'*He did.*'

'*Had he made her his mistress? Were they lovers?*'

'*I do not think so, no.*'

'*That,*' *said Cameron,* '*is a most difficult thing to accept.*'

'*Eunice did not want a lover. She wanted a husband.*'

Cameron considered Clare's statement carefully, then said, '*How much of this matter did you impart to Mr Walcott or to Mr McKay?*'

'*Not much of it,*' *Clare admitted.*

'*In that case, why have you told me?*'

'*Because I do not want to hang,*' *said Clare.*

The sea voyage from Liverpool to Dublin in June was pleasant enough but the welcome that he received at Kildrennan was less warm than the weather.

To say that Frederick was impressed by Kildrennan would have been to under-state the effect it had upon him. He had not depicted in his mind's eye Gabriel Geary's policies as so extensive or so well-tended. Even the ride down the long drive that led out of mature woodlands towards the headland upon which Kildrennan House stood in solitary splendour thrilled and quickened Frederick's blood. He had been shut away in poor lodgings in Liverpool for weeks, eking out the last of the readies and supplemented, where possible, by billiards for cash or judicious betting at cards.

If Kildrennan was far better than he had supposed it would be – £2,000 in income was conservative – then Gabriel Geary's annoyance at the lack of 'family' was far worse. Oh, Frederick was given a spacious bedroom overlooking the sea, was fed like a fighting cock, plied with whisky, was taken to the races at Blackrock, to a mid-summer ball at Castle McGonigle, but none of that show of Irish hospitality could quite disguise Geary's disappointment that Frederick's good-looking sister had stayed at home. Marianne too, more beautiful than ever now that she was out of bud and into bloom, had gone cool on him and would not permit him to catch her all alone, out of sight of the Aunt or a grizzled old nurse.

Even the mid-summer assembly at McGonigle Castle, as wild and drunken a spree as Frederick had ever attended, cast up no opportunity for Frederick to ply his trade as a seducer. He had not the breath left after endless jigs and reels to lure Marianne away from the company of the roguish young men who surrounded her and did what he could not, made her laugh. From the Aunt he learned that there were other suitors, younger than he, well-connected, and from Irish families. Frederick could not make up his mind whether the Aunt was for him or against and when he walked out around the estate, alone, his confusion curdled readily into melancholy.

On the eighth day of his stay he was informed by Gabriel Geary that he, Gabriel, was unfortunately obliged to leave for business in Cork and would ship directly from there to England for a summer in London and Tunbridge Wells. The hint was too broad for Frederick to ignore. He was being brushed off, sent packing.

That early evening Frederick gathered his resources, tippled himself back into arrogance and broached the subject of marriage to Marianne.

Discussion was short and sharp. Mr Gabriel Geary had no objection to Mr Frederick Striker throwing his hat into the ring for his daughter's hand but he, Mr Striker, must

give proof of his worthiness and his financial stability
before he, Mr Geary, would consider him a serious con-
tender.

Were there other 'serious contenders'?

Several.

Would Mr Geary allow him grace – say three months –
to prove himself and to make himself acceptable not only to
Mr Geary but to Marianne?

Mr Geary would.

Encouraged by this small progress, Frederick left Kildrennan the following morning to return to Liverpool to
rake up a salt cargo.

Back in Kildrennan Gabriel Geary put pen to paper and
wrote a letter of enquiry regarding Mr Striker to the only
man in Scotland with whom he had nodding acquaintance,
a certain Lord Drumfin.

Peterkin made all the difference to Clare's outlook on life.
At first the distance between Saltmarket Lane and Tobago
Street had seemed like a gigantic abyss that separated her
from her child. As summer gathered around Glasgow,
however, and the gardens came into full flower, Clare
watched her son put on weight and become attentive to
the world about him with a feeling of satisfaction, almost of
contentment. She quickly lost her resentment of Mrs
Handyside, even of the wet nurse, Sally, who had lost
her own third bairn at birth but was loving towards the
surrogate and glad of the modest sum that Mr Andrew
paid for her services.

There were two other fosterlings in Mrs Handyside's
care, a girl and a boy, each about two years old. She had
reared them with such devotion and care that they were
sturdy and lively as any child anywhere in the city, a fine

advertisement for how Peterkin would grow and develop, even without his mother's constant care.

Clare did not neglect her duties to the Purves's children. If anything, she was more attentive to them than ever, lavishing on Margaret and Dorothea the feeling of tenderness that having Peterkin had released in her. Dorothea was at an age to be curious about Clare's infant and, with Andrew's permission but without Edwina's knowledge, was taken out to Caltoun one fine August afternoon to see the baby for herself. The memory of that day, above any other, Clare clung to when winter came.

The air was hot and still, redolent of larkspur and lupins and the honey-sweet scents of alyssum and stock. Mrs Handyside had made lemonade spiced with mint. She brought the jug out to the garden where the children played under the shade of the wall. Peterkin, in a cool dress and shady bonnet, lay against Clare's knees where she sat upon the grass on a spread blanket. He gurgled and goo-ed up at her and reached for the frill of fine French lace, Frederick's gift, that she had stitched to the bodice of her cotton frock. Dorothea had been fascinated by the little pink baby and had been permitted to hold him, like a doll, until he cried to be put down again. She had soon been diverted by the energy of the other fosterlings, however, and had been willingly dragged off by them to look for earthworms in the borders and to steal succulent pods from the pea-rails when Mrs Handyside wasn't looking. And then, after they had been summoned to drink cups of lemonade, all three children and Peterkin fell asleep on the plaid, shaded by the awning of sail-canvas that Mrs Handyside had put up to protect them from the hot, hazy sun. For an hour Clare was there among them, Peterkin cradled in her lap, the older children sprawled against her too, their little grubby hands upon her skirts, cheeks against her knees, in the heavy-scented cottage garden remote from the reek and bustle of the August town.

In all of her time with Frederick, Clare had not felt as she felt then, at peace. Vanity had led her into his arms, into the bed in the Linden Tree. She had supposed herself to be irresistible, her beauty as binding upon him as a spell. All of that had been but childish fantasy. He had wanted only pleasure from her, not to seek in her and with her what *she* desired. She did not have to put Frederick from her thoughts. It occurred without will or effort. He was gone from Glasgow, gone from her mind too.

All that concerned her was what would happen when Frederick returned to claim her and to claim Peterkin as his own.

'When did he come?' said Cameron Adams.

'In October.'

'To marry you? To take you away with him?'

'No,' Clare answered. 'I would not have gone with him even if he had asked it.'

'Did you not love him?'

'I did not want him to have an influence on Peterkin.'

'Were you afraid of Frederick Striker?'

Clare shook her head. 'Only of what he might do to Peterkin.'

'Why would he want to harm the child?'

'Frederick harmed everyone.'

'Surely the child posed no threat to him,' Cameron said, 'unless as an impediment to an aristocratic marriage? Was that the reason?'

'Reason?'

'Why Frederick gave you the arsenic?'

'I did not say that Frederick gave me the arsenic.'

'He did, though, did he not?' Cameron said.

'No. Frederick had nothing to do with it. He cared for Peterkin.'

'From what you have told me, Striker did not even clap eyes on his child.'

'He did, yes, he did.'

'Oh? When? In October?'

'Yes,' Clare said, too quickly.

'So he called at Tobago Street?' Cameron said.

'Yes.'

'With you?'

'Yes – no, alone.'

'That does not tally with Mrs Handyside's testimony. Perhaps, she is lying – though I cannot think what benefit it would be to the woman to lie. Can you?'

'I . . . I'm mistaken,' Clare said. 'I fetched Peterkin from the cottage. I took him into Glasgow to meet Frederick.'

'Now this is new,' said Cameron.

'It had escaped my mind.'

'What other matters have escaped your mind, Clare?'

Clare got to her feet, the blanket draped over her shoulders. Quietly she said, 'I would like you to go now, Mr Adams.'

'Why?'

'Because it is very late. I am weary for sleep,' Clare said. 'Besides, I have told you all that I can.'

'Not all that you can, Clare: all that you will.'

'Please leave me.'

In the dim light of the single candle flame she looked more beautiful than ever. The strain of weeks in prison had paled her cheeks and thinned her and when he reached for her hand he found it weightless as paper. He gripped her fingers gently but would not let her go, would not let her turn away from him.

'Clare, what happened in October?'
'I cannot tell you that.'
'Why not?'
She seemed to lean into him. For an instant Cameron was tempted to put an arm about her waist, to sit her on his knee like a child. He could not be sure but he thought that for the first time tears glistened in her eyes.
'Why not?' he said again.
'Ask Eunice Bates,' said Clare.

Great gales had all but stripped the trees and chill rains lashed the stubble fields and dunned the turnpikes into seas of mud, driving autumn hard away with their ferocity. At Eunice's request Clare had brought Peterkin to visit her on several Sundays in the harvest month and, for an hour or two, the girl and the woman had entertained themselves by playing with the child and spoiling him.

They would put his 'Grahamston cradle', a wicker wash basket, by the side of the pianoforte and together would tap out simple tunes on the keys while Peterkin, wriggling and gurgling, would press his little palm against the instrument's panel to feel the vibrations. With that lack of inhibition which small children often induce in stiff-backed folk, Eunice would warble songs in her flat, clacking voice, while Clare held the baby in her arms and danced him up and down in time to the beat.

'He'll be a prodigy, you'll see, a musical master at the age of ten. He'll be ringing bells before he has a beard,' Eunice would shout then, taking one hand from the keyboard, would wiggle a finger into Peterkin's middle and coo, 'Wonee, wonee, wonee, wonee, den?'

Frederick was seldom a subject of conversation. Clare had the distinct impression that Eunice would be relieved if her brother never showed his face in Glasgow again. There had been not so much as the scrape of a pen from him since his departure, not to Clare, to Eunice or even to Andrew. Once, and only once, Eunice offered the theory that Frederick had slunk back to Liverpool to find comfort with his own kind.

'Women, do you mean?' Clare had asked.

'Oh, yes, I expect so.' Eunice had tactfully changed the subject in case it was painful to Clare which, of course, it was not.

Eunice, like Clare, was content with her life in those summer and autumn days. She had her house to keep, marketing to do, Peterkin to visit, Andrew and Clare to call upon her. Andrew met the cost of the house now and provided a modest sum, which was all that Eunice required, to keep her in food and fuel. He even talked of hiring a servant to keep her company for he did not care to think of Eunice being alone in the villa in the long winter nights.

It rained all day on that October Saturday. Sheets of rain blown by a rising wind rattled grapeshot on the villa's windows and Eunice, after checking her cupboards, elected to stay indoors. She did not expect Andrew that evening. He had indicated that he had a duty to attend a gala supper at the Tontine in aid of a Provost's charity. Eunice consoled herself with the thought that, if the wind dropped and the rain ceased, she would have Clare's company, and Peterkin's, come Sunday.

She lighted a fire, the first of the winter, in her bedroom, and lay by its glow, listening to the battering of the storm, snug and comfortable yet disappointed that no change in the weather would mean no nephew to amuse and adore tomorrow.

The day passed slowly but not unpleasantly. It was
around half past eight o'clock in the evening when Eunice
heard a sound at the kitchen door. She had cooked and
eaten a large breakfast, had neglected dinner and was in
process of bathing a chop in fine flour to make supper. The
sound distracted her. It was still raining but the wind had
reduced its force and backed westerly. The loudest noise
now came from the torrent of water that gushed from the
eaves. Eunice had no opportunity to speculate on who
might be calling upon her at this hour. She had barely
slipped the chop into the pan of hot pork fat and wiped her
hands on her apron when the wooden door broke inwards
and leaves, twigs and globules of rain billowed in upon her.
From the midst of the whirl of debris a man stepped over
the threshold, a man with a bullnosed mallet raised in one
fist.

Eunice screamed. She might have turned and fled
through the house and been out of the front door into
the rain if the man had been a split second slower. She had
seen him before: the horse man. He strode and stretched
and grasped her by the throat before Eunice could even
think to react. He pulled her down, bending her from the
waist as if he intended to behead her. She waited for the
blow. It did not come. Instead she was dragged forward to
the door and with her head tucked into her belly by the
pressure of the man's hand, she saw him kick the door shut
and brace it with the hammer. He pulled her back towards
the table, lifted her, and crushed her, face down, against
the table's edge.

'Where is he? Where's Striker?'

Flour dusted the table top and tickled Eunice's nostrils.
She sneezed, sneezed again. The man pressed hard upon
the nape of her neck.

'I want Striker,' he said, his mouth to her ear.

She could smell drink on his breath, the sodden cloth of his peajacket, the stench of moleskin breeks black with rain.

The hand on her neck was large enough to encompass the back of her head. She felt so much pressure on the bones of her skull that she feared that he might crush them even without a weapon.

'He – hasn't – been here for months. I – don't know where he's to be – found.'

'Oh, I know where he's been,' the man said. 'He's been squealin' to the excisemen. My brother's in jail because of bloody Frederick Striker.'

'What?'

'You're the sister, ain't you?'

'I am, but I don't know where—' Eunice struggled ineffectually. Out of one eye she could see his hairy cheek, his lips and nostrils. 'Tell me what Frederick's done.'

'He squealed to save his own bloody neck.'

'But – but – where?'

He placed his free hand on her thigh. She felt him stiffen against her and at that moment realised what had come into his mind.

'Don't play the idiot wi' me,' the man told her. 'You know fine well what your precious brother's been up to.'

'Salt?'

'Aye, salt. A fortune in salt.'

'Paying no tax?'

'All sailin' smooth as a summer sea,' the man told her, pressing not with his hand but with his body, rubbing himself against her. 'But he had to go an' get himself tangled wi' Drumfin. When the excisemen came, with armed officers, we had no choice but to cut an' run.

We lost the ship an' the cargo. They got Jericho, my brother. They took him away in irons.'

'Won't they come for you too?'

'Never saw me. Jericho won't squeal, not him.' He slackened his hold on her neck and let her ease herself up a little. 'But I've got a message for your brother. An' since he ain't here to collect it, I reckon you'll have to collect it instead.'

'I know nothing of all this,' Eunice said. 'You must believe me.'

'Oh, I believe you,' the man said. 'But believin' ain't goin' to make no difference.'

Eunice managed to turn her hip against the table's edge but he had trapped her with thighs and forearms. The violence excited him. His unshaven cheeks were flushed and his full red leathery lips were pushed out. He might have done what he willed with her, and taken his time about it, but he was not that sort of man. He wasn't cunning or patient; not like Frederick.

Eunice shuddered but did not resist when he began to knead her breasts. He was too large, too strong to struggle against. She let him do what he willed, waiting for the instant when his hands would be busy with her skirts, when he would edge her backwards across the table.

From the tops of her eyes she could see the frying pan's smoke and could smell now a corporeal odour of burned pork fat. Behind her and a little to her left was the thin-bladed knife she had used to trim rind from the chop, its narrow handle bound with twine and plastered with white flour.

Deliberately Eunice splayed her knees to make it easier for him. She heard him grunt when his hands found bare flesh. She stretched, tipping up her legs and when he bent his head to nuzzle her lips, she tickled the knife into her fingers, clasped it, swung it and stabbed.

If his father had not been half-seas over then Andrew would not have dared slip out of the supper room on the Tontine's second floor. Meat had been consumed, speeches made, plates put round to collect for the Provost's charity, glasses raised in toasts to various pompous members of the Trades' Hall faction by various pompous members of the Merchant's House and raised again in a round of reply before really serious drinking got underway.

The revel would go on far into the night. There would be empty pews aplenty in the kirks tomorrow morning and some damned whey-faced penitents nodding off during the afternoon sermons. Andrew had no head for drink, no taste for unbidden carousal. He was bored by it and wished now that he had turned down the invitation. To assuage his guilt – for he already knew what he was going to do – he made a ridiculously generous contribution to the Provost's Fund then sat tight, waiting his chance to slip away unobserved. Peter-Pierre was tucked below in the servants' hall. He would see to it that the old master was stuffed into a chair and carried home. Nobody would be particularly surprised that Andrew Purves, sober, sour and arrogant puss that he was, had slunk off. An hour in Eunice's company was worth the minor risks involved, risks which added spice to his truancy.

There were no lights in the windows at the front of the villa but Andrew was not deterred. He knew that Eunice would welcome him, whatever the hour. He approached the door, stood in the lee of the house, removed his dripping cloak and hat, then reached out to knock upon the door. He found it was unlatched. It swung open before him. Puzzled, he let himself into the hall.

An unpleasant smell of burned fat greeted him. He felt a certain apprehension about Eunice's safety. Down the passage-way he could make out a glimmer of candlelight and when he quietly called out her name, she answered almost as if she had been expecting him: 'Andrew, I am here.'

The kitchen was newly swept and sprinkled and, apart from the lingering odour of charred pork, sweet. The table top looked as if it had been recently scrubbed. Eunice was seated on one of the rush chairs, a plate and an empty gin glass by her hand. Stuck into the table was a knife. She wore a plain, spotless linen nightdress with a frilled collar, sleeves buttoned at the cuffs. Her hair was gathered behind her in a loose fall, fastened by a pearl-silk ribbon.

'Andrew, I hoped you would come.'

'It's so late,' he said. 'I escaped from – what happened to the door, Eunice?'

'A man came looking for Frederick. He would not be denied entry.'

'Eunice, are you—?'

'I fended him off.' She nodded at the knife. 'With that.'

'You didn't kill him?'

'No.'

Andrew draped his cloak upon the chair-back and set his hat upon the seat. Frowning, he came to her and put his hand upon her shoulder. She covered it at once with her hand, arm folded over her breasts. It was the first time that he had seen her unclad. He was startled by the fullness of her figure, the hint of flesh through linen. Her skin was warm, her hand warm, her normally pale complexion rouged with some inner fire.

With a shrug she said, 'I drew blood. I wounded him. Oh, not badly, but enough to send him packing. He will think twice before he bothers me again.'

'Eunice,' Andrew said, 'this will have to end.'

'I know.'

'I cannot see you persecuted for Frederick's misdeeds.'

'Yes, he will have to be dealt with,' Eunice said. 'He'll have to be stopped.'

'If we knew where he was,' said Andrew, 'I would write to him, tell him, man to man, what must be done.'

'No, dearest,' Eunice said. 'Leave it to me. He's my brother, after all.'

Her hand tightened on his. She swivelled in the chair to stare up at him and then, gently, drew him down until his arms were about her body and her cheek rested against his.

'Andrew,' she whispered, 'take me to bed.'

'Now?'

'Now,' she told him. 'Now, now, without delay.'

Obediently he lifted her into his arms and, without once faltering, carried her upstairs.

'What question,' said Cameron Adams, 'must I ask Mrs Bates? Will it shed light on the events of the thirtieth December?'

Clare shook her head.

Impatiently Cameron Adams said, 'Do you mean that you do not know, Clare, or that you will not tell me?'

Again she shook her head. She had told him too much already. She should not have been coaxed by his kindnesses. She should have kept her secrets all to herself, in silence.

He said, 'Are you telling me that you did not see or hear from Frederick Striker after October?'

'I am.'

'In October, what occurred?'

'I saw him only once, and only for a half-hour.'

'Where did the meeting take place?'

'At his villa in Grahamston.'

'Did he summon you there by note or letter?'

'No,' Clare said. 'He sent a messenger to tell me.'

'Did you ask permission to go?' said Cameron.

'I made an excuse, went out on an errand.' Clare too lost patience. 'Why do you ask me such trivial things? Does it matter how I heard that he was home?'

'It may,' Cameron said. 'Nothing can be considered trivial in this case.'

'You've read my account, sir. That is precisely what happened. I purchased a quantity of sulphur in a packet from the Apothecaries' Hall to administer to Peterkin for the cure of an itching rash about his little forehead. I was given, by accident, by mistake, another substance.'

'Arsenic.'

'I do not deny that I administered the substance. But I did not know what it was. I thought it was a remedy, a safe remedy. I had used sulphur before. On William when he had worms and on Dorothea who had a tormenting itch at the time of her teething.'

'Why did you not keep a quantity of sulphur in the nursery cupboard in Purves's Land?'

'I did. But I purchased a separate little packet for Peterkin, to make sure that it was fresh.'

'And gave it to him after your walk on the afternoon of the last day of December?'

'Yes,' Clare said. 'Yes.'

'Why does nobody, neither the man nor the boy, remember you purchasing sulphur in that week?'

'I cannot say.'

'Why, also,' said Cameron, 'does Mrs Handyside not recall the administering of the medicine?'

'She was out when I returned from my walk. She had taken the other children somewhere. I do not know where.'

'You gave Peterkin the tip of a spoonful, in water?'

'I have stated that I did.'

'Arsenic does not dissolve as sulphur does.'

'I moistened the spoon, that was all, then gave him the water to sip.'

'Did Peterkin not reject it?'

'I rubbed it on his gums.'

'Forcefully?' said Cameron Adams.

'Gently. He was troubled by the itch. Mrs Handyside will tell you that he had scratched himself across the brows.'

'She has confirmed that much,' Cameron said. 'But she found no trace at all of cup or spoon.'

'I washed them clean and put them away.'

'Why?'

'Any tidy person would do the same, especially in another woman's house,' Clare told him.

'The packet of sulphur, however, has vanished,' Cameron said. 'One ounce of fresh sulphur powder in brown paper, with only the merest tip taken from it. What did you do with the powder, Clare?'

'I threw it away.'

'In your statement you said that you left it at Mrs Handyside's.'

'Perhaps I did. I cannot remember.'

'It was not found.'

'Then I lost it.'

'It was never yours, Clare, was it? Frederick gave the medicine to Peterkin and you knew nothing of it.'

'No.'

'*Frederick wasn't in – where – Liverpool? He was here in secret in Glasgow.*'

'*He was not,*' said Clare.

'*Why are you protecting him if you do not still love him?*'

'*I am not protecting him. He was not here. I've told you what happened,*' Clare said. '*When I left Peterkin he was well and sturdy. Near midnight that night the officers came to tell me that he was dead and that I had done for him. Do you think, do you truly think, that I could have deliberately killed my own son?*'

'*It is not what I think. It is what I can prove that matters now,*' Cameron said.

He got to his feet, buttoned his greatcoat and reached for his hat.

Clare said, '*Will you come again tomorrow, Mr Adams, with more questions?*'

'*I doubt it. I have a very great deal to do before the opening of the court.*'

'*In that case, I will thank you, sir, for supper and for listening to me,*' Clare said. '*Even if your efforts prove fruitless, I am grateful, Mr Adams.*'

'*My efforts will not prove fruitless.*'

'*Do you believe that I am innocent?*'

'*What I believe, Miss Kelso, is largely immaterial. There is one man in court who can, if he chooses, save you. But we do not know whether he is friend or foe.*'

'*Lord Drumfin?*'

'*The same.*'

'*What shall I wear to please him?*' Clare asked.

'*Deep mourning,*' the lawyer answered, then he shouted impatiently to the turnkey to come and let him out.

It was so still in the great vertical stone building that Clare could hear not only Mr Adam's footsteps echoing up from the stairs but even the murmur of voices as he was accosted by Hinchcliff outside the jailer's rooms. Hinchcliff, she thought, would scrounge for money, some tip or gratuity for the services that he had rendered that night. She could imagine him, though she had never seen him so, in dirty nightshift and tasseled cap, arguing unctuously by the light of a lantern while Billy, yawning, waited to unlock the door and gate.

She had light now, three candle stumps, one lit. She rose from her position on the bed and dug the stumps from the candelabra with a fork, hid them quickly beneath the straw mattress. She poked about among the pile of dishes and plates to see what else she could save before Hinchcliff or the turnkey clattered upstairs to rob the remains. How Hinchcliff would love to appropriate one of the handsome silver servers. He would not dare do so, however, for footmen from the Tontine would be round at the double, come daylight, to check the inventory and carry all away.

She poured the very last of the wine from the bottle, scooped the glass into the melted ice and drank the mixture thirstily. Just as she set the glass aside she noticed that Mr Adams had forgotten to take away the little wood and leather stool. She seated herself upon it for a moment and then, on impulse, got to her feet and pushed the table noisily towards the window. Using the stool as a step, she climbed up on to the table and hoisted herself the last few inches by fisting the window's iron bars. Balanced on toe-tip, she looked down into the Trongate.

A dog, black and silent as Cerberus, snuffled along the line of the market drain, his progress observed by two or three crouching cats, shadowy as wraiths. When the chain of the gate of the Tolbooth rattled the dog raised his head, sniffed, then slunk away without bark or bay into the lane that led to the churchyard.

Faint moonlight defined the highway, not enough to silver it but sufficient, just, to show her Cameron Adams when he emerged from the gate below the tower. He did not duck under the arches of the piazza but walked out into the middle of the street and, turning, looked up at the window, at Clare. He gave no sign of recognition, however, no signal of farewell. He simply stared at her for a minute and then, with an impatient toss of the head, turned away and headed for the Tontine Hotel to pass, restlessly, what remained of the short spring night.

BOOK TWO

9

King's Yellow

In spite of his late night Cameron was up early. He found a
barber and the services of a valet and appeared none the
worse for wear when, on the stroke of half past nine, he
joined McKay for breakfast in the Tontine's crowded
coffee-room.

McKay was not alone. Jonathan Brown had travelled on
the 'growler', an infamously slow overnight coach from
Edinburgh, and had arrived early at the Saracen's Head.
Without pausing to shake the dust from his garments,
Jonathan had hurried along Gallowgate to the Tontine to
join his colleagues in making final preparations for the
presentation of Kelso's case. He brought news, and views,
from Walcott, together with a sheaf of papers which
included a list of witnesses that the fat lawyer had drawn
up, a list that Cameron rejected out of hand.

Jonathan was of an age with Cameron but very lithe and
light and so fair that he seemed almost boyish, not at all
grave enough to be a dedicated Writer to the Signet, let
alone to serve as an agent in a criminal trial. While McKay
interrogated the male servant about the origin of the
Tontine's eggs, Jonathan quietly asked Cameron what
he had thought of their client.

'Is she not very lovely?' Jonathan said.

'Indeed, she is,' Cameron said, giving nothing away.

'Are you not impressed?'

'I am impressed by the fact that she is lying.'

'Do you think that she killed the child?' Jonathan raised his pale brows until they almost disappeared under the edge of his unpowdered wig.

'I think that she administered the poison,' Cameron said.

Having settled on what would be eaten, McKay caught the Edinburgh advocate's last statement and smugly wagged his finger. 'Did I not say so all along, sir?'

'I do not think, however,' Cameron went on, 'that Clare Kelso was aware that it *was* poison.'

'She loved the child,' said Jonathan.

'She did,' said Cameron.

'Pshaw!' McKay snorted. 'Perhaps she killed it in a frenzy of "love", then. Will you plead exclusively on the utterance of witnesses for exculpation?'

'No, I will not,' said Cameron.

'That's what Walcott intended to do,' said Jonathan.

'Walcott was not aware of all the facts.'

'The facts are plain as pikestaffs,' said McKay. 'The female remains infatuated with her seducer, this scoundrel Striker. At some point or other it came into her head that he would only marry her if she had no encumbrance – namely, a squalling brat – and she fixed so firmly on the idea that she decided to do for the child.'

'The letter,' said Cameron, 'denies that hypothesis, Mr McKay.'

'The devil it does!' McKay said. 'She declared herself full mad in love with him.'

'When?' Cameron said.

McKay opened his prim little mouth and closed it again. He was relieved when the arrival of breakfast delayed his need to reply. All three watched as two round trays were unloaded and dishes placed upon the table. It took several minutes for the meal to be served and McKay busied himself with buttering bread, salting fish stew and tucking his napkin neatly into his vest. He had just begun to eat when Cameron repeated his question.

Dabbing gravy from his lips, McKay answered testily, 'During the course of the affair.'

Cameron shook his head. 'Not so. Only at the *beginning* of the affair, sir.'

'What is your point, Cameron?' Jonathan said.

'My point is that she did not love Striker at the time of the child's death. She loved the child more than anything.'

'That may be true, but why then did Striker write as he did?' said Jonathan, stealing the question from McKay's lips.

'Letters without dates?' said Cameron.

'Liverpool, Dublin, Doncaster,' said McKay. 'Business took him to those places. If you suppose that he was not there, sir, then how do you explain his rapid and fulsome replies to letters of enquiry from Mr Walcott and also from the Solicitor General, Ordway?'

'But what does he say in those replies? Only that he was not in Glasgow at the time of the murder, that he left Clare Kelso in the care of his sister and her master, Andrew Purves, that it was always his intention to make provision for the child, and so forth,' said Cameron. 'Not one expression of regret, of horror at what happened. Not even of surprise.'

'You mean . . .' said McKay.

'He knew,' said Jonathan.

Cameron filled his mouth with soft brown bread and savoured the taste and texture of it after the ham had gone down.

'Do you mean, sir, that Frederick Striker murdered the

child?' said McKay. 'How could that be so if he was in another country, two hundred miles away from Glasgow at the least?'

'We have only Striker's word on that,' said Jonathan. 'He could have left a letter with some inn-keeper or amiable whore to put into the post.'

'While he was really in Glasgow,' McKay clapped a hand on the table. 'By God, Mr Cameron, that is ingenious. Is it then your intention to impeach Frederick Striker for this crime?'

'It's one thing to suspect that Striker duped Clare Kelso into administering poison to the child, quite another to prove that he did,' said Cameron. 'In fact, gentlemen, I do not believe that it is within our power to do so.'

'But if Striker was in Glasgow on the day of the murder somebody must have seen and recognised him,' said McKay.

'Somebody who has chosen to remain silent,' said Jonathan.

'Kelso?' said McKay. 'But why?'

'Out of fear, perhaps,' Jonathan suggested.

'Or love,' said McKay. 'Female infatuation has no bounds of reason that I've ever discovered.'

'There is nothing in Clare Kelso's declaration to hint that Striker tricked her into administering the arsenic,' Jonathan pointed out.

'There wouldn't be, not if she was intent on protecting him,' said McKay.

'At the cost of her own life?' Cameron said. 'No, gentlemen, whatever her other failings Clare Kelso is no fool. She has remained consistent throughout a whole series of interrogations. As you know only too well, Kelso's voluntary statements should be the prosecutor's trump cards, the means whereby he can expose her in falsehood through her ignorance of what other witnesses have said against her.'

'He will cast doubt upon her statements, yes,' McKay said.

'And so shall I,' said Cameron Adams.

'What then will be our line, Mr Adams?' said McKay.

'Striker.'

'Kelso will not support that defence,' McKay said.

'Then we must defend her in spite of herself,' said Cameron Adams. 'The complete absence of motive is much in our favour. Ordway will imply that she was carried away by an unreasoning passion for Frederick Striker. To make that argument convincing he will have to prove that Striker disliked the child or was unwilling to take on the financial responsibility for it and that Kelso was in desperate straits.'

'None of which can be borne out by the evidence,' said Jonathan. 'Striker never even saw his son, did he?'

'According to all statements, he did not,' said Cameron, 'though Clare Kelso claims that he visited the child, Peterkin, on one occasion in October.'

'The woman, Handyside, makes no mention of such a visit. I am certain she would have remembered it,' said Jonathan.

'If indeed Striker did see his son in late October then he did not call upon the child at Mrs Handyside's cottage,' said Cameron. 'Which means that somebody fetched the boy out. Somebody familiar enough to be unremarkable to the honest foster mother.'

'Clare Kelso,' said McKay.

'Or Eunice Bates,' said Cameron.

'Do you infer, sir, that Eunice Bates colluded with her

brother in the commission of the crime?' McKay said.

'I make no inference,' said Cameron. 'What remains the most puzzling aspect in all of this tangle is the complete absence of motive for murdering an innocent ten-month old child. There are no sane reasons to account for it. Striker had none, for the child was not a burden to him. Eunice Bates had none for, on Kelso's word, the sister was greatly attached to the bairn.'

'Which brings us back to Clare Kelso,' said Jonathan.

'Or another, unknown hand,' said Cameron.

Jonathan Brown and Angus McKay stared at the Edinburgh advocate in astonishment. 'Who?' they said in unison.

'That remains to be seen,' Cameron Adams said. 'Meanwhile, with your assistance, gentlemen, I must make myself known to the witnesses and see what they have to say for themselves.'

Mr McKay pushed away his plate, supped a mouthful of tea from his cup and, discarding his napkin, got at once to his feet. 'Pray, sir, where do you wish to begin?'

'With Andrew Purves,' Cameron answered. 'And his wife.'

'Edwina Purves has been sent away,' said McKay.

'What?'

'To Moorfoot, with the children, yesterday,' McKay said.

'For what reason?' Cameron demanded.

McKay shrugged. 'Out of harm's way?'

'Who else went with her?'

'Only her servant, Pym,' McKay said. 'Shall I fetch them back?'

'At once,' said Cameron Adams. 'Servant and mistress, both.'

*   *   *

The coming of the Circuit Court to Glasgow was an event celebrated with much pomp and ceremony. The Lords of the Justiciary had for many years taken up residence in the Saracen's Head inn in Gallowgate from where, magnificently robed in scarlet and ermine, they would walk along Trongate to the Justiciary Hall for the long sittings that the process of the law demanded.

The judges were accompanied in the foot procession by the Provost in his velvet dress, bailies with cocked hats and golden chains, and a large military escort, including a band which, in terms of racket, bowed only to the two state trumpeters who could make a simple fanfare sound like the knell of doom. The town officers wore long wide-skirted coats and blue breeks and shouldered halberds as lightly as if the weapons weighed no more than barbers' strops, while the sheriff-officers, in seamed coats, pink breeches and matching cocked hats strutted and pranced like dancing dogs. Ahead of all paraded the macer, carrying 'the tin', a humble appurtenance of iron topped with Crown and Thistle in peeling gilt, which, heavy with tradition, would be hung on the middle panel behind the judges' bench for all to see and wonder at. In the rear, very last of all, came Hanging Johnnie Harkness, a silly, cadaverous, show-off creature, all nerves, in tatters of yellow silk and blue flannel, who, egged on by the crowd, discarded dignity to skip and dance his prophetic jig.

Up the broad flight of steps to the small hall just west of the Tolbooth the judges went, there to work their way through a dark roll of robbery, assault, sheep stealing, rape, fraud, conspiracy, fire-raising, poaching and murder, all crammed into sessions of ten or twelve or fourteen hours in each of the six days allotted to the burgh's spring assize.

Preparations were complete within the cramped hall, the

echoing jail and its antechambers. Prisoners had been
served with final indictments. Lists of witnesses, writings,
articles to be used against the panels had been offered in
advance by prosecutors in exchange for details of special
defences, like alibi or impeachment. Intricate technical
arguments on relevancy and precedent had been cobbled
up, polished with Latin until they shone like new, and
papers by the ton, cauled in buckram or ribbon-bound,
were strewn about the lawyers' desks to impress the
'assizers' from which the judges would select each fif-
teen-man jury, with its chancellor and clerk.

The crowd outside the court that Saturday morning was
the largest seen in many a year. For weeks wild rumours
had been circulating among the hoi-polloi that famous men
had been involved with the Banker's Beauty, that intimate
details of seduction and defilement would be revealed in
course of the trial. What spark there was to fan the flames
of public imagination remained, as always in such cases, a
complete mystery. But those who knew Clare Kelso, even
on the nod, could not think of her without a mingling of
pity and desire. What jailer Hinchcliff had told her was
untrue. The tangled tales about her that had entertained
marketmen and stallholders as well as burgesses and their
wives came down, for the most part, on Clare's side and
emphasised the unity of the masses in siding with an
innocent who had been duped and exploited by a monied
class. None of this had been imparted to Clare. Jonathan
Brown and Cameron Adams did not have ears tuned to
Glasgow gossip and Dry McKay would not deign to
unbutton himself to a woman whose guilt was so apparent.

Clare heard the early gathering of the horde. Some keen
souls had been up before dawn to push and shove for
preference about the court's narrow High Street entrance

or to fight for a place in the queue in the corridors of the courthouse itself. Hundreds of common folk seemed to believe that they had entrée and were entitled to seats in the gallery or on the tiered benches that gave the small hall the aspect of a cockpit. Hundreds more, deserters from honest toil, had found silver to spare to bribe the town officers who had charge of the admission of 'visitors' at the court's Great Door. It seemed to Clare that the citizens of Glasgow had not come to see her judged but condemned. She had again that dream – drowsing fitfully, not quite asleep – of death on Hanging Johnnie's rope.

At the clatter of the bolt, she sat upright in the bed, one hand to her throat, the other pressed into her lap to hold her petticoats down. They had come together, Andrew and Eunice, and by their manner Clare knew that they had been together, close together, at some point during the night.

Eunice had brought her a hat with a black lace veil, too coarse to be pretty in spite of its needlework. Clare's jet black dress was hung by the window, clean underwear and stockings draped on the chair. She had dyed her kidskin slippers with soot and spit. She intended to confront her accusers like a dark angel, with only a pure white cambric handkerchief to offset the sombre raiment.

Eunice was paler than ever. The eruptions on her face glared on chalky white skin. She looked elegant, though, in autumnal brown and clung to Andrew's arm as if her poise were of his making. Andrew too wore umber suiting, pockets and cuffs faced with black embroidery, waistcoat traced with an underthread of bottle green. His wig, professionally curled and powdered, had been settled on his head dead square so that no trace of his own dark hair showed, even at the ears. They had little, very little, to say.

Yet Clare knew that they had somehow managed to make love in the night and that, together, they had brought some of that sad affection to share with her now.

She was glad of it. Their presence calmed her. She was not ashamed, not before them. She felt a strange, sly pride at what she was about to do, pride that she had known this man, this woman and, as fate had allowed, been given what measure of respect each of them could afford to give a girl who had been not quite a servant and not quite kin.

Lips cold as ice, Eunice kissed her. But when Andrew hugged her, Clare was again aware of the palpable warmth that hid beneath his autocratic stuffiness. He had always been good to her, always kind. She had cost him dear in money and harassment and she hoped that he might find his reward, not in heaven but on earth. Fleetingly, she wondered if Eunice Bates offered recompense enough, ransom for duties and demands. For Andrew's sake, she hoped so. She could offer him no more. She had been burden enough.

Even so, when the door closed behind him Clare threw herself against it and, in dismay, cried out for Andrew to save her, somehow, from the ordeal that lay ahead.

An hour later, or a little more, Clare heard the trumpet fanfare blare out from the Tolbooth's steps. Very soon after that town officers came clumping on the stairs. Unlocking the cell, Hinchcliff declared, 'Here she is, lads, all ready an' waiting.' She took one last look at her image in the water bowl. She composed her expression as best she could to hide her fear and, just as the door swung open, dropped the black lace veil across her face. She picked up the little Testament from the table and, holding it to her bosom, turned to confront the men.

'Ready, lassie?'

'I am.'

'Come along, then.'

The lace veil created distortions, separated her from the men, from the staircase. She stumbled a little. One of the officers steadied her, hand on her arm. She seemed to be imprisoned by the veil now. Thus enclosed, her fear increased to a numbing terror as she was led down to the lobby of the jail, steered to the right along the passage that led to the justiciary hall. Her stiff black skirts rustled, her petticoats clung to her knees with the speed of her step. She was vaguely aware of the crowd in the hall, of shouting. Her name. Shouted. She clutched the Testament close to her breast. A low, square door at the end of the passage faded as she approached. Light and space seemed to suck her forward. Her slippers clipped the wooden stairs that carried her upward into open court and directly into the prisoner's box. The silence that greeted her appearance was like a blow. She had not expected it. There was no sound even from the citizens that packed the galleries. They were all staring at her, every eye in the hall upon her. Standing at the rail, Clare slowly lifted one hand and raised the black veil from her face. The silence was broken by gasps followed by a hot mutter of voices. She looked out at them and at the lineaments of the courtroom bravely for a moment then, with the cambric handkerchief pressed to her eyes, softly began to cry.

The hall was not as she had expected. She was on a level with the judges' bench, public galleries to left and right. Behind the dock, row upon row of seats crowded up to the roof. In a niche at the north end was a figure of Justice with balance and sword, the royal arms above it. The ugly mace, like a claymore, was hung behind the judges while below the scarlet bench, separated by a railing, she saw the lawyers, Mr Adams and Mr McKay among them. She recognised too the man who had interrogated her several times on behalf of the Advocate Depute, His Majesty's Advocate Robert Hume. He was leaning back in his chair, watching her with a faint smile upon his little moon-shaped face and his fingers steepled against his chin. To Clare's left, tucked just below the gallery and close to the lordships' bench, were the jurymen, who had already been selected and briefed. The tall venetian window that admitted light from the High Street blinded her. Teary as she was, she could not bring herself to study those grim-featured men in any detail, to mark them as individuals.

Cameron Adams had come away from his desk and advanced to the step by the side of the dock. He sought for and found Clare's hand, took it down from her face and patted it with an expression of great sympathy and compassion. Weeping even more copiously, Clare was drawn back and seated upon an armless upright chair close enough to the rail of the dock to see and to be seen.

Now, and only now, did Clare raise her head and peer across the pit of the court to the bench where Lord Pole and Lord Drumfin lolled like lions, maned by ermine collars and wrapped in scarlet robes. Huge curled wigs added not dignity but animal power to their appearance. Drumfin could carry it. His beefy, cheery red face was well suited to the weight of high office, his vast bulk to its official robes. Pole, however, was shrivelled by the judicial garments. Pinched and sallow, he stroked a long feather quill with fingers like a kestrel's claws.

Clare tried to recall what Mr Adams had told her, that Pole was a true jurist, obsessed with the technical correctness of legal findings, fair to a fault in his decisions and judgments. Drumfin was the danger. His fat and ruddy features masked an impulsiveness, a cruel and casual disregard for the niceties of Scots law. He had obtained his office by preference and held on to it by the exercise of convivial generosity to his brothers on the bench. It was Drumfin who returned Clare's guarded stare. His head was cocked back and he regarded her down the half-length of the hall with speculation, sizing her up with bulbous yellow-tinged eyes.

She put her handkerchief to her face again to hide from him, then quickly tugged down the lacey veil and retreated inside the purled and latticed twilight that it created. She choked back a sob, balled the handkerchief in her fist, gripped the Testament tightly and straightened her shoulders as if to say that she for one was ready, even eager, to begin.

The jury was sworn and the chief prosecutor, Advocate Depute Robert Ordway, rose to his feet and in a clear melodious voice read out the Indictment against Clare Kelso, servant to Andrew Purves of Glasgow, in the county of Lanarkshire.

Ordway was a handsome man. Born to the manor he had an inbred refinement that made him seem at times languid and effete. He was, however, known to be a master of trial procedure, precise and ruthless in his practices. Long-chinned, full-lipped, he held the papers from which he read in his left hand and seemed able to recite them from memory, a trick of reading that, Mr Walcott had told Clare, he had learned by rehearsal but one that never failed to impress.

'Indicted and accused at the instance of William Millar of Harvie, Esquire, His Majesty's Lord Advocate, for His

Majesty's interest, for the crime of wilful murder, in manner mentioned in the criminal indictment raised thereanent, bearing that whereas, by the law of God, and the laws of this and other well-governed realms, the crime of wilful murder is a heinous crime and most severely punishable; and particularly, by an Act passed in the Parliament of Scotland in the year of—'

From the corner of her eye Clare noticed Mr Shenkin. He was in the first row of the gallery. He had leaned so far forward that his head seemed balanced upon the railing there, ready to topple into the body of the court if he so much as nodded. She thought that Mr McCoull was by his side, but she could not be sure. She had an outlandish impulse to wave to them but, of course, resisted it. Surreptitiously she looked about her. She wondered where the witnesses were kept apart and why it was that some whom she had thought of as friends had been called against her and others who were enemies were on Mr Adams's list, not that of the Crown.

'– and at the time and place aforesaid, the said child of the accused was murdered or did die by poison wilfully administered to him; and of which murder or poisoning the said Clare Kelso is guilty, in art or part; and that being found so proven by the verdict of an assize before the Lords and Commissioners of the Justiciary, she ought to be punished with the pains of the law, to the terror of others from committing the like in time coming.'

Ordway seated himself again, legs crossed. He let the papers slide from his fingers, to be scooped up and filed by the Crown's agent, Writer Henry McAllister.

Lord Pole stirred himself and put down the quill with which he had been toying. On the bench beside the judges were several black bottles of port wine, with glasses, carafes of water, tumblers and a basket of biscuits, all presented without the slightest attempt at concealment. Drumfin had already helped himself to a tumbler of water, tinted with wine, and he sipped from it lightly as Pole, with arm extended, gestured at Clare.

'The netting, take up the netting, girl,' Pole said in his squeaky voice.

Clare hesitated. She glanced down at Cameron Adams who signalled her to lift her veil. She did so, nervously, and stood up.

'Now, Kelso,' Lord Pole went on, 'you have heard the charge against you read. How do you plead to it?'

Clare cleared her throat and timidly uttered the first words, and the last, that the court would hear from her that day. 'I am not guilty of it, sir.'

She waited. But there were no more questions. Clerks by the right side of the bench scribbled furiously, as if she had made a lengthy speech. She inclined her head, saw Lady Betté Sinclair and Mr Malabar and one of the other young gentlemen that she had met at the February ball seated behind, to her left. She wondered if Frances Purves had travelled up from Moorfoot and, if so, if Frances thought her guilty or innocent. After ten or fifteen seconds, Clare brushed down the veil and seated herself upon the chair once more.

Lord Pole addressed the defence counsel. 'Do you wish to question the relevancy of any part or parts of the indictment, Mr Adams?'

'I do not, your ludship.'

'Do you have the list of witnesses that Mr Ordway intends to call?'

'I do, ludship,' Cameron said.

'Do you find them all admissible, Mr Adams?'

'I do not object to any named, ludship.'

Pole glanced at Drumfin who, tumbler to his lips, nodded.

Pole said, 'In that case, perhaps we might ask Mr Ordway to proceed with his first witness.'

There was a briskness to the business that surprised Clare. She watched a side door open and, almost before the macer had called the name, saw Mrs Handyside ushered across the floor and assisted up three worn steps to a witness box, which was no box at all but a raised dais like that used by the conductor of the city's military band for concerts on the Green.

Mrs Handyside was not her usual self, not easy. Courtrooms were far from her element. She was more than just nervous, she was terrified.

Solemnly sworn and purged of malice, Mrs Handyside was interrogated by Robert Ordway.

Ordway said, 'Has any person on the part of the prisoner been speaking with you lately?'

This very first question caught Mrs Handyside completely off her guard and flummoxed her immediately. She glanced helplessly from Cameron Adams to Lord Pole but got no assistance from either party.

'Come now,' said Ordway, with the languid impatience that was his trade mark. 'Is that such a poser for you, madam?'

'Yes.'

'Yes, it is a poser?'

'No. Yes, I have been spoken to lately.'

'When might that have been?'

'Yesterday afternoon, at – at my cottage in Tobago Street.'

'Were any particular cautions or admonitions given you and, if so, what were they?'

'No, nothing of that sort,' said Mrs Handyside.

Cameron Adams got to his feet. 'M'luds, I object to this mode of examination. It is perfectly within the rules of process for counsel to address and examine Crown witnesses, as I am sure my learned friend the Advocate Depute knows.'

Ordway did not wait for ruling or intervention from the bench. He waved his hand airily as if to dismiss, for the benefit of the jury, such pettifoggery. 'Very well, very well. I shall proceed.' He turned to the witness and then, after a hesitation, swung again to look up at the judges. 'I merely wished to establish that the panel's counsellors had not by some means or other intimidated or played upon the sympathy of this witness by the manner of their inquisition.'

Lord Pole sighed. 'We are, I believe, well aware what your motives are in putting such a question to the witness, Mr Ordway. Witness has, however, given satisfactory answer. Further advance along this line would, we feel, impugn the good woman's honesty. I am sure that is not your intention.'

'Her evidence is very vital, sir,' said Ordway.

'Then, for God's sake, let the court hear it,' Drumfin put in, with less patience than his bench companion.

'How long have you known the panel, Clare Kelso?' said Ordway hastily.

'Near ten months, sir,' Mrs Handyside answered.

'In what circumstances?'

'I was foster to her son.'

'Her *natural* son, do you mean?'

'Aye.'

'What was the child's name?'

'Peterkin.'

'Peterkin?' Ordway rolled his eyes by way of comment and, looking at the jurymen, repeated, 'Peterkin!'

'That was his name, sir,' said Mrs Handyside stoutly.

'Then we must accept it,' said Ordway. 'What age was the child when he was brought to you?'

'Two or three weeks old.'

'I see. Did you nurse him yourself?'

'No, I am too old for milk now.'

There was a stirring of laughter in the galleries and it might have risen higher if Drumfin had not forestalled it by lifting his upper body grandly, planting both fists on the bench before him and glowering round the court.

Ordway continued. 'A wet nurse was employed?'

'She was, sir. A decent girl, named—'

Ordway interrupted. 'Who paid her?'

'Clare's – the panel's patron.'

'Ah! A patron,' said Ordway. 'Did this "patron" also pay your fee for minding the child?'

'He did,' said Mrs Handyside. 'Seven shillin's the week.'

'A not inconsiderable sum,' said Ordway. 'How were the payments made to you, Mrs Handyside?'

'In money, every month.'

'By whom?'

'Clare – Miss Kelso brought it – or sometimes another.'

'Another?'

'Mrs Bates brought it once.'

'Who, pray, is Mistress Bates?'

'She is – she was the baby's aunt.'

'Indeed!' said Robert Ordway. 'Sister to the accused?'

'I was told – I mean, sister to the baby's father.'

'So, the father was known?'

'Aye, sir.'

It was Mr McKay who climbed to his feet, not Cameron Adams. His voice had the granular quality of old sawdust. 'M'luds, the paternity of the child is not at issue here. If it will save Mr Ordway time, let it be admitted that the father was Frederick Striker of Grahamston.'

Drumfin said, 'He has acknowledged this fact?'

'In letters to the court, m'lud, as well as by word of mouth. He – Striker – has not endeavoured to deny his paternity.'

Drumfin said, 'Did Mr Striker then also contribute toward the cost of the child's keep?'

'No, not to my knowledge,' said McKay.

'It seems that Mr Striker's purse is tighter than his mouth.' Drumfin grinned, pleased at the roar of laughter that greeted his remark.

Pole scowled, rapped his mahogany chock upon the bench but could do nothing to still the galleries' mirth. Robert Ordway put his hands on his hips and fanned out his robe, waiting. He had been put off his line by the judge's interruption and had a sinking feeling that Drumfin was somehow against him.

Lord Drumfin was not, however, quite finished yet. When laughter had quieted he addressed another question to the bar. 'Is Mr Striker not present?'

McKay got in first. 'No, m'lud.'

'Why is he not present?' said Drumfin. 'Do we know the fellow's reason for not being here, Mr Ordway?'

'Mr Striker has been out of Scotland in pursuit of business for several months. Since, I believe, October.'

'October?' said Drumfin. 'What is the nature of Mr Striker's business?'

'He is a merchant and trader, m'lud,' said Robert Ordway.

'Therefore not short of shillings, we would assume,' said Lord Drumfin.

'I cannot answer that question,' said Ordway and, before Drumfin could queer his pitch further, added, 'Mr Striker has been in every way co-operative with the Crown counsel and has been in correspondence with its agents since he learned of the arrest of the accused.'

'Yet he has not returned from his "business"?'

'It is impossible for him to do so, m'lud.'

'I will not ask you to explain further, not at this point,' said Drumfin. 'For the benefit of the jurymen we have now established that the child, Peterkin, was fathered by the absent Mr Frederick Striker and that the child's aunt – Mrs Bates – showed commendable concern for and interest in her brother's offspring. Does that satisfy your objection, Mr McKay?'

'It does, m'lud.'

Affably, Drumfin spread his palms. 'Proceed, Mr Ordway, if you will.'

Ordway paused long enough to allow the court to settle then snapped out his questions quickly, tapping them at the witness as if with a cobbler's hammer.

'Who was the generous patron to whom you referred?'

'Mr Andrew Purves, of Saltmarket,' Mrs Handyside answered.

'Did he too visit the child?'

'No, sir, he never came.'

'The panel, however, did visit?'

'Regular, sir. One time or two times every week. She came Sundays, often on Fridays too,' said Mrs Handyside, adding anxiously, 'She was very fond o' the wee boy. Very fond.'

'What did she do for him?'

'Fed him, dressed him, took him out for walks.'

'Fed him?'

'When he was weanin',' Mrs Handyside explained.

'Did she feed him that particular Sunday?' said Ordway.

'I never saw him fed, sir.'

'Oh, she did not feed him?'

'Clare – she had him out.'

'Perhaps she fed him while she was out or when she returned?'

'I could not say if she did, sir, since I was out too.'

'You saw no plate, no dish,' said Ordway, 'no tumbler, nor cup nor glass nor spoon to suggest that he had been fed?'

'I never saw anythin' like that,' Mrs Handyside said.

'Nonetheless, Clare Kelso was alone with her child, out of doors and also within your cottage, for several hours?'

'About two hours.'

'So food or drink could have been administered in that time?'

'Aye, but Clare said—'

'We will come to what the panel said in due course,' Robert Ordway told her. 'Meanwhile, it would be to the advantage of the court, Mrs Handyside, if you would inform us in your own words what precisely did take place that afternoon, the last day of the year.'

Mrs Handyside primped her gingham, smoothed the folds of her skirt and adjusted the sit of her bonnet, as if her honesty would be judged on neatness of appearance.

She said, 'It was about half past two of the clock when Clare came. She was a wee bit later than was her usual and said she had been kept back by her duty in the nursery in Mr Andrew's house at Purves's Land. I had Peterkin all nice in a wee cap an' pinafore an' a clean cloth about him.

She said she would take him for an airin'. At this I told her I would be takin' out the others, my other fosterlings, to visit my mother in King Street an' if she was back before me she would find the latchkey on the shelf above the door. She went away wi' Peterkin, an' I left shortly afterwards with the other two.'

'Did she say where she was taking him?'

'No, just for air.'

'Did she seem distressed?'

'Maybe a wee thing flustered.'

'Flustered?' Robert Ordway repeated.

'Because she'd been late,' said Mrs Handyside.

'What sort of day was it?' said Ordway. 'Do you recall the weather? Was it clement?'

'Grey, it was a grey day but dry, not very cold.'

'The last of the year, though,' said Ordway, 'so darkness would come down early, particularly as it was clouded.'

'Aye, dusk was well down before I got back from my mother's house.'

'To find Kelso and her child in your kitchen?'

'That's right, sir. She had just arrived, she said.'

'How was the child, Peterkin? How did he seem in himself?'

'Fine. He was a bit cranky, that was all.'

'Cranky?' said Ordway.

'Frettin', girnin'.'

'So he was not, even at that time, himself?'

'He was tired, that was all. He needed a wee nap to set him right.'

'Before we go on to the events that followed, Mrs Handyside, perhaps you would be good enough to indicate to the court something of the child's general health?'

'He was a fine healthy boy.'

'No ailments at all?'

'A rash, just a wee rash across his brow.'

'Not severe?'

'He scratched at it with his nails. It was not so bad as it looked.' Mrs Handyside paused. 'Clare thought it was hives.'

'Did she tell you so, and if so, when?'

'She asked what I'd given him for it.'

'What had you given him for it?'

'Nothing at all,' said Mrs Handyside. 'I put some butter fat on it, that was all.'

'But you administered no internal medications, not that evening or previously?'

'No, Mr Ordway.'

'Nonetheless, some remedy or other had been administered.'

'Aye, Clare said she had given Peterkin a tait of sulphur.'

'A tait? How much is that?'

'A touch. I'd have thought about a third of an eggspoon.'

'Have you given children in your care sulphur?'

'Once or twice,' said Mrs Handyside. 'I'm not much for doctorin', unless they're real sick.'

'Peterkin was not "real sick"?'

Mrs Handyside shook her head. 'But Clare was fair concerned about the rash, the itch.'

'What did the panel tell you, exactly?'

'That she had given Peterkin a small dose of fresh powdered sulphur.'

'What did you think of that?'

'I thought nothing of it, sir.'

'Did Kelso tell you *where* she had given the child the powder?'

'She did not say, sir.'

'Or when?'

'No.'

'When did the panel leave your cottage, and what were the circumstances of it?' Ordway said.

'She left about half past five o'clock.'

'Was that a usual time for her departure on Sundays?'

Mrs Handyside paused. 'It was earlier than her usual.'

'How much earlier?'

'An hour, or three quarters of an hour.'

'Did she tell you why she was leaving early?'

'She said she had to get back.'

'How did she behave? Was she still "flustered"?'

'A wee bit, maybe.'

'Noticeably?'

'Aye.'

'What did she do before she left?'

The pause this time was longer. A thin thread of tension increased in the silent courtroom. Beneath the rail of the witness box, quite visible to all, Mrs Handyside's fingers kneaded and twisted at her gingham skirt.

'Madam, will you answer, please?'

'She kissed him.'

Clare, without calculation, began to cry.

She did not display it, did not lift the cambric to her eyes or remove the partition of the veil. She squeezed her eyes shut and let the tears trickle soundlessly down her cheeks.

She remembered the kiss, the final kiss, the way that Peterkin had fallen peacefully still when she had lifted him up and put her cheek to his and how he had sought her mouth with his soft little mouth and made the noise that was his name for her. She could almost feel the weight of him in her arms again.

Mrs Handyside had come to the cottage door with him

in her arms. She always did. She had pointed out Mama as
Mama had gone along the narrow road between the lowering privet hedges. The sky had been thick as grey velvet
and the smell of suppers, of chimney smoke, was strong in
the still air. By the light of the lantern at the cottage door
she had seen the last of Peterkin, struggling a little in his
foster-mother's stout arms.

Mrs Handyside said, 'She always kissed him. She did not
want to leave him. It hurt her so to leave him, even though
she knew he was safe and sound in my care.'

'And then?'

'I took him in again, took off his pinafore and changed
his bandage.'

'You mean the cloth about his parts?'

'Yes.'

'Had he, had the child fouled himself?' Ordway asked.

'In the ordinary way, aye.'

'What did you do with him?'

'I put him down to play with the others while I poked up
the fire and filled a pot for supper.' Mrs Handyside waited
for a question but it did not come. She knew what was
required of her and, though obviously agitated and distressed, pushed on. 'It was about a half-hour later when I
heard Peterkin cryin'. He was cryin' sore, so sore. He had
his brow to the stone floor and his hands against his
stomach. When I picked him up he was sick.'

'You mean he vomited?'

'Yes.'

'Violently?'

'No. He was just – just sick. It trickled down his chin on
to his pinafore bib. I took him to the fireside chair to wash
him. He was sick again.'

'What colour was the vomit?'

'Yellow.'

'He purged too, did he not?'

'Aye, sir.'

'Violently?'

'Very violently.'

'Were you concerned?'

'A wee bit. I thought it was something he had eaten.'

Ordway, who had remained in or near the lawyers' desk, advanced now towards the witness and stood below her, one hand raised and upon the rail. He did not address himself to the woman, however, but turned towards the jurymen and repeated loudly, as a statement, the woman's last words.

'Something he had eaten.' He swung round. 'What did you suppose that to be?'

'I didn't know, sir.'

'What did it look like, madam? What did you *think* it might be?'

'Sulphur, sir,' Mrs Handyside hung her head as if ashamed of her opinion.

'What did you do?'

'I washed him clean again and put on him a gown, a cotton gown, an' another clean flannel. Then I gave him a spoonful of magnesia with some milk.'

'Did he, did the child imbibe this remedy?'

'Imbib . . .?'

'Drink it, madam,' said Ordway, with a sigh.

'He did, sir. But he sicked up directly.'

'And then?'

'He seemed easier when he had purged, so I put him to his bed in the kitchen, where I could keep an eye on him while I made a bite of supper for the other two.'

'The other children were perfectly fit, perfectly well?'

'They were just their usual selves,' said Mrs Handyside. 'It was a half of an hour or so before I saw that Peterkin had turned worse. He had not been sick again but he had soaked his flannel an' had gone fit with his breathin'. I was fair worried now, so I ran out to Mrs Lumsden's house, along the gardens by the toll. She sent her man, Mr Lumsden, to run an' fetch Doctor McCorkindale from his house in Caltoun Main Street.' She looked down at the Advocate Depute who nodded for her to continue. 'It was the best part o' an hour before the doctor came. He had been at the kirk but he came as soon as he got back.'

'It was now what hour?'

'About a half-hour after seven.'

Robert Ordway said, 'We will hear shortly from Doctor McCorkindale but I would be grateful if you would conclude your account first, Mrs Handyside. Tell us when you decided to send for the child's mother, for Clare Kelso?'

The woman began to weep. She had furnished herself with a large handkerchief of spotted blue cotton, of the kind that gardeners wore about their heads in hot weather. Delicately, she dabbed her eyes with it.

'When – when – the doctor said Peterkin was dyin'.'

'Who went to fetch the mother?'

'Mr Lumsden.'

'And?'

'She was not there.'

'Not there? Not at home in Purves's Land?'

'No, sir. Mr Lumsden left a message with Mrs Purves sayin' for her, for Clare, to come at once to Caltoun. But she never came.'

'I wonder why she did not come?'

'I do not know, sir. It would have been too late in any

case.' Mrs Handyside sniffed and sobbed. 'By a quarter past eight o'clock the poor wee bairn had gone.'

'Gone?'

'To heaven, sir,' said Mrs Handyside and burst, at that moment, into a flood of tears.

Perhaps Advocate Adams did not trust himself to examine the first of the witnesses on behalf of his client. Mrs Handyside had been rendered almost inconsolable by the nervous strain of Ordway's interrogation and by the memory of the fateful night. For whatever reason, Advocate Adams left it to McKay to sift out points as best he could from the sobbing foster mother.

McKay was well prepared, firm but not bullying. He was a little more firm, though, with Mary Lumsden and her husband Oliver, a tile-worker long resident in Caltoun, whom Ordway had impannelled to give factual substance to Mrs Handyside's testimony. Lumsden was a small, coarse fellow of fifty or so. He had no gift of the gab and seemed thoroughly bemused by even the plainest language that the lawyers used. It was not Lumsden's account of the seeking and finding of McCorkindale that interested the defence but details that might explain the curious fact that Clare Kelso had not been informed by Mrs Edwina Purves that the child was ill and that she, Clare, had been sent for urgently. There was just enough confusion in Mr Lumsden's mind to transform his declarative statements into little mysteries on their own account.

Though Mr McKay picked away at the tile-worker he managed to establish only that Clare Kelso was not to be found within the precincts of Purves's Land. Mr Lumsden – who, it seemed, had not had his supper and was fair ready for it – left a message with the lady of the household – or was it her servant – and returned post-haste not to the cottage in Tobago Street but to his own dwelling where, on his demand, his wife fed him. This sort of behaviour, McKay knew, would not seem unduly callous to half of the men in the hall, including some of the jury members. In consequence, he did what he could with Lumsden and then let well alone.

Cracking Doctor McCorkindale was altogether a different matter. McCorkindale had no great medical expertise except that gathered by a lifetime of practice among the poor folk of the Caltoun and Blackfaulds. He was cynical, conceited, and revelled in the limelight that the death of Peterkin had shed upon him. His face was as wrinkled as a crab-apple kept too long in store and he looked far older than his fifty-three years.

After some preliminary, he declared, 'When I reached the house of the woman Handyside, which was, incidentally, known to me from a previous visitation there some years before, I found a male child of about ten months laid in a wicker bed before the kitchen fire. It was clear to me from a glance that the child was excessively ill. He was restless, breathing hard – labouring for breath, in fact – and had no pulsation at the wrist. His skin was cold and clammy to the touch and, thinking to restore pulse to his blood, I ordered a warm bath to be prepared. Before this could be accomplished, however, the child fell into convulsions and very swiftly thereafter died. There was nothing, I assure you, that I or any other doctor could have done to bring the infant back from the brink of expiry.

'The following forenoon at the ordering of the resident bailies and in the presence of two of them, I opened the child's stomach and examined the contents. In this I was assisted by Doctor Thomas Sowerby who, as you will see, has attested and signed the medical report.

'The child's stomach was much swollen and the membranes inflamed. From the stomach I removed a quantity of a substance which, when analysed, proved to be king's yellow; that is, sulphuret of arsenic. In quantity there was about a quarter ounce remaining in a dry and powdery state. I have no hesitation in stating that it was the presence of the poison in the stomach that was the immediate cause of the child's death.'

'A quarter ounce, how large a dosage is that, sir?' asked Mr Hume, Ordway's junior counsel.

'About a teaspoon's full.'

'Did you and your colleague also examine the clothing of the child?'

'Indeed. I removed from the premises of Handyside's cottage the clothing that the child had been wearing before it was washed and dressed in nightgown and flannel.'

'What did you find, Doctor?'

'Traces there too of king's yellow. Not upon the flannel but upon the bib and breast of the pinafore.'

'In terms of what might be sold across the counter of a druggist's or apothecary's shop, Dr McCorkindale, how much of that would have found its way into the child's stomach?'

'In terms of king's yellow, it is sold as a rule by the dram, for three pence. But it is not much asked for except in the height of the fly season, which December is not, of course.'

Before Hume could phrase his next question and utter it, the chancellor of the jury shot to his feet and, after being sanctioned by Lord Pole, put a question on the jury's behalf. 'How is sulphur sold? Could we be told?'

Though he might have expected a similar question from the defence counsel in their questioning, Hume was slightly nonplussed by the interruption.

McCorkindale answered, 'It is sold, usually, in a penny packet of about one ounce.'

The juryman, a majestic looking and well dressed gentleman, persisted. 'But one ounce was not found within the body of the child, or upon its clothes?'

'It was not such a large amount, no.'

The majestic juryman and several of his brethren in the box were looking now towards the bench. Drumfin took up the matter on their behalf. 'What I think we wish to know, Doctor McCorkindale, is what effect the substance in the found quantity would have had upon the child *if* the substance had been sulphur and not arsenic.'

'It was not sulphur, your lordship.'

'We know that, sir, but if it *had* been sulphur?'

'It would not have had any effect, not in that quantity.'

'Except to cure the child's rash?' Drumfin said.

'Perhaps, perhaps. That's the common belief,' McCorkindale answered.

'Sulphur is commonly given for hives and rashes, is it not?' said Drumfin.

'Personally I do not prescribe it,' said McCorkindale. 'But, yes, it is a common remedy.'

After another spate of questions from the prosecutor, none of them of moment, it was Cameron Adams' turn. He rose swiftly and without ado tackled the matter of the cause of death and prudently left the circumstances surrounding it alone.

'Have you ever known a death caused by overdosing with sulphur, Doctor?' he began.

'I cannot say, personally, in my experience – no.'

'It is a very common remedy and liberally used by the lower ranks.'

'It is.'

'Who are therefore on the whole quite familiar with the correct amount to administer?'

'Yes.'

'Would you expect a woman who had been a nursery-maid for five or six years to be acquainted with the purposes and properties of sulphur?'

'It would seem right.'

'Upon examination was Peterkin – the child – found to have any other ailment?'

'He was in all respects a healthy boy.'

'In all respects?' said Cameron. 'Was there no blemish, however minor, upon him, sir?'

McCorkindale pursed his wrinkled lips. 'A rash, a simple irritation upon the brow, nothing serious.'

'But a blemish, nonetheless,' said Cameron. 'Was the surface of the skin broken?'

'Here and there.'

'The child had been scratching the spot, had he?'

'That would be my judgment, yes.'

'Now, I'm sure we are all here painfully familiar with sulphur – have we not all had it thrust down our throats at one time or another, to cure everything from pimples to growing pains? But we are not familiar, I suspect, with sulphuret of arsenic. Tell us about king's yellow, if you will.'

'I expect you wish me to say that it is similar in appearance to sulphur?'

'I do not wish you to say anything that is not the truth, sir,' said Cameron. '*Is* king's yellow similar to plain sulphur?'

'Only in superficial appearance. It is heavier than sulphur in the ratio of three to one and, thus, in comparative bulk. It is less soluble in water. In fact, it sinks in a cloudy sediment when entered into water, which is not a property of sulphur.'

'Ah!' said Mr Adams. 'So sulphur is more soluble?'

'I have just said so.'

'Therefore sulphur would also be absorbed more readily from the stomach, taken in by the gastric juices?'

'What? Yes, yes, I suppose it would.'

'In the contents of the child's stomach you found no traces, however slight, of sulphur as such?'

'I did not.'

'Which is not to say that such traces did not exist?'

McCorkindale opened his lips to protest the slur upon his thoroughness but Cameron Adams rode over him. 'Which is not to say that the dose of arsenic was not mingled with some quantity of plain sulphur since the sulphur would be more swiftly and completely absorbed than the arsenic?'

McCorkindale was honest enough to hesitate and consider his answer. The possibility had patently not occurred to him. Seconds passed, a half-minute. Both judges hung forward, leaning upon their elbows, and the court and its galleries were quiet, though the significance of the counsel's question was lost upon the vast majority.

'I can only say that I did not find sulphur,' McCorkindale answered, at length. 'It is, however, possible that if some sulphur had been mingled with the arsenic it would have been taken in by the digestive system and would not have been evident in the stomach contents.'

'Or upon the bib of the pinafore?'

'I – I did not test that garment for sulphur.'

'Or any garment?'

'No, it did not seem necessary.'

'Did not seem necessary,' Cameron Adams repeated, with great clarity. 'Why did it not seem necessary?'

'Because the child had died of arsenic poisoning.'

'How could you be sure?'

'Damn it, sir, I witnessed the death with my own eyes.'

'And you read in the signs an indication of poisoning?'

'Have I not said so time and again?'

'And therefore were looking for poison. *Only* for poison?'

'I—'

'Thank you for your evidence, Doctor McCorkindale, that will be all the defence requires from you.'

At the Advocate Depute's desk there was a little flutter of robes and papers, a muttered *tête-à-tête* between Ordway and Hume which was disturbed by Lord Drumfin's sleek and tender enquiry, 'Well, Mr Ordway?'

In a tone that indicated that he was not at all sure what had been gained or lost in the trudge towards the truth, Robert Ordway said, 'I think I am finished with the witness, m'lud.'

'I would think so too,' said Drumfin and, with a small, fat, enigmatic smile, paused to pour himself a full glass of port.

The apothecary was graced with the odd name of Kellerman Rettie. When quizzed about it, he shrugged his bony shoulders and said that his name was so registered in Gorbals Parish, where he had been born, and that to his knowledge he had never had any other.

He declared that he was the son of an apothecary, had been trained by apprenticeship to his father in the Old Hall in the Briggait in Glasgow and by attendance at classes in the College for a period of one year, when he was sixteen. He had been principal druggist at the Apothecaries' Hall for thirty-one years, since his father's death, also manager after the Hall had removed to its commodious new premises in Virginia Street, which supplied many famous professors and surgeons from Hutchesons' Hospital and the Lock Hospital for unhappy females.

Drumfin could not resist. 'Tell me, Mr Rettie, are there many "unhappy females" here in Glasgow?'

'Indeed, my lord,' the apothecary answered, 'far too many.'

The Advocate Depute did not begin his examination until the laughter had died down.

Did the witness know the panel by sight?

Yes, he did.

Did the witness know who she was?

Yes, nursery servant to the Purves family.

Had the witness ever served her with chemical substances from the stock in the Apothecaries' Hall?

Yes, many times.

What was the nature of the drugs bought?

Simple preparations, mainly of a herbal nature. Remedies such as would be needed to care for the health of children. Examples: camomile, St John's wort, magnesia, poppy oil for toothache, aconite powder, senna, and so on.

Sulphur?

On occasions.

Did the witness recall a visit to the Hall from the panel in the last days of the old year?

The witness did not.

Could the witness, after such a lapse of time, trust to his memory?

The witness had been questioned on that very matter on the third day of January and several times in the days that followed, when his memory was fresh. Besides, the panel was a pretty girl, a very pretty girl, not the sort of customer that one was liable to forget. The witness, however, was not constantly and continually upon duty at the counter of the Hall. He could not say upon his oath that the panel had not visited the Hall and made a purchase or purchases. He could only say that he himself had not seen her there for several weeks before the closing of the year.

Several weeks?

Five or six. More than a calendar month at the least.

How many apprentices or assistants did the witness employ within the Apothecaries' Hall?

Four, in addition to himself. He had personally questioned them about Miss Kelso, who was, he thought, known to all of them as they were young or youngish men. They had also been questioned by a representative of the magistrates and by a representative of the Lord Advocate soon after the beginning of the year. None of them remembered selling sulphur, or anything, to Miss Kelso in the course of the fortnight before New Year.

How is plain sulphur sold?

The witness answered that sulphur was sold as a rule in a parcel or small packet of one ounce weight, which cost one penny. The sulphur was drawn from a jar kept handy on the shelf beneath the serving counter in the Hall, for it was asked for frequently. It was measured into a copper pan with a spoon, weighed and packaged in brown paper at the counter.

Sulphuret of arsenic: king's yellow?

King's yellow was not much in demand, except in the season of high summer when the weather was hot. It was used, on sugar, to trap and kill black flies and other bugs.

Some folk used it too to eliminate cockroaches if their dwelling was plagued by them but it was, as a rule, used for flies and there was little call for the poison in December.

Where was the king's yellow kept?

In a jar in the third shelf to the left of the serving counter, along with other less popular substances.

All of a poisonous nature?

Not all, no.

So the sulphur was in a jar below the counter and the arsenic in a jar high above the counter and away from it?

That, the witness agreed, was accurate.

Mr Kellerman Rettie was asked several other questions about the management of the Hall and about conditions which sulphur was used to treat.

To everyone's surprise he was released from the box without interrogation by defence counsel; after which, one by one, in order of age and experience, Mr Rettie's assistants were tediously trotted out, briefly questioned and released, unchallenged, to sink back into obscurity.

The last of the apothecary's assistants, however, was not let off so lightly.

James Taylor, aged sixteen, had been two years with the Hall, had taken no classes yet and earned his keep mainly by washing pots and stoking charcoal fires in the laboratory. He was small as a leveret, had a short upper lip, prominent teeth and a pinkness about his eyes that suggested he wept often and long. He was a pathetic soul and Mr Hume was quiet and swift in extracting from him the same facts as he had extracted from the others. Hume was about to stand the witness down when Cameron Adams got to his feet.

'Tell me again, James, do you know Clare Kelso by sight?'

'I've – I've seen her in the Hall, aye, sir.'

'And you remember her particularly?'

'Aye.'

Lord Pole interrupted. 'The witness has already answered these questions, Mr Adams. I trust that you will be moving forward very soon. The bench cannot bear wasteful repetition, you know.'

'Thank you, m'lud. I will endeavour to reach the heart of the matter as soon as I can,' Cameron said. 'Now, James, how often do you serve behind the shop counter?'

'Sometimes.'

'How often?'

'When Mr Rettie tells me.'

After a to-and-fro exchange Cameron finally ascertained that young Master Taylor was left alone in the public part of the shop on two or three evenings each week, always at a late supper hour, when Mr Rettie and his eldest apprentice went out to eat. An hour and half to two hours seemed to be the spell in which young James Taylor was in sole command. He was adamant, however, that he had not sold Miss Kelso anything in the two or three weeks preceding New Year. Not sulphur. Not nothing.

'Why do you remember Clare Kelso so well, James?'

'Because I do.'

'Because she is pretty?'

'Bonnie, aye.'

'Because the other young men, your peers in the establishment, talk about her?'

James blushed. The pinkness seemed to spread outward from his eye sockets and run like flannel dye to the very tips of his ears. 'A . . . a . . . aye.'

'What do they say about her?'

'That she's awful bonnie.'

'What else do they say about her?'

James Taylor glanced helplessly about him, pink turning to rose on his skin, upper lip nibbling nervously.

'You must answer, young man,' Lord Pole told him.

'They say they'd fair like t'be her master.'

'Who is her master? Do you know that, James?'

'Mr Purves.'

'Do you know Mr Purves? Have you seen him?'

'Nah.'

'Why do you suppose your companions would like to be this gentleman, Mr Purves?'

'For to get to bed wi' her.'

A beat of utter silence at the boy's statement was followed by muffled uproar laced with hissing and shushing as Mr Adams advanced remorselessly upon the witness, poised with his next question. Pole rapped the mahogany chock and the macer shouted for silence and respect.

'Is that what they say, James?' Cameron Adams asked. 'Do they say that Miss Kelso's master sleeps with her?'

'Aye.'

'What reason do they have to suppose that?'

'She had his bairn.'

More uproar, impervious to the judge's rapping, the macer's cries and the clash of ceremonial halberds at the doors behind the galleries.

Cameron Adams was patience itself. He leaned his elbow up on the edge of the witness cage and kept his head down until, after several minutes, a semblance of order was restored. He had known what the boy would say if led aright. Angus McKay had spoken with all of the attendants at the Hall and had come back outraged at the apprentices' salaciousness and lack of respect for their betters.

Trading mercilessly on young Taylor's naivety, Cameron Adams changed course. 'Where is the sulphur kept, James?'

'On the shelf below the drawer.'

'And the king's yellow?'

'Back high on the left.'

'In a jar?'

'Aye.'

'What colour is the jar?'

'Blue.'

'What colour is the jar in which the sulphur is kept?'

'Blue.'

'What colour is sulphur?'

'Yellow.'

'And sulphuret of arsenic?'

'Yellow.'

'Do you never make mistakes, James?'

'I never made a mistake. She never come that week, not for anythin' '

'Do you serve customers with arsenic, as well as sulphur?'

'Serve what they ask for.'

'Measure it, weigh it, parcel it, take the payment?'

'Aye. Mr Rettie taught me a' that.'

'Have you sold many packets of king's yellow, James?'

'Nah.'

'So you would recall a customer asking for it?'

'Aye, sir.'

'Even if that customer was not a "bonnie lassie" like Miss Kelso?'

'Aye, sir.'

'Did you sell king's yellow, in any quantity, to anyone in the closing weeks of last year?'

'Nah.'

'When did you last sell a quantity of king's yellow?'

James Taylor had recovered enough to put on a little show of concentration. He twitched his upper lip and scratched his ear.

'Last summer, for the flies.'

Cameron Adams said, 'To whom did you sell it?'

'I canna remember that.'

'Man or woman?'

James Taylor shook his head, stumped.

Cameron Adams said, 'On the last Wednesday of the old year, James, did you sell a quantity of king's yellow to anyone?'

'Nah, nah.'

'On the tenth day of January, James, which was also a Wednesday, did you sell a quantity of sulphuret of arsenic to anyone?'

'Nah.'

'But selling king's yellow is a very rare event, by your own admission. Do you not have to climb on the stool to reach down the blue jar from the high shelf and measure out with excessive care a dram of the yellow powder? It is not something that a bright lad like you is liable to forget, James, is it?'

'Nah.'

'Are you quite certain of that?'

'Aye, sir.'

Cameron turned to the defence desks and made a little signal and Jonathan Brown, who had been writing steadily throughout, got to his feet and faced towards the witness.

'Do you know this gentleman?' Cameron asked.

'Nah.'

'Are you sure?'

'Sure, sir.'

'If I were to tell you that Mr Jonathan Brown, which is this gentleman, entered the Apothecaries' Hall at approximately a quarter past the hour of nine o'clock on the evening of Wednesday the tenth day of January and purchased from you, James, not one dram but one full ounce of king's yellow would you deny it?'

'I canna remember him.'

'Would you deny it?'

'I – I never saw him before.'

'Mr Brown, if you will,' said Cameron Adams, and Jonathan produced from his vest pocket a perfect, tight, little package which he held up between finger and thumb.

'King's yellow. One full ounce. Bought from you, James. Bought from you,' said Cameron Adams.

Lord Pole, annoyed by the trick, snapped, 'Do you intend that we should enter this package as a production in evidence, Mr Adams? If so, I must inform you that it is against the rules of procedure to do so at this late date and I cannot allow it.'

'I do not intend to do so, m'lud,' said Cameron. 'However, if the court requires it I will be prepared to swear Mr Brown, the agent in this case, to the stand as a witness for the panel. He will then attest, on soul and conscience, that the substance is in fact sulphuret of arsenic and that it was purchased in the manner and quantity which I have described.'

'At whose request was this purchase made?' Pole demanded.

'At the suggestion of Mr Walcott, who was, before his illness, the panel's counsel.'

'Hah! The devil!' Drumfin exclaimed.

At that moment, after hasty consultation with his colleagues, the majestic juryman got to his feet and addressed himself to the bench. 'My lords, the members of the jury are willing to accept the veracity of Mr Adams' statements without the bother of listing and swearing in the agent.'

Pole glared at the juryman. 'It is not then evidence.'

Hamilton, the majestic juryman, was, in fact, a Writer to the Signet who had been called for duty from the register in the regular manner. It was already becoming clear to all concerned that one member of the jury, at least, had a bias towards finding in favour of the panel and that he was intent upon stamping his authority and his will upon the others who, being lesser men, were in awe of his erudition.

'It does not have to be evidence, my lord,' said Hamilton, while other worthy gentlemen in the jury nodded, 'for counsel's point to be taken.'

'If it is not evidence then the point must be ignored,' Pole shrilled.

'How may we do that, my lord?' Hamilton asked.

'Put it from your minds.' Pole clacked the mahogany chock upon the bench, though there was no noise to silence. 'Put – it – from – your – minds.'

Hamilton did his best not to smirk. He glanced at his fellows in the jury-box, who pulled faces at him and shrugged shoulders. He turned again to the bench. 'Very well, my lord, we have put it entirely from our minds.'

Laughter from the gallery grated upon the estimable Pole like flint on steel. It was all he could do to contain himself. Lord Drumfin patted his arm and murmured a few soothing words, then gestured to the juryman to sit down quickly before the learned judge saw fit to have the soldiers clear the court with swords and bayonets.

Smouldering, Pole signalled Mr Adams to continue. But

the defence had all but done with poor, confused James
Taylor.

The advocate asked the boy once more if he could recall
having sold a quantity of king's yellow to any person in the
last weeks of December and received the same reply as
before – a reply invalidated by doubt.

Clare was aware of what her counsel was about. Her
nervousness had diminished enough for her to be drawn
into the unfolding of Cameron Adams' defence of her life.
Even so, she was as tense and coiled as a watch-spring
during the advocate's examination of the apothecary's boy
and was relieved when, at last, the lad was dismissed.

Robert Ordway gave no outward sign that he had been
rattled by the dubious tactics of his opponent. Nonetheless
he took his time in summoning his next witness and
embarking upon the second phase of his prosecution of
justice – an establishment of motive where it seemed there
was none. He called first young Madelaine Butters who
told the court, in her own inimitable style, of how the panel
lived in Purves's Land and what her duties were and how
well she carried them out. Cleverly led on by the Advocate
Depute, Maddy let her animosity towards the panel show,
particularly when she reached the matter of Mr Striker.
Led on again, Maddy made it plain that Clare Kelso had
been attracted to Mr Striker and had set her cap at him as
best she was able, considering her position as a servant in
the banker's house.

When asked about the events of the night of December
31st, Maddy was rock-like in her affirmation that Clare
Kelso had not returned to Purves's Land before eight
o'clock of the night and that she had taken her supper along
with the two older children before putting them to bed.

It was this part of the spoken testimony that Cameron Adams elected to attack in his cross-questioning. 'Do you say that my client was not in Purves's Land until eight of the clock?'

'Aye, sir, that's what I said, because it's true.'

'Not in Purves's Land, or not in the nursery?'

'Well, I never saw her.'

'No, but where were you between the hours of, let us say, six of the clock and eight?'

'I was lookin' after the bairns.'

'In the nursery?'

'Aye.'

'You did not leave the nursery?'

'No.'

'So, for all you know, my client might have been else-where within the confines of the house?'

'Elsie Gollan told me—'

'We will hear from Mistress Gollan soon enough, I expect,' said Cameron Adams. 'Let me be firm on the point, however, that you can state only that Miss Kelso was not *in the nursery* before eight o'clock. You cannot say for an absolute that she was not elsewhere in Purves's Land?'

Much put out and sulky, Maddy shook her head. 'No, I canna.'

'Did Miss Kelso say anything to you when she entered the nursery, anything that was of an unusual nature?'

'No. She was quiet.'

'Was she usually other than quiet?'

'She—'

'Particularly as the younger child, Margaret, was already asleep: was that not reason for her to be quiet?'

'Aye, maybe.'

'Did she seem distressed? Did she seem – what's the word that the Advocate Depute prefers – "flustered"?'

Maddy hesitated. 'A wee bit.'

'Come now,' said Cameron Adams. 'What does that mean? Was she in tears?'

'Och, no.'

'In a temper?'

'No.'

'She came in quietly and went about her duties with the older children – quietly.'

'Aye.'

'She was not distressed at all, was she?'

'When I asked her about Peterkin she was worried.'

'Oh, indeed! And what did she say in answer to your enquiry?'

'That he had a rash.'

'She was worried about the rash?'

'Aye – an' somethin' else too.'

'Is that perhaps an opinion formed in hindsight?' said Cameron Adams. 'Because I cannot see that you have any basis, in what you have so far said, for such mysterious conjecture. Did she tell you what this "something else" might be?'

'No.'

Maddy had already informed the court that Clare had told her that she had been late because Peterkin was unwell with a rash, and that she had given him sulphur for it while at Mrs Handyside's house. Guided by Ordway, Maddy had also told that there was no sign of bottle or packet and that, as far as she was aware, the chest of remedies in the cupboard in the nursery had not been opened by Clare Kelso that day or that night, though there was a box of sulphur powder within it.

Cameron had almost finished with Maddy now.

He said, 'At what hour did the officers of the Watch come?'

'About ten,' said Maddy. 'Ten or half past.'

'In that period of two hours did Miss Kelso receive a visitation from Mrs Edwina Purves or from anyone else in the household?'

'No, she did not.'

'Who brought in the officers?'

'Mr McIntyre, the coachman. He had seen the magistrates' order for her arrest.'

'How did Miss Kelso behave?'

'She screamed – an' then she was quiet again.'

'Did she say nothing at all?'

'She said "Peterkin, oh my wee boy", or somethin' like it. She was fair shocked.'

'Because nobody had brought her word that her child was gravely ill?'

'Nobody that I saw,' said Maddy.

Morning had long ago waned into afternoon. March had shown its inconstant character in the tall window that faced the jury. Blinks of sunshine, spatters of rain, dust and old leaves whirled high on gusts of the cold east wind.

The parade of witnesses continued. Clare watched them listlessly now, emotions dulled by the memory of that last afternoon with Peterkin and Frederick. She had not known that Edwina had received a message from the cottage in Caltoun, that she had been summoned to her son's deathbed. Somehow, it did not seem to matter. It was no more than evidence of a malice that she had grown used to over the years. She listened to the questions, the answers. Heard her own words quoted by one witness after another. Heard her letter to Frederick read aloud by Mr Hume and a letter that Frederick had written to the prosecutors quoted by Mr Ordway in a voice that mocked the sentiments contained in the words. Heard recent letters from Frederick cited, his statement, his acknowledgment that Peterkin was his son.

Clare heard Lord Drumfin enquire where Mr Striker was to be found now. And Mr Ordway answer that he was in Ireland. She heard the majestic chancellor of the jury demand an explanation as to why this paragon of responsibility had not deemed it necessary to present himself to the court and support the mother of his child in her time of trial. And she heard Lord Pole inform the juryman that his question was not in order, that Mr Striker, being a merchant trader, could not simply abandon his business ventures no matter how much he might wish to do so. Business. Business: the word was bruited back and forth in angry exchanges between bar and bench.

Clare was brought a round of buttered bread and a cup of water and, like many in the gallery, ate a meagre dinner while the arguments rumbled on. A bowl of broth was brought in for Lord Drumfin. But Lord Pole would have none of it and contented himself with an orange and a glass of plain water.

Mr Lewis, chief officer of the Watch, who had accompanied Clare to the Tolbooth, reported what had been said on the way. Mr Rossmore, Elsie Gollan and Mrs McNab all gave evidence. The court was told of the servant's infatuation with Mr Striker, of her encounter with him at Sinclairs' Land, her acts of intimacy at the Linden Tree, her belief that Mr Striker would marry her. Casual conversations that Clare could not recall were quoted verbatim by servants: gossip and chit-chat dignified by the grandeur and gravity of the courtroom.

All honest stuff, however. And most of it true.

Finally, without comment or embellishment, Clarc's initial declaration was read out in full by Mr Hume.

And the case for the Crown was complete.

On Soul and Conscience

—————◆◆◆—————

If the case against Clare Kelso was woven from a web of facts, rumours and deceptions, the trial itself was seamless. There was no interval between the prosecutor's last words and the first words offered by Mr Adams' witnesses as exculpatory proof of the panel's innocence.

There was much clearing of throats, murmuring of opinions and shuttling out of the rear doors of the court-room in search of public closets. Mr Ordway and his assistants munched handfuls of nuts and dried fruits from a bowl, sipped a little sweet wine and shuffled papers into order for the second act in the drama. Cameron, however, was on his feet almost before the door had closed behind the last prosecution witness. He remained so, robed and wigged and grave as a pallbearer, for two or three minutes until Lord Pole instructed him to commence and continue, and the macer called Doctor Ure to the stand.

Doctor Alexander Ure was a lecturer in chemistry in Glasgow and a Fellow of the Royal Society, no less. Duly sworn, he declared on soul and conscience that he had examined and analysed the king's yellow purchased by Mr Brown from the stock in the Apothecaries' Hall. It floated in water and mixed with water only when stirred, at which time it formed a cloudy sediment. The sample given was lighter in colour than might be expected for pure sulphuret of arsenic as it had been mingled, in small part, with magnesia which, even to a semi-skilled eye, would give it the appearance of medicinal sulphur.

Cameron asked, 'Why did Dr McCorkindale not mention to us that the king's yellow sold in the Apothecaries' Hall had been mixed, however lightly, with magnesia?'

'Perhaps he did not test it for magnesia?'

'Yes,' said Cameron, 'or perhaps his analytical sample did not come from the Hall at all.'

Robert Ordway was on his feet at once, tendering a strenuous objection and pointing out that Dr McCorkindale's sample had come from the stomach of the deceased infant.

Mr Adams demurred. To the witness he said, 'Are mistakes sometimes committed at the counter of the Apothecaries' Hall?'

'M'luds, I vigorously object,' Ordway called out. 'The question is not relative to any particular mistake but to errors in general. In fact it is only upon the word of the panel that we are led to believe that the deleterious drug was purchased at the Hall at all.'

Cameron said, 'Am I not to be allowed to prove any facts that might tend to exculpate and alleviate the guilt of the prisoner? After all, it is her contention – crucial to a fair judgment – that she purchased sulphur at the Hall and was given king's yellow by mistake.'

'There is no proof or corroboration that the panel purchased sulphur at the Hall at all. We have heard nothing to that effect,' said Lord Pole.

'Perhaps not directly, m'lud,' said Cameron. 'We have heard from a boy who cannot remember selling an *ounce* of the obnoxious article.'

'*After* the event, sir,' Ordway shouted. '*After* the dreadful event.'

'Very well,' said Cameron. 'If it is necessary, gentlemen, then I will take the high ground on this matter. It is no very difficult thing to produce a skein of witnesses who will swear that mistakes of this kind are a frequent occurrence not only in the Apothecaries' Hall but in every blessed druggist's in the city.'

Lord Pole said, 'We are not here to sit in judgment on the competence of apothecaries. The Advocate Depute's objection is clearly valid and will be sustained.'

Lord Drumfin was not prepared, quite, to let it go at that.

In a swaddle of ermine and scarlet he leaned over the bench and in a reasonable, almost consoling tone, told Mr Adams, 'We would not wish to prevent you introducing direct proof that king's yellow was substituted for sulphur. Implication is not proof, Mr Adams, not *for* the panel nor *against* her. If, however, the jury desires to be horrified by stories of how mustard was sold for magnesia or gunpowder for cayenne, the bench will bow to its wish.'

None of the jury, not even the contentious Mr Hamilton, wished to be bothered with that diversion, and the expert testimony of Dr Ure drew to a dreary close without further interruption or debate.

Clare's eyes were wearied by peering through the veil. She had not wept since the first hour of the morning and would not weep again. She felt arid within, though she was not without hope that Cameron Adams would contrive a miracle and secure her acquittal; that he would do so without uncovering the truth that she had striven to hide, not from herself but from the world at large. She was a little afraid of Mr Adams' zeal and perspicacity, and of his kindness. She lifted the lace from her face and looked out across the dusky hall at Edwina Purves who, to Clare's astonishment, had taken her stance in the witness box. She had known that Andrew and Eunice had been listed to speak in her defence but she had not expected to see Edwina there, for Edwina was, and always had been, an enemy.

The woman was dressed in an expensive printed cotton gown in mauve and wore a bustle pad that, in the nakedness of the witness cage, made her seem shorter and stouter. She had gone to great pains with trimmings, though, and had topped an elaborate hair-do with a hat that was far too luxurious for the occasion. She was highly nervous and wrung her hands over and over each other, stammered as she repeated the oath and, even before Mr Adams got down to serious questioning, swayed almost as if she would swoon.

Edwina told who she was, and how the panel had been brought into her employ and what duties the panel had done within the household and, when prodded by the advocate, admitted that she had few faults to find with Kelso as far as service went. She made it clear, however, that she did not find the girl at all agreeable and thought her 'forward' in the extreme. No, not garrulous or impudent the way some low-bred servants were, just lacking in proper humility and respect.

When asked if her husband, Mr Andrew Purves, regarded the young woman as servant or kin, Edwina managed to give no sort of answer at all but hemmed and hawed until Mr Adams put her out of her misery by suddenly changing direction.

'On the evening in question, Mrs Purves – that is the last day of December – at about the hour of seven o'clock or a little time after, did you receive word from Coachman McIntyre that a man had called to see Miss Kelso?'

'I did not know who the man was.'

'Did you not ask Coachman McIntyre to discover the man's name?'

'No, he – I – no name was given. He – the man – did not know enough manners to give a name. He waited in the yard.'

'Did you not ask McIntyre if it was Mr Striker?'

'I may have done. Yes – I think – I may.'

'What were you doing when the visitor arrived?'

'I was in my dressing-room.'

'Not at supper?'

'No, it was too soon for supper.'

'Where was Mr Purves, your husband?'

'I really do not recall.'

'Was he not at home?'

'No, I believe that he was out, supping out. Really, I do not know.'

'What did you do?' Cameron said.

'What could I do? I didn't know where he was. I do not keep a rein upon my husband, sir. He is perfectly well able to look after himself and come and go as he pleases, when he pleases.'

'I meant, madam,' said Cameron, 'what did you do about the stranger waiting in the yard?'

'Sent Pym – my servant – to see what he wanted.'

'How long was your servant gone?'

'A few minutes only.'

'She returned with a message, did she not?'

'Yes, directly.'

'What was that message?'

'Some garbled nonsense that Kelso's child was unwell.'

'Did the caller – who was Mr Lumsden, as we know – did he impart to your servant any sense of urgency, of the seriousness of the child's illness?'

'Children are always unwell.'

'You did not speak with the man in person?'

'Certainly not.'

'Did you send to look for Clare Kelso?'

'I did not have to do so,' said Edwina. 'I knew that she was not at home.'

'Do you mean that she was not in the nursery?' said Cameron. 'Had you been to the nursery?'

'No, but I knew –' Edwina paused. 'One knows these things.'

'Did you instruct your servant Pym to tell the other servants to let you know as soon as Clare Kelso returned?'

'I may have done. I cannot recall every trivial item of conversation.'

'Trivial? I would not have thought that a sick child was a trivial matter,' said Cameron. 'Be that as it may, you did not tell *anyone* about the message, did you?'

'I cannot recall.'

'In fact,' Cameron said, 'did you not give your servant Pym specific instructions that nobody was to be told?'

'N . . . n . . . no,' Edwina stammered.

The hand-wringing had become so rapid and rolling that every eye in court was drawn to it, including those of their lordships. The plump, gloved fingers roiled and twisted as if they had a life independent of Edwina Purves, like two small uncontrollable animals that had escaped from her sleeves.

'You did not, however, leave a verbal or written message for Clare Kelso, did you?' Cameron said.

'I – I forgot. I meant to do so but I – it slipped my attention.'

'When did you take supper?' Cameron said.

'About half past eight o'clock.'

'With the family in the dining-room?'

'Yes.'

'Who was present at supper?'

'The family.'

'Tell the court who was present, please.'

'My father-in-law, my mother-in-law.'

'And?'

'That – that was all.'

'Your husband did not return for supper.'

'He did not.'

'Was it not customary for your son William to join the family at the supper table?'

'Only now and then, when my husband was present. I will confess that I do not approve of my husband's insistence that a small, boy be granted the privileges of supping with adult persons.'

'An eccentricity, of course,' Cameron agreed. 'Supper was served, eaten and cleared by what time?'

'About half past nine o'clock.'

'And then?'

'I retired to my room.'

'You did not go first to the nursery?'

'No, it was not my habit to disturb the children so late into the evening. I went to my room, with my servant.'

'Did you ask her if Clare Kelso had returned?'

'I may have done. I cannot recall.'

'If I may make the observation, Mrs Purves, you did not seem at all perturbed that your nursery servant had not returned from her afternoon call. Let alone that her child was unwell.'

'Kelso was a law unto herself,' said Edwina. 'My husband saw to that, sir.'

'Ah!' said Cameron. 'Did you, perhaps, suppose that Clare Kelso was *with* your husband?'

The galleries buzzed. Pole clacked on the bench and Edwina's answer was almost lost in the din.

'*Certainly not,*' Edwina cried, loudly. '*Certainly not. How dare you suggest it?*'

'I suggest nothing,' put in Cameron, quick but innocent. 'When did you next see Clare Kelso?'

'I did not see her again. I retired to my bed about ten of the clock and was wakened from my sleep some time later by the officers when they came to take her away,' Edwina said. 'By the time I attired myself decently, she had been taken downstairs. I may – yes, I do believe I glimpsed her as she was led off. But I did not speak with her.'

'So, Clare Kelso did not know, because nobody had told her, that her child, Peterkin, was sick, let alone that he was dead?'

'She would know if she killed him, wouldn't she?'

'That, madam,' said Cameron stiffly, 'is what we are trying to ascertain by polite and diligent enquiry. I will put it into other words: was Clare Kelso told by you or any of your servants that her child was ill?'

'I do not think she was.'

The buzz in the court was muted, puzzled but sympathetic. Even Pole did not have the gall to smother it. He let it continue until Advocate Adams loudly cleared his throat and, standing close now, addressed the witness once more.

'As the lady of the house of Purves were you not concerned to learn what had taken place, not the least curious?' Cameron allowed half a minute for Edwina to muster a reply but she gave none. She wrung her hands furiously and pouted. He said gently, 'Perhaps your husband told you what was going on?'

'Pym told me.'

'Not your husband?'

'No.'

'Your husband was too occupied attending to the matter, reading the warrant and the like, I suppose,' Cameron
turned away as if he intended to let the matter slip.
Edwina's bosom heaved under the mauve cotton, her
hands became suddenly still, fingers knotted. Cameron
glanced back over his shoulder. 'Or was your husband not
there at all?'

Any one of a dozen witnesses could have testified that
Mr Andrew Purves had not been at home that whole
evening and that the arrest of Clare Kelso had taken place
without the permission or intervention of anyone of higher
authority than a male servant and a lady's-maid. But the
revelation would do only from Edwina Purves's mouth and
Cameron had no intention of letting the woman retreat
again into embarrassed silence.

'Was your husband there, madam?'

'No, he was not.'

'He was not in the house?'

'He had not returned, no.'

'When did he return?'

'After – after midnight, I think.'

'Do you not know?'

'About a quarter past twelve.'

'On the first day of the New Year?'

'Yes.'

'Did he tell you where he had been?'

'He was too concerned with what had happened.'
Cameron said, 'What *did* he do?'

'He went at once to the Tolbooth to talk with the officer
and then, I believe, he returned to the house and instructed
our male servants to make the chaise ready for a journey to
Edinburgh.'

'To Edinburgh?'

'To hire a lawyer.'

'Why did he do that, do you think, Mrs Purves?'

'Because he is a fool,' Edwina said.

It was clear, not only from the swell of her belly but also from her cowed and waddling demeanour that Pym was well advanced into pregnancy. In the welter of more important events, it seemed, nobody had thought fit to burden Clare with mere domestic gossip and she had not known of Pym's condition. In spite of her own fatal predicament and the animosity that Edwina's lady's-maid had shown towards her in the past, Clare felt a pang of sympathy for Pym. There was, as yet, no wedding band upon her finger and, in her face, none of the smug triumph of a girl who has netted a valet for a husband.

Clare wondered if Peter-Pierre had fled rather than square up to fatherhood. It would be one more problem for Mr Andrew to deal with, though Clare did not doubt that her master would do his duty as a decent and honourable man, and see Pym delivered and settled again into the household as he had done for other servants in the past, Clare herself included.

Coachman McIntyre had already given evidence. Very brusque, he was, and to the point. He had not known what news or information the man Lumsden had carried for Clare Kelso. He had fetched word at once to the mistress of the house, Mrs Edwina Purves. She had sent her maid who had talked with the man, said nothing, paid the man nothing for his trouble and had instructed that he be shown out of the yard.

Cameron Adams enquired politely after Pym's condition, about which, of course, the public was by now exceedingly curious. Lord Pole, however, suggested that, as the hour was wearing late, Mr Adams move along to relevant matters; at which point Mr McKay was brought from his seat to extract from the witness in as short a time as possible corroboration of the tale that her mistress had spun.

Unusually, Pym was weepy. It might have been a fine face-saving act, Clare supposed, but Mr McKay was certainly not going to be softened by tears.

He concluded, 'The man Lumsden told you that Clare Kelso's child was ailing and that a doctor had been sent for to the cottage in Caltoun?'

'Aye.'

'You gave this report to your mistress without searching for Clare Kelso?'

'Aye.'

'What did your mistress tell you to do?'

'No' t'say nothin' to nobody.'

'And did you obey your mistress?'

'Aye.'

'Did you not return to the nursery to discuss the matter with the servant Madelaine, or to the kitchen, perhaps?'

'Nah.'

'Where did you sup?'

'In Mrs Purves's dressin'-room.'

'Why did you not sup in the kitchen, as was, I believe, the customary thing?'

'Mistress Edwina told me not to. She fetched me a tray herself.'

McKay allowed himself an audible groan. 'After supper, did your mistress dismiss you?'

'Nah, sir,' said Pym, dolefully. 'I was t'sleep on the cot in the dressin'-room that night.'

'Why? Were you sick? Did your mistress wish to make you comfortable, keep an eye on your welfare?' McKay suggested.

'I was no' t'talk wi' the others.'

'Was your mistress not concerned about the plight of Kelso's child?'

'She was pleased.'

'I beg your pardon?' said McKay.

'She was fair pleased.'

'At a child being ill?'

'She never liked Clare,' said Pym.

'So, the panel – Clare Kelso – did not hear from your lips that her child was ill and attended by a doctor?'

'Nah.' Pym lowered her head and let tears splash upon the rail of the box. 'She never knew. I should've told her, sir, but I had my orders, y'see.'

'Were you there when the officers came for her?'

'I saw it, aye.'

'What did you think had happened?'

'I thought her bairn had died.'

'Why did you think that?'

'Because I heard her cry.'

'Weep?'

'Cry out, sir,' said Pym.

'From within the nursery?'

'Aye. She cried loud.'

'What did she cry out?' said McKay.

'She cried out t'God. An' then she shouted – *He's dead. Peterkin's dead. My wee boy's dead.*'

Whether it was the memory of the panel's suffering or from some guilt within herself, Pym dissolved into such hard and racking tears that the majestic juryman rose to his feet and suggested that the witness had been subjected to too much strain already and that it would be humane to dismiss her unless further testimony was absolutely crucial. Kind hearts in the gallery applauded and whistled. Pole was beside himself at the unwarranted usurping of judicial authority. He would have called down the wrath of the court upon Mr Hamilton if Lord Drumfin had not placated him and, with the Advocate Depute's permission, had the unfortunate female escorted from the box.

'Mr Adams?' Pole hissed.

'M'lud?'

'I will not have this bullying of witnesses,' Pole said. 'What you have offered to us throughout the course of this long day bears very little legal weight. I trust that the good men of the jury will recognise the flimsiness of what you are about and will take heed when the time comes.'

'With respect, m'lud,' said Cameron, 'I am obliged to make what defence I can for the panel.'

'Indeed you are, sir.'

'And to present a case for acquittal without the evidence of the one person who could ensure that acquittal.'

'Who do you mean, sir?' said Pole.

'I mean, m'lud, the father of the child.'

'Oh!' said Pole, falling into the trap that he had baited for himself. 'And why have you not sought fit to summon the father here, business or no business?'

'Because the father – Mr Frederick Striker – cannot be found.'

Drumfin leaned forward. 'Have you tried to run the fellow to earth, Mr Adams?'

'I have, m'lud, but entirely without success. He is not to be discovered in those places where his letters were put to the mail. Mr Walcott and I have had agents seek for him in vain.'

'What does the absence of the father, of Mr Striker, have to do with it?' Pole demanded. 'He was not here in Scotland when the poison was administered. He has not been in association with the panel since the autumn of the year. You cannot possibly expect the court to infer that Mr Striker had anything whatsoever to do with the murder. That was not the line of your defence at all.'

'Mr Striker is everywhere in this case, m'lud,' said Cameron, bravely. 'His influence, as we have seen, is perniciously displayed, not only upon the unfortunate girl but upon many of the witnesses who have passed before us.'

'Pish and tosh!' Pole's anger turned to impatience. 'I for one would like to be out of here before kirk tomorrow, Mr Adams. How many more witnesses have you to call?'

'If your lordship will consult the list, you will see that the answer is two,' said Cameron. 'Two witnesses upon whom the influence of the absent Mr Striker was very strong indeed.'

'His sister, I suppose,' said Pole.

'Yes, m'lud.'

'Call her then,' said Drumfin.

'As soon as we have light,' said Pole.

Small though the hall might be, when glittering chandeliers were roped down and rings of candles lighted, the scene in the court became one of gilded splendour. It was reflected and projected outward into the night by the tall glass windows and the lords of the Justiciary seemed to have guardians seated like angels in the sky, and jurymen, inquisitors and witnesses to have acquired doppelgangers in the dark air above the High Street.

In appearance, Eunice Striker Bates was perfectly in

tune with the hour, a person not suited to daylight but to the oily theatricality of glowing candles and polished brass.

Broad-shouldered and full-bosomed, face pale as a mask, she looked like some Drury Lane tragedienne hired to perform from a repertoire of classical speeches. She held her head high, her chin out. Her hands, in contrast to Edwina's, rested white and motionless upon the rail. Even her flat and unfamiliar accent gained a kind of depth from the quiet, packed surroundings as she was sworn to speak only the truth before God and the assize.

Her account of herself was brief and modest. She had been brought to Glasgow by her brother after the death of her husband. Her brother had been her protector since youth and had taken responsibility for her welfare since the death of her mother and, later, her father, many years ago. She resided now with her brother in a villa in Grahamston and kept house for him. She had known of her brother's liaison with the panel and had heard from Frederick's own lips that he intended to marry Clare Kelso. But he had vacillated in that intention towards the fulfilment of Miss Kelso's term, and afterwards.

Had there been a reason for Mr Striker's change of heart?

It was Mrs Bates' belief that her brother intended to marry another girl or woman, one who had more to offer him materially.

Did Mrs Bates know this woman or girl?

Only that she was the daughter of a landowner in Ireland.

Was Frederick Striker free with this information?

As free as he was with any information, which meant that he was not open or expansive about his plans and intentions.

When had Mrs Bates last seen her brother?

Mrs Bates answered without hesitation that she had not seen her brother since the latter part of October, when his visit had been short. Nor, Mrs Bates volunteered, had she heard from him by letter in the time between his departure and the tragic events which had brought her here today.

Unlike her brother, Mrs Bates had evinced no coolness towards the panel because of her condition. Indeed the child had been born in her presence in the villa at Grahamston with a midwife in attendance. Mr Andrew Purves had paid for the midwife and had paid, a little later, for the upkeep of the child at Mrs Handyside's cottage in Caltoun.

Yes, Mrs Bates continued to entertain Miss Kelso at her home. Yes, Mrs Bates was a regular – even frequent – visitor to the Handyside cottage to visit her brother's natural heir and to observe his welfare and progress, which she found most satisfactory. No, her brother had not instructed her to attend and to observe the upbringing of his son. She visited the child because she wished to do so, not out of a sense of duty or obligation to any of the parties.

Did she, in fact, love Peterkin?

Mrs Bates thought that the court might take it that she loved the child almost as if he was her own.

She had never borne children, however?

No.

Did Frederick Striker offer any form of material support for the child?

He did not. It was left to Mr Purves to provide. Which Mr Purves did without hesitation or complaint. Yes, she did know Mr Purves and he had called on two or three occasions at her house before and just after the birth of the infant. She was not well acquainted with him, however, and could judge his character – honest and generous and responsible – only from his actions towards the panel.

Did Mr Frederick Striker transact business with Mr Purves or with the Captains' Bank?

Mrs Bates believed that he did, or had done so, but she was not party to the details of any such transactions and felt that such a question might best be answered by Mr Purves.

Did Mrs Bates see or communicate with the panel upon the fatal day of December thirty-first of last year?

She did not do so, on either count.

Or with Mr Andrew Purves, perhaps?

No, she had no reason to communicate with Mr Purves or, as far as she could tell, he with her.

When was the last time that Mrs Bates had seen Mr Purves?

Some weeks before.

And the child, Peterkin?

Three days previously when he had seemed to her well and thriving.

And the panel, Clare Kelso?

Two weeks backward from Sunday.

What could Mrs Bates tell the court about the attitude of Clare Kelso to her child?

Clare Kelso had loved the child more than she had loved life itself. She had been a caring and attentive mother, in so far as circumstances allowed her to be. She, Eunice Bates, had heard no cross word directed towards the child from Clare Kelso, nor did she detect the least sign of bitterness or transfer of anger towards the infant for the untoward circumstances of his birth. She had borne her burden at first with hope and then, as that faded, with resignation, a fortitude gained from and revolving around the child that had been born to her.

Had the panel spoken harshly or bitterly against Frederick Striker within the hearing of or directly to Mrs Bates?

No, Mrs Bates had heard no such feelings expressed.

Clare Kelso bore her circumstances and her rejection with stoicism?

With fortitude.

Out of her friendship with the panel and her fondness for the child, in her experience, did Mrs Bates believe that Clare Kelso had administered poison deliberately, with the intention to murder her babe and do away with him?

Mrs Bates did not believe Clare Kelso capable of such an act.

She had nothing to gain from it?

Nothing at all to gain from it. Indeed, she had lost by death the only thing that, in Mrs Bates' judgment, gave meaning, purpose and wholeness to her life.

By 'the only thing' did Mrs Bates mean the child?

Of course Mrs Bates meant the child.

Not Mrs Bates' brother, not the lover?

Certainly not.

Could it not be that Clare Kelso had taken the life of her child to free herself of an encumbrance?

The child was no encumbrance.

An impediment then?

Impediment to what, pray?

The return of her lover, of Mrs Bates' brother.

Such a suggestion was, in Mrs Bates' opinion, utterly without foundation. Her brother had no animosity towards the child. He might be indifferent to it, perhaps, but there had been nothing in her communications with him, or with the panel, to suggest that it was the child that kept him abroad.

Finally, Mr Adams put to the witness a question that allowed Mrs Bates to reiterate her belief that Clare Kelso was incapable of murdering her son and that the death could not be other than accidental.

Robert Ordway was on his feet before his opponent at the bar had time to find his seat.

'Madam,' Ordway said, 'from your observations of the accused woman, would you say that Clare Kelso is still in love with your brother?'

'I would say that she is not.'

'Would you say that she has come to hate him?'

'I do not know that I would use the word "hate".'

'What word then would be appropriate?' said Ordway.

For the first time in the giving of her evidence Eunice was at a loss. The white hands moved up the rail together, then apart and she let her neck muscles slacken so that, for an instant, her head was curiously cocked.

'I cannot think – I cannot say—'

'I put it to you, madam, that Clare Kelso *did* hate your brother, however much she may have endeavoured to hide the emotion from you.'

'No, I would have known.'

'How would you have known?'

'Because I am thoroughly familiar with that emotion.'

'What?' said Ordway, caught a little off balance.

'I have experienced hatred, sir, and I have experienced malice. And I will state in answer to your question that Clare Kelso was possessed of neither feeling towards my brother.'

'Do you not then believe that she might have put away the child to take revenge upon the child's father?'

'Ridiculous!' said Eunice Striker Bates.

'Do you not suppose—'

Cameron intervened to object that the witness had answered the question and given an opinion and that neither she nor the esteemed Advocate Depute were in the business of dealing in hypotheses. Pole grudgingly upheld, and Robert Ordway was left lame in one leg of his examination.

Clare watched and listened intently now. She had, at some point, edged forward to balance on the very edge of the chair, veil lifted, knuckles of one hand poised to support her chin.

'Mrs Bates, did you not see the panel at all upon that fateful day?'

'I have said that I did not.'

'Therefore you have no knowledge of where she might have been or what she did between the hours of six and eight o'clock?' said Robert Ordway.

'None at all,' Eunice answered, lying with a smoothness and efficiency that Clare now saw as a family trait, one of which Frederick would have been proud.

It being New Year's Eve there had been a stir in the streets and the stalls along the Trongate had stayed open late, lit by lanterns and tar dips that cast swarming shadows on the pavé under the awnings. The homing instinct was stronger that night than at any other time in the year and porters and caddies, coachmen, carters and their vehicles had been thick along Argyll Street and out towards the toll beyond Grahamston.

Clare had walked fast, a shawl cowled over her head, eyes down, face hidden, nothing but another small, scurrying figure in the ebb and flow of pedestrian traffic, unnoticed and un-remarked. She had not been more than twenty minutes or a

*half-hour behind Frederick and yet, when she had been ad-
mitted to the villa and had asked, 'Where is he?' Eunice, with a
shake of the head, had told her, 'He's gone.'*

*Eunice had put an arm about her shaking shoulders and had
led her into the parlour. There had been a candlestick upon the
piano lid and music littered about the floor and, as Clare had
come up the path from the gate – before that – she had heard the
huge, infuriated sound of the instrument's keys being thumped
as if with fists, and had thought that Frederick, in his clumsy
way, had taken to practising too.*

*Eunice had seated her upon a round chair amid the clutter
and, standing just behind her, had asked, 'Did he meet with
you?'*

'Yes.'

'Did he see Peterkin?'

'Yes.'

'Did Frederick hold him?'

*'For a moment, yes.' Clare had glanced round. 'Why,
Eunice, why has he run away again? He did not seem to
mind me or the baby. Why can he not stay, just for a little
while?'*

'Did Peterkin cry?'

*'No, not when his Daddy held him. Frederick had sweet-
meats to give him and he held him on his knees and gave him
them himself.' Clare had begun to cry. 'I thought he would
stay.'*

'I sent Frederick away.'

'Why, Eunice, why?'

'Because he will harm you. He will harm us all, Clare.'

'No, he loved—'

'This time,' Eunice had said, 'he will not return.'

*Clare had put her hands into the pocket of her dress, had
fished and fumbled for a handkerchief, for her eyes were*

*streaming and her nose running. Eunice had leaned across her
and had held out a clean, lace-bordered handkerchief for her
and Clare had just reached up to take it when the woman said,
'What's that?'*

*'Frederick's, I will leave it here. I used only a teaspoonful.
There's plenty left. Though –' more copious tears ' he will not
need it now, if you say he has gone for good and all. Is it true?
Did you send him away?'*

*Eunice had not been listening. The lace-bordered hand-
kerchief had fallen from her fingers and lay upon the carpet
in a crumpled pyramid, crushed when Eunice had kneeled on
it.*

*The action of kneeling had not seemed voluntary, more like a
collapse, a stiff, wooden-jointed folding, like a puppet with
frayed strings.*

'Frederick gave you this?'

'I had none. I meant to buy fresh, but—'

'What – what is it, Clare? What did Frederick say it was?'

'Sulphur, for Peterkin, for his rash.'

*Eunice had clutched the little smooth blue glass jar in both
hands, had held it up before her eyes like a holy relic. She had
keened and rocked on her heels, had pressed the jar to her brow,
bent over. 'Oh, God! Oh, God! Oh, God!'*

*'What? What?' In alarm Clare had put her arm about the
woman's body and had felt through the garments the quivering
of her flesh. 'What is it? What's wrong?'*

'I sent him away, God, I sent him away.'

'Perhaps he'll come back. He usually does.'

*Eunice's face had been down almost to the carpet, her voice
thick and clotted as if her throat had filled with dust. All Clare
had seen had been the strong bent back and the hair, greying
along the nape of the neck and about the ears. She had not seen
the anguish or the sudden iron fixing of the mask over it, nor*

had she noticed that the blue glass jar had gone, vanished into a sleeve or a pocket.

She had slipped down to comfort Eunice and they had wept together for a moment or two, Eunice with her face hidden in the folds of her skirt, Clare leaning upon her in the belief that they were both weeping for Frederick who, selfishly, waywardly, had hurt them both in fair measure.

After a minute, Eunice had got to her feet. Her face was bloodlessly white, and her eyes had sunk back deeply into their sockets so that Clare could not see them at all, as if a vizor had been pulled across them. Eunice had reached down a hand and had drawn Clare to her feet.

'I must go,' Clare had said. 'I only came to talk to Frederick, to ask him if he thought our child bonnie.'

In a voice flatter and harder than marble, Eunice had said, unforgivably, 'We will take tea first, my dear. Before you go back to town, you must tell me what happened this afternoon. What happened between you and my brother. Leaving out no detail at all.'

'Concerning Peterkin?'

'Yes,' Eunice had said. 'Especially concerning Peterkin.'

In spite of his best intentions and all his experience as an advocate Mr Robert Ordway could not keep Frederick Striker's name out of the courtroom. The gadfly nature of the Englishman was not, of itself, a mark against him, nor was the fact that business kept him permanently on the hop. Even the fathering of an illegitimate child contained only the kernel of scandal for the jurymen fancied themselves as worldly-wise. What had come forth about Striker was that he had neglected his responsibilities towards the servant girl and her child. Duty was the ethic that made a fellow a gentleman and it had become clear, or at least implicit, that Frederick Striker, for all his airs and graces, his promises and written testimonies, was a chap who did not know his place or how to behave in it.

The jurymen were local to Glasgow. A number of them had seen Clare about the town or had heard of her through the gossip of wives and servants. She was too fine looking a girl to have merged with the grey throng and, whatever the masses might think of her, the lawyers and judges could tell that the jury had swung behind her, almost regardless of evidence.

What axe against the justiciary the majestic Hamilton had to grind was a mystery. He, however, had been too voluble in his support of the panel's cause to ignore, too well-spoken and well-educated to be cowed by their lordships. How Hamilton's name had cropped up on the jury list was never revealed, and it was assumed by all and sundry that it had been pure random chance that had brought him into the small hall that Saturday to buzz like a bee in Lord Pole's bonnet.

It was Mr Hamilton who would interrupt the final witness for the defence and, by his pertinacity, throw a cloud of confusion over the trial's closing hours. By then, however, Mr Andrew Purves had been in the box for some time and had impressed all those present with his dignity and honesty.

Andrew had explained the circumstances of Clare Kelso's arrival in his household and come close to wringing tears from the more sentimental folk in the gallery when he described the death of Clare's mother and how he had tended the orphan. He had told too of her thirst for knowledge and her ready learning, and how, this past year or so, she had been tutor to his children as well as nurse. His testimonial to Clare's character and worth was too down-to-earth to be glowing and had no ring of falsity to it.

The court then heard how Mr Andrew Purves, acting
for and on behalf of the interests of the Captains' Bank,
had advanced a loan to Mr Striker for the purchase of a
cargo of printed calico and how, after the conclusion of
that transaction to the benefit of all parties, two or three
other small arrangements of business had been conducted
between the bank and the English gentleman.

Mr McKay, who was steering this easy course, tactfully
did not press Andrew Purves to reveal confidential details
on these later transactions.

'Are you still engaged in financing aspects of Mr Striker's trading ventures?' said Mr McKay.

'No, sir, I am not.'

'Is there a reason for that, sir?'

'I do not believe that Mr Striker is an honourable man.'

'In business or in matters of the heart?'

'One reflects upon the other,' said Andrew.

Mr McKay sat down at this juncture and gave over the
witness to Mr Adams who, with considerable delicacy, led
Mr Purves to tell of the 'courtship' of Clare Kelso by
Frederick Striker and how he, in small ways, had encouraged it.

It was towards the end of this phase of Andrew Purves's
evidence that Mr Hamilton, sanctioned by Lord Drumfin,
put the first of his two questions on behalf of the jury
members.

'May we enquire of the witness, m'lud, how he regarded
the panel – as servant or as kinswoman?' Hamilton said.

'I do not see that the question is pertinent,' Pole said.

'Will Mr Purves not be allowed to answer it?' Hamilton
persisted.

'He may answer it only when you inform me what is its
pertinence,' said Pole, 'beyond mischief.'

'No mischief, my lord, I assure you,' said Hamilton. 'It is a matter of judging how the girl was treated.'

'You are being *told* how she was treated. She was being treated with great consideration and generosity.'

'Aye, my lord – for a servant.'

'That is what she was,' said Lord Pole.

'She was also a kinswoman of the witness, a cousin germane,' said Mr Hamilton. 'She may have been well treated as a servant but as a cousin to the Purves family she was treated with less than her due.'

'That is a matter of judgment and opinion,' said Pole.

The Advocate Depute got to his feet and put in his pennyworth. 'I believe, my lord, that the good juryman is asking if the witness had the right to give Miss Kelso away to Mr Striker. If she was a servant, he had not. If he thought of her as a cousin then he was acting as he saw proper.'

'Mr Purves did not give her away,' said Pole. 'She gave herself away.'

Andrew spoke out. 'My lords, I will answer the juryman's question, though perhaps in a less clear-cut manner than he wishes. With permission, I will do my best.'

'Please do,' said Drumfin.

'I regarded Clare Kelso as my cousin, as a kinswoman. I was inclined to treat her as such and would, perhaps, have given her more of the liberties of a family member if it had not been for my wife. My wife did not agree with me that Clare Kelso had claim to the priorities of kinship. My wife saw her as a servant and for that reason I naturally took regard for my wife's wishes and trod a line between, as best I could do.'

Mr Hamilton opened his mouth but Pole had had enough of it and silenced him emphatically with a gesture.

Mr Hamilton sat down, willing to bide his time.

Cameron Adams continued with the witness. He extracted an admission that he, Andrew Purves, had misjudged the integrity of Frederick Striker and had encouraged the fellow's courtship of Clare Kelso. No, he had not contrived at being rid of her. She had told him that she was in love with Mr Striker and wished nothing more than to marry him and to be his wife and tend to his household.

When had the witness changed his view of Mr Striker?

Gradually, over the months, culminating in the birth of the child out of wedlock and by Striker's reluctance to shoulder his responsibilities to Miss Kelso and to fulfil his promise to her and to those who had her interests at heart.

Did the witness reprimand or remonstrate with Mr Striker over these breaches of decency and civility?

The witness had no opportunity to do so. Mr Striker was absent for most of the period and returned only briefly and with a certain secrecy.

Did the witness believe that Clare Kelso was still infatuated with Mr Striker?

He did not believe so.

Did the witness believe that Clare Kelso regarded her child as an impediment to marriage to Frederick Striker?

From conversation the witness was of the opinion that Clare Kelso no longer wished to marry Frederick Striker at all, that she was settled with her lot and with the lot of her child, as it had fallen.

Did the witness believe that she had killed the child with forethought, malice and deliberation?

The witness could not imagine it, nor the reason for it. Nor could he believe that under any circumstances Clare Kelso would take the life of any living thing, let alone her own son, whom she loved with a mother's protective passion.

On that positive note Cameron Adams declared himself finished with the witness.

The Advocate Depute did his best with the meat that remained on the bones of the banker's testimony but found precious little there. He picked and scraped for a time at this and that but, weary perhaps after the long, long day and a little careless, missed the question that was burning on the lips of the majestic juryman.

Clare too, like many of the others who had been in the courtroom since the morning hour, was fatigued beyond belief. Her concentration had shrivelled. She found herself annoyed by trivial questions. She wanted out, wanted back to her cell in the Tolbooth, to be alone and quiet and away from the attention of lawyers and judges and jurymen, from the glances of fidgeting spectators and the weight of their sympathy. She felt now that the trial itself had become a cruel punishment. Her back ached and her neck, and a throbbing pain niggled across her brows. She prayed silently that the advocates' closing arguments, though they were arguments upon which her life depended, would not be windy and wordy, that mercy would be shown to the paralysing discomfort that had become worse to bear than grief and guilt and fear. Even the sight of Andrew, the sound of his steady voice extolling her virtues and taking upon himself some of the blame for her foolish vanity, could do no more than delay the long, night-time slide into something close to indifference.

She sipped water, ate the last dry biscuit from the basket that had been brought to her, and heard the drone of voices as from afar, monotonous and mechanical and remorseless now as the chime of the Tolbooth clock.

'My lord?'

Lips pursed, Pole said, 'What is it now, Mr Hamilton?'

'A question on behalf of the jury, my lord.'

'May I say that in all my years on the bench I have never known a more inquisitive or interfering jury. Why can you not be content to hear the evidence as it is exposed by the learned counsels?'

'The witness has not been asked, my lord. And I – we – are rather afraid that the opportunity may pass.'

'Asked what?' said Drumfin.

'Where Mr Purves was on the evening and night of December thirty-first,' said Mr Hamilton.

'We have heard from Mr Purves's own lips how he heard of the tragedy and what he did then,' said Pole.

'But we have not heard where he was until that late hour,' the juryman said, 'or if in that time he encountered Clare Kelso.'

The question, and its answer, revived at once the flagging spirits in the courtroom. Gallery and tier, the lawyers' pit, even the ermine on the bench all stirred at the awkward and indiscreet implication of the juryman's request. Lord Pole had no time to fume himself into a refusal to allow the witness to be humiliated, however. Robert Ordway was first to recover and quick to turn the question to the man in the box.

'Mr Purves,' Ordway cried, 'will you answer?'

'I will, sir,' said Andrew.

'Did you encounter Clare Kelso that afternoon?'

'I did, sir.'

The stir grew to a murmur, the murmur to a soft, astonished roar. 'When did you see her, Mr Purves?'

'Between six o'clock, when she returned from Caltoun, and five or ten to eight o'clock, at which time she went upstairs.'

'Upstairs?'

'Yes,' said Andrew, without flicker. 'From the office behind the banking hall.'

'You were not out at all?' said Drumfin.

'No, m'lud. I was in the banking hall.'

'And you claim that Clare Kelso was with you for almost two hours?' said Ordway.

'I do not "claim it", sir,' Andrew said. 'It is the truth. Clare Kelso and I were together for that period of time.'

'Alone and undisturbed?'

'Yes.'

Over the oceanic waves of speculation that filled the hall, Ordway shouted his question. 'And what, Mr Purves, were you doing with Kelso – alone and undisturbed – for all that while?'

'Talking, sir,' Andrew said.

'About what, pray?'

'Frederick Striker,' said Andrew.

'For two hours?'

'Other matters too.'

'What matters, may I ask?'

'Her child, her mother, her sense of disappointment in how affairs had turned out. Many things,' said Andrew.

'Why was all mention of this meeting omitted from Kelso's declaration?' Ordway shouted through the hub-bub.

'To protect my reputation,' Andrew stated calmly.

'Protect it from what?'

'Scandalous gossip.'

'Even at the risk of her life?'

'Even so,' said Andrew.

*   *   *

Shortly thereafter Robert Ordway addressed the jury.

'Gentlemen, I cannot help feeling that you are reluctant to hear of the evidence of the behaviour of this young and interesting woman to her infant son who could and should not have been less dear to her because he was a natural child. However you may feel, however painful your duty may be, you have sworn to judge and decide by the evidence in the case. Giving weight to the probabilities or improbabilities of the charge, it must be confessed that the accusation against the panel at the bar can only be proven by circumstantial evidence which, I must point out to you, is very often the case in crimes of murder by poisoning.

'Gentlemen, you must make up your minds whether the poison was given willingly or by mistake. Into the heart of the prisoner we cannot see; yet there is such a body of small matters ranked against her, which are in every way legal and convincing, that you might feel that the prisoner would have done well to plead guilty to the crime and depend upon mercy not facts for her life.'

During the half-hour it took the Advocate Depute to review the facts that pointed to her guilt, Clare heard little of the carefully marshalled arguments against her.

She was puzzled as to why Andrew had perjured himself on her behalf. What reason could he have at such a late stage in the trial for risking a dangerous lie. She wondered too why it was that none of the lawyers had thought fit to question Andrew on where he had been *after* she had returned to the nursery, how he had occupied himself in the four hours or so between eight o'clock and midnight. Did they assume that he had remained alone in the office behind the banking hall for all that length of time?

It was a nonsense to suppose that she would have

protected her master's reputation by lying under the pressure of the advocates' gruelling questions. At the time she had been too shocked and stricken by grief to do other than tell them the truth. What she had omitted from her declarations had been other facts, other occurrences, not connected with decency or with loyalty to anyone other than herself.

Robert Ordway concluded by expressing his regret that it was necessary to invite the ultimate penalty of the law against a young woman who was, in his opinion, as much a victim of the crime as its perpetrator but that he could not see, in all honesty, how the jury could avoid granting his plea for a verdict of guilty on the strength of the evidence that had been presented.

If Cameron Adams had been set up for a flourish of oratory and had harboured his strength and concentration for a final eloquent rebuttal of his adversary's summing up, then he obviously thought better of it. It was now almost midnight. The night sky was black as pitch and the courtroom's reflections had become sharper in and beyond the window glass. There was, within the hall, a great feeling of exhaustion mingled with relief. The curiosity that held the majority of aching spectators to their seats had dwindled into a steely resolve to see the thing through to the bitter end, to be revived by the drama of final judgment and, just possibly, sentence.

Sensing the jury's fatigue, and armed with the perjured evidence of at least two of his own witnesses, Cameron Adams was brisk and decisive.

He said that he felt considerable embarrassment in rising to combat the able statements made by the Learned Gentlemen who had just addressed them and that he felt himself totally unfit to do justice to the importance of the case under consideration. But he relied that anything in which he might be found wanting would be supplied by the integrity and intelligent compassion of the jury. He felt – nay, he knew – that it would be impossible for fifteen honest men to return any other judgment than that of acquittal of the prisoner, for to do so would completely violate all the principles of moral justice and human nature. He admitted that in all probability it was the prisoner's hand that had measured and administered the poison but, as the learned Advocate Depute had pointed out, the balance of judgment lay in her intention and, behind that intention, in her motive.

Mr Adams was very quiet, very grave, as he singled out for the jury the areas of doubt that had been thrown to the fore by the evidence; facts that did not seem to fit together *because* there had been no intention and no complicity on the part of the panel to murder the child whom she loved. Had a fatal error taken place in the dispensing of the medicine? That was for the jury to decide. Could they in all conscience, however, imagine the young woman before them being cold and calculating enough to return to her duties in a nursery and to pause to engage in conversation with her master, *knowing* that at that time her son was in his death throes?

What gain was there for the panel?

What reason for making a murder?

Did she seem, from what they had heard and what they could see with their own eyes, like a moon-maddened beast, to kill her own flesh and blood for no purpose at all?

Cameron Adams left them with that hollow in the heart of the Crown's case, a final passing mention of the absence of the child's father and a reminder that the killing of a child by its mother was one of the most heinous and unnatural crimes in the whole gory catalogue of crimes. One which required more proof than the circumstances which had been led by Learned Counsel on the other side of the bar.

Clare roused herself to look towards the bench. She had expected Lord Drumfin to deliver a directive to the jury but to her dismay it was Pole who hunched forward and inclined himself to face the jurymen, all of whom were wide, wide awake now, as stiff with attention as guardsmen on a parade.

'May I say,' Pole began, in his high-pitched little voice, 'that I have found the matter of this trial distressing in the extreme. It is, however, the sacred duty of jurymen not to be led away by their feelings but to judge the case solely on the evidence adduced. Motive,' the judge went on. 'It is indeed difficult to find a motive in this case, a point made much of by the panel's learned counsel.'

Clare listened with a mounting sense of panic. She had anticipated that Drumfin would stand for her with the jury and instead Pole was presenting a directive for a guilty verdict, undoing all the good that Mr Adams had done for her case. She looked towards Drumfin who was shaking his head, fat red cheeks blown out in mute disapproval.

Pole said, 'You dare not disregard the strong circumstances that point against the prisoner simply because you cannot deduce motive. Many crimes are perpetrated where there appears to be no earthly inducement whatsoever. Circumstantial evidence is of all others often the most convincing and is without doubt the very best sort of evidence, for there is no possibility of the witnesses laying out their prejudices in an improper and impartial manner, as is the danger with exculpatory witnesses, useful though their evidence might be.'

The macer got quietly to his feet from his stool by the

bench and at the doors the officers were ready with their hands upon the bolts.

'You must have regard to the law, gentlemen,' Pole concluded. 'In the light of the hardest of the evidence and of the law of Scotland, it is a judgment and decision not of the heart but of the head, not of sentiment but of intellect that I ask of you, and that you return a verdict which will prove satisfactory to yourselves and to your country.'

Lord Pole bowed, rose, instructed the jury to be enclosed together until the court reconvened at half past nine o'clock on Monday morning, at which time a verdict would be given.

Seconds after their lordships had departed, Clare was touched by the jailer's hand and lifted from her seat. She glimpsed Mr Shenkin's face in the gallery, in the pit the faces of Mr Adams and his fellows. She could read nothing at all in them and they gave her no sign of what they felt had happened.

Only Robert Ordway was looking in her direction. He had his robe fanned out about him, fists on hips. He stared at her with such severity that he seemed to be telling her that he would have his will after all, that he knew her to be guilty.

Clare felt frozen again, aching not with discomfort but with the fear that somehow, at the last, it had all gone wrong and that, in spite of all she had done, she would never see Frederick again.

As one of the last of the 'old school' of convivial judges, Drumfin thought nothing of laying on a Circuit supper for the Provost and his magisterial henchmen in the depths of the Saracen's Head. It mattered not a jot to the jolly lord that it was two in the morning, that exhausted jurymen were quartered nearby or that Lord Pole detested and despised such irrational and expensive feastings. When Drumfin undertook to show himself and the law in its most imposing attitude every shut eyelid in the inn started open at his cheery bellowing and the fanfare of trumpets with which he insisted on declaring the Royal toast. What galled Lord Pole most of all was the fact that his rumbustious colleague did not seem to suffer from his excesses but would be up with the lark, dressed and barbered and ready to lead the long procession uphill to the cathedral before he, Pole, had finished his gruel.

Pageantry, even of the Christian sort, did not sit well with Pole's plain temperament. He was obliged out of duty to head the trail to kirk of magistrates, civil authorities, sheriffs and lawyers. He did not enjoy the occasion, solemn though it was, for his head ached with lack of sleep and his back with the burdens of jurisprudence. Not so cocky Lord Drumfin who, like some chubby Teutonic saint, smiled and gestured beneficently, did everything short of cavort to the strains of the band of the Dragoon Guards and the clump of the boots of the 77th Foot.

Divine service was performed by the Very Reverend Principal Gilchrist who had the temerity to pray for the young woman, Kelso, who currently languished in distress in the Tolbooth and whose judgment before heaven would surely be tempered by mercy by those who judged her here on earth.

The devil it will! Clement Pole thought irreverently, pressed his thumbs to his throbbing head and muttered his prayers like a threat.

After the sermon the judges had been invited to drive out to Garscube, residence of the Right Honourable Sir Islay Campbell, a man of great distinction in both sport and law.

But Pole could not face a whole day in the company of Drumfin and endless talk of gamebirds and gay ladies. He pled indisposition and went instead to the house of Professor Lawrence Crawford, just down the street in the College grounds, to dine frugally and discuss the New Philosophy of Newton and Locke; while the jury were rounded up by the Dragoons and herded back to luxurious confinement within the walls of the Saracen's Head.

'How do they look to you, Mr Brown?' said Angus McKay, anxiously watching the receding column of good men and true.

'Weary,' said Jonathan Brown.

'And hungry,' said Cameron Adams.

'Resolved, do y'think?' said McKay.

'No, I expect they will spend an hour or two after their dinner deciding what's what,' said Jonathan.

'Aye, well, our client has one champion among them, that is for certain,' McKay said. 'And a very persuasive champion he'll be, or I miss my guess.'

'I do not doubt that they will find Clare innocent.'

Both Jonathan and McKay glanced in surprise at the Edinburgh advocate. They had let the parade, or what was left of it, disperse into the High Street. There was little now to hear except the pulse of the drums and an occasional ghostly fanfare echoing in the lanes.

'Acquittal?' said Jonathan.

'How can you be so confident?' said McKay.

Cameron Adams said, 'Because she did not do it, a truth that must be glaringly obvious even to fifteen citizens of the west.'

'I'm not so sure,' said McKay.

'That she is innocent or that they will find for her?' said Jonathan.

'That they will find for her,' said McKay. 'Och, I admit that I am prejudiced against her and have been from the start. I do not like such pretty, empty-headed creatures. I think that they are dangerous enemies of social order and bring nothing but havoc in their wake.'

'Servant girls?' said Jonathan, trying not to smile.

'Women, pretty women,' said Mr McKay. 'However, our learned friend here seems to believe that the case is sealed in our favour. So, since there is nothing more for us to do, may I invite you back to my lodging to partake of a bite of dinner and a glass of good Madeira?'

'Why, we would be delighted. Would we not, Cameron?'

Cameron Adams hesitated. 'I regret, sir, that I have still a little business to attend to which will engage me for most of the afternoon.' He saw McKay's teeth clench in anger at the insult of a refusal and quickly added, 'However, with permission, Angus, I would be only too pleased to take supper at your house. By which time, gentlemen, I may have something interesting to impart.'

'Indeed?' said Jonathan. 'And what might that be?'

'The name of the person who poisoned the child.'

'What! Not Clare Kelso?' said McKay.

'Oh, no,' said Cameron. 'Not Clare.'

Someone, some friend, had paid for a dinner to be sent up to her from the Saracen's Head, a succulent spread of hot meats and cold pies, with a pudding of almond cream. Clare could not do justice to it. It lay congealing on the plates on the table in the cell when Cameron called upon her and, soon after he had gone, was taken away and consumed by turnkey Billy Turner, while Clare lay face down on the bed and wept.

'Is there word?' Clare asked, as soon as Cameron entered the cell.

'No, there is no word. There will be no word before morning,' said Cameron Adams. 'For what comfort it will give you, I will tell you now that I think you'll get away with it.'

'Away with what?'

'With lying.'

'I have told you the truth, sir.'

She was seated at the table, much of her defiance punched out of her by the tension of the trial and the long night of worry that had followed it.

Cameron did not offer an arm to console her. He had shed his generous manner and had in him now an anger that she had not seen before, not even during his performance in court. He leaned over the neglected dinner, took her chin in his hand and lifted her head so that she faced him square. Her blue eyes were still piercing but the lids were puffy with weeping and the sockets bruised with fatigue. He refused to let her look away.

'Frederick *was* here, wasn't he?' Cameron said. 'On the afternoon of the murder Frederick was here in Glasgow, with you.'

'No, I have not seen him since . . . since October.'

'How did he do it? He must be as stealthy as mist when he chooses to be. McKay has asked about the city, has enquired of boatmen and coachmen and hire-carters and nobody saw him. Yet I know he was here,' Cameron said. 'Why do you persist in protecting him? Dear God, Clare, do you not realise that you might have sacrificed your life for him?'

'I will not be hanged. I do not think Lord Drumfin will permit that sentence,' Clare said.

She straightened her back and stuck out her chin. The delicate lines of her throat were drawn by the light from the window, just as they had been when he had first clapped eyes upon her. Damn it all, Cameron thought, perhaps McKay is right, and pretty women are dangers to moral order.

'There's little even Drumfin can do against a guilty verdict. The law is specific,' Cameron told her. 'But devil take the law! I want to know how Striker got here and why you let him give medicine to your child. Did you not realise that the child was a tie, a chain binding Striker to you and to Glasgow?'

'No, Peterkin was no bond at all on Frederick.'

'He did not even *see* his child.'

'Yes, yes he did, and loved him.'

'Ah!'

She bit her lip with teeth as small as seed pearls then swung about and stared out of the cell's high windows.

'Why did you lie to protect him?' Cameron said. 'Do you not see how evil he is? How was it done? How did Frederick persuade you to administer the arsenic? Did he tell you that it was sulphur?'

She gave a little nod.

Cameron said, 'Did you know he was coming to see you that afternoon?'

She nodded again.

Cameron said, 'Where did you meet him?'

'On the riverbank by the New Green.'

'And he asked you to bring the boy?'

'Yes.'

'Did nobody see you there?'

'We went into the Gallow Wood and sat among the black trees. He put his coat upon the ground. It was cold and we did not sit for long. He played with Peterkin, held him on his knee and threw him up and made him laugh.'

'How long were you with him?'

'A half-hour or less.'

Cameron said, 'Did he give a reason why he had not returned to marry you?'

'No. He said that he would stay in Glasgow now. He said that he would come to visit Peterkin and that we would be married. He admired his son very much. And loved him.'

Cameron said, 'Loved him so much that he fed him poison? He did give Peterkin the arsenic, did he not?'

'He told me it was sulphur.'

There was not a tear in her eye now. Her pale lips were firm. She stared out of the window while she spoke, face tilted away from him.

'Did you not think it strange that Striker had sulphur conveniently in his possession?' Cameron said.

'He told me that he took sulphur regularly for hives upon his body. I had no reason to disbelieve him.'

'How was the powder contained?' Cameron said.

'In a small blue glass bottle,' Clare said.

'But it could not be taken without water, surely?'

'Frederick had a silver flask with him, a silver cup fitted to the top of the flask. We used the cup and took water from the well as we walked back towards Caltoun.' She spoke with strange matter-of-factness. 'Frederick also had a spoon, a snuff spoon. We washed the cup and spoon in the bowl of the well and dried them on Frederick's hand-kerchief. He was used to making the mixture, he said. He said it would cure Peterkin's rash overnight.'

'And you suspected no wrong?'

'He seemed so caring. He was solicitous towards Pe-terkin, as concerned about the rash as I was. He mixed the

powder in the tiny cup, just a small measure, and had me
hold Peterkin while we put it in his mouth.'

'Did the child take it willingly?'

Clare gave a murmuring laugh. 'No, he fretted at the
taste of it. He would have spat it out if Frederick had not
pinched his nose until he swallowed. He made such a wry
face and didn't cheer up until Frederick gave him a sugar
sweet to take the taste away.'

'A sugar sweet.' Cameron shook his head. 'He came well
prepared. What then?'

'We went back to Tobago Street, to the cottage.'

'Striker too?'

'No, Frederick left us at the corner of the gardens. He
kissed Peterkin and chucked his cheek and told him that he
was a brave boy,' Clare said. 'Peterkin cried when his
daddy went away.'

'Did you believe Striker when he told you that he would
come back to visit the boy?'

'Yes.'

'Did you also believe him when he declared that he
would marry you?'

'No, I did not believe that.'

'Because of what had gone before?' said Cameron.

'Because I no longer wanted to marry him.'

'Did you tell Striker that?'

'No.'

'Why not?'

'I intended to wait,' Clare said. 'I intended to wait until
he had been captivated by Peterkin, until I could be sure
that Frederick needed us.'

'You realised immediately that it was Striker who had
poisoned your son, Clare. Why did you not accuse him?'

She shrugged with a gesture of indifference that shocked

Cameron. He backed away from her a step, steadied
himself against the edge of the bed. Clare said, 'I was
better without him. Frederick was an expert in betrayal. If I
had tried to make anyone believe that Frederick had killed
my baby, somehow Frederick would have turned the
accusation against me. And I would have been proved
guilty on *his* word.'

'You have a low opinion of the law, Clare.'

'For gentlemen like Frederick the law is lenient, not the
same law that comes down upon servant girls. In any case,'
Clare said, 'Frederick left Glasgow that same night.'

'He escaped that night,' said Cameron. 'How do you
know?'

'I went to Grahamston.'

'When?'

'After I had left Peterkin with Mrs Handyside, as soon as
she returned from her outing.'

Cameron said, 'And Frederick was gone?'

'Vanished. Eunice told me that she had turned him out,
but I did not quite believe her.'

'What did you do then?'

'I returned the sulphur bottle and then I stayed and took
tea with Eunice, at her insistence. She was exceedingly
distressed at Frederick's departure, even although she
claimed to have been the cause of it. I admit that I was
not entirely surprised to find Frederick gone. It was his
way. It will always be his way.'

'Wait,' Cameron said. 'You *returned* the sulphur bottle?'

'Yes, I had it in my pocket.'

'Frederick left the bottle with you?'

'I told you that.'

'And you took it back to Eunice?'

'Yes.'

'Good God!' Cameron exclaimed, and slumped down astonished upon the bed.

At first Andrew had been furious at the Edinburgh advocate for fetching Edwina back from Moorfoot. There was nothing he could do to prevent it, however, without implicating himself further.

It was at his insistence that Edwina, Pym and the children had been sent away. He made the excuse that he did not want them involved in the sordid affair and warned them that if, by chance, Clare was found guilty and sentenced to hang he would expect his family to remain safely out of town until after the execution. Uncle Jamie was perfectly willing to take in lodgers, though he did not personally share Andrew's revulsion for the machinery of justice and made no attempt to prevent Frances from descending upon Purves's Land to see her erstwhile companion tried for her life.

Mr Walter Malabar was considerably excited by the trial for murder of someone connected to the family into which he would eventually marry. He had expressed a wistful, if undiplomatic, hint to Frances that it would be 'awfully thrilling' to think that he had danced with a girl who had actually poisoned her child. Fran had boxed his ears at the very suggestion that Clare Kelso might be guilty of that or any other serious crime and, chastened, Walter had thereafter pretended to be entirely devoted to Clare's cause and eager for her innocence to be proved.

Two youthful-chatterboxes at the dinner table that Sabbath afternoon was almost more than Andrew could bear. The long day's wait in the antechamber of the court, sitting only two or three feet away from Eunice yet unable to talk intimately to her, had worn him to a thin edge. The giving of evidence in the late, last hour of the evening had so charged his blood that he had slept not at all. He had been so snappish with Frances that she had not pressed her suggestion that the family toddle up to the cathedral to hear the sermon on Sunday morning and had, instead, settled for another dreary harangue from Mr Brimston at St Matthew's.

Andrew would have preferred to have been rid of them all, mother, father, wife and children. He would have swept the servants away too if it had been practicable. Instead he had been landed with a guest, with Edwina returned, and the social responsibility that went with being head of the household.

Meat and drink had been provided in lavish quantity; his father had seen to that. But Andrew had no appetite, picked at the pork steaks idly and drank nothing but water. He felt, quite literally, sick with a longing to be with Eunice in the quiet, well-ordered house in Grahamston. He was choked not by lust for her body but by anxiety for her safety. Eunice now with a knife stuck into cork on the table by the bed. She kept an old sword on a nail by the house door. She declared that she had no fear at all of Frederick's enemies now she had drawn blood. She said that she would not hesitate to do so again.

Andrew watched Edwina sneck at the piece of pork with her fork and snap it into her mouth. Edwina had been surly since the discovery of Pym's pregnancy. Andrew realised that he had no notion what Edwina expected from him, what he could give to her that would make her happy. His father, who had taken him aside, told him plainly that there was nothing he nor any other man could do to make Edwina happy and that fretting about failure was a fair way to ruin one's own life.

Sometimes he wondered if his father knew of his liaison
with Eunice and tacitly approved of it. Time would not
provide him with an answer to that question, though he
would depend upon his father to do what was right in the
days ahead, particularly in regard to the children. If it had
not been for the children – and the trial – he would have
fled Purves's Land long since.

'You know Striker better than anyone here, Mr Andrew,' Walter Malabar said, switching the conversation in
his host's direction. 'Where do you think the errant father's
hidin' himself?'

'I really have no idea,' said Andrew.

'Hiding? Who's hiding?' old Mrs Purves said. 'Is Pym
hiding? Should do too, in her condition.'

Old Mr Purves wiped her greasy chin with a napkin,
speared a cube of pork and offered it to his wife on his fork.
She consumed it greedily, munched and mumbled and soon
forgot what it was that had drawn her into the table talk.

'I mean, sir,' Mr Malabar went on, 'if it was me, I would
not abandon my lover in her time of need.'

'Aye, but you're a gentleman, Walter.' Frances patted
her intended's hand.

Edwina put down her fork, and rinsed her teeth with
sherry. 'I'm sure Andrew is a gentleman too.' She gave her
husband a vinegary smile. 'Too much of a gentleman to
betray confidences.'

'Confidences, Auntie?' said Fran, not quite innocently.

'Mr Striker may have abandoned his little harlot without
a word or the scrape of a pen but I'm sure that he has not
abandoned his dear sister. What do you think, Andrew?'

Old Mr Purves said, 'I think we have had too much talk
of this damned trial. I for one would be glad if the subject
was dropped, at least until we have eaten our dinners.'

Edwina ignored him. 'Has Mrs Bates not heard from her brother?'

'I do not know what Mrs Bates has heard,' Andrew replied.

'Did she not give you some little hint, slip you some news that is not known to others?' said Edwina.

It had not occurred to Andrew that his wife might have guessed that he had taken Eunice to be his mistress. The sudden attack was disconcerting.

He saw how futile it would be to hesitate. Indecision was what Edwina expected of him, a quality above all others that would ensure his loyalty, not to her but to habit. The only thing of value that Striker had taught him was that a man is not a miller's mule. He was not strapped to the yoke of the shaft by anything other than his own cowardice.

'*Did* Mrs Bates tell you something, sir?' said young Mr Malabar, eager for secrets. 'Something that did not emerge in front of the court. About where Striker is, for instance?'

'What *did* you talk about when you were alone, Andrew?' Edwina said.

The pork steak had a heavy grey gravy that had begun to crust like candlewax. Beneath it, though, the meat was tender and still quite warm. Suddenly Andrew found his appetite. He cut the steak and ate a large mouthful, gave a hum of approval at the flavour of the herbs that had been used in the sauce. His father glanced at him and, without request, filled an empty glass with sherrywine, put it down by Andrew's hand. It was almost as if at some point in the past old William Purves too had been driven to the same desperate edge. Confidently, Andrew met his father's eye and, cheek bulging like a greedy boy's, gave the old man a wink.

'I presume you mean in the witnesses' room?' he said.

'Wherever it might have been,' said Edwina.

'Well, I will tell you,' Andrew said. 'We talked of far-flung places. We discussed America and its opportunities, how big the moon might really be over the beaches of the Caribbees, and how well a gentleman and his lady might live there on little else but love.'

Fran was first to break the silence, first to see the humour in Andrew's uncharacteristic lyricism. She gave a little chuckle. 'The Caribbees! Aw, Andrew, you never did?'

'Indeed I did.'

'I do not believe you,' Edwina snapped.

'That is your prerogative, my dear,' Andrew said and, still with that curious smile upon his face, tucked in with relish to the rest of his steak.

Wind from the south brought soft billowing rain to the city. As afternoon drifted into evening the river and its guarding hills merged into pearl-grey tinged with green whorls where woodlands leafed above the ebb-tide's brown daubs. The wicket stood open. A piano played a strident, tuneful welcome, loud as a band, to escort him to the villa's door. She had obviously been watching – if not for him for someone – from the darkened parlour.

She answered at once in response to his knock. Echoes of the military air jarred the stillness of the villa's rooms as if she had played all night, all day to fill the vacancies with tremulous vibrations. She wore silk, a gown the colour of tobacco leaf. She had pinned up her hair in thick braids to show off the shape of her poor pitted face. She had painted her mouth and brows, fine and gaudy and defiant as a prince's mistress paid to bestow all that was asked of her but remain forever untouchable.

'I had a premonition that you might call,' Eunice Bates said.

Cameron Adams took off his hat and, at Eunice's invitation, crossed the hall into the parlour.

The entire house was dark. No fires burned in the grates, candles remained unlit. He could smell nothing wholesome from the kitchen and, peering, saw nothing cheering in the parlour except a pewter-coloured bottle of Holland gin, a carafe of water and a glass.

Cameron wondered if the woman was drunk. If so – *in vino veritas* – would it benefit his purpose, or act against it? She seemed, however, stone cold sober as she seated herself upon the stool by the piano, hands in her lap.

'You are a clever fellow, Mr Adams,' she said. 'Too clever to be denied the truth for long, I fear.'

'The trial is effectively over, Mrs Bates. There is only the small matter of a verdict to round it out. I am no longer under restriction of the law, or even of politeness.'

'Surely you are not going to bully me?'

'No, madam, that is not my tactic.'

'What has she told you?' said Eunice.

'She admitted that my suspicions were correct, that Frederick *was* here upon the day of the murder.'

'Murder? Oh, you still believe that it was murder, do you?'

'What else would you call it?' said Cameron. 'He took the child and gave it poison in the guise of a medicine.'

'Perhaps you are not so clever as I imagined,' Eunice said. 'Does Clare believe that Frederick would deliberately put the poor baby away? No, Mr Adams, my brother would not do that.'

'I may not be so clever as you give me credit for,' said Cameron, 'but I am not as gullible as young Clare Kelso. I do not think that your brother would shy away from murder.'

'Oh, quite, quite!' said Eunice. 'You read his character very well for a stranger. No, Frederick is by his very nature a poisoner. Everyone he meets is poisoned by him. It is his nature. He is ambitious, but has no talent and no capacity for honest toil, you see. What he has obtained in this world, meagre scraps of happiness and satisfaction, have come through charm, charm and deception.'

'And murder too?'

Eunice nodded. 'Yes, murder too, Mr Adams.'

'Why then should I believe you when you tell me that he did not return to Glasgow for the purpose of ridding himself of an unwanted infant?' Cameron said. 'Do you expect me to accept that a man who is capable of murder in the general is too tender to apply the principle in the particular?'

Eunice touched a hand to her brow as if the lawyer's lack of acuity made her irritable. 'You have answered your own question, Mr Adams. I ask you to accept that Frederick did not put away little Peterkin, for the sole and simple reason that he had nothing to gain by it.'

'His freedom?'

'He had his freedom. There are no chains binding Frederick to anyone.'

'Not even to you?'

'Alas, not even to me.'

'Did you send him away?' Cameron said.

'Yes.'

'Because you no longer love him?'

'Oh, I expect I will love Frederick until my dying day,' said Eunice. 'The truth is, Mr Adams, that I can no longer afford to love him. I told you, Frederick is destructive. Besides, I no longer need him.'

'Because Andrew Purves will look after you?'

'Did Clare tell you that too?'

'She did not put it quite so directly,' Cameron said.

'Andrew will look after me,' Eunice said. 'And I will look after him.'

'Does he not have a wife to do that for him?'

Eunice let that question slip away into silence.

After a while Cameron said, 'Why did she protect him, Mrs Bates? Is her motive something that only another woman could comprehend?'

'You flatter my sex, Mr Adams,' Eunice said. 'Have you not found the answer yet?'

'I cannot say that I have,' Cameron replied.

'Then,' said Eunice, 'it must remain a mystery to you.'

Cameron leaned forward and placed one fist softly upon the woman's knee. He noticed how his touch made her flinch. She wanted this interview, needed it to happen, yet she required near darkness for it. It was as if he was a priest of the Roman persuasion and the grille of the confessional must be between them at all times, reducing him to nothing but an ear, a voice. He said, 'Clare does not truly believe that it was a fearful and tragic mistake.'

'I know she does not. She is too clever for that.'

'Is she lying to protect you, Mrs Bates?'

'Ah!' said Eunice.

'If not you, then Andrew Purves?'

'No, not Andrew. Not, in fact, either of us,' Eunice said. 'I do not think that Clare is capable of recognising the truth.' She hesitated. 'But I think that you are.'

'I know about the bottle.'

'Ah!' said Eunice again.

'I know where the bottle came from and to whom it was returned.'

'And what that means?'

'Yes, I think so,' Cameron said.

'Then you know everything,' said Eunice.

'Not quite,' Cameron said. 'I do not know why.'

'Why?'

'Why you tried to murder your brother and brought about the death of his child instead,' Cameron said.

'Why do you think I did what I did?'

'To protect Andrew Purves?'

'Quite right,' said Eunice.

Since the stabbing she had felt more confident in herself. The long-handled knife remained her constant companion, tucked into her skirt when she was alone in the house and, at night, embedded, unsheathed, in an old cork float she had scavenged from the riverbank. It was a pretty knife now that she had cleaned the steel blade with vinegar and had honed the edge and refined the point upon the stone cope of Ninian's well.

The memory of striking, of stabbing, remained with her. It jockeyed her spirits when low moods threatened and despondency drew her down. Vividly she recalled the look of indignation on the man's face when the knife entered his body, how he had reared back from her. The second blow at his belly had been more fierce. The blade had puckered and checked against his clothing before it had broken through and slipped in and out, and in again. She had driven it hard, very hard. Though the bull-nosed hammer had hung poised over her head, he had not dared to bring it down. Perhaps, she told herself, he thought that she was a demon whose head might not crack open and whose rage would be all the worse for his assault. He had fled before her darting knife.

Afterwards she had been filled with a sense of that sort of power which must fill men when they have no guile and no conscience and their strength runs unfettered like a beast let loose. For days she'd waited for the man to return, longed for it. She made love to Andrew with a passion that was unfettered and violent too.

There was no such violence in her brother. He was all guile, all wiles and scheming, a coward at heart, He would have pleaded with his enemy, abased himself like a woman, would have coaxed and cajoled, lied and promised and if those tricks had failed he would have wriggled free and fled. She had not fled. She had stood on her nature. She should have done so before now, and she would do so again, willingly.

On that day at the year's end, Eunice had not been thinking of her enemy. Andrew had come early. They had sat by the blazing fire in the parlour and drunk mulled wine together. They had taken an early supper and had talked of the future. About eight or half past she had gone upstairs to the bedroom and had taken off her clothes and, bathed in firelight, had laid herself upon the bed to wait for him. He had come to her soon and she had watched him undress. She was flattered by the fact that he was eager for her. She moved this way and that upon the counterpane to please and attract him. She had no modesty when it came to Andrew. He benefited now from the tricks of seduction that had been forced upon her by other men. As a lover he was both tender and powerful. He had the patience and the heart not to be greedy. He pleasured her more than any other man had ever done. He would wring from her soft cries and groans and, in due course, would bring her to great heights of abandonment when, for long minutes at a time, she would thrash and gasp beneath him and care not that loving had become a contest. She knew that each battle would end in mutual surrender, immediate reconciliation, in kisses and caresses and declarations of love. He would turn her on her belly; would stoop and kiss the pale scores that marked the flesh of her back and buttocks, touch with his tongue the old scars that had once pained her and that had once bled. He would mount her carefully, lay his comforting weight upon her, would lift her hair in his hands and splash it like water against his chest, rub his cheek against her shoulder, seek out her mouth with lips that tasted salty sweet and soon she would beg him to battle with her again, in any way he willed.

Cocooned in body sounds and lost in themselves, the first she knew of Frederick's arrival was when he brushed open the bedroom door.

'Now there is a sight to see,' Frederick folded his arms and leaned against the wall by the doorway. 'A fine spectacle to greet a man just returned from the bosom of the deep.'

Andrew cried out and rolled from her. She could not forgive Frederick for his stealth and coarseness, for his calm, insolent manner. She bounced on to her knees and shouted at Frederick to get out. When Andrew fell from the bed on to the floor Frederick laughed again and shook his head.

'I've been listening to you, old fellow.' He lowered his head to address Andrew who was crawling on all fours towards his clothing on the chair by the fire. 'What a trumpeting and roaring. Dear me! Like the mating of elephants. Cover yourself, Eunice. You know that I cannot abide lewdness and you are, believe me, exceedingly lewd at this moment.'

Eunice reached for the quilt and held it pinned with one fist just above her breasts. The element of high comedy that had so tickled Frederick receded as Frederick kicked the wood chair and toppled it in Andrew's direction. She watched Andrew grope for his shirt, pull it on and get to his feet. He had no dignity at all. She hated her brother for robbing such a man of dignity.

'Leave us, Frederick,' Eunice cried.

'Oh, no,' Frederick said. 'After what I have just witnessed it would be remiss of me to condone further turpitude. If you wish *to make yourself decent, though, I will turn my back. See.' He covered his face with his hand and swung himself round until he faced the door, which he closed with a motion of his knees.*

Trembling, Eunice slid from the bed. She gathered her clothes to her breast, looked round helplessly for a private corner, found none and was forced to wrestle with ribbons and ties there by the bedside.

When Eunice looked round again she saw that Andrew had put on his breeches and had tied his shirt but that he had gone no further towards dressing. He slumped on the chair by the fire, right hand pressed flat against his chest as if taking an oath.

Frederick wore a coat of heavy cloth that hung over a stained suit of frivolous cut and weight. He had ugly hessian boots upon his feet and his shins appeared shrunken, bony bands below the dainty buckles of his knee-breeches. His head, unwigged, was bound about with a raffish red bandanna. Plain upon him were signs of travel, a sea journey, perhaps.

She deliberately stepped around the foot of the bed and stood by Andrew, a hand upon his shoulder.

Frederick glanced round. 'Ready to talk?'

'How did you gain entry?' Andrew asked.

'With my little latchkey.'

'I have had the lock changed, Frederick,' Eunice said.

'Very wise of you, Eunice, very prudent. It would not do for just any Tom or Dick to gain entry, would it? It's fortunate that I have a key that will fit any lock.'

Eunice said, 'Must we remain here, Frederick? I would prefer to go downstairs.'

'Would you indeed?' Frederick said. 'Well, I prefer to stay here. What do you say, Andrew?'

'I say you had no right—'

'No right!' Frederick exclaimed. 'It is my house. The woman

you had beneath you is my sister. I have a perfect right to protect that which is mine. In fact, sir, I have a perfect right to take my whip to you, or my sword.'

Andrew raised his hand and Eunice clasped and squeezed it. 'If you attempt any such thing, Mr Striker, I guarantee that you'll regret it sorely.'

'A bold statement from a man who has taken advantage – persistent advantage, I suspect – of a defenceless widow.'

'The advantage was mine, Frederick,' Eunice said.

Frederick came away from the door. He seemed both relaxed and tense at one and the same time. His manner was no longer bantering, however. He moved a step or two to the bed and placed his hands upon the end of it. She, and Andrew too, watched him as if he was an animal of uncertain temper who might spring upon them without warning. He said, 'Honour is involved, sir, whether you care to acknowledge it or not. My honour.'

'I do not believe you have any honour,' Andrew said. 'Certainly you have exhibited none of that quality in your dealings with my cousin.'

'Suddenly Clare is no mere servant girl. She is your cousin,' said Frederick. 'I do not doubt that she will be flattered by this abrupt elevation in rank. Will you take her and her child into your dining-room, into your drawing-room? Will she dine with you, sup with you?'

'Clare and the child are, or should be, your responsibility,' Andrew said.

'And your wife and children – are they not your responsibility?' Frederick said. 'You see, sir, what we have here is bare-faced and inexcusable adultery between a married man and a vulnerable widow. You cannot cloud the issue with my misfortunes. They are as nothing compared to the predicament that pandering has put you in.'

'*Clare*—'

'*Clare, Clare, Clare!*' Frederick shouted. '*At least I am free to marry if and when I wish. You, Mr Andrew Purves, are not. You cannot even hide behind a promise of marriage.*'

'*What do you intend to do, Frederick?*' Eunice said.

'*The possibilities are intriguing,*' Frederick said. '*I cannot, of course, do nothing at all. That would sit too much against the grain of all that I hold decent. I must do something, mustn't I? Perhaps I should take an action against you, Mr Andrew Purves, perhaps I should bring the matter to the attention of your wife and let her do what must be done to punish you.*'

'*I presume,*' said Andrew, evenly, '*that what you will do, sir, is to suggest a settlement?*'

'*Why, I never thought of that,*' said Frederick. '*What it is to have a banker's brain which can function so clearly even under duress. What sort of a settlement?*'

'*A sum of money,*' said Andrew.

'*Paid to her or to me?*'

Andrew said, '*I do not believe that you regard Eunice as the injured party.*'

'*To me,*' said Frederick. '*Would you pay me a sum of money to maintain my silence about this filthy affair?*'

'*I would,*' said Andrew.

He was no longer slumped. He sat tall on the chair, legs spread, his bare feet solid upon the boards. He continued to grasp Eunice's hand, though, and she could feel his grip tighten with each exchange.

Frederick broke away from the bed, circled behind it, then threw himself face down upon the rumpled quilt. '*How does one place a monetary value upon the honour of a man and his family?*'

'*By discussion,*' Andrew said. '*And agreement.*'

'*Like gentlemen?*'

'Yes.'

Frederick propped himself on his elbows. 'Of course, there is no guarantee – even if you do give me your solemn word – that you will not betray my family's honour the moment my back is turned. Alas, I will be obliged to be away from home for much of the approaching year and, knowing my sister's warm disposition as I do, I could not be certain that this relationship will not continue. A settlement would have to take account of that factor.'

'It would do so,' said Andrew.

'What a lot you have to gain, Andrew,' Frederick said. 'And what a lot to lose. Not only your reputation and your family's reputation, the good will of your wife and the respect of your servants, but the companionship of my sister too.'

'How much?' said Andrew.

Frederick spread his palms. 'How much do you think she's worth, my friend?'

'All that I have,' said Andrew.

'At that moment, I knew I would have to kill him,' Eunice said. 'If I did not he would bleed Andrew dry. Worse, he would destroy us both in the process.'

'Were financial terms reached that night?'

'One hundred pounds, as a binder to the agreement,' Eunice said. 'Tom Moresby delivered it here the following morning, before my brother had gotten himself out of bed. But I was well aware that that was only a beginning.'

'Is that when you sent him packing?'

'No, later,' Eunice said. 'It was too dangerous for Frederick to settle in Glasgow. He had cheated his partners in the salt smuggling venture and had incurred the wrath of a powerful and ruthless landowner—'

'Lord Drumfin?'

'The same,' said Eunice. 'Frederick could not safely appear on the streets of the towns of the west of Scotland ever again. I knew Frederick of old. I knew what he would do. He would milk Andrew for thousands, a hundred or two hundred at a time, and then he would take me away.'

'Did Purves see how it would be?'

'Of course he did,' said Eunice. 'Andrew told me that I was worth all that he had and that he would not abandon me, no matter how demanding Frederick became.'

'Fine words,' said Cameron.

'He meant them, every one.'

'How did you obtain the arsenic?'

Eunice shrugged as if the practice of murder was a simple matter and hardly worth mentioning. 'My brother has been ill, several times ill. He has been infected by street women at least three times and possibly more often than that. He keeps a little quilted leather satchel of medicines that he carries in his luggage with him. It contains six or eight simple remedies.'

'King's yellow is hardly a simple remedy,' said Cameron.

'It depends what condition you intend to cure,' said Eunice. 'But no, the arsenic was not with Frederick's treatments. It was kept elsewhere, safely hidden in a sealed jar in a box of old snuff; a box that has travelled with us for many years.'

'Mrs Bates, do you mean to tell me—?'

'Nothing ever proved, no charge ever made. Poison is a silent friend when properly employed.'

'Your husband?'

Eunice Bates did not answer Cameron's question. She sighed at the lawyer's assumption that she would yield up everything. He was too decent to understand a half, a tenth of what she was telling him. She did not feel compelled to colour the grotesque design of her days with Frederick just to appease the Edinburgh advocate's need for detail.

She said, 'I had forgotten, you see, that it was my brother's habit to dose himself regularly with quantities of the substances. I had not been with him enough in recent years to have observed the habit. He would take one or two of the remedies at a time, over a period of weeks. He would carry a small flask of pure gin with him, mix the powder in the alcohol, swig it down and wash away the aftertaste with another sip from the cup.' She paused. 'I chose the brimstone bottle, the little blue jar. Sulphur.'

'Because of its colour?'

'Frederick was negligent. He would measure, stir, toss off the medicine. In time and out of my sight I hoped that he would fall sick and die.' Eunice gave a chuckle, parched humour. 'Half-hearted, was it not? I should have stabbed him or choked him with a cord. But I could not do it directly.'

'Instead you changed the sulphur in the bottle for king's yellow and hoped that would be enough to do the murder for you,' Cameron said. 'Is that why you sent him away? So that you would not be implicated? After all, nobody had seen him here in Glasgow, nobody except Clare and Andrew. Did it not disturb you that your brother might be found dead at an inn in Doncaster or a Liverpool lodging house?'

'Not in the least,' Eunice said.

'Did Frederick tell you that he was going to visit Peterkin?'

'No,' Eunice answered. 'He was too concerned with counting the money that Andrew had had delivered. He sat at that very table, barefoot and tousled, counted it out and made a tally of it in a little book. I told him he had his money and would have more but that I did not want him near me. I *asked* him to leave. He laughed and said that he would consider the matter. He suggested that Andrew might pay for every visit, that he might issue a ticket for each performance, as if it was a play. When he went out in daylight, I was surprised but glad to be rid of him.'

'But you did not realise that he had taken the medicine with him, the sulphur?'

'It did not occur to me to open the satchel again. It had cost me effort enough to do the thing in the first place. I did not even know if he had the itch. For once, he did not describe or talk of his ailments. He was too elated, too arrogant and satisfied with himself.'

'When he came home again, did he inform you that he had seen Peterkin?'

'Oh, yes.'

'And were you not apprehensive then?'

'No, I – I was too angry. I was blind to that other possibility, that remote and tragic chance,' Eunice said. 'Frederick had just remembered where the child's name came from. He teased me for my sentiment. He laughed at my folly, my silliness, and at Clare too for humouring me.'

'Was he not taken with the child? Clare said that he was taken with the child.'

'He was taken only with his own good fortune. His luck at finding me with Andrew,' Eunice said. 'He told me nothing of what had taken place between Clare and he and, of course, made no mention of medicine. He was far too full of himself, wild with new plans. Do you know what he proposed?'

'No, I do not.'

'He proposed that I might marry Andrew and become

heir to the Purves's fortune. Edwina Purves, my brother said, might fall ill or meet with an accident. And the way would be clear for me to marry the man I loved. Had the thought not occurred to me? Frederick asked. Nothing was ever enough for Frederick.' Eunice paused. 'I do not regret that I tried to poison him. He is all poison as it is. He would have died of his own disease. I regret only that I did not do it properly.'

'And took away Clare Kelso's child instead.'

'Frederick's child too.'

'How did you persuade Frederick to leave?'

'I threatened him with a knife. I told him I would kill him if he did not go,' Eunice answered, wearily. 'He was amused at my outburst. The knife did not frighten him in the least. No, I think he had already decided to leave that night. He had his valise packed and strapped, the money that Andrew had given him safe within it.'

'And his medicines?'

'Yes, the satchel too,' Eunice said. 'He was gone from here less than an hour after he returned from his visit with Clare and Peterkin.'

'Gone where?'

Eunice shook her head. 'Why should he tell me? I was old, was I not, staid, worn out, useless to him now. Besides, he never did tell me where he went or what he did.'

'And you did not know that the child had been poisoned?'

'Not until Clare came here,' Eunice said. 'By then it was too late.'

Cameron said, 'Will you tell me—?'

Eunice got to her feet abruptly enough to startle him. He rose too, stumbling a little towards her in the unsettling darkness of the parlour.

'I have told you enough,' she snapped. 'I will tell you no more.'

He was rough with her. He caught her by the shoulders and inclined his head until his face was only an inch from hers.

'You will,' Cameron said. 'You will tell me one thing more before I leave or I will drag you to the magistrates and let them wring it out of you.'

'I will deny every—'

'Even if Clare is found guilty?'

'Ah!' Eunice said and went slack. Cautiously he released her. 'Ah yes!'

'If Clare *is* found guilty and sentenced to execution what will you do then?' Cameron Adams asked.

'Confess,' Eunice answered.

'And if she's acquitted?'

'Then you must depend upon God to punish me,' said Eunice Striker Bates.

Fine Lawn, French Lace

———◆———

At nine o'clock on Monday morning the bells of the city rang anew, announcing that the procession of judges was coming forth from the Saracen's Head to finish the trial of Clare Kelso.

Magistrates and military went forward along the Gallowgate to escort the ermine through the pack of palpitating mortals that surrounded the Tolbooth. Infantry and dragoons were out in force and there was a good deal of flaying of batons and heaving of horses to shape the mob into orderly lines. Lord Pole was both dismayed and puzzled by the enthusiasm of the Glasgow citizenry to be present to hear the doom of Clare Kelso. But Drumfin, refreshed by his day in the country, explained to his prissy colleague that 'neck or nothing' situations held a natural fascination for the human animal and that he, like the herd, was jumping keen to hear what verdict had been rendered.

It was some minutes after the hour of ten before Pole established order in the jam-packed hall. He commanded that the doors be shut and locked and, amid breathless silence, called the Diet of his Majesty's Advocate for his Majesty's interest and ordered the prisoner to be brought upstairs to the dock.

To the spectators it seemed that reason had fled from the mind of Miss Clare Kelso. She was stiff and white and brittle as an icicle and had to be forced down upon her seat by a turnkey and an officer, one to each arm. The black web-like veil had been parted and framed her sweet, numb features perfectly, adding a penitent fatalism to her appearance that brought stifled gasps from some of the more tender hearted. There was an uncommon and uncanny stillness among the legal fraternity in the pit of the court and no signal of reassurance, not even a passing glance was directed towards the prisoner by her counsellors.

Clare had not lost her reason. She was stiff with tension, pale from lack of sleep. In the wake of her admissions to the Edinburgh advocate, judgment for her cause no longer seemed inevitable, no longer seemed just. She had betrayed Frederick to Cameron Adams, and had betrayed herself too, perhaps, in the process. For Clare it was no longer a simple matter of whether she would live or die. Dying, even on a rope's end, would be in some ways preferable to living with the knowledge of her own stupidity, with the responsibility that she had taken upon herself all those weeks ago.

Mr Hamilton, chancellor of the jury, had in his hand the long envelope that contained the written verdict, prepared, signed and sealed in a closed room early that morning.

Clare scanned the faces of the jury to read there what they had decided. They were implacable and the chancellor himself kept his hand over the wax seal to hide its colour from prying eyes. Black wax meant guilty; red, an acquittal. The majestic juryman delivered the package into the hands of the justiciary clerk who in turn transported it up to the bench.

Drumfin, smiling, leaned on an elbow and watched the expert manner in which Lord Pole pressed the slender packet down upon the surface of the bench and, still without revealing the colour of the wax, struck the seal a smart blow with the mahogany chock. He covered the

fragments with a cupped hand, slid the verdict from the
envelope and shook it open. His thin nostrils flared. He
heaved a sigh, took in a breath and, in a shrill tone declared,
'By a plurality of voices the jury finds the prisoner *not
guilty.*'

McKay was on his feet at once, applauding. Jonathan
Brown clapped Mr Adams upon the shoulder. The Edinburgh advocate was motionless for a moment then turned
his head and looked up at Clare. To her dismay he gave no
sign of pleasure or triumph but only a small frown and a
shake of the head which was totally lost in the general
hubbub: Cheering, catcalls, whistles, applause, a deafening
affirmation of the verdict's popularity but also of the
theatrical nature of a trial in which Peterkin, snuffed
out, was remembered only as a faint poignant chord.

Clare felt her mind cloud over. In spite of her determination to be strong her head was forced downward and to
the side until, in a half-swoon, her brow rested upon the rail
of the dock and the tears fell, splashing, to the footworn
boards.

For a minute or more there was nothing but a blur of
tears, wreathing an image of Peterkin's happy face, and
clouds of sorrow upon her. She heard the *chak-chak-chak*
of the mahogany chock as through a rushing rain and felt
the hand of an officer upon her, gently now, as he lifted her
from the rail and supported her so that she could see and
be seen by the judges.

Although the verdict had been recorded, Lord Pole had
not yet dismissed the prisoner. Apparently it was not his
intention to do so without reprimand. He had a point to
make, and make it he would, with all the authority he could
muster from scarlet robes and lofty stance. He did not
order the doors to be opened but proceeded to address

Clare Kelso and the court before public excitement had diminished.

'Nothing,' he piped, then repeated loudly, '*nothing* could be more disagreeable to my feelings than the verdict which has now been returned. The verdict, however, is not unanimous and I am bound to say that a portion of the jury thought the panel guilty of the charge brought against her. Whether she is or not, is known only to herself and her Maker. But it is my belief that it will cost her the rest of her life to atone for her past conduct which, as has emerged, has not been by any means decent or blameless. In fact, if I had been on the jury I must declare that I would have gone along with the minority.'

Faint cries of 'Shame, shame' from the depths of the public gallery were stifled instantly.

Pole went on, 'There have been no niceties in this case which has been marked by innuendo and an excess of sentiment. I must also take this opportunity to animadvert on one of the jurymen, *viz* Mr Hamilton, its chancellor, who, there can be no doubt, ruled the verdict and got it down in favour of the prisoner. It is the duty of a jury, even its chancellor, to hear evidence patiently and for the most part in silence and to restrict observations on the conduct of the trial until he has retired from the box.'

Mr Hamilton, not in the least chastened, grinned broadly and then, to cheers from his supporters, bussed his fingertips and threw a fluttering kiss towards the bench in silent scorn at the reprimand.

'In conclusion, might I say again that in my heart I feel the girl to be guilty, and though she has been found otherwise in relation to the crime of murder she is still a transgressor in the eyes of God. I advise you most strongly, young woman, to be both penitent and circumspect throughout the remainder of your days.' Lord Pole paused. 'You are now entitled to be dismissed from the bar.'

Clare was momentarily at a loss what to do. In the stampede from the galleries she seemed to have been forgotten. The stately progress of the assize would continue. Lead-stealers, sneak thieves, burglars and resetters would follow her into the dock. But she had been cast up, cast aside by the tidal surge of justice and was free to go again into the daylight and about her lawful business. What that business was Clare had no clear idea, nor did she know how she would set about her mission.

The officer, a bearded fellow in a brown uniform adorned with umpteen metal buttons, touched her lightly upon the arm and with deferential politeness said, 'Step down this way, Miss Kelso, if you please.'

She managed to turn. Her legs were like straw beneath her. She trembled all over as if with a fever. She paused for a moment at the top of the steps and glanced back at the court. Strangers, lawyers, were already crowding the desks in the pit but the galleries were emptying rapidly and neither of the judges was to be seen upon the bench. She looked up to the gallery on her left in the hope of catching sight of one friendly face, of Mr Shenkin or Mr McCoull, but they too had vanished into the crowd.

The officer said, 'I must ask you to hurry, Miss Kelso.'

'Where – my clothes from the jail, where are they?'

'They will be fetched down,' the officer assured her. 'In the meanwhile, if you will be so good, Lord Drumfin craves a brief word in private with you before you leave.'

'Where is he?'

'This way.'

Steps, a narrow passageway, at the end a huge conglomeration of people; she followed the officer towards them and ran against him when he stopped. He opened a small door in an arched recess and ushered her into a room.

The room's one lead-paned window looked out into a tiny paved courtyard with a single unleafed tree in it. Calf-bound books lined the place from floor to beamed ceiling, and there was no furniture except a small ornately carved table and a single Jacobean chair. Arthur Nye, Lord Drumfin, still bundled in ermine and scarlet but with his wig removed, leaned a haunch against the table. He sipped from a tumbler of wine and munched oatcakes and cheese from a plate by his hand. He looked much redder and fatter than he had done across the breadth of the hall, and his smile was oily.

'Do sit down, Miss Kelso,' he invited. 'I take it that the relief of being released from Hanging Johnnie's clutches has left you a bit weak at the knees. Natural, natural.'

Clare seated herself demurely upon the Jacobean chair, knees together, skirt tugged tightly down, hands in her lap. She was not in the least shaky now. Her strength had returned, a cold calm strength. She had not the slightest inclination to flirt with this sensual heap of male flesh. There was no need for it. She was free again, restored. She met his admiring gaze without flinching.

'Is he waiting for you?' Drumfin asked.

She thought of pretending not to understand but there was no need for that either. 'If you mean Frederick Striker, your lordship, no, he is not waiting for me. Not to my knowledge.'

'Where is he?'

'He has had what he wanted from me, sir, and I doubt that I will see him again.'

'Oh, aye, lass, you will, you will,' Drumfin said.

'Is it so obvious, Lord Drumfin?'

'To me it is,' the judge said. 'Why do you suppose I put Mr Hamilton, for that is his name, into the jury? To be *friendly* towards you. Just in case your advocate did not do what was necessary to put you out into the world again.'

'Are you saying, sir, that you think I murdered my child?'

'I'm not saying that at all. The contrary is true. I have been convinced from the first that it was friend Striker who did the dirty deed.'

'I know, sir, that you and he are acquainted.'

'Did he tell you in what manner?' said Drumfin.

'He is in your debt, I think.'

'Aye, but he is not so much in my debt as he is in yours, Clare Kelso,' Drumfin told her. 'To keep your mouth shut fast about his role in it was a daft thing to do. He is not worth it. He is a fast fellow, too fast, too loose for his own good or the good of anyone who encounters him. By God, I tell you if my agents had laid hands upon him he would not have survived to poison your bairn. That's why you want him, is it not? That's why you will wait for him and find him?'

Drumfin was as fat as Mr Walcott but the judge was not like the lawyer in any other respect. His cheeks emanated a glow of exuberant good health and he displayed none of the slow, solemn charm of the famous old advocate. However much Drumfin was attached to the ladies, however lecherous, he did not want her. He was oblivious to her in that respect. He only wanted her to be his instrument, to extract revenge upon the man who had cheated and demeaned him.

'Striker will come back this way again, you know,'

Drumfin went on. 'Oh, perhaps not this summer or next, but in time he'll return. I think your instinct tells you so. Back our Frederick will come, running round and round like a buck hare in a big field, darting hither and yon.'

'Yes,' Clare said. 'And I will wait for him.'

'I knew it, damned if I didn't!' Drumfin slapped his knee. 'And when our quarry comes close enough to catch, what will you do then, lass?'

'That remains to be seen.'

'Did you know about his romance with the Irish heiress?'

'No, sir.'

'Hah!' said Drumfin. 'I almost had him there. Would have had him if that fool Geary had not written and warned him off. Be that as it may, between us we'll snare him yet.' He put his hand inside the fold of his robe and brought out a packet wrapped in brown paper and sealed with the same brittle red wax as the jury had used on her papers of acquittal. 'Take this,'

'What is it?'

'It is money, a little money. Also, a list of the places where I might be found. You are literate and can write. If Striker drifts into your ken before he drifts into mine then I ask only that you write to me at once.'

'And how will you respond, Lord Drumfin?'

'Swiftly and very, very quietly.'

'What if I do not choose to give Frederick to you?'

'Then you're more of a fool than I take you for,' Drumfin said.

He was still holding out the packet, not urging it upon her but awaiting, with patience, a willing acceptance. 'Pole did not exaggerate when he said that you must not come within the ambit of the law again. The crowd were with you and I was there to protect you. And, it must be said, your advocate stirred enough mud about to blind everyone to the truth. The truth of the *law* is that you should have been found guilty. That, in the absence of the perpetrator, of Striker, was where the evidence inevitably pointed. On this occasion you were fortunate. You will not be so fortunate next time, Clare Kelso.'

A tentative voice outside the little door called, 'Lord Drumfin? Lord Pole conveys his compliments and begs to remind you that—'

'Tell the old fool to suck another orange,' Drumfin shouted, 'and to hold his water.' To Clare he said, 'I can do what you cannot. I can be rid of Frederick Striker without a ripple. I promise you justice, lass, rough but thorough, as soon as you tell me where to find him. Now, what do you say?'

Clare paused for a fraction of a second then reached out, took the packet and hid it in the pocket of her skirt.

Gleefully, Drumfin slapped his knee again. 'I knew my judgment was correct. Damn it, lass, between us we'll have the scoundrel yet. We'll make him pay, will we not?'

'Indeed, sir,' Clare said, 'I hope that we will.'

The lawyers were waiting for her at the end of the passage. Mr Adams seemed to have shed his sulkiness. He shook her hand warmly and received her thanks with grace. She was also congratulated by Mr McKay and by the Writer, Jonathan Brown, but there was in them and between them an awkwardness, a reserve that had not been present before. Clare understood at once. Before the verdict her position had been very clear, her relationship to these professional gentlemen defined by it. Now she was loosed from that role and had no status but that of servant.

She kept the packet that Drumfin had given her tucked

out of sight and when McKay asked her directly what the
learned judge had said to her she answered that his lordship
had merely sought an opportunity to wish her well and to
enquire, as was his right, about her treatment as a prisoner
in the city jail. Cameron Adams would not be deceived by
her lie, but there was no help for that. In the weeks and
months ahead she would be obliged to practise much
deception and the sooner she learned the art and craft
of it the better.

Fay Hinchcliff had brought down her clothing from the
cell. It lay on the floor in a great untidy bundle, fastened
with cord like a tinker's pack. The jailer's wife hovered in
the shadow of the stairs, simpering and grovelling to the
magistrates and sheriffs who bustled past, keeping a weather eye on Clare and her gentlemen friends in the faint, fond
hope that she would be paid for the excellent service that
she and her dear husband had rendered to the little prisoner.

To Clare's disappointment there was no sign of Andrew
or Eunice in the crowded hall. She had no idea what she
would do now, what would be expected of her. She had
been proved innocent of murder, but guilty of transgres-
sion. She had brought shame to the banker's house and she
surmised that there would be no great welcome, no cele-
bration of her release to be found in Purves's Land.

'They are waiting for you?' Cameron Adams said.

'Who?'

'The public.'

'But why?'

'To cheer you.'

'I've done nothing,' Clare said.

'Ah, but you have, Miss Kelso,' said Jonathan Brown.
'You have escaped from the clutches of authority, an act

that inevitably wrings sympathy from the great mass of the people.'

'But where will I go, what will I do?'

'Wave to them, smile at them,' said McKay. 'Let them pat your back and steal kisses if they wish. In their eyes you are famous now. I tell you, Clare, you will not be without friends in the city from this day forth.'

Cameron was watching her, judging her response.

She said, 'I do not wish to be famous.'

'There is no help for it, Clare,' said Cameron.

'Will you come out with me?'

'No, I have other business, as does Mr McKay.'

'And I, alas,' Jonathan Brown said, 'must hasten back to Edinburgh on the noon fly as I have a client to see first thing tomorrow.'

'Then we will part here?' Clare said.

'So it would seem,' Cameron told her.

'Will you not come with me as far as the house?'

He hesitated. 'I cannot. It is best, under the circumstances, if you go alone.'

'Very well, sir,' Clare said. 'It only remains for me to thank you all for what you have done for me. I will not forget you for it.'

'Nor will we forget you, Miss Kelso,' said Jonathan Brown.

She did not care about the Writer or McKay. She searched Cameron Adams' face for some fleeting sign of warmth, an indication that she meant more to him than a court triumph over the Advocate Depute and a handsome fee in his pocket at the end of it. But, she realised, Frederick stood between them, more real, more redoubtable now than ever. She was not for the likes of the Edinburgh advocate. She had no right to expect him to protect her.

'Goodbye, Mr Adams.'

'Goodbye, Miss Kelso.'

Swiftly she lifted the bundle of clothing. At least she went out without rags on her back, dressed in the wardrobe of a lady. Fine lawn and French lace, roped and toted like a tinker's sack. She paused, looked out at the broad step bathed in gelid sunlight and at the oblong slice of Trongate and its crowds. She went forward into the air, into the bellow of applause that greeted her appearance.

Two mounted dragoons and a half-dozen soldiers kept the mob at bay at the foot of the steps. Across the broad highway aristocrats and burgesses' wives watched from the shelter of sedans and carriages, too grand to dirty their shoes but too vulgar to miss the last of the show. Above Clare the Tolbooth soared into the sky. On its balcony, filling in behind her, the city fathers showed themselves, glasses in hands, as if they had magnanimously released her at the crowd's command.

The cord of the bundle bit into her hand. Its weight on her shoulder was considerable, causing her to stoop. In the pocket of her dress, Drumfin's flat, sealed packet pressed against her thigh.

They were screaming for her, not for her blood now but for her recognition. She descended three steps and stopped. Deliberately she put down the ignominious bundle. She straightened her dress, her hat, her hair and then, with a pointing finger, selected from the ranks a lad of nine or ten, a thin, pea-headed urchin with dirty hair and greedy eyes. 'You, boy,' Clare called, 'fetch me a chair.'

Ten minutes later, just as the clock in the tower mechanically chimed the hour, Clare was lifted safe away from the Tolbooth steps and, with the crowd about her already beginning to disperse, was carried down to Salt-market and deposited at the gate of Purves's Land.

'They're gone,' Tom Moresby told her. 'Left ten minutes ago. In the diligence. For Moorfoot. Bob at the helm.'

'Were they not in court?'

'Oh, aye,' Moresby told her. 'Did you not see them?'

Clare shook her head.

She had not expected a warm reception but she felt a strange, glazed anger at such total neglect. She had been glad to climb into the sedan chair and close the door. Faces pressed about the window had been blurred and unrecognisable, neither friends nor enemies. Here, though, in the place where she had lived almost half her life, she had anticipated some greeting, some expression of pleasure, however grudging.

Sensing her disappointment, the porter dared to put an arm about her shoulder and there, on the pavement before the bank's door, hugged her. 'You're free now, miss, an' that's what counts.'

'Has Mr Andrew gone too?'

'No, he's upstairs with his father. It's the women that went. Sailed off in the coach. All arranged first thing this mornin' before they went to the court.' Tom Moresby pulled a face. 'She, it seems, would be havin' it no other way.'

'I take it,' Clare said, 'that you mean Edwina?'

'Aye, what tantrums!' said Moresby. 'She's been squabblin' with everybody: Miss Frances, Mr Andrew, Pym, even with old Mr Purves.'

Clare was relieved to learn that Edwina was not at home. She wondered at the cause of the woman's outburst, if the strain of the trial was wholly to blame or if some word had

finally filtered down to Edwina about Andrew's relationship with Eunice Bates. 'What should I do, Mr Moresby?'

'Talk to the master,' the porter advised and courteously
opened the door for her.

The banking hall was empty of custom. Mr Shenkin and
Mr McCoull were seated together at the long desk, eating
bread and cheese from a brown paper and drinking mild
beer from a jug that they passed between them. When
Clare entered the clerks glanced up guiltily, like schoolboys
caught at mischief, and the beer jug vanished from sight
beneath the desk.

'Clare?' said Mr Shenkin. 'Is that you?'

'In the flesh, it is,' Mr McCoull wiped crumbs from his
lips with the back of his hand. 'By God, it's good to have
you back with us so soon. Are you hungry? Will you have
cheese?'

In spite of the clerks' pleasure at seeing her again, and
their obvious delight at the verdict that had freed her, there
was a reserve in their greeting, a distancing that made Clare
uncomfortable; part and parcel of the stunning effect of
being out of the cell in the Tolbooth and back here, back
home.

Everything was the same; yet everything was changed. It
was she who carried change with her. She too was awkward
when Mr Shenkin hugged her and Mr McCoull bussed her
cheek. She listened to them chatter about the trial, express
certainty that she was as innocent as a lamb, express
mumbling regret at the death of her child, admiration
for the wiles of her lawyer, anger at Lord Pole.

To the clerks' conversation Clare responded with a
warmth that was largely feigned. She was distanced from
her friends by her purpose, her mission. During the short
journey in the sedan chair she had opened the packet that

Drumfin had given her. In it she had found twenty pounds in Scots banknotes and a sheet of legal parchment upon which had been copied three addresses. She had counted the banknotes, barely glanced at the addresses, folded the parchment and tucked it and the money into separate pockets of her dress. She had used one pound to pay the carriers and was careful to collect exact change from them.

Upstairs, in her chest in the nursery, were sundry articles of clothing, three pairs of slippers and two good pairs of shoes, in addition to a little money that she had saved. The dresses and gowns in the bundle were stylish enough to see her through the summer, however, and she felt herself to be adequately equipped to begin her journey. There was just one matter that required attention, something that had to be done.

After a few minutes she made her excuses to her friends in the banking hall and climbed the stairs to the domestic apartments.

The nursery was empty. It smelled of lye soap. The room had been scrubbed from floor to ceiling, as if Edwina thought it had been contaminated. Clare trod nervously on the polished boards as if they were ice that might crack open and reveal water beneath. Not one crumb, not one tangled stocking or fragment of chalk was to be seen. The grate, polished to a gloss, was empty of fire, and the little beds that flanked it had been stripped to the mattresses.

Clare set down her bundle. The startling emptiness of the nursery was disturbing. It tore at some membrane of control in her breast and let out a sudden hot bubble of pain.

She leaned forward over Margaret's empty cot and wept.

'Clare?'

Andrew stood in the open doorway, tall and solemn. His sad, dark, Purves eyes conveyed a pity that he could not put into words. Though she had no reason to be so, Clare was ashamed of her tears. She hid her face in her arms, away from him. She heard the clean squeak of the boards, felt his hand upon her shoulder.

'Oh, Clare!' Andrew said and, drawing her to him, let her rest in his arms and weep.

Jonathan's rush for the midday flyer meant that a hearty dinner at the Tontine or the Saracen's Head was out of the question. Instead the legal gentlemen celebrated like drovers, with a glass of whisky apiece from the counter of the dramshop in the coaching yards. They raised, clinked and toasted the verdict and the jurymen who had brought it in and then, coughing at the taste of strong, raw malt, clinked again and soberly toasted Clare Kelso, as if she were a queen or empress.

'Why will you not come with me, Cameron?' Jonathan asked. 'You could be home by midnight.'

'I have a fancy to see a little of this quaint town, since I am here and have no brief in Edinburgh that will not wait until the week's end,' Cameron answered.

'I would have you to supper, sir,' said McKay, 'but, alas, I must ride out myself to Partick to visit my aged mother.'

'Your mother?' Jonathan said in surprise.

'Aye, Mr Brown, did you think I did not know the lady?'

Jonathan and Cameron exchanged a glance, unsure whether this was a reprimand or Glasgow wit. McKay gave them a wink each and a hoarse chuckle by way of a clue. He said, 'I know her well, too well. If you think that I am dry, you should encounter the matron; a desert for feeling, is she. We will exchange ten words or less between supper tonight and dinner tomorrow but she will scowl at my wig and the modernity of my apparel and we will be happily miserable together. I would invite you there with me, Mr Adams, but I fear that you would not be able to stand up to the pace.'

'I fear that I would not,' Cameron said.

'Besides,' said Jonathan, 'I have a suspicion that our learned friend does not intend to sup alone this evening.'

'Ah!' said McKay, nodding. 'The girl. I see.'

'I am done with the girl,' Cameron shrugged. 'It would not be prudent to meet with her again.'

'The devil with prudence,' said Jonathan. 'She might be willing to show her gratitude. Does that prospect not tempt you, old fellow?'

'I am sure Mr Adams is too conscious of his professional position and his rank to take advantage of a servant,' said McKay, this time without wink or chuckle.

'What will become of her?' Jonathan asked.

'No good will become of her, in my opinion,' said McKay. 'She is both pretty *and* educated. That is a combination in a woman that can lead, as we have seen, only to bad ends.'

'Perhaps you're right, Mr McKay.' Jonathan finished his whisky at a swallow. 'But I would wish her more good than harm after what she has endured.'

'Harm of her own making, sir.' McKay swept the dram down his throat too. 'However it is with her, I must be off, gentlemen. Perhaps we may do business again now that you have found the way to the Glasgow assize?'

When McKay had gone, when the small, high-riding coach had been wheeled into the yard and the horses secured in the shafts, when only seconds remained before the horn was blown to announce departure through the arch, Jonathan leaned from the open window and grasped Cameron's hand.

'It is the girl, is it not?'

Cameron said, 'I cannot leave things as they are.'

'Why, why not?'

'I have something to tell her. Something that I think she must know before too long.'

'Concerning Striker?'

'Yes.'

'He killed the child.'

'No,' Cameron said. 'That's the devil of it. He did not.'

Jonathan's brows climbed in amazement. He would have clung longer to his friend's hand as if to drag the truth out of him if the horn had not blared and the driver's whip cracked over the horses' curried manes. Cameron stepped back quickly from the wheel as the fly swung, swivelled and headed for the gate.

Craning out of the open window, Jonathan shouted, 'Dine with me on Sunday. At my rooms.'

And Cameron, tipping his hat, mouthed the words, 'I will.'

Clare ate ravenously from the plate of cold meats that Andrew ordered from the kitchens. She could not believe that her appetite had survived the storms of emotion that had racked her and felt something of a hypocrite for tucking hungrily into her dinner. Andrew too ate well. He forked slices of roast mutton into his mouth as if he had laboured hard at an anvil or in the fields all morning. Clare noticed, though, that he watered the wine and drank sparingly of it. To keep her wits sharp too, she took nothing to drink but a mug of small beer.

Andrew looked drawn. There were dark circles about his eyes. For the first time it occurred to Clare that the ordeal had not been hers alone but had been shared by those who cared for her.

They ate from a table before the fire in the library, tucked away safe and snug at the corridor's end. They discussed the trial, but rather casually, as if they had been spectators to it and not participants. It was not until the last scrap of meat had been eaten and the last slice of buttered bread devoured that Andrew, to Clare's relief, brought the conversation round to the matter of her future. 'What will you do, Clare?' he asked.

She said, 'I presume you mean that I can't stay here?'

'It would be foolish to pretend that nothing has changed,' Andrew said. 'No, you cannot stay on here.'

'Because of Edwina?'

'Oh,' Andrew said, 'my wife is in a rage, of that there's no doubt. But her temper is not the reason. If that was all there was to it, Clare, I would weather it and keep you on.'

'I have no right to ask you for reasons,' Clare said. 'I did not expect, or intend, to stay on at Purves's Land.'

'Where will you go?'

She hesitated. 'To the north, I think. Thanks to all that you have taught me I'm not without skills. In fact, I think I could pass myself off as a governess, if the household was not too rich or particular.'

'I am sure that you could,' said Andrew. 'You will, of course, carry a reputation with you, though not as far as you think, perhaps. I will give you letters of recommendation, if you wish.'

Again Clare hesitated, 'That will not be necessary. I will try myself in Perth or even further away from Glasgow. Inverness, I hear, is a very fine town.'

'At least let me give you some money, your wages and a little more,' Andrew offered.

'No, you have done more than enough for me as it is,' said Clare. 'Much more than I had a right to expect. Besides, I have a small sum saved.'

Andrew did not press the point. He took the plates and put them upon the tray and carried it to the door. He opened the door and, on the pretext of putting the tray out into the passageway, looked this way and that to make sure that no eavesdroppers lurked there. He closed the door and leaned against it. 'Clare, I will not be here in Purves's Land. If you require assistance of any kind, you may write to my father and he will forward the letter to me, wherever I might be. I would not want you to think that I had abandoned you.'

'Not here?' Clare said. 'Where will you be?'

'It's my intention to make an extended visit to the seaports of the east coast of America, to see what sort of business I might pick up there now that the war is over,' Andrew said. 'I leave this afternoon.'

Clare stiffened. 'Does your father know of your plan?'

'Yes, he has given his approval,' Andrew said. 'He has agreed to take care of Edwina and my children until such times as I return.'

'You do not intend to return, do you?' Clare said. 'Have you told *her* yet?'

'Edwina will be told after I've gone. I've left her a letter. I do not think that she will be too disappointed to see the back of me.'

'I didn't mean Edwina,' Clare said. 'I mean, have you told Eunice Bates that you are leaving Scotland?'

Andrew shook his head at the girl's perspicacity, gave a fleeting smile. 'Eunice will be with me.'

'Will America be far enough for Eunice?' Clare said. 'Far enough from Frederick?'

'It had better be,' said Andrew.

'Do you love her?'

Clare saw that the word embarrassed him. She rose from the chair by the fire and went to him. She was his servant no longer, nor he her master. 'Do you think that she loves you?' Clare asked.

'I believe she needs me.'

'Does she not know of your plan?'

'No, but—'

'Do not delay,' said Clare. 'Tell her that you love her and take her away with you. Tonight. Away from that house, away from Frederick. Far away.'

'Do you imagine that Frederick's here, hiding somewhere near at hand?'

'I'm afraid of him,' said Clare. 'I'm afraid of him as I am of the devil who might appear in any place, at any time.'

'I thought you may still have been in love with him.'

'Love him! I *hate* him,' Clare said. 'He poisoned my child. Did you not know?'

'I suspected as much,' said Andrew. 'Eunice will not talk of it but she is wounded by what happened. She loved the little boy too, Clare. Grief has all but devoured her sanity these past weeks. You are not alone in hating Frederick Striker.'

'Does your father know of this part of your plan?'

'He has guessed it,' said Andrew. 'But he is too downy a bird to bring it out. If it was declared between us then he would be morally obliged to warn me against it.'

'I'm sorry I brought all this upon you, Andrew,' Clare said.

He sighed and gripped her hands tightly, as if to steady

himself. 'If it had not been for you, Clare, I would not have met Eunice and my life would have filtered away like sand in a glass, grain by dry grain. You asked if I love her. I do. I did not believe that it was possible to love someone as much as I love Eunice.'

Clare stifled the envy that was in her at Andrew's declaration. If only she'd had someone like Andrew to love and cherish her instead of being trapped by her own vanity into loving Frederick Striker.

'In that case, go with her,' Clare said.

She knew that the taint of dishonour would cling to Andrew Purves from this day onward; a man who had abandoned wife and children for another woman. But the Purveses would look after their own and old Mr Purves would protect Edwina and his grandchildren and provide for their futures. There was something brave, not cowardly, in what Andrew was about to do and she wished only that she could have been the woman in Eunice's place.

'I have left instructions for the lawyers' fees to be paid,' Andrew said. 'I have taken all that I will need. And it is curious how little that turned out to be.' He fished at his waist for the silver chain upon which he kept his keys. 'All that remains now is to see you provided for.'

Clare watched him cross to the narrow cupboard that hid halfway behind a bow-fronted bookcase. He unlocked the cupboard and drew the door ajar. He stooped and straightened and brought to the table a strongbox. It was a heavy object, bound in iron and fastened by two huge brass clasps locked to a padlock.

Andrew placed the box upon the table, worked the key into the padlock and broke the links of the clasps. He opened the lid. Clare was close enough to see piles of deeds and documents within, nestling against two packets of banknotes and several purses of coin. He plucked out one of the purses and offered it to her. 'Twenty pounds, Clare. Will that be enough to see you on your way?'

'More than enough,' Clare said.

She held the purse against her breast. 'There is, however, something else that I require from you, if you will give it me.'

Andrew glanced at her enquiringly. 'What?'

'The letter that Frederick left with you,' Clare said. 'I want you to give it to me.'

'How did you know of it? Did Frederick tell you?'

'It's Frederick's protection against his enemies, against the men he cheated, is it not?'

'Something of the sort,' said Andrew. 'But I cannot, in conscience, let you have it, Clare.'

'Why not? Frederick gave it into *your* keeping, not to the bank. Do you intend just to leave it here?'

'I had not thought of it, to tell the truth.' Andrew frowned. 'Do you have any inkling what it contains?'

'Names,' Clare said. 'Names and places.'

'What possible value can it have for you, Clare, now that you are free?' Andrew's frown deepened. 'It was given to me on trust and I cannot break—'

'How can you talk of trust?' Clare said. 'It was given to you by Frederick Striker, who murdered my child and who would have let me hang for it. It's the last thing I will ever ask of you, Andrew. Besides, you will be all the safer if you leave that letter with a friend.'

Again Andrew drew in a long breath and held it in his lungs. He looked proud for a moment, proud in the manner of the burgesses. For an instant Clare thought that the habit of honour would defeat her, that he would refuse.

'Yes,' Andrew said, at length. 'I see what you mean, Clare. I see exactly what you mean.'

She felt almost faint when Andrew sifted through the documents in the strongbox and drew out a slender packet of pure white paper. Upon it in Frederick's marching hand were written the words: *Frederick Striker, To be Opened by a Magistrate in the Event of His Death.* Brown wax seals coated the packet's three folds, each bearing the impress of Frederick's monogrammed finger ring.

Andrew held the packet across his palms as if finally to weigh its lightness against conscience. Then he put it down upon the table, quite deliberately turned his back upon Clare and stared out of the room's tiny window at the afternoon sky.

'Take it, Clare,' he said, and added coldly, 'then go.'

She had no hesitation. She lifted the weightless white packet and hid it too in the pocket of her skirt, closing her left hand across it. There could be no turning back now. She experienced one faint, receding moment of sorrow at what she had done, what Frederick had forced her to do.

She did not try to touch him. 'Where is my son buried?'

'In St Matthew's kirkyard,' Andrew said. 'In a corner of my father's plot.'

'Is there a marker?'

'Yes, a little stone.'

'Thank you, Andrew,' Clare said. 'Thank you for that. For everything.' Then she left him.

Advocate Adams had tried his level best to be calm and rational. He was weary to the bone after his tussle in court. Waiting for the verdict had taken a final toll on his nerves; not, he knew, the sort of thing that a successful defender should ever admit. He needed rest, a nap on his bed in the

Tontine. After a light dinner he had gone upstairs to compose and settle himself, clarify his thoughts before he went in search of Clare Kelso. However, he had hardly kicked off his shoes, unbuttoned his waistcoat and laid himself down on top of the quilt before all manner of mental twitchings drove sleep from brain and body.

Clare Kelso troubled him. He could not fathom her at all. Sometimes he saw her as a natural victim, felt a rush of desire to know and to protect her. Moments later, though, he would be convinced that she was a devious schemer who had plotted with her lover to be rid of an embarrassing encumbrance, and that all conclusions based on the sister's confession should be discarded as fantastical dross.

The fact that he, Cameron Adams, rising star of the Scottish bar and a respected member of Edinburgh society, could harbour longings for a girl of such low class, let alone one who had borne a bastard child, put all his lessons in logic out of joint. And that irked him. He wondered if, in time, he would wind up like fat old Walcott, chasing every pert and pretty miss who drifted his way.

Whatever opinion was held by Lord Pole, whatever manipulations of justice Drumfin had brought about, Cameron knew that Clare was innocent. He knew the truth. And damned few others did. Not even Clare herself.

Clare had professed to the court the child's death was accidental. But she did not believe it. She thought she had been deceived, twice over, by Frederick Striker. She thought that the Scottish judicial system was incapable of judging and punishing the seducer. She had, Cameron realised, risked her life to retain that privilege for herself.

He groaned, rolled on to his side and stared out of the hotel room's window at the eaves of the tenement that backed the Tontine. Pigeons roosting on the edge of the

tiles reminded him uncomfortably of a row of little hang-
men; not a prospect to soothe or inspire.

'Devil take it!' Cameron said suddenly, swung himself
from the bed and groped with stockinged feet for his shoes.

Old Mrs Purves had no awareness of the turmoil that was
taking place in the household. Her reign was well and truly
over. She had had her day of laying down the law, of
tantrums, threats and sulks. She had kept her husband in
his place and had aged and withered in the process. More
spry in body and whole in mind, he was having his last fling
at a kind of freedom. Naturally, old Mrs Purves realised
that Edwina and the children had gone to Moorfoot but she
was hazy as to the reason for it. Something to do with the
Kelso girl's trial. When she enquired of her servant, Lowther, what was afoot below stairs, the woman placated her
with half-truths and distortions.

For this reason old Mrs Purves failed to realise that her
son had come to say goodbye.

Andrew's kiss was certainly less perfunctory than usual
but she put it down to boyishness, to relief that Edwina and
the noisy brats had been swept from his ken for a while. She
was more interested in what had been prepared for supper
than in interrogating her lad. She knew nothing of him, of
what he did, what he needed and desired. She did not detect
the frog in her husband's throat when the kiss upon her cheek
was planted and Andrew, pausing, brushed from her brow a
sprig of brittle grey hair that had escaped her cap. Indeed,
before the menfolk had gone from her chamber she was
grumbling to Lowther that Andrew had appeared before her
in boots and what wear they would inflict upon her carpets.

Mr William Purves went just as far as he dared, to the
foot of the stairs of the house's first storey. There, without

blessing or reprimand, he nodded to Andrew, and blew his nose loudly into a handkerchief.

He watched his boy descend to the side door, waited motionless for three or four minutes then went down to the banking hall to bury his sorrow as best he could in business and the money trade.

Andrew had not been able to predict how he would feel when the moment of departure came. He covered it briskly, feigning efficiency. The truth of it was that he had but a broad plan for the flight – for that's what it was – to the far side of the world. He had organised efficiently for everybody else but could get himself no further than the moment when he would confront Eunice, sweep her up and carry her off.

Hard cash was no object. Savings amounted to some eight hundred pounds Scots. He had taken the precaution of writing to several shipping clients of the bank to establish *bona fides* and to ensure himself of credit through their offices if it became a matter of necessity. Passage for the Atlantic crossing would be booked through an agent in Liverpool. He did not want to linger in the port of Glasgow to await departure. Besides, Scottish cargo vessels were, as a rule, quite small and confining. In Liverpool he would be sure to find berths in a brigantine bound for New York, as much comfort as money might buy. Baggage was packed into two stout canvas valises which he had purchased for the purpose from a chandler's in the High Street and in one small chest, roped and secure. The dunnage had been transferred from the library to the fly that Moresby had found for him and which waited in Saltmarket Lane, out of sight of the windows of Purves's Land.

Tom Moresby had been his confidante all along. Only Tom Moresby knew for certain where his master was going and whom he would take with him. Only Tom Moresby was there to wish him God-speed and good fortune, to shake his master's hand and receive, as well as a guinea, an embarrassing hug and a slap upon the back.

Once he was aboard the fly, the flap dropped, Andrew did not look back at the sooty walls of Purves's Land or its chimneys receding behind the steeples and tenements of Argyll Street. He sat forward, elbows on knees, and let knots of tension in his belly unravel. He sucked in a deep breath, then another, and waited for guilt and fear to catch up with him as the fly rocked, the horses found pace and the street fled away towards Grahamston. The only emotions that rose in Andrew Purves were positive ones, a great singing in the blood, the tingle of adventure, an expansive feeling of relief that, for a time at least, he had stoppered the neck of the hourglass, choked the granular ebb of tedium and responsibility. It took several minutes to realise that he was not going to feel bad, that the lightness in him was pure and selfish, but also something to be enjoyed. When he strode into the villa, he would lift Eunice up with him, kiss away her terrors, caress her until grief and melancholy departed like dust from fine cloth. And before the sun dimmed and afternoon was lost to dusk he would be away, alone with her at last along the road to a future in which love would be permanent and assured.

Whistling cheerfully, Andrew hopped down from the fly. He instructed the driver to wait right where he was. He vaulted the wicket gate and sped down the path to the villa's front door. He called out to let Eunice know who had come calling but, in his eagerness, did not wait for her to open the door. He slipped his key into the lock, pushed his way into the hall and called out, 'Eunice? Eunice, darling, it's Andrew.'

Eunice was hanging from a length of rope knotted to a stanchion of the staircase. She had arrayed herself in lawn and lace. Gravity had drawn out the folds of the dress, refined her sturdiness, maintained her modesty. A shoe from a silken foot lay awry on the floor where some unthinkably violent spasm had projected it. Her hair had come loose from its ribbon. It wisped coyly over her face, veiling bulging eyes, a protruding tongue, the final unpeaceful rictus that had followed the breaking of her neck.

Andrew stood stockstill. He watched the draught twist her a little this way and that, as if her corpse was something to be appraised and admired. He did not have to touch her to know that she was beyond a surgeon's aid, beyond his reach, and Frederick's. He staggered, put out his hand to steady himself. He sank slowly down into a hunkered crouch, face buried in his hands. There he remained for three minutes or four, dry and silent, without a sob or a groan or a prayer to give evidence of his shock. He felt no more alive than Eunice and his limbs, when finally he moved again, had in them the same deadly stiffness. He pulled open the door, stepped out, bent to the lock and turned the key. He walked down the path, opened the gate and clambered stiffly into the fly again. Stiffly he seated himself, sat back and crossed one knee over the other.

'Are you feelin' ill, sir?' the driver enquired.

Andrew's expression was grave, his pallor white, but he gave nothing else away. For an instant, when he had first caught sight of her and knew that she was dead, he had thought that his life was over too, that he would follow her, drowned or hanged or poisoned, into that better world. But he was too much of a coward to escape that way – or not coward enough. He knew exactly what he must do. He would return to the bank, to the deserted house upstairs and unpick the plot that he had contrived, remove all the letters, all the signs that he had loved someone enough to kick over the traces. He would hide suffering behind a mask of sombre respectability, absorb without a whimper the punishment that a god in whom he did not believe had meted out to him. Nothing had changed, nothing would ever change. Eunice's terrible gesture of despair had damned him for daring to love her, had condemned him to infinite loneliness.

He scowled at the driver. 'I'm perfectly well, thank you.'

'Where to now, sir?' the man asked, shrugging.

'Back to the Saltmarket,' Andrew answered, and rode away from the garden cottage, leaving Eunice to the attentions of officers and magistrates, while he mourned alone at home.

The kirkyard of St Matthew's church did not seem like a community of the dead. It was a place of soft angles, secluded corners, shady trees and weathered monuments all tucked away in the shadow of a church whose mellow stone gable and lichened walls seemed quietly protective but not remote from the rattle of horse-drawn traffic and the garrulous voices of pedestrians.

It was as if past history and present reality were rooted one in the other and neither separate from God. On the Sabbath psalms would reverberate across the kirkyard. On Wednesday afternoons the praise of angels would ring in voices from the markets across Kentigern Street.

Clare found the little tablet of raw granite laid flat upon the ground. Fresh spring grass edged it and daffodils were nodding into bud on the mound that rose to the drystone wall that bordered the street. Five upright stones stood to the left of the tiny grave, not far away. They did not seem in the least supercilious, grandfathers and their wives, Purveses all, and, oddly, a scattering of rounded stones about them like loaves half buried in the ground; children too, a nursery of infants caught as they dropped from the womb or, after a year or two, drawn back by their Maker to play about His knee. Clare put down her heavy wicker hamper with a sigh. She eased her shoulders and slipped to her knees on the moist unmown turf. The ochre smoke of the tannery in Brandon Lane drifted lazily through unleafed boughs. She could hear the faint rhythmical clang of hammer and anvil from the forge by the Ramshorn gate, lively but not loud enough to waken Peterkin from his soft green sleep.

She had brought nothing. She could think of nothing that would last. There was frost still in the mornings, early summer rains would come, the sun would wither whatever she might lay as token on the stone. She had other things to give him, though, things that would grow as gradually as he had grown inside her and be delivered, perhaps, with just as much pain. It was not maudlin sentiment that drove her now but anger. She would grow old in fulfilling the vow that she had made to herself that night in the Tolbooth when she knew that her son was dead.

She could not, however, leave him neglected. She needed a sign, not for the child but for herself, a transient marker to say that she had passed. She looked about her, found daffodils acceptable. She cut five or six sticky stems with her thumbnail and, kneeling, bound them with ribbon taken from her hair.

Smiling, she laid the posy across the letters that Andrew had had pricked into the stone, the unfathered name: *Peterkin, an Infant, Died Dec.* 1787. No name to indicate that he was an intruder here, a stranger to the Purveses.

She nodded to herself at Andrew's generosity and then, all done, rose from her knees, brushed dirt from her skirts, looped the hamper's leather thong about her shoulder and settled its weight upon her hip.

'Goodbye, my dearest boy,' she whispered and, just as the clocks struck four, turned to leave the kirkyard for the Clydeside shore.

By the time he found the graveyard, half-hidden behind the church, Cameron Adams' anxiety had reached fever pitch. He realised that he had erred. He should not have let her go. He should have been close by her when she left the court, stuck close by her side thereafter.

It had not occurred to him that Clare would be resilient enough to shake off weeks of confinement and the dreadful strain of a public trial and pick up the direction of her life in a mere matter of hours. He had carelessly assumed that she would be there in Purves's Land, awaiting him, awaiting direction and momentum, awaiting the imposition of purpose. How he had misjudged her. Her composure had stemmed not from female silliness or shock but from determination.

'I wish to speak with Clare Kelso.'

'Clare has left our service, sir,' the old banker had told him. 'She has packed her bags and gone.'

'May I enquire, Mr Purves, where she has gone?'

'I have no idea of that, Mr Adams.'

'Perhaps your son would know?'

'My son – my son has left too, to travel abroad.'

'What! Have they left together?'

'Certainly not, sir,' old Mr Purves had told him angrily.

'Do you think, perhaps, that Clare has gone to Mrs Bates' house?' Cameron had asked.

'I greatly doubt that, Mr Adams. In fact, I can tell you that she has not.'

'May I ask what makes you so sure?'

'Because that's where my son has gone,' old Mr Purves told him.

'To take his leave of Mrs Bates? Do you suppose I might catch him there before—'

'I think, sir, that you are too late,' said the banker. 'Unless I miss my guess, my son and the lady will already be speeding towards a destination unknown to me.'

'And Clare – have you no notion of where she went?'

'None at all, Mr Adams.'

He had paused, considered, then had asked, 'Where is the child buried, Mr Purves?'

'Behind St Matthew's kirk.'

If there was even a grain of truth in what old Purves had told him then Andrew and Eunice Bates, in the tradition of fleeing lovers, would be hastening away from Glasgow. Clare Kelso would certainly not be with them. She would follow a different destiny. He had now a glimmering of what that destiny might be. Cameron cursed himself for not reading the signs more accurately. It was suddenly imperative that she be informed of his discoveries, made to understand that, believing it to be a lie, she had told the court the truth and that Frederick Striker, however black his character, however numerous his faults, had not murdered her child.

As he came within sight of St Matthew's steeple Cameron broke into a run. It was exceedingly undignified behaviour, unsuited to an Edinburgh gentleman, but he did not give a damn about appearances. Mingled with his need to divert Clare from her vengeance was need of another kind. The late-night supper in the Tolbooth had become more than a tale to tell his sisters and his fellow-advocates. Realisation that he would not see Clare Kelso again had occasioned his restless agitation, had driven him out to find her.

Secluded and shady, St Matthew's kirkyard would be a perfect spot for a tryst. He could not have selected a better place to encounter Clare. There were many things he wanted to say to her and, though he remained unclear as to his personal intentions, he acknowledged now that he had fallen under her spell. He had met, flirted with and separated from several young women before now and it shocked him to have to admit that he did not want Clare Kelso to become one of that lost flock, remembered, like the dead, only with wistfulness and longing. He paused at the iron gate in the breast-high wall. He straightened his hat and patted dust from his breeches, buttoned waistcoat and coat and then, as if mere chance had brought him here, sauntered on to the flagged path that meandered between the leafless trees and mossy memorials, in search of the corner plot where Purveses lay.

Within seconds of rounding the corner of the church gable Cameron knew that he had come too late. Burying ground, mounds, dips, banks of spring flowers, all were deserted. Driven once more by urgency, he hurried on, calling out as he went, 'Clare – Clare Kelso – are you there?', nurturing the faint hope that he would find her kneeling by Peterkin's grave.

She did not rise at the cry of her name and, when he saw the posy of daffodils and snatch of ribbon that bound them, he knew that he had come too late. He had lost her.

There were many roads out of Glasgow, gates and tolls

and bridges. The river too was a turnpike of escape, filled with wherries and small sail-craft that would carry a traveller down to the ports of the estuary, to snuggling towns on islands and seashores, communities too numerous to count. *He* did not know where Frederick Striker might be found. But *she* did. She had kept it from him all along, from all of them.

Clare wanted Striker for herself.

In one last despairing attempt to stop her, Cameron Adams set out at a run for the quays.

Custom House and bonding warehouse, the bulging brick cone of the bottle factory all caught the sad slanting rays of March sunlight. The old bridge hung suspended on a drifting haze that mirrored the currents that coiled about its piles and made the harbour boats bob skittishly as if they were eager to be off to sea before nightfall. Deepening of the river had opened the heart of the city to herring yawls, coasters and smacks whose bulk loomed over the fretting host of lighters and small craft that crammed the long jetties by which the course of the river had been changed.

The square cast-iron shape of a dredging machine plunged its pole into sharp sand south of the bridge-end and rose with water dripping from its fangs, while the crane on the Broomie Quay shrieked and heaved enviously and plucked a net of bales from the bowels of a big-sailed barge. Coal and sand, fish and timber, coils of tarred rope and stringy sailormen jostled for space beneath painted hoardings that announced tides and sailing times and chalked boards offering space for passengers and light cargo.

As always, Clare felt Glasgow's energy rise like sap. She remembered the talk in the banking hall of growth and prosperity, of the gobbling up of green pastures, the tearing down of hedges, the swift shrinkage of the pretty fields and gardens that flanked the Clyde. She experienced a pang of regret at leaving the lengthening town, the place that had been her home since that autumnal afternoon, eight years since, when her mother had bravely led her up to Purves's Land.

She had been too young to have a future then, or much of a past. Now she had both. Each was fixed and immutable as the other. The past was locked away under Glasgow's rooftops and buried behind its shady kirk. The future was set out and sealed in Frederick's letter.

She kept the shawl about her head for fear of recognition and did not dare put the hamper down though it bit hard into her shoulder bone and rubbed, bruisingly, against her hip. She walked slowly along the quay's edge looking for a vessel to carry her away.

Manned by a father and son, the *Swan* was a long, low, raffish craft with a half-furled mainsail on its mast and a little canvas tent drawn taut across its stern. The boy, aged twelve or so, caught Clare's eye and yelled out to her, shrill as a gull, 'Sail-boat, miss, sail-boat. Take you anywhere, we will, for half a fin.' Clare hesitated. He was so eager, the boy, a wide white smile splitting his brown face. He was all gab and confidence. She noticed how the father, bent and silenced by the hardships of his trade, watched with a glint of admiration in his grey eye as the boy cajoled her merrily. 'Show you mermaids, miss, an' whales, grampuses an' conger eels, flyin' fish an' desert isles, cannibals an' crocodiles.'

'In Greenock?' Clare said.

'Greenock! Aye, we'll whisk you there an' back again, dry as a cornhusk.'

'How long will it take?'

'How long's your arm, miss?'

'Will you take me now, right now?'

The father straightened. He was hardly taller than his lad but had equally candid features. He glanced upwards at the sky, towards a sun blurred by March haze, then sniffed the breeze that stirred the riggings round about.

He nodded.

'We'll have you suppin' broth at Turvey's Tavern before you can say knife,' the boy said. 'Step down, miss.'

The ladder was made of rope and slats. The man poled the boat closer, nudging its bow against the beams. Legs spread, the boy reached up to take the hamper and put it down behind him. He reached next for her hand and guided her, like a gallant, down the four steps. His hand was moist and calloused but it was not a man's hand. She had no fear of him in spite of his chatter, or of the father who, with apology, asked if she had money enough for the fare.

It felt strange to be there on the river below the pilings, in among the hulking crafts. Clare was relieved when the little vessel was cast off and steered out into the stream, the boy on the pole, the man on the tiller. Her hamper had been stowed safe beneath the tented awning and she had been seated in the stern. From there she watched the skill with which the sail was spread to catch the east wind, how the ropes were tugged and slackened to pull round the bow and head the boat down the channel.

There were so many new sounds that Clare could not be sure that she heard her name being called above the guddle of the stream, the slap of sails, gulls' cries and the shouting of men. At first she paid no heed to a voice that she thought might be entirely a figment of her imagination.

'Clare?'

The boy stared back at the quay. It was receding rapidly now, swivelling away behind her between hulls and bulwarks.

'Clare, wait, wait.'

It seemed almost as if the town itself was calling out to her, begging her not to leave. She twisted her body and stared back too at the quays. She glimpsed him: not Andrew.

Mr Adams spread his arms akimbo and frantically waved his lawyer's hat to attract her attention. For a moment no longer than a catch of breath Clare was tempted to tell the boatman to put about, to take her back. But it was too late. She let the vessel surge on unchecked into a current that was as brown and flowing as a stallion at the gallop, and watched ropes and riggings, sails and spars rank in behind her and diminish, closing off sight of the Edinburgh advocate and smothering his desperate cries.

'Your husband, miss?' the boy asked impudently.

'I have no husband.'

Clare cut him off, reached into her pocket and took out Frederick's letter. She crushed it against the gunwale to break the seals and then, holding it fast in the keen night wind, read where she must go to find him, and patiently craft her revenge.